**Praise for the Novels
of Ann Aguirre**

Hell Fire

"Riveting. . . . Full of well-drawn characters, a nearly tangible setting, and the threat of death around every corner, this spine-chilling paranormal mystery is sure to keep readers turning pages—and glancing over their shoulders."
—*Publishers Weekly* (starred review)

"A well-paced plot with a satisfying amount of suspense. Aguirre mixes the supernatural with real-life details and makes this well-crafted story feel authentic." —*Romantic Times*

"Fans of the first book, never fear; this is a good, solid follow-up that left me hungry for more." —Calico Reaction

"Reading *Hell Fire* is a completely sensory experience that would be half as immersive in the hands of a lesser writer."
—All Things Urban Fantasy

"Sets a new bar for Ann Aguirre." —Fantasy Literature

"*Hell Fire* has a searing triangle romance, breathtaking paranormal elements, intimate adventure, mature point of view, and solid writing craft." —Lightworks

Blue Diablo

"Ann Aguirre proves herself yet again in this gritty, steamy, and altogether wonderful urban fantasy. Outstanding and delicious. I can't wait to see what she comes up with next."
—#1 *New York Times* bestselling author Patricia Briggs

continued . . .

Also by Ann Aguirre

ANN AGUIRRE

SHADY LADY

A CORINE SOLOMON NOVEL

A ROC BOOK

ROC
Published by New American Library, a division of
Penguin Group (USA) Inc., 375 Hudson Street,
New York, New York 10014, USA
Penguin Group (Canada), 90 Eglinton Avenue East, Suite 700, Toronto,
Ontario M4P 2Y3, Canada (a division of Pearson Penguin Canada Inc.)
Penguin Books Ltd., 80 Strand, London WC2R 0RL, England
Penguin Ireland, 25 St. Stephen's Green, Dublin 2,
Ireland (a division of Penguin Books Ltd.)
Penguin Group (Australia), 250 Camberwell Road, Camberwell, Victoria 3124,
Australia (a division of Pearson Australia Group Pty. Ltd.)
Penguin Books India Pvt. Ltd., 11 Community Centre, Panchsheel Park,
New Delhi - 110 017, India
Penguin Group (NZ), 67 Apollo Drive, Rosedale, North Shore 0632,
New Zealand (a division of Pearson New Zealand Ltd.)
Penguin Books (South Africa) (Pty.) Ltd., 24 Sturdee Avenue,
Rosebank, Johannesburg 2196, South Africa

Penguin Books Ltd., Registered Offices:
80 Strand, London WC2R 0RL, England

First published by Roc, an imprint of New American Library,
a division of Penguin Group (USA) Inc.

First printing, April 2011
10 9 8 7 6 5 4 3 2 1

For Sharon Shinn,
whose words made me sigh
and wish I could ever write so well.
She has since proven herself as gracious
and charming in person as one would imagine.
Thanks for everything.

ACKNOWLEDGMENTS

Once more, I'm starting with Laura Bradford, who goes beyond the call. Thank you for the DMV, *District 9*, and the Toys "R" Us Bakugan mission. I hit the jackpot the day you said, "I don't know if I can sell a science fiction novel, but I think I want the challenge."

As always, I thank Anne Sowards. Her notes make every book better and I am so lucky to work with her, along with all the other talented people at Penguin.

Next, there's Lauren Dane. She never fails to make me feel better when the chips are down, and she's first to cheer me on when I score. Lauren is so talented and so smart, and I am so lucky I can run things by her while I'm working. My books wouldn't be as good if I didn't have her ear.

Here's a shout to Bree and Donna. Both of you have been there, and I appreciate it more than words can say. I'd give either of you my seat in the lifeboat any day.

The incomparable Ivette takes meticulous care that everything in the book makes sense.

I also need to thank Stacia Kane. She convinced me to write what I wanted and not worry about convention. The book is better for her bravery and its daring.

Then there's Laura Bickle. She gets my work from the ground up; thanks for being a sounding board during revisions.

Additionally, thanks to the fine staff at La Finca in Catemaco, who made my research trip a fabulous vacation, and thanks to the real "Ernesto," who took us out in his *lancha*, showed us the sights, and did *not* suffer a dire fate.

Thank you to Teté, a New Age expert, and Estelle, a real-life *curandera*, for insights that enriched this book and brought Tia to life.

Finally, I thank my family. If they weren't so awesome, I'd never be able to keep a schedule. My kids are fantastic, and

I'm so proud of them. They're smart, capable, kind, and a whole lot of fun. I'm lucky to have them.

Then, of course, there's my husband. To give you an idea the kind of guy Andres is, when he comes home from a long day of work—and a longer commute—to find I'm cranky because my draft isn't going well, oh, and I've been interrupted eleventy-four times by peddlers, he listens and then cooks dinner. I'd never ask it, but how cool is that? He also has an epic ability to plot logical consequences for the messes my characters find themselves in. Without him, this book wouldn't be as good.

Many thanks to my fabulous proofreader. You know who you are.

As always, I must convey my utmost appreciation to my readers. You guys are the best. Please keep writing; that's ann.aguirre@gmail.com. I love hearing from you.

If Death Is the Answer,
What Was the Question?

Lust sizzled through me. There were two of them, a matched pair. I knew a woman wasn't supposed to want such things, but sometimes we had desires—dark desires—that couldn't be denied. There was no doubt about it.

That was the sexiest set of salt and pepper shakers I'd ever seen.

Briefly, I imagined Chance's reaction to my infatuation. *Corine*, he'd say, *why don't you make love to them? You're making me jealous, woman.* With some effort, I put him from my mind. My ex didn't deserve to be the voice inside my head.

Instead I focused on the treasures I'd found outside my back door. Crafted of pure silver, they depicted lovers reaching toward each other, separated by whatever distance their owners dictated. I studied the artful lines and the graceful arches of the spines. These were classically inspired, likely a representation of Eros and Psyche. On closer inspection, I noted that the pepper flowed from holes in Psyche's fingertips. I couldn't believe where the salt came from.

Wonderful. The designer had a sense of humor.

I didn't expect trouble from these two. Mentally bracing myself, I curled my left palm—now marked with a flower pentacle—around Psyche, lifting her out of the pretty white box. Heat flared, but it brought no pain. As I'd thought, there was no trauma attached. Though I would have loved to keep these, my gift whispered of the fortune I'd make selling them to a professor visiting from Spain. In my mind's eye, I saw a flickering image of my prospective buyer. I'd recognize her when she came in, and make sure to show them to her.

After the mess in Georgia, I was happy to be in Mexico. Things hadn't been the same since I found my mother's necklace; for a moment, I saw myself kneeling in that demon grove, shadows gone green from the Spanish moss, the smell of verdant decay in my nose like a damp, mildewed rag. I reached out and took the necklace—against Jesse Saldana's warnings—and lived my mother's death. I hadn't survived it, or at least, when I came back, everything had changed. My ability was no longer the simple "touch" it once was; I thought I'd received my mother's power, but I wasn't a trained witch. Nor did I know who to trust with the revelation. At this point, I didn't know how to discipline my new power, and that was made for a bad situation, considering the cost at which I'd gained it. In time, I'd move beyond the pain of all those deaths in Kilmer, and these peaceful months at home had helped.

But I was curious about these salt and pepper shakers. As a handler—someone who could read the histories of charged objects—sometimes I wanted to see the stories, even when I didn't have to, especially when there was no grief or trauma involved. I didn't read every item that came across the counter in the pawnshop, but when I thought something might have a happy story to tell, I wanted to see it for myself.

As I reached toward Eros, the bell above my door tinkled. Sunlight cut through the shadows, golden motes of dust whirling in the air and hinting at how hot it was outside. The heavy rock walls and cool plaster interior made it possible for me to stand my shop with just a simple oscillating fan. In fact, it was cooler than any un-air-conditioned building I'd ever seen in the U.S.

I recognized the man standing in the doorway, though he

was not either of the ones I might've expected. Kel Ferguson stood well over six feet and he was heavily muscled. Tattoos covered his skin, even on his skull, written in angelic script. He had eyes like shadowed ice and he professed to be the Hand of God, tasked with killing those who would push the world toward the end of days. Once, in Laredo, he'd claimed if he had been on the job at the time, he could've prevented the Holocaust.

I didn't know if he was crazy, but I did know the man was damn near unkillable. In Texas, I had watched him take multiple wounds so deep they showed bone; I saw him fall. And then he rose again, ready to fight on. Whatever else he might be, I was pretty sure he wasn't entirely human. I also wasn't sure whether we were still on the same side. I froze, eyeing him across the counter.

"Corine." He inclined his head toward the saltshaker. "Don't touch that."

My right hand rested on the counter, mere inches away from Eros. I'd intended to read him, now that Psyche had told me where they were destined to wind up. Another thirty seconds and it would've been too late, assuming he was right in his warning. Somehow I didn't think Kel had come all this way to mess with my head.

"Why not?" There was no point in remarking on his lack of niceties.

"It's hexed," he told me.

Damn. Despite my uncertainty about his motives, I didn't doubt him. After what I'd seen him do in Laredo, I had to take him seriously. His reactions and recovery came from something greater than insanity; that was for sure. I wasn't ready to admit he had a direct line to the divine or anything, but his presence had saved my ass once before. There could be no discounting him now.

It was lucky I hadn't lifted Eros out of the box he'd come in. In all honesty, I didn't know who had sent the set. I'd found them this morning and assumed they comprised part of Señor Alvarez's last shipment—that could've been a costly mistake.

Alvarez had done a stellar job running the pawnshop while I was gone, but he seemed relieved to be out of the store. Much as I didn't understand it, he preferred being on the street looking for lost riches. *Hm.* On the other hand, maybe I knew why he didn't want to deal with customers all day. That was my least favorite part of running the place.

Belatedly, I realized I was fixating on the mundane to keep fear from paralyzing me. A hex meant nothing good, but it remained to be seen how *bad* it was. I squared my shoulders and edged the white case away from me with the heel of my hand.

"What kind?"

"The killing kind."

A shudder rolled through me. "So if I'd picked it up, I'd be dead on the floor. Right now."

Dammit, I owed him my life. *Again.* I hated having unpaid debts. Right now, I could think of better positions to be in: I owed my life to both God's Hand and a demon who said to call him Maury, which wasn't his real name, but he didn't want me summoning or binding him. Talk about your grandiose games of tug-of-war.

"That's why I'm here," he said, and the tattoos against his skull glowed just a little, as if bearing witness.

I raised a brow. "To save me?"

"I've been assigned as your guardian until the immediate danger passes. I'm told you're going to be important."

"Oh, no." I shook my head. "I helped Chance find his mother. I took care of business in Kilmer, and now I'm *finished.* I run a pawnshop. That's all I want or need. It's a good life."

"Very well," he said. "For the moment, put aside the matter of whether you have a role to play in things to come. Do you think you'll survive to enjoy the quiet life if you don't deal with Montoya?"

Montoya. Christ on a cracker, that name brought back memories I didn't want. In rescuing Chance's mother, I'd pissed off the *jefe* of a major cartel. It wasn't like television, where it was all automatic weapons, either. These days, the cartels used warlocks, shamans, and voodoo priests—any advantage to get their merchandise to market and crush their rivals. Chance's luck would keep him safe, even if his mother hadn't forced Montoya to swear off pursuing vengeance against her son—and she'd called the Knights of Hell to witness the agreement.

So Chance was fine. Like a cat, he always landed on his feet. And I didn't miss him at all. Really, I didn't. He'd expected me to give up everything I'd built on my own here, just slide right back into the life I had left behind. But I was a different person. I wouldn't go back, and if he'd wanted me as much as he claimed, he would've considered making some changes too, not expected me to yield everything for the joy of being with him.

Unfortunately, that left me as a scapegoat. Any good practitioner could've scryed for information on those responsible for the raid on his property. That meant Jesse, Chuch, and Eva might be vulnerable too. Me . . . well, crap. Kel was right. I was screwed.

"So he knows where I am. Why didn't he send someone?"

"You know why."

As I considered, I realized the hexed saltshaker was cleaner than a thug with a machete. Severed heads made the news, but some cartels didn't want that kind of press. It interfered with business. And if Kel hadn't come in, I'd be a silent statistic; Montoya could not have planned for God's Hand.

I sighed. "What now?"

"You muster your allies," he answered. "And plan for war."

Allies, hm. There's always Booke, and Jesse will be happy to consult. Shannon won't let me keep her out of this, if I know the girl at all.

Booke was my occult expert in the U.K. whom I'd met online through mutual friends. Currently I didn't know *what* role Jesse Saldana played in my life; he wanted to be my boyfriend, but long-distance relationships were too hard, so right now he was my friend and mentor with an eye on a relationship upgrade, if one of us ever decided to relocate.

As for Shannon, I met her in Kilmer, and I wouldn't have survived those dark woods without her; in the end, her ability to summon and speak to spirits had saved us all. Like me, she bore an unusual gift and came from a painful past. I saw a lot of myself in her, which was part of why I cared about her. I wanted so much better for her than I'd managed at first on my own.

So I took her under my wing; she went with me to Texas and then accompanied me from there to Mexico City. Although she was young, I couldn't claim she was immature. I'd been like that too. Growing up different in a tiny, cursed town squashed the child right out of you.

I went on with the mental inventory, thinking of the coolest married couple I knew, Chuch and Eva Ortiz. *But I refuse to drag them into my problems. It's been months, and she's about ready to have her baby. I can't permit more than peripheral contact, in case Montoya doesn't know about them already.*

And he might. *It's impossible to judge.*

Which meant I'd accepted Kel's assessment. I wouldn't be thinking of who I could turn to for help if I didn't believe him about the threat. *Shit.*

I glanced up to find him watching me in silence; doubtless he knew the exact moment I worked out the fact that my options were limited. With a frown, I handed Psyche over, and he set her back in the box. In a gesture more symbolic than helpful, I put the lid on it.

"We should go see someone who might be able to tell us what kind of spell was used on this thing."

He nodded. "Do you have any contacts here?"

"Yep."

Tia worked on Tuesdays and Fridays at the market, where she kept a stall selling charms and potions. On other days, she cleaned houses. She was a wizened woman with wispy gray hair that she wore in a messy bun, and her clothing consisted of housedresses covered with aprons in competing floral patterns.

I loved her.

"We should go."

"Not until Shannon gets back. I can't leave the store unattended."

Kel gave the impression of incredulity without shifting his expression. "You don't think this is more important than selling a few gewgaws?"

"Actually, no. If I don't have money to pay my bills and eat, then I might as well fondle Eros, because I'd rather die fast than starve in the streets. You probably don't have to worry about such things, being God's Hand and all."

To my surprise, he said, "Point."

"If it comes to another extended journey . . ."—I so didn't want to go—"I'll make alternate arrangements."

His mouth twitched. "As you think best."

Right, because you're just a holy warrior and you'd never tell me what to do. I wasn't buying that for a minute. Oddly, I realized I wasn't scared of him. This time, I didn't ask him to swear he meant me no harm. If he said he had been sent to protect me, however little I understood that call, then I believed him.

I got us both some *limonada* from the fridge upstairs and we drank in silence. Shannon returned a few minutes later, arms laden with plastic grocery bags. She liked doing the food shopping—and since I didn't, I was happy to let her.

She was talking when she came through the front door, something about the way the sun hit the bougainvillea on the adobe walls, but her words dried up when she spotted Kel. I took a couple of the bags from her, not that she noticed. Two spots of color burned on her cheeks; though we'd been here a while, she stayed out of the sun, preferring her pallor and dyed-black Goth hair.

"Who's this?" she asked, eyes wide and avid.

Good lord, she was smitten. I'd never seen her look at anyone this way, and we had some sexy neighbors. I tried to see him through her eyes—maybe it was the muscles and the tats? Along with a pair of jeans, Kel wore a plain white dress shirt, but most of the buttons were open to reveal a clean undershirt. Through the fabric showed glimmers of dark ink, as if he were a secret work of art ready to be unveiled to the right hands.

Sure, he was bald, but he had a strong jaw and those icy, mysterious eyes. Damn, now I could see it too. This was the last thing I needed.

Clearing my throat, I answered belatedly, "Kel Ferguson. He's an old friend."

That was true enough. With my eyes, I told him not to go into the whole Hand of God business with her. She'd probably decide his modern-day-paladin status meant he was perfect for whatever she had in mind. I didn't like to think about it; she was almost nineteen and a boiling cauldron of hormones.

"Nice to meet you." Kel extended a hand. Apparently, he was capable of pretending to be normal, at least for short stretches.

She shook his hand with a little quiver of pleasure. I wondered if he noticed. "I'm Shannon, Corine's roommate."

That was a good way to describe our situation to an outsider. I was also her mentor, helping her learn about her gift—which was summoning and speaking to the dead via vintage radio—as best I could. So far, we seemed to be doing all right. She was a lot happier and safer than she'd been in Kilmer, at least.

"You never told me about him." She cut me a reproachful look.

I grinned. "The better to surprise you with. Now, we have an errand to run. We'll wait until you get the food put away and then I need you to mind the shop."

"Give me a minute. I'll be right back."

True to her word, she didn't linger upstairs. In short order she took my place behind the counter and I picked up the white box. Maybe Tia could tell us something, and that would give us a place to start. Magick left a trail, and all its practitioners possessed an astral tell. If Tia couldn't provide any insights, I'd call Booke, who could examine the object in the planes.

"Thanks. We'll be back later."

"It's my turn to cook," Shannon said. "Should I make enough for a guest?"

Subtle. I slid him an inquiring look. From what distance did he plan to guard me? Would it be up close and personal or did he prefer to sit outside in an SUV like they did in the movies? I felt pretty sure that holy warriors didn't operate like spies, though.

"I was hoping you'd invite me to sleep on your couch, so dinner would be welcome."

She brightened. "Consider yourself invited."

"Ready?" I asked him.

He responded with a nod, so we headed out the back, which led us through a jumble of crates and piles of junk I had yet to examine. The metal door opened into an alley littered with broken pavement. Two stray dogs fought over food scraps, and I gave them a wide berth. There was no point in unleashing the fearsome fury of God's Hand on a couple of hounds.

Heat hung in the air, making it feel dry and sharp in the lungs. Kel didn't appear affected by it—of course he wouldn't— but I was sweating by the time we reached the corner. He must've known the market was within walking distance, because he never suggested we drive.

A tangle of electrical wires hung over my street with shady trees guarding the parrot-bright buildings. Sun dappled the concrete and found bits of crystal to make it sparkle. The sidewalk was rough and uneven; he took my arm a couple of times to help me over slabs of overlapping cement. Houses with their high walls and sturdy gates gave way to businesses: a doctor's office, a dry cleaner's, an OXXO—a convenience store—and the *comedor*, where I bought my beans and rice. Overhead, the sky was too blue and beautiful for me to want to believe that somewhere in this lovely country, a powerful man wanted me dead, but if I didn't take action, he would get his wish.

We came to a busy street, the one with the *farmacia* on the corner, and waited until it was clear. An old man sold flowers and magazines in the median; he raised his hand in greeting. Everyone recognized me around here, most likely because of the hair. Once a week, I walked down to buy a copy of *Muy Interesante* and practice my Spanish reading. Sometimes I bought *un ramo de rosas* too—it seemed criminal *not* to when one could do so for ten pesos.

At the first gap between zooming cars, Kel shepherded me across as if I'd never done this before. I cut him a look, eyes narrowed against the sunlight, and I would've sworn for a brief instant that God's Hand was smiling. By the time we passed into the side street shaded by tall buildings and stately laurel trees, I decided I must've been mistaken.

The *avenida* that led to the marketplace took us up a steep incline; walking in the mountains was much harder than hiking on level ground, and by the time we reached the top, I was puffing a bit. So much for my resolution to work out—in some regards, I didn't have much discipline.

Acacia and rubber trees lined this backstreet, and a park opened up inside the framework of buildings, after we crossed one more road. From here I could see the red awnings, where people sold fresh fruit, vegetables, cleaning supplies, clothing, knockoff designer handbags, and homemade food, along with even more interesting items. Tia offered some of the most intriguing selections you could find anywhere in the city, in fact.

Kel broke the silence at last, following my gaze up the mountain, where the market sat at the far end of the park. "Is that where we'll find her?"

I thought he knew the answer already, but he studied my face, as if seeking confirmation. So I nodded and led him across the brownish grass. Four kids were swinging as we passed by, their cries echoing as we climbed the final hill.

My palm sweated where I held the white box; it was a

little unnerving to carry something that could kill me. I didn't want this, but Montoya's gambit signaled an end to my hard-won peace. Deep down, I always knew the confrontation was inevitable. You didn't do what I did and get away with it.

When we drew closer, I inhaled the scent of hot melted cheese, chorizo, and tacos al pastor. At the far end of the market, a man had set up a grill, and he was serving a queue of customers who devoured his food standing up. Kel glanced that way, and I shook my head, smiling.

"Shannon will never forgive you if you eat elsewhere. Come on. Tia's over here."

There's No Dave Here

Since it was almost four when we arrived, Tia was putting away her wares. Her hair drifted in silver wisps out of its customary bun, and she had on a blue and white flowered dress with a red apron atop it. Part of her stuff sat at her feet in two bags, charms and potions to solve any ill. I wondered how she had intended to get them home, prior to our arrival.

She smiled when she spotted me. *"Buenas tardes."*

Kel returned her greeting in perfectly accented Castilian Spanish. My brows rose; I wouldn't be able to keep secrets from him in Mexico—that was for sure. Tia studied him for long moments and then extended a gnarled hand, which she rarely did. He accepted the handshake, only to have the old woman spin his palm upward and peer at it. She made a noise as if she were sucking false teeth, but those that remained in her mouth belonged to her naturally.

"Mucho gusto," she murmured.

When she let go, I had the feeling she knew things about him that I never would, but the knowledge swam and drowned in her murky eyes; she'd never tell me what she'd seen. Tia told us to finish packing up the stall's contents. Her home wasn't far. Since we were here, we could help her carry things. I didn't argue; it never did any good.

We made quick work of her potions and charms. Before
long, we were following her down the street that paralleled
the park. Her house sat farther up the mountain, the levels
built into the rock itself, but she had an amazing view. Kel
said nothing, merely carried three heavy bags with an ease
that said he could bear any burden. It was a reassuring quality in a guardian.

I had visited her home before; sometimes I gave her things
to sell in addition to her own wares. This time, I tried to see
the place through Kel's eyes. The house was terraced, the
adobe whitewashed pale as milk so it glimmered in the sun,
contrasting with the black wrought iron on the windows. The
upper level had cement-and-plaster balconies, gently curved.
As we stepped through the latticed front gate, I noted Tia
had planted new flowers in the front—hibiscus and dahlia,
angel's trumpet and flowering sage. Her garden was beyond
lovely, the courtyard paved in ornate terra-cotta tiles. Some
of them had cracked, but it didn't give the sense of disre-
pair. With moss growing green against the clay, it was more
of a natural reclamation.

Tia handed us the rest of the bags so she could unlock
the door. Within, it was dim and cool. My shoes made no
sound against the marble floor. It was a nicer home than
you might expect from a woman who cleaned houses for
a living, in addition to selling potions and charms, but Tia
worked so hard because she claimed it kept her young. Given
how well she moved, I couldn't argue with the results.

"Put everything on the table," she instructed in Spanish,
and then led us into the sitting room, where she met with
clients.

Here, the furniture was so old, it felt different from modern couches in the lack of springs. With its solid wood frame
and plain cushions, this was more like a futon, only it didn't
flip to form a bed. Everything in her home belonged to the
rustic hacienda style, and had been crafted by hand.

Kel sat down beside me. He seemed to take up more
than his half of the sofa, due to presence more than physical

size. Which was impressive. But unlike most men, he didn't sprawl; he contained himself in as little space as possible, as if he were accustomed to being confined.

Like any good hostess, Tia offered us refreshments, which I declined. We needed to get down to business. The social stuff would have to keep for another time, assuming I survived.

I hefted the white box. "I have an item for you to examine," I said in Spanish.

"¿Qué?"

"It's a saltshaker, but it's got a killing hex."

She crossed herself and regarded the case dubiously. "What do you think I can do with it?"

"I was hoping you could tell me something about the kind of magic used."

Tia considered for long moments, brow furrowed, and then nodded. "I have one charm that might prove useful. Do you know if it's meant only for you, or will it work on anyone who touches it?"

I glanced at Kel, who answered, "It's keyed to Corine."

Wonderful. From my mother—who had been a witch—I knew such specificity required sophistication and finesse in the casting. In most cases, it also required a personal effect or some physical tie, like locks of hair, blood, or nail clippings.

Damn. I probably shouldn't get my hair done at the salon until this is over.

"I would rather not test that," Tia said with a grin creasing her weathered cheeks.

She stood up and headed for the kitchen. A few moments later, she came back with a tray, including a crystal bowl, salt, a cup of mixed herbs, and a slender stick carved out of green, fragrant wood. She was also wearing a pair of long black satin gloves, perhaps a remnant from an old *Día de los Muertos* costume of *La Calavera Catrina*, which came from a zinc etching by José Guadalupe Posada in 1913. It had since seeped into Mexican celebrations, a feminine skeleton in silk and tulle—death all dressed up.

I gathered she was taking no chances with poor Eros. Given my track record in romantic relationships, I couldn't help but wonder if there was a warning in the form of the would-be instrument of my death: *Love will be your doom*. Smiling at such hubris, I watched as Tia perched on the edge of the sofa and arranged the items.

First, she rimmed the bowl with salt and then sprinkled the remainder into the water. Next, she scattered the herbs, and finally, she stirred the mixture with the stick, all while whispering what sounded like broken fragments of a prayer.

I caught snippets, like *"en espiritu sancti"* and *"el buen Señor,"* but mostly, it was too soft for me to understand. When she finished chanting and mixing—the water was a cloudy pool by this point—she picked up the white box, opened it, and—with one thumb holding Pysche in place—she tipped Eros into the bowl.

With a hiss, the herb-and-salt-infused water turned black as ink and it roiled as if a thousand tiny snakes swam in its depths. Tia cupped her hands, guiding the liquid, which solidified into a substance that resembled black Jell-O.

Gross.

Beneath the permanent suntan, her face paled as she worked, air-sculpting the lines into something she saw only in her mind's eye. Before long, the thing in the bowl began to look human; she was crafting a viscous bust of the spell caster.

Holy crap, all Booke can do is tell us what the person's astral sigil looks like.

It wasn't a perfect image, of course, but I would most likely remember this face, if I saw him—and it was most definitely a man. Kel stood up and, without bothering Tia, went looking for a pad of paper. Shortly, he sat down and started sketching in quick, bold lines—good on him; there was no telling how long this spell would last.

As he was putting the finishing touches on the drawing, the creation wavered. Tia swayed, and then Eros came spurting out of the thing's mouth, landing in a wet, slimy spatter on top of the tray. Now we just had a disgusting saltshaker and a bowl of dirty water. My friend looked worse for the wear, so I made her a cup of tea. I had been to her house often enough to know to manage.

When I returned, she seemed a little stronger, but her voice was hoarse. *"Magia negra, muy negra."* Bad magic, very dark: as if I couldn't have guessed that by the reaction to the water she'd blessed. *"Magia sangrienta."*

Blood magick.

That actually helped. Certain voodoo traditions used blood, and so did the darkest hermetic traditions. Practitioners like my mother never used blood; neither did Tia. I also knew of a few shamans who used it, but in sympathetic magick, not baneful.

Most would laugh at the idea of magick and hexes. The world was divided into three groups: practitioners, those who *wanted* to believe in the paranormal, and those who scoffed at it. Skeptics comprised the vast majority; practitioners were rare, and the ones who wanted to believe or had seen something unusual tended to get lumped in with those who claimed aliens had abducted them or that the government had put hardware in their heads to make sure they always bought American cars.

At any rate, Tia's work gave us a place to start.

Area 51, a message board used by the gifted community, offered untold resources. People there could likely tell me some names of practitioners who could—and would—craft such a special blood-based spell. After all, not all sorcerers, witches, and warlocks were willing to hire out as mercs; many felt that demeaned their gifts.

While Tia sipped the hot tea, I cleaned up the mess. I was careful not to touch Eros; I merely carried the whole tray to the kitchen and left him alone while tidying up. I could hear Kel talking in his low bass rumble and I marveled at his perfect, elegant Castilian accent, so different from the one I'd picked up here. It sounded like he was reassuring her. With Tia, he showed gentleness I had never seen from him before, and I made a note to question him about it later.

She had more color in her face by the time I came back to the sitting room and her hands were steady. But the air felt thick and cloying, as if her spell had some residual effect. No breeze whipped through the open windows, and this high on the mountain, that stillness was unusual at this hour in the evening. It seemed as if the world held its breath.

"How much do I owe you?" I asked in Spanish.

"*Quinientos.*" Five hundred—it was more than she'd ever charged me before, and yet it wasn't as much as it sounded.

I dug into my purse, which felt light, since Butch—my hyperintelligent Chihuahua, whose ability to sense supernatural threats had saved my bacon more than once—was with Shannon at the shop, got out my wallet, and peeled off a bill. I loved the colorful Mexican currency; my favorite was definitely the twenty. The old ones were a charming shade of purple, and the new ones blue, both so beautiful they didn't even feel like money.

"Is there anything else we can do?" I asked, because she looked very tired, more than I had ever seen her. For the first time in our acquaintance, she looked not old, but ancient, as if a strong wind could sweep her away.

"No," she said. "Just take the cursed thing when you go."

After picking up the white box, Kel went to the kitchen to fetch the saltshaker. I was happy to let him take care of it.

"Are you going to be all right?"

"No." Probably reading my expression correctly, she went on. "But because I'm an old woman, not because of this. I hope I was some help. If you want more answers or for someone to remove the curse, you need to go to Catemaco."

I'd heard of the place, a legendary town of witches set on the mystic shores of one of Mexico's largest lakes. "Say I do—who would I speak with?"

"Nalleli. She is the island witch. Any boatman should know of her."

"And she'll be able to help me?"

Tia smiled, her eyes shadowed and deep in her lined face. "Much more than I can, child."

Kel appeared in the doorway, the white box in his hand. Presumably he had washed and stowed Eros back in the compartment alongside Psyche. Maybe it was the inveterate pawnshop owner in me, but in addition to those answers about the man who had crafted the spell, I also wanted the curse removed.

It would be irresponsible of me to sell the set to the Spanish professor, knowing one of the items was cursed. Though nothing should happen to her, since the hex was keyed to me, one never knew what might happen as spells started to decay. I didn't want to be the reason she wound up on her kitchen floor, bleeding from the eyes, two years from now.

I also wanted to make that sale; the Spanish professor would *love* these. Maybe Chance thought I bought the pawnshop for lack of other options, but I really enjoyed hooking people up with junk they never knew they always wanted.

God's Hand bowed to Tia and then we let ourselves out. Her garden smelled sweet with the freshness of growing things as we passed through. Outside the gate, the street was quiet. She lived high enough on the mountain that there wasn't much traffic, and the park had emptied when the sun went down. It was dark and silent enough that I was glad for his presence at my side. The walk back to my shop from Tia's place was always easier, since it was almost entirely downhill.

"We're going to Catemaco?"

I guessed he had overheard everything, but I couldn't get used to the idea that someone so dangerous and otherworldly would be content following me around until he received alternate orders. "Well, *I* am."

"You won't last the week without me," he said quietly.

An odd sensation took me then, as if I'd been living on borrowed time for longer than I knew. I was supposed to perish in Kilmer, but I survived the fire that caused my mother to take her own life—only to die there so many years later— and be resuscitated by Jesse Saldana. Again I nearly died, only to be saved by the very demon I was meant to feed.

Reflexively, I rubbed the hard spot on my side. It was barely perceptible, but since I knew where to touch, I could find it.

A knife went in there—and now the weapon is part of me.

"That's good news," I said sourly.

Kel's gaze followed my movement; his jaw tightened. "I know about that, and it gives me no pleasure to be sworn to one so demon-touched."

"Where were you, then? So it didn't happen."

"I had other orders."

Well, of course you did.

I didn't want to hear how much I sucked in comparison to his other jobs, so I changed the subject. "You were different with Tia. How come?"

"I behave in accordance with proximity to grace."

It took me a minute to work that out. In that time, we cut across the silent park. In the dark, you couldn't see the brown patches in the grass, but I heard the difference beneath my feet. "You're saying she's a holy woman?"

More than me, certainly. I have earthly tendencies of which a paladin could never approve.

"And shortly destined for . . . better things."

"You mean she's going to die soon?" My heart twanged.

I didn't want to lose Tia; in the time I'd lived here, she had become important to me. When I came back from Kilmer, heartbroken all over again, I'd spent more than one night on her sofa, listening to her stories. Sometimes Shannon came along. In her quiet way, Tia had done more to teach me how to be self-sufficient and complete unto myself than anyone else. She'd taught me that work was often a cure for what ailed you, and that unless you learned inner contentment, you could never truly be happy.

"Is that so surprising?"

Given her age, no. Not at all. I just wasn't ready to lose her. I'd never known my grandmother. If my dad's parents weren't dead when he disappeared, I never met them, and my mother might've been born from the forest for all I'd ever known of her family.

"I'll miss her, that's all."

"You should be happy for her."

"Oh, shut up." Maybe it wasn't the best idea to antago-
nize my protection, but as I understood it, he wasn't going
anywhere until his orders came from on high, so it didn't
matter what I said anyway. It wasn't like he *wanted* to be
here.

To my surprise, he did. We walked down the side street,
which seemed much darker and scarier at this hour. There
were no lights on inside any of the buildings, and as we passed
a house with an outdoor light, something popped like a fire-
cracker, and the lamp went out. *Gunshot.* This wasn't the
kind of neighborhood where that happened on its own. Weapons fire was pretty rare in this part of Mexico City, because
laws regarding illegal guns were harsh as hell, and nobody
wanted to wind up in prison here.

I couldn't see; I didn't know if I should run or try to
hide. The street was bathed in complete darkness, and if there
was a sniper on the roof with night-vision goggles, this would
be like shooting fish in a barrel. As I moved, the shooter
nailed me in the upper arm. The pain nearly blinded me. I
swallowed a scream; if I hadn't shifted, I'd be dead now,
and he might finish the job at any second.

But I'd forgotten about Kel. He slid in behind me and
used his own body as a shield. With his hands on my shoulders, he pushed me into a run. I might've expected him
to bound off looking for the shooter, but no—his mission
was clear. He had orders to protect me, and he intended to
do so.

I stumbled over the broken cement and he said right beside my ear, "I can see fine. I'd lead but I need to stay behind you. So you'll have to trust me. I'll guide you."

Like hell, I thought, but when he said, "Up," I lifted my
feet and managed to scramble onto the higher part of the
sidewalk.

Another shot rang out, and Kel stifled a sound.

"You're hit." Because of the injuries I'd seen him recover
from in Laredo, I knew he would live no matter where they'd
gotten him, but that didn't mean he felt no pain. I knew

firsthand just how much it hurt; the warm blood trickling down my biceps made me wonder how bad my arm was.

Flesh wound, I told myself. *Just a graze.*

"Keep moving," he ordered.

I needed no second invitation, and I sprinted as fast as I could toward the distant lights of the busy *avenida* just a block and a half from my store. It was strange with him running right behind me, but with his greater size, he found it no problem to keep up, even when he'd been shot. Each step sent a fresh jolt through my wounded arm.

We burst onto the sidewalk, and I had never been more reassured to see the glowing red and yellow OXXO sign. Men milled about here, drinking, and smoking. They gave us a glance, and then their gazes slid away, partly because of my pale, sweaty face, partly due to my big, bleeding companion.

As soon as we caught a break in traffic, we ran across. I had a sharp stitch in my side by then, and a dull throb in my biceps, but I was sure it was nothing compared to Kel's problems. Not that he would complain. I suspected whining meant being kicked out of the paladin club. I could so see him in armor, wielding a giant sword. And things could have been worse on my end too. At least I didn't have a bullet in me; when I rotated my arm, I felt an intense ache, not a foreign presence.

"They had a guy watching me," I panted. "In case the hex didn't work."

I wanted to take a break, but we were almost to the safety of my shop. *Keep moving. You don't know where the sniper is.*

"Insurance."

That made sense, I supposed. But the shooter would tell Montoya I had protection. *Worse and worse. Better to focus on what I can do to help him.*

"How does this go? Do I need to dig that out of you or will it work its way out as you heal?"

Shadows played over his bare head, but his face revealed no particular emotion beneath the streetlights. He hesitated, and when he spoke, his tone reflected a quiet surprise, as if nobody had ever asked him that before. "If it's not removed, it will stay beneath my skin."

A constant irritant—yeah, I knew all about that, and fought the urge to rub my side again. I wouldn't do that to him.

Looks like I'll be playing doctor tonight.

Playing Doctor

The shop was closed, so we went through the back door and up the stairs. I could smell the spicy marinara sauce before we hit the second floor. Shannon was making spaghetti, her best dish. Admittedly, it was hard to screw up: boil the water, time the pasta, microwave the sauce—not rocket science. But tonight, she'd gone to some extra trouble with grated Parmesan cheese and a Caesar salad.

It looked very impressive.

Butch raised his head from where he lay napping on the sofa and growled low in his throat, but I think he smelled the blood more than objected to my companion. He'd always liked Kel. I went over to give the dog a soothing stroke on the head, and once I got closer, he settled down. For a tiny breed, he could be quite protective. Of course, that could be because if I got myself killed, he'd be homeless.

Shannon came down the hall brushing her hair. "Are you guys ready to eat?" She glanced from me to Kel. "Let me guess. Something went horribly wrong."

"Got it in one."

"Is that blood?" she asked, stepping closer.

I covered my upper arm with my fingers and watched the red trickle through. With grim determination, I blocked the memory of how stepping to the left narrowly saved me from a bullet in the chest. I could've died, just like that. The knowledge sank into my stomach like a fisherman's hook. "Yeah."

Her pale face went a little green, but she squared her shoulders. "What can I do?"

"I need my wound cleaned and bandaged."

"I'll take care of it," Shannon said, heading down the hall to get first-aid supplies.

"After she patches me up, I'll operate on you," I told Kel. "How long do you think we have until he makes another run at us?"

"Not long," Kel answered.

The girl paused and turned, eyes wide. "Another run? Don't you think it's time you clued me in?"

He answered succinctly, "A drug lord is trying to kill Corine over something she did before she met you. Someone took a shot on the way here and nailed both of us, but since he didn't kill her, I suspect he'll arrive soon to finish the job."

The girl had stones. She folded her arms and demanded, "Shouldn't we be, oh, I don't know . . . *running for our lives*?"

Oh, crap, I hadn't wanted to tell Shannon about Kel being God's Hand, so now she didn't know there was anything special about him. But circumstances made it necessary to fill in the blanks for her. "We need to talk."

It was best if I explained things to her. I made the request silently, leveling a significant look on Shannon. He acknowledged that with an inclination of his head.

Ignoring his injury, Kel strode toward the door. "Before we take off, I'll put the gunman down."

I didn't like sending him out to hunt a human being, but I had to be pragmatic. *The man who shot us works for Montoya; he accepted money to kill me. He's not going to stop until I'm dead.* However I rationalized it, though, I couldn't feel good about it, and knowing it was necessary didn't lessen the sickness in my stomach. So I focused on the burn in my biceps and told myself, *He'll do worse to you—and to Shannon—if you let him.* That so wasn't on. But I loathed the ruthless decisions being forced on me in the name of survival, and I wondered if the woman I'd been, the one Chance loved, could've made these choices.

"Do what you have to," I told Kel.

"I'll handle it," he said quietly.

I should be thankful for small favors. There were a number of places nearby where he could stash a body, and I wanted to be long gone before the authorities started asking awkward questions. In our favor, if this guy worked for Montoya, then he had a record, and the *policía* would assume the death was drug related. Lucky break. Funny, right then I didn't feel fortunate.

"Come up when you're done. I'll fix your back, and then we can go."

Kel smiled—and that was terrifying. "This won't take long."

His movements carried an awful grace as he slid out of the apartment. Shannon gave a shiver, but she wasn't panicked. Another girl might be freaking out—not Shan. But then, like me, she grew up in a cursed town, where people died mysteriously and disappeared all the time. She was nearly sacrificed to a demon by her own mother, who developed a conscience only at the end; Sandra tried to claim innocence, but her daughter knew better. I could only try to be there for her and help pick up the pieces. Part of me thought she needed a more stable life, but I couldn't offer that right now. I could only give her support and affection.

"Come on," she said, leading the way to the bathroom.

I stripped off my bloodstained shirt and stood in my white bra while she cleaned the wound. As she worked, I sucked in a sharp breath, gritting my teeth. In old Westerns, the hero always had a bottle of rotgut to take the edge off. I just closed my eyes and tried not to scream.

"How does it look?" I asked eventually.

"It got the outer edge of your arm."

"A graze?"

"I guess," she said. "There's no hole, if that's what you're asking."

That was good news. At least I didn't have to worry about

muscle damage. If she cleaned it and wrapped it, I should heal well enough. The last thing I wanted to do was see a doctor in Mexico, who might report me to Montoya.

With gentle hands, Shannon took care of the wound and I went up to the bedroom to get a clean shirt. When I returned, she was dumping the spaghetti and salad in plastic containers. She opened a drawer and got out a plastic bag to stow the food and then added napkins and plastic silverware.

"Should I bring bowls?"

In answer, I located three plastic ones and handed them to her. If they didn't make it back here, no big loss. I couldn't say the same about Shannon. Though the gunshot wound should've alerted her to the fact that this situation was no joke, she still needed to know what she was getting into in order to make an informed decision. I took a deep breath and then summarized my history with Kel: how I met a holy warrior in a hundred words or less.

"Damn. Seriously?"

I had to nod. "It's all true, my hand to God."

"Pun intended?"

"Of course."

"He's really downstairs killing somebody for the Lord?"

My lips twisted. "Welcome to my world."

"I'm thinking he's not my type after all."

"Well, that's one positive that came out of this. He's not exactly human, Shan." I turned. "I'll go get our stuff."

"You said the same thing about your ex," she pointed out.

I was on my way to the stairs, so I called over my shoulder, "Hence the 'ex' part."

Our two bedrooms were up one level; the bilevel flat had the sitting room, kitchen, and half bath downstairs. Upstairs, we had two bedrooms and a bath, with balconies off each room. The split design made the place seem spacious, and when one of us had company, we could give the other privacy.

Though she'd been here only a few months, Shannon had more visitors than I did. I resisted any neighborly attempts to get to know me. It didn't take a shrink to figure out why.

Two guys claimed to care about me, yet neither was here. They both wanted me to give up the life I'd built and come live somewhere else. With Jesse Saldana, it would be Laredo, Texas. As he'd pointed out, I could open a pawnshop there, but he couldn't be a cop in Mexico, and he had a large family he didn't want to leave behind. I couldn't blame him. Chance, on the other hand, had business interests in Florida, where his mother lived. He was a dutiful son and he wanted to take care of her, a feeling that got stronger when he almost lost her.

Regardless of whether it was a reasonable hope, I wanted someone who didn't expect me to give up everything, a guy willing to do whatever it took to be with me. I'd spent my whole life settling, trying not to attract attention, and generally doing whatever it took to keep other people happy. I didn't want to do that again. I *wouldn't*. Not when I was comfortable in my own skin at last.

Sure, there were certain challenges, like a drug lord who wanted me dead, and the fact that I owed a demon a debt that he could call due at any moment. *But everybody's got problems, right?*

Within a few more moments, I packed our bags. Shannon's was a parti-colored black backpack with feminine skulls on it. Mine was less interesting, just a simple gray duffel that had wheels if you unzipped the bottom compartment. As we hurried around, Butch whined; I think he recognized signs of impending travel.

"Don't worry," I told the dog. "I won't forget your stuff."

He did not look particularly reassured. While he leaned against my legs, I plugged in Shannon's laptop and went online. Because I didn't check as often as Shannon, I had messages waiting. The first was from Yi Min-Chin. *Things are going well at the store. Came up with a new cream, and I'd love to see how it works on you. Love, Min. P.S. Chance misses you.*

Yeah, right. I wrote back quickly, asking about the cream.

I ignored the mention of her son. She had been hinting, none too subtly, for months that I needed to come to Tampa for a visit. Much as I loved her, that wasn't happening.

I read on. I could hear Jesse Saldana's drawl as I skimmed the words.

Hi, sugar. Worked late tonight and I was thinking about you just before bed. I tried to call, but I got voice mail. I sure am missing you. Just as soon as I can swing it, I'll take some vacation time and come see you. I have a bit saved up, even with that trip to Georgia. I figure I need to check out your shop. My mom's birthday is coming up. I bet you could help me find the perfect thing for her. That's if I'm welcome. Anyway, I'll call again soon. Love, Jesse.

I also had a quick note from Booke, the magickal expert I'd met online while trying to find Chance's mom. He was a proper mystery; I knew him only by his voice, as he appeared to be trapped somehow in Stoke. I'd give a lot to unravel his secrets, but this wasn't the time. I skimmed his message detailing his latest project. Since we'd perfected lucid dreaming and then moved on to the next level, object translocation, he wanted my help in testing a new theory. For now, the idea would have to keep, but I was game once things settled down.

The rest of my mail didn't amount to much. I deleted and then started typing. I couldn't say anything specific without risking giving too much away, but I didn't want Jesse or Booke to worry. I let them both know I was taking an un-scheduled trip, showing Shannon some of the sights, and that I'd be sorry to miss our regular chats. Knowing he was lonely, I talked to Booke weekly on IM and about once a month on the phone. Jesse, I spoke to more often, since we were "dating," though not exclusively. We'd agreed a monog-amous long-distance relationship couldn't work, but we should get to know each other better in case one of us—meaning me—wanted to relocate. Before a few months ago, I'd never heard of virtual dating, but it was better than nothing. I did miss him.

When Kel returned, he stopped in the shadows and said softly, "I recommend you avert your eyes."

We both squeezed our eyes shut, and I felt the breeze of his passing. I smelled the sweet, coppery tang of blood, and a shiver worked through me. In the bathroom, the water ran for a good five minutes; I imagined the crimson diffusing in the sink, swirling down my drain. Pretty soon I felt a little woozy.

"Is this how it begins?" she asked.

"What?"

"One of the adventures you told me about."

I wasn't sure I'd call anything that'd happened to me an *adventure*, but I could see how a not-quite-nineteen-year-old girl might view it that way. She was young enough to find all of this exciting as well as terrifying and disturbing. If nothing else, I'd have some crazy stories to tell my grandkids—assuming I lived to see them.

"Pretty much. See what you can find out about hotels in Catemaco." After she nodded and sat down with her laptop, I went down the hall to the half bath and knocked. "You ready for me?"

"Almost," came his low response.

The noises from within indicated he was still washing up. *Damn, what did he do, bathe in the shooter's blood?* I was sure I didn't want to know the answer.

Eventually, he opened the door and I stepped inside. His shirt was off and it was wet where he'd scrubbed it. To his credit, there wasn't a speck of blood anywhere in the place. After all, it wasn't his first time cleaning up after himself.

In the hall, Shannon's soft tread said she was coming down the hall to watch, so I closed the door. Outside, she muttered in annoyance, and I heard her retreating. Given Kel's broad chest, powerful shoulders, artful tats, and incredible delts—along with a mass of old scars from fighting evil, or so he claimed—that seemed like a bad idea. I didn't want her romanticizing him. As long as I remembered how scary I'd found him in that orange prison jumpsuit, my hormones wouldn't overwhelm me, making me forget that he was, no matter how you spun it, first and foremost a killer.

He'd assembled the supplies on the edge of the sink, everything I needed to dig a bullet out of him. The knife was bigger than I felt comfortable using; nonetheless I picked it up, and my hands were steady. I took a few deep breaths to prepare myself for the coming ordeal. There was a reason I didn't go into health care, after all.

"Brace yourself, Bridget." He didn't tense or otherwise react, so I went in.

Shit. His skin had already started to seal over the wound. No wonder he'd given me the big knife; I had to cut him. *Dammit. I don't know if I can—*

"I'll be fine," he said with a touch of impatience. "Just do it."

"How much will it hurt?"

"Would it make you feel better if I told you I feel no pain?"

God, could that be true? Maybe you could blast him down to bone and he'd never know the difference, just continue with his assigned task until the flesh repaired itself.

"Yeah."

"Pity I can't claim that, then."

Yes, it certainly was. I wished he'd lied. But that wasn't going to happen. God's Hand was nothing if not scrupulously honest, even when the truth was weird, unwelcome, and terrifying.

The tattoos didn't extend to his back, so there was no fear of the scars marring the designs. He had angelic script on his chest, arms, shoulders, and head. For a fleeting instant, I wondered what the writing said. Eva had said he had angel names on his skull, but she hadn't seen the rest of him.

This isn't helping. Each second I stand here, the wound heals a little more.

Another deep breath, and I sank the knife into his back. The blade was sharp and silvered; his flesh gave way with sickening ease. Rich red blood spilled from the wound, darker

against his scarred skin. He braced an arm on the sink, muscles bunched. The other he wrapped around his midriff in a
protective gesture. When I glanced around him, I saw agony on his tense features reflected in the mirror.

Hurry. You don't want to make him mad.

By the time I finished, I felt nauseated and shaky, but I
dropped a twisted lead pellet in the trash beside the toilet.
Mechanically, I blotted away the blood and started to tape a
bandage over it, but by the time I got the gauze and tape
ready, the injury had already scabbed over. I stared at that
for a moment, unblinking.

This was indisputable truth, as I'd first glimpsed in Laredo.
He might be crazy, but he had unnatural powers. I didn't
want to contemplate where those abilities might come from.
At least he possessed none of the aromatic tells to suggest
he'd made some infernal pact.

"You're all set," I said quietly. "Feel any better?"

In answer, he rotated his shoulders, testing. "Yes. Thank
you."

He turned then, and I saw why he'd been covering his
abdomen. There was an angry red scar there, a new one. While
Shannon and I stood outside, wondering what he was doing, he had literally been holding his guts in and mopping
up his own blood.

Sickened, I stared at the evidence of my own cruelty.
Neither of us had wondered if he'd been hurt. We'd been
confident he could handle whomever Montoya had sent to
kill me—and so he had, but not without cost.

"Why didn't you let me help you?"

He reacted as if I had proposed something shocking and
inappropriate; his whole body stiffened, and he took a step
back. "Because I could handle it myself. I *cannot* dig a bullet out of my back."

"So you accept aid only if you can't perform the task
yourself?"

"That's one way to look at it."

I didn't understand him at all, and now the bathroom
seemed too small. I took a step back and flung the door

open. "Then I'll let you finish up in here. Shannon and I are ready to go anytime."

Out in the living room, I made a call. This time Señor Alvarez didn't seem surprised that I needed him to watch my shop for a while, but he sounded more resigned than pleased. In fact, I had to offer him a higher commission on daily sales to get him to agree.

By the time Kel came out, Shannon and I had our stuff lined up at the door, along with my purse, which contained a slightly unsettled Chihuahua. Shannon carried our dinner in one hand and a laptop bag in the other. Since her arrival, I'd sprung for wireless Internet—growing up in Kilmer had left her starved for the normal accoutrements of modern life.

"We can eat in the car," she said. "And I washed up the dishes so we don't get bugs. I also found a place for us to stay once we get there. I wrote down the address."

She was a good kid. I knew better than to put it that way, however, because I could still see residual interest in him simmering in her eyes, no matter what she'd said about him not being her type. Kel was fascinating, whether I liked it or not.

"Thanks, that's great. But you proved yourself in Kilmer, so I already knew you're kick-ass in a crisis."

Shannon flushed with pleasure at my comment, but she shrugged it off. "So we're set?"

"Let's move," he said.

As we went down the stairs, I studied him. There were faint lines of weariness and pain about his eyes, though nothing I would've noticed before. He led the way to a vehicle parked on the street a few houses down. Kel had been smart enough not to cover their gate, which caused a lot of trouble here. It was so annoying to back out, only to find some asshole had blocked you in.

His ride wasn't a macho SUV. Instead, it was a nondescript sedan in black or midnight blue—hard to tell in the dark. He loaded our bags into the trunk with an ease that belied the fact that he'd nearly been eviscerated; that injury suggested an opponent who had some skill with knives. I had a particular horror of blades. Over the years I'd handled a number of them, and they *never* told a happy tale.

"Shotgun," Shannon said, and climbed into the passenger seat.

The back was fine with me. It had been a long-ass day, and I wouldn't mind taking a nap. Butch whined, so I put him down to do his business. We'd given him dinner and a drink before leaving the apartment, so he should be good for a while yet. Afterward, I picked him up and tucked him back in my purse, where he snuggled in.

When I opened the right rear door, Kel put his hand on my arm to stop me from climbing in. "Why don't you drive?"

I couldn't have heard him correctly. "Really?"

He pitched his voice low, so Shannon—who was already in the car and fiddling with the radio—wouldn't hear. "The healing takes a lot out of me. We need to get to Catemaco, but I don't know how much longer I can stay alert."

I remembered how he'd practically gone catatonic after the fight with the warlock. Yeah, it wouldn't be good if that occurred with him behind the wheel of the car, especially one that contained Shannon, Butch, and me. While Kel might be able to recover from anything, the rest of us were all too human and fragile.

"Okay," I said. "Will you have something to eat before you pass out?" I glanced at Shannon's dyed-dark hair. "She wanted to impress you."

"That's absurd." In the half-light, I could almost swear his mouth pulled into the hint of a weary smile. "But yes, I'll eat the spaghetti if it will make the girl happy."

I smiled at him. "Thanks."

"One more thing, Corine."

Oh, I was sure I didn't like where this was going.

"When he fell, I took his weapon, an expertly crafted dagger. I thought you might handle it once we're in Catemaco."

Lovely. Something to look forward to. He took my silence for assent and slid into the car. I made sure Butch was comfortable in the back with Kel before rounding the vehicle and hopping into the driver's seat. The car had GPS, which would make our lives easier. Though I knew the general direction of Catemaco—and that it wasn't too far from Veracruz—I had never been there.

After buckling my seat belt, I programmed the address Shannon provided into the device and drove into the dark.

Hard to Handle

Once we left the highway, the night turned dark as sin. There were no lights on the narrow road that led to Catemaco. My companions were both out, so I had to trust the GPS knew what it was doing. If it didn't, there was no telling where we'd end up.

I drove past signs for cigars and giant lake shrimp, but none of the stalls was open at this hour. Though it wasn't quite midnight, it was certainly late enough for everyone else to be off the road. I had seldom been more relieved than when I made the last turn, and the gizmo claimed that the hotel Shannon had chosen lay a mile and a half up ahead on the left. Surprisingly, it was a nice place.

Floodlights illuminated the careful landscaping, and tall trees shaded the parking lot. It was a big, bright blue building with the name spelled out in flowers. I pulled into a space near the lobby, and turned the key in the ignition. As I stepped out of the car, I could taste the soft, clean air, so different from the city.

Shannon stirred as I pulled my bag out of the car. I slung the duffel over my shoulder, and then opened up the rear door. Butch hopped down, sniffed a few things, and then trotted over to the nearest tree. It was dark, so I didn't worry about what was he doing, or the mess he might leave behind. He was a small dog—how bad could it be?

My guardian was still unconscious. I hovered, unsure whether I ought to touch him, but I couldn't leave him in the car, either. Though it seemed self-serving, we might need him, and he couldn't defend us from the parking lot. At last I set my hand on his shoulder and gave him a gentle shake. It took two tries to get him to open his eyes, and when he did, they looked oddly sunken.

But despite appearances, he came alert in an instant. "We're here, I take it?"

I nodded. "I'm going to see about a room. It might be best if you stay outside while I do."

Kel glanced down at his white, bloodstained shirt. "I think so too."

"Do you have anything else to wear tomorrow?"

"Yes—my bag is in the trunk. I just didn't think it was worth slowing us down."

"Good call," Shannon said. "Am I allowed to come in with you?"

"Of course."

I whispered Butch's name and he came trotting out of the shadows wagging his tail. He'd no doubt sniffed everything nearby, and if there were anything to fear in the vicinity, he would've communicated that. Which meant I strode into the lobby with all confidence, despite my wrinkled clothing and gummy eyes.

The foyer was small, but immaculate. Beyond a glass wall I could see the restaurant, now closed for the night, and beyond the interior dining room, more tables sat beside the pool. At the front desk, the man looked tired, but he perked up when I started the registration process.

Our business didn't take long. I told him we needed a room with two double beds, and I wasn't sure how long we were staying. Judging by the dearth of cars in the lot, that shouldn't be a problem. And indeed, it wasn't. I paid for a couple of nights, and he gave me a key.

"You have a room on the second floor," he said in Spanish. "Lake view."

I nodded, listening to the rest of the amenities. Butch knew to stay in my bag until we left the lobby. I praised him and scratched his ears as I slid behind the wheel. After moving the car, I led the way to the stairs, and then Kel took point. He checked the place out thoroughly before motioning us up.

The room surprised me in a good way. It was large with a balcony facing the lake. Perhaps it was sparsely furnished in contrast to American hotels, but I preferred the sense of space. And we still had a TV, a desk, and a bureau, along with a mirror outside the bathroom. Not that I imagined we'd be spending that much time in here.

"You want a shower?" I asked Kel.

"Please."

I could wait until morning. When the water cut on, I set the chain and the dead bolt on the door and changed into my pajamas. Shannon was doing the same. She really was a remarkable girl.

"I'm thinking we take the bed by the inside wall," she said. "If I was trying to break in here, I'd come through the balcony. The other door has a steel core, and those are good, heavy locks."

I followed her train of thought. "So if someone does try to get in that way, it won't be quiet, and Kel will have a chance to get between them and us."

"Exactly."

God, I was tired. I slid into bed and curled onto my side. The double bed was big enough—and Shannon was small enough—that we shouldn't bother each other. My eyes closed.

I had the sense of being out of my body, light as air; I had to be dreaming. As I floated, the darkness melted away, coalescing into a combination of red-velvet brothel and roadhouse chic. This was Twilight, run by a woman named Twila, who ran San Antonio. Anybody with a gift who arrived in her demesne and planned to stay had better ask her permission. I'd been here before.

I'm dreaming.

The bar was nearly full, rowdy and loud. The music banging in the background I recognized as the Dropkick Murphys, an interesting choice for a joint in Texas. Jesse Saldana sat on a bar stool, nursing a beer. I recognized the bartender, a pretty woman in her forties who sported a ponytail. *Jeannie.* I'd met her myself. On this occasion, Saldana looked none too cheerful, thumb rimming his mug in slow circles.

"I don't think she trusts me," he said.

She served a draft and collected money from a guy I didn't recognize and then answered, "From what you've told me about her, I'm not surprised."

"She was hurt tonight." He took a long pull from his beer. "Don't know how bad. I was about to call her when she e-mailed me. No mention of the pain. Just 'I'm taking an unexpected trip; don't worry.' Like I can help it."

Jeannie gave him a kind look. "Sounds like she has issues with authority, hon, and like it or not, that's *you.*"

Shit, they're talking about me.

"So what do I do?"

"Show her you care, and you're willing to do whatever you can. But trust takes time. You can't demand it."

"I know," he said sadly. "I just have this feeling she's in deep, and it's going to get really bad before it gets better."

She touched him lightly on the hand. "There's nothing worse than seeing someone you care about suffer."

The despair in his face astonished me. I didn't know he felt this way, or maybe I only wanted him to. This was just a dream, after all. Not a true thing. Right? Nobody seemed to notice me; I might as well be a ghost. Wishing I could comfort him and explain why he couldn't be involved further, I touched Jesse on the shoulder, and he spun around, dark eyes haunted.

Shannon nudged me awake. The sun shone brightly through the curtains, patterning the tile floor. "You okay? You were whining in your sleep."

"Yeah. Thanks." I swallowed a moan as I slid out of bed. No point in telling her what I'd dreamt. I was pretty sure it was just a guilty conscience anyway.

A shower woke me up fully. I dressed in whorls of steam, so my clothes felt damp and sticky when I stepped out of the bathroom. I put down breakfast and a drink for Butch. The crunch of him enjoying his kibble sounded, but I didn't have to worry about waking the other two; they were both up before I stumbled into the bathroom.

Shannon stood on the balcony, her eyes wide with awe. "Look at the pool!"

Sometimes I forgot how young she was. But in all fairness, it was impressive. From our vantage point, the waters gleamed azure; there was a pale blue waterslide and a stone waterfall. Flowers bloomed in the center, lending the impression that we'd awakened in some tropical paradise.

The lake itself caught my eye. It was so big I couldn't see the opposite shore, and it lapped right up to the edge of the property; the land behind the hotel was a narrow slice. There was no pier, but I could see a place where the boats presumably pulled up. Down some distance, there was an earthen hut and a small swimming beach.

I considered before I made the offer, but it should be safe enough, and the waiters circulating among the guests looked fit and strong. "If you want to stay here and swim while we go looking for the island witch, it's fine with me." I did glance at Kel for confirmation. "That would be okay, right?"

He nodded. "I have no reason to believe they know where we are right now. Of course, that could change."

Yeah. Whomever Montoya had found to hex my Eros saltshaker might be able to scry our location. That was a pretty powerful and specific spell, however, and so it wouldn't be accomplished with a flick of the wrist. Such things took time and preparation; we couldn't waste our head start.

"That'd be cool," she said. "I've never really been on vacation."

I didn't let my emotional response to that show on my

face. My mom had taken me camping. Maybe we'd never gone anywhere like this, but I had those memories, at least. I didn't envy Shannon's recollections of her own mother.

"You have a suit?"

"Duh." She grinned. "I looked this place up, remember?"

"Then just charge your food to the room when you get hungry." I managed not to tell her to put on sunscreen. Besides, Shannon didn't want to lose her Goth pallor, so when she wasn't swimming, I was sure she would sit in the shade.

It was early, and she hadn't showered. If it were me, I wouldn't bother if I was going to the pool in a little while. Butch hopped into my purse, which answered my unasked question—it seemed he wanted to go in search of the island witch with Kel and me.

The guardian waited by the door. "I arranged a boat downstairs."

Wow, that was fast.

"So they know Nalleli here?"

"I didn't ask about her. They do, however, handle lake tours for their guests."

It made sense. Tourists who came looking for the famous Catemaco witches would be referred to charlatans in the *zócalo*. Likewise, those who wanted the grand tour of the lake . . . well, the staff helped out with that too. I wasn't sure if the locals knew the name Tia had given us, but we didn't want to leave a trail a mile wide.

"Are you sure Shannon will be all right?" I asked as we went down the stairs.

We passed through the small garden and through the lobby out into the pool area before he replied. "Do you want a detailed analysis?"

"Please."

"Should Montoya manage to uncover your location by arcane means, the spell will be keyed to you, so as long as you're not with Shannon when the attack comes, then she'll be fine."

"You're saying this is safer for her." *Damn.* I wished I'd

left her in Mexico City to run the shop. Not that she would've agreed to it.

"No question."

There were a few sunbathers already, and some Europeans were eating on the patio, basking in the sunlight. They spoke German, as best I could tell, and the older woman in the group had painfully fair skin. I hoped she put on sunscreen too.

Palapas lined the lakefront, the kind you usually saw in beach towns like Cancún or Puerto Vallarta. Here, there was no white sand; instead the little shelters sat atop rich green grass. The soil was damp beneath my soles, but not enough to sink. It had been raining, so the lake lapped nearly to the top of the concrete rim. There was no fencing, so you could fall into Lake Catemaco pretty easily. I didn't know how deep it was here.

To the left lay an impressive play area. There were no kids running around yet. If Shannon were a bit younger, she'd get some use out of the swings and the slide. Of course, if she were younger, she would still be with her father.

Today, I wore a pair of long cargo shorts and walking boots, paired with a yellow cotton peasant blouse. The bugs would be bad out on the water, but I didn't have any repellent on me. Somehow I doubted insect bites would prove a problem for Kel.

"It'll be a while," he said. "I thought you could read the dagger before we go."

I'd almost forgotten. With trepidation, I sat down at one of the white wrought-iron tables; the paint had peeled in spots, showing the darkness beneath. Placed just beyond the patio, they sat on the grass, where parents could watch their children at play. At this hour, the place was quiet, the sun only just starting to warm the day.

Kel handed me the weapon. A waiter came over, but he waved him away with a terse request for *café*. I gazed at the blade for a few seconds, and then braced myself. Knives were never good.

I reached for it and wrapped my fingers around the han-

dle. Fire blasted me as if I'd stepped into the heart of a vol-
cano. How my skin could still be on my body, I had no
idea; my vision washed red, and then I fell into a nightmare.

So many killings.

I saw them all, one by one, superimposed like ghostly,
silent reels shown in some infernal theater. Agony streaked
through me with each death. The cries felt like they must
surely choke me, and it got worse. The man had last used
this weapon to murder a child—an object lesson. I caught
some of the words, mouthed with angry gestures. I watched
the shock and grief, and could do nothing to stop it. It was a
past thing, untouchable, immutable.

I bore it and held my silence.

Then it showed me something new. Not a death. An argument. The man spun the blade in his hands, and his anger
suffused me. He got up in another man's grille, someone
who bore an unmistakable resemblance to the face Tia had
crafted. But before he could strike, the other man gestured;
the assassin slammed to the ground, and the knife dropped
out of his hand. I lost the thread there.

Finally, the dagger flashed the killer's fight with Kel,
lightning-fast and fierce. By the time I returned to the world
of lake, pool, and *palapas*, and Kel came back into focus,
I sat doubled over, breathing in raw, ugly gasps. Nausea
racked me. He touched my back, tentative as the brown bird
hopping around the base of the table, hoping for scraps. My
hand burned, but something had shifted in my gift. The
flower pentacle scar from my mother's necklace absorbed
the damage—and that was new.

"Take it away," I said hoarsely. Not his hand. The knife.

To my vast relief, he did.

"Nothing helpful?" he asked at last.

"Only that the man who used it is a professional. He
killed on orders, not for pleasure." I'd seen no signs of en-
joyment, but those rare flashes when I saw his reflection in
windowpanes, he had eyes like death, hollow and empty.

"We could have guessed as much." He paused, frowning and thoughtful.

"I'm glad you killed him." The last death—the child—would haunt me. "But at least I got a good look at the man who hexed me. I have a few corrections for your sketch."

"We'll do that when we get back. It's time to go." He stood up and headed toward the lake.

Voyage to Monkey Island

The morning sun warmed my skin as we waited for the boatman. In the distance, I spotted a flat-bottomed *lancha* churning the water; white spume sprayed in its wake as if it were propelled by fire-extinguisher foam. A large awning shaded the boat, which he piloted from the back. It was a bit battered but seaworthy. This vessel could hold eight more people, but we'd hired a private tour.

"He's ten minutes late," Kel said.

That was pretty good. In the city, if I scheduled an appointment with a repairman, I'd be lucky if he showed up on the promised day. Punctuality was an individual judgment more than a social imperative.

"How much is this costing me?" I whispered, as the boatman pulled up. The prow nudged the cement rim gently, and the man leapt onto shore with rope in hand. Steps led down into the launch, making it easy for us to board.

The other man answered—so he understood some English. "Four hundred pesos."

That was reasonable, thirty bucks or so, depending on the exchange rate. Catemaco wasn't a big tourist spot, so they hadn't jacked up the prices. The food probably wouldn't cost a fortune while we were here, either. Good thing, as the pawnshop took care of Shannon and me, but I wasn't rich.

I peeled off a couple of bills and passed them over, and

the boatman beamed at me. His teeth were very white in a sun-weathered face. *"Me llamo Ernesto. Bienvenidos."*

As we boarded, he seemed so pleased, chattering about the sights he would show us, including Monkey Island, that I couldn't bring myself to cut him off. So we listened while he practiced his English until he came to a word he didn't know, and then he substituted in Spanish.

Obligingly, I supplied the word for him. "Monkeys."

I always found it funny that there were two words for monkey in Spanish: *chango* and *mono*. I'd asked if one meant ape, but though *chango* was more slang, it still meant monkey. Spanish was weird that way: two words for monkey, and *esposas* meant both wives and handcuffs. That said a lot.

Ernesto had a thick accent. "You're going to love the Monkey Island."

I didn't share his certainty. Monkeys struck me as sinister, falling under the category of things that looked almost human, but weren't, really, like dolls and clowns—all creepy in my book.

Shannon looked so small from this distance, capped with a shock of black hair; she waved from the balcony as we got under way. I waved back and took a seat in the middle when the boat accelerated. Ernesto was still talking. We would stop first at the city market, he said, and for a mere fifty pesos more, he would disembark to buy fresh fruit for us to feed the monkeys.

I glanced at Kel, who murmured, "It might be best if we let him give us the regular tour in addition to going to see Nalleli. That way, our destination isn't so singular."

And we wouldn't stand out in his memory if someone questioned him later. It made sense, though I wasn't keen on the delay. There must be other tourists who asked to visit Nalleli. Otherwise, I wasn't sure how we'd find her.

"Do we know which island she's on?" I asked in a whisper.

"I'm sure *he* does," he answered, tilting his head back toward our guide.

It made sense. The island witch might be the only true *curandera*—or *bruja*, depending on the type of magick she practiced—in the area, though Catemaco was famous for its witches and warlocks. But tourism dictated that most were performers and charlatans more than true practitioners. I needed someone with real power, and I hoped Tia knew what she was talking about.

The boat gathered speed, leaping out toward the middle of the lake. Wind whipped across my face, and Butch popped his head out of my bag. I clutched him to my chest. If he got overly excited and jumped, I'd never see him again in a lake this size. It was *enormous*.

Buildings on the shore looked strange and exotic—as we neared the *zócalo*, a gold cathedral edged in red caught my eye. It rose above the palm and mangrove trees, and the bright-painted boats that crouched at its feet seemed as supplicants to the stately structure. We passed an orange and white building on the way to the mooring place. The reason it drew a second look? On the concrete wall below, it read, HOTEL DEL BRUJO, in black block letters, and the architecture reminded me of an old houseboat.

Shortly, Ernesto pulled up to a shallow point in the lake, not a dock so much as a sandbar. I gave him fifty pesos, and he leapt lightly down into the water. The boatman waded ashore, leaving Kel and me to watch the old woman doing her laundry nearby. She grinned at us from a nearly toothless mouth—and for a moment I was afraid she was going to come over begging. That was one of my least favorite parts of living in Mexico, because I never knew how much to give. However, with Kel at my side for protection and Butch in my lap to read the nuances of the situation, we'd be fine. Sopping clothes in hand, she came over to make small talk—and she didn't ask for money.

Maybe she had cataracts, because she didn't appear afraid of Kel, though she directed her greeting to both of us. *"¿Es un buen día, no?"*

I gazed up at the blue sky. It was, actually. I hadn't noticed because of the fear and necessity driving me. The gentle slosh of the water made the *lancha* rise and fall beside the sandbar, soothing me.

He answered in his precise Castilian Spanish. As it had been with Tia, his manner was gentle and almost courtly. *"Sí. ¿Como estáis vos?"*

"Muy bien, gracias."

She chatted with him as she washed. A bag sat beside her on the shore, clothing spilling out upon the sand. She used a bar of soap, but it wasn't the regular kind; I'd seen it in the cleaning aisles for use in laundry. You could shave it for use in machines or rub it on stains for washing by hand. I couldn't see that the lake water was doing her delicates any good, but it was doubtless better than nothing. I wondered if she lived nearby.

"Do you know the island witch?" Kel asked eventually.

Ah. Clever.

"Nalleli?" It seemed she did. I suspected she knew most things around here. *"Sí."*

"¿Donde vive?"

The old woman turned and gestured, giving complicated directions. I wasn't sure I'd be able to find the spot, based on what she was saying, but Kel appeared to follow it all. He smiled and thanked her. By the time Ernesto returned with pineapple, papaya, and cantaloupe for the monkeys, the washerwoman was giggling like a young girl.

She stepped back as Ernesto powered the boat in reverse, and then we headed back out onto the lake. Since it was relatively early, we saw a number of fishermen trying their luck—and one man asleep in his boat with a hat drawn across his face. Imagining what his wife would say when he came home empty-handed put a smile on my face.

This reminded me of a trip I'd taken with Chance. We'd crossed the channel by boat, Dover to Calais. To a girl from the Georgia backwoods, he'd seemed so impossibly charming and urbane, and I had to work to make myself worthy of him. I suspect he sensed that insecurity and it gave him leverage. It saddened me, thinking about that girl clutching his hand with each bounce of the waves. He'd wanted to be all things to me, and for a while, I permitted him to be.

After the way he'd left me in Kilmer—and no word

from him since—I didn't love him anymore. But some exes carved out space in your heart that could never be filled.

Oh, Jesse tried. And sometimes I felt like letting him. He represented security and normalcy, all the sweet and wholesome things I'd never known. Trouble was, I had self-destructive inclinations, and I didn't always heed what was best for me. Sometimes my instincts were purely imperfect.

The increase in speed roused me from reverie. Mountains rose in the distance, shrouded in clouds, as if the lake had been poured from their great heights. The islands appeared densely wooded, small strips of jungle rising from the water. I could see why the locals thought this place was magical—so astonishingly remote and unspoiled—and when the sun hit the water, it shone blue as a tropical ocean. But when the sun slid behind the clouds, it went dark and sullen.

As we went farther from town, we saw more wildlife. A snowy egret perched on a wooden pole rising from the water, the remains of a pier long since fallen into the *laguna*. Laughing gulls followed the boat, probably hoping for a treat tossed into the wind.

Butch studied everything with great interest, his big eyes shining with what I took to be delight. Kel was harder for me to read, just a wall of heavily muscled silence beside me. Luckily, Ernesto didn't have a shy bone in his body, and he regaled us with old stories while pointing out everything of interest. En route, we passed Heron Island, an inlet filled with water lilies, and an ecological preserve, which housed native art and a nice restaurant on the water.

"We should go," Kel said, as if we *were* tourists.

His attempt to pass as a vacationer amused me. But our guide had clearly seen weirder things than Kel, because he didn't stare at the tats. Then again, ink sometimes indicated some underworld ties, particularly when done in certain patterns. Ernesto couldn't know these were written in angelic script.

The boatman nodded. "If you do, try the eggs. Such a lovely sauce! And it is very nice to eat by the dock and watch the birds."

"*Quizá*," I said, which means *maybe*.

"You must see Eyipantla Falls as well," Ernesto added. "Sadly, I cannot take you there, but if you have a car, it is not far from your hotel, and the route is well marked."

"Noted."

It was getting harder for me to appreciate the scenery and rein in my nerves. Soon I'd find out whether Nalleli could help us, if she could tell anything about the hex or at least remove the curse from my damn saltshaker. The professor from Spain would be arriving in a few weeks.

But maybe I was fooling myself that I could go back to my shop. Since Montoya knew to find me there, it would be the height of stupidity to return. Instead I should keep moving, preventing his pet caster from getting a lock on me. It worried me that we'd paused in Catemaco, but I couldn't see a way around it. I needed to hear what the island witch had to say.

Lunging, Butch yapped at a bird that dove too close to the boat. I wrapped an arm around him and tucked him beneath it.

"Oh, no, you don't," I muttered.

The dog had the grace to look abashed.

I bounced with each wave until I learned to brace myself with my other arm on the green poles that held the awning aloft. The engine slowed as Ernesto downshifted, letting the boat glide close to the island. At first I didn't see anything, and then big simian faces poked out from the undergrowth. Two of them dangled above the boat, their weight causing the branches to hang so low as to brush the awning. I'm not sure what I expected, but these were not the tiny, adorable animals that perch on people's shoulders in the movies.

These monkeys were too big to be rightfully called cute—and as Ernesto put the fresh fruit on the yellow seats at the bow, they boarded.

Heaven and Hell

"Don't worry," Ernesto said in Spanish, doubtless reading my look. "They'll eat the fruit and go. I do this all the time."

Well, sure. Who wouldn't *want to invite enormous feral monkeys onto their boat?*

Beside me, Kel tracked their movements as the animals squatted and tore into the pineapple. The two largest ones fought over the last piece, shrieking until I thought they'd come to blows. Eventually the smaller yielded and picked up some melon. They were huge and greedy, their eyes darting back and forth as if they were angry about being forced to live on this island. But I was probably reading too much into the situation. They were animals.

Normal people probably snapped pictures right now, but I didn't have a camera. Mostly, I wanted to get this over with so we could ask Ernesto to take us to see Nalleli. It didn't help my nerves that Kel was carrying a hexed salt-shaker that could kill me. I'd started to put it in my bag earlier, but he'd extended a hand, wordless. I couldn't claim I was sorry to turn Eros over to his care.

A thump overhead rocked the whole boat—and I wasn't a fan of the idea that there were now giant monkeys on top of us. The one that climbed down the pole was bigger than the rest; it had a scarred muzzle and patchy gray fur. It should've been funny with its muddy red ass, but instead it looked mean and angry. Without meaning to, I moved a little closer to Kel. He put his hand on my arm—caution or reassurance, I didn't know which. Either way, it wasn't working.

I smelled something burning.

Please, oh, please, let that be nothing more menacing than a part we don't need.

Unfortunately, the sun slid behind a cloud—clouds that hadn't been so present or so dark a few minutes before—and the wind kicked up, classic signs something hideous was about to happen. To make matters worse, the smolder intensified into the stink of rotten eggs. Nothing good ever came of that stench. For the first time since I'd known him, Butch howled. It was a tiny, despairing sound, which I took to mean: *We are all kinds of fucked.*

"They're scrying," Kel said softly. "Using the water all around us."

An actual witch would know how to block that. It sucked that I wasn't one. "But how— Oh, *shit.* A tracking spell."

It only made sense. Still, I couldn't regret keeping the saltshaker. The curse needed to be removed before it decayed and struck somebody else. Only a selfish son of a bitch would discard a hexed item for someone else to trigger, and it wasn't like discarding an item guaranteed nobody would ever touch it again. Some people made their living picking through the garbage.

The monkeys screamed, showing yellow teeth. There were six animals, so big and heavy that they weighed down the boat. All around us, the air turned thick, heavy as chilled molasses; it had an actual viscosity, as if I could slice it and peer through. I struggled for oxygen, but it was no use. I couldn't breathe, couldn't move, and it was the worst thing ever, even worse than the cold life-sucking shades the warlock in Laredo had conjured. Oh, I didn't want to face *worse* than Nathan Moon.

Not like I had any choice.

The boatman seized. His whole body went rigid, and then the convulsions started. A bloody froth poured from his mouth, bubbling over his T-shirt. I fought the icy paralysis, but couldn't break free. *Poor Ernesto. He's dying because of me . . . for four hundred pesos.* I wanted desperately to look away, but I owed him that much—to bear witness to his suffering.

"What's happening?" The words weren't clear because I couldn't move my lips, but Kel took my meaning.

"A summoning," he said. "Passing over takes a lot out of any demon, so they're feeding on him before they attack us."

The paralysis was probably insurance, assuring that its prey didn't scamper off before it was ready to fight. Tears streamed down my cheeks as I watched the boatman writhe in unspeakable agony; it seemed like an eternity before he stilled. Eventually, the air cleared, releasing my locked muscles, but I didn't see anything we could fight. Kel tensed beside me, and his gaze cut every which way. Regardless of what he sensed, he didn't leave my side. I could never repay him for that.

His hand tightened on my forearm as the world around our boat went dark. I could still hear the rocking of the lake, but as if from great distance. He flashed, his white light shooting skyward like a beacon, and everything snapped back into focus, the darkness swirling away like windblown smoke.

I'd almost forgotten he could do that. He'd saved us at the airstrip outside Laredo with undead swarming all around, but it appeared his brightness worked best on zombies and shades, not demons. The wrong in the air didn't dissipate. Black columns of darklight poured into the monkeys' eyes, and they dropped their chunks of pineapple and papaya. The sweet-smelling pulp smeared all over the seats overlapped the sulfur stink, creating a truly horrific fruit salad. Hairy limbs jerked as the fiends learned how to puppet their new meat suits.

"Lesser demons," Kel breathed.

Oh, Christ. They must've been sent through the tracking spell by the foul practitioner Montoya had hired, and they'd eaten Ernesto's soul, as Kel had predicted—and they would've gotten me too, if he hadn't driven them back with his divine light. Not long ago, I would've felt ridiculous thinking along those lines, but it was nothing more than the truth today. People had been saying the eyes were the windows to the soul for centuries, but that wasn't strictly true. They were more like doorways, and if you weren't well protected, anything could get in.

At least they can't possess me or devour my soul anymore. But we weren't out of the woods yet. Not by any means.

"What's the game plan?"

We had no driver, and as soon as these monkey-demons worked out how to use their new bodies, we'd be up to our asses in attempted murder. I'd never seen animal possession before, but these beasts weren't natural, and they had the size and strength to do serious harm. Much as I hated to see Kel kill creatures in the wrong place at the wrong time, I wanted them to eat my organs even less. And it didn't seem right to leave a host of demonic monkeys on the island for the next batch of tourists.

Why couldn't I do anything *useful* in situations like this?

"Stay back. I may be able to perform an exorcism."

It went without saying that he was going to take some hideous damage in the process. I scrambled, looking for a place to hide, but the best I could do was to crouch down between the seats in the stern of the boat. A flat-bottomed *lancha* like this didn't offer much in the way of cover. I shuddered as I squatted next to Ernesto, who was horribly, undoubtedly dead. Grief for his fate and for his family's loss rippled through me.

The monkeys came at Kel as a unit, a whirl of claws and teeth. He rocked but did not give ground. Blood poured from the wounds they tore in his sides, greedily feasting on his flesh. They were something other now. Not animals. Fiends. I bit down on my thumb to keep from crying out.

His voice rang like a clap of thunder and warmth showered over me. *"Deus, in nómine tuo salvum me fac, et virtúte tua age causam meam. Deus, audi oratiónem meam; áuribus pércipe verba oris mei."*

Latin. Of course it would be Latin. The cadence rose and

fell, fueled by the strength of his will. But I made some sound—drawing attention to myself—and one of the demons broke away from the rest, bounding down the aisle toward me. I threw out my branded palm, intending to shield my face, and words that were not my own erupted from my mouth:

"In the name of the north, south, east, and west, in the name of the once and future queen, in the name of the smoke and the air, and the wind and the water, I name you the *Klothod*, who were banished from light of the daystar and may not walk this earth without my leave. I turn and bind you, back from whence you came. *Tsurikshikn!*"

A flash of light went up; I didn't know if it came from Kel or me. My eyes blazed white, a sort of crazy snow-blindness, and when my vision cleared, I saw the guardian crouched before me. The ash littering the boat blew away in the gentle breeze. Even the smell was dissipating in wind that carried the scents of fish and freshwater.

"How did you know that banishment?" he demanded.

I dropped to my knees, shaken and bewildered. "It just came to me."

"Like magic." His tone belied his blank expression.

I had succeeded in upsetting or surprising him; I wasn't sure which. Considering he didn't seem bothered by the deep wounds in his torso, it must be major. Reaction set in—the summoning, Ernesto's death, the demons, and the possessed monkeys. From head to toe, I trembled.

Through chattering teeth, I offered, "Maybe I read it in one of my m-mother's books?"

"Unlikely," he said quietly.

"Then how?" With my eyes, I begged for a logical answer.

Using the driver's seat, I pulled to my feet and stepped away from poor Ernesto. There were other monkeys on the island; we hadn't killed all of them. More faces peered at us through the bushes, but none of them looked likely to board. *Good.*

"For those of the proper lineage, the knowledge comes

from blood and bone, a dormant part of you until such a time when it is needed."

Proper lineage? I frowned at him, trying to keep my emotions in check. "That makes no sense. What are you saying?"

"Those words were excised from the Testament of Solomon thousands of years ago. They were deemed too powerful to remain in this world."

Holy crap. I wasn't sure I wanted to know, but I asked anyway: "How come?"

"Because in the right hands, conjoined with a true name, they can be used against *any* creature, not just demons. Imagine that." He paused. "I'll give you a minute."

My jaw tightened; I wasn't stupid. If I could use that incantation to banish humans, angels, shades, wraiths, or whatever else I might run across, that was simply too much power. I understood why it had been culled. But what was such knowledge doing in my brain? From Kel's expression, he had some idea about the answer too. Ordinarily I'd be making some attempt to patch up his wounds, but he seemed in no mood to have me change the subject.

"But you recognized it because—"

"I'm not of this world," he finished. "At least not entirely."

What the hell? What are *you, then?* But I didn't figure he would answer me, even if I asked. This wasn't the time to discuss his origins; he wanted to talk about that ancient banishing incantation, and truth be told, so did I.

"So why didn't you use that instead of doing a regular exorcism?" It would've saved him some pain—that was for sure.

His eyes were reflective and cool as a glacier. "Because it only works for one of Solomon's blood. It was magic granted to his line by the archangel Michael. Your family has long been given dominion over demonic forces."

Shit. His expression said he believed it, one hundred percent. I sought detachment to process the new information. Allegedly, the words came because I needed them, because

I was descended from King Solomon. No way to verify that, not after all these years. According to my mother, my dad, Albie Solomon, had been a traveling salesman, but I'd never dug into the histories on my father's side, so I had no more knowledge than that, and it was unlikely I could trace it all the way back in any case.

I didn't know much about the old king, except that he'd threatened to split a baby in half in order to tell who the real mother was. There were other legends as well—that he'd built his famous temple by summoning and binding demons to do the hard labor. Could I believe I was born of his line? Nothing else made sense. Yet I preferred *not* to come from a special lineage, or be destined for big things, because that would obligate me to all kinds of shit not commensurate with a quiet life. At this point, I might not have a choice.

I cleared my throat, more freaked than I wanted to admit. "Moving on. We still need to talk to the island witch. The sooner we get this saltshaker situation handled, the better off we'll be."

"Agreed," he said. "We covered a lot of territory." The old woman had given us directions from the shore, not from Monkey Island. "How do you propose we locate her from here?"

"I was thinking I'd handle the wheel. If Ernesto has been running tours a long time, he may have left impressions. He seemed to like his job, and strong happiness soaks in as well as the bad stuff."

Kel nodded. "Good idea."

Anyone else would've attempted to talk me out of it, like, say, Jesse or Chance. They'd seen me read a whole house in Kilmer and knew how much this would hurt. I rather doubted Kel cared, as long as I lived through it. We needed the information; this was the way to get it.

"Could you move Ernesto?"

I just wasn't cold enough to hop behind the wheel on top of his body. Christ, I didn't know what we were going to tell the Mexican police. I didn't look forward to all the questions. Everywhere I went, it seemed I wound up on the wrong side of the law. Except Mexico City. The place was clearly charmed, and the only spot where I could consistently stay out of trouble.

In answer, he bent and scooped the man into his arms. He whispered a few words—probably a blessing of some kind—and then tossed the body over the side of the boat. There was a splash, and Ernesto sank from sight. I'd forgotten how fucking heartless God's Hand could be.

"Doesn't he deserve a service?" I demanded.

His customarily blank face showed a shimmer of emotion. "I have the blood of angels in my veins, Corine Solomon. I defy you to find anyone more worthy to send a soul to his rest."

Blood of angels? What does that even mean? I hoped it didn't mean he'd been drinking it. *Because . . . gross.*

I tried once more to explain why I found this course objectionable. "But what about his family? They're going to wonder."

"Explaining the circumstances behind his death would prove impossible. The Mexican police would discover that I have a record and they would attempt to extradite me. Such events, while not catastrophic, would interfere with my ability to protect you."

"Yes, I understand that, but—ah, never mind." It wasn't like I could change anything now. Ernesto had sunk as if he had a pocketful of stones—and for all I knew, maybe that was what Kel had been murmuring, a magickal rock-whispering spell.

I might as well handle and get it over with. But as I sat down, he touched my arm lightly, his fingers patterned gruesomely with blood in the bright sunlight. "His mother is devout, so I can touch her dreams. She will not wonder."

Small comfort, maybe, but it did help. I acknowledged that concession with a nod, took a deep breath, and curled my hand around the wheel. Pain surged through me, laced with heat, but it wasn't the *I wish I were dead* kind. This contained joy at its core, as if I'd held a sparkler too long.

Because Ernesto had gripped this wheel for so many

days, it had absorbed a great deal of his memories. They flickered before me in quick succession. I saw that he'd taken us on a standard tour, but he sometimes took people to see the island witch too. With great determination, I fixed the course in my mind and marked which island before the images melted away.

My hand was red and sore, but it wasn't marked; I thanked my mother's power for that and called this a good reading because I could stand the burn. Sometimes handling left me crippled with pain for days after, if the charge left behind was traumatic enough. When I opened my eyes, I found Kel's attention split between the remaining monkeys and me. I couldn't blame him for that. Talk about culling the local primate population.

He brushed his fingertips lightly across my palm. The resultant tingle banished any residual pain, leaving me pleasantly light-headed. "Wow. How come you never did that before?"

"I wasn't sure you were worthy." *Ouch.* "We are taught not to waste our gifts. But you hold heaven in you as well as hell, and you have yet to choose your course."

Sometimes he sounded utterly crazycakes—and sometimes I feared the world he lived in because it was *real*, simply layered above and below my own. At a loss, I muttered, "Thanks."

"How much does your arm hurt, by the way?"

"It's a constant throb, low like a toothache. Don't worry; I'm keeping it clean, and I won't let it slow me down."

He nodded. "If it becomes too painful, tell me."

"So, do you know how to drive a boat?"

"I can get us there, if you remember the way."

As the boat engine fired up, the monkeys shrieked and beat the trees, showering us in falling leaves. They hadn't gotten anything to eat, but from their size, they would last until more tourists arrived, no problem. I had never been so happy to put a place behind us.

"I do." I glanced back and was sorry I did when I saw

the new alpha male posturing on the shore. "Man, that's not a happy sound."

"They're trapped," he said, "and like any creature, they protest it."

No doubt.

"What are we going to do with the boat?"

He considered for a moment, his big hands strong and sure on the wheel. "We'll leave it where Ernesto paused to buy fruit. Someone will claim it. And we should be able to get a taxi back to the hotel from the *zócalo*."

I had to admit—that was very clever.

Kel guided the launch skillfully through the water. With the sun out, Lake Catemaco was beautiful again, pure majesty and shining blue water, but I remembered all too well how easily it could turn dark. Geographically, the island wasn't far, but there were a number of wooded isles in the lake. Without Ernesto's specific knowledge added to the old woman's directions, we would never have found it.

On arrival, there was no dock, just a makeshift pier constructed out of scrap wood and fallen trees. We cut the engine and drifted in. When we reached a safe distance, Kel jumped first, rope in hand, and then he lifted me down by my waist. I was happy not to make the leap.

A young boy melted silently from the shadows and took the line, mooring our boat to a curved mangrove tree. Its roots bowed upward, creating a lagoon within the lagoon. I chose my footing carefully until I could scramble out of the water onto the mossy ground. The trees were heavy and marched up the hillside like resigned soldiers; the air itself carried the scent of decomposition, a soft green scent that somehow did not smell of death, but more like renewal.

"*Buenas tardes*," the child said. He was reed-thin and sun-browned, not more than ten years old. "*¿Estás aquí para ver a mi mamá? Nalleli?*" he clarified, as if there might be ten other island witches.

"*Sí, por favor. Es muy importante.*"

White teeth flashed in his thin face. "*¿Como siempre, no?*"

I felt a flush starting. Doubtless everyone who showed up begging her aid claimed it was a matter of life and death. In our case, it was true.

"*Claro*," I muttered.

The boy beckoned for us to follow. Deeper in the undergrowth lay a primitive staircase, no more than planks cut into the soil to help with traction in the climb. I didn't like how deep into the jungle this path appeared to go, but we needed answers and Nalleli could provide them. Moreover, I needed a curse and a tracking spell removed. I had no other leads in Mexico; nor did I dare let wretched Eros out of my sight. *Rock and a hard place, once again.*

"Let's go," Kel said. "Before we lose track of him."

The Island Witch

"You're crazy powerful," I said as we went deeper into the jungle. The dirty yellow T-shirt on the back of a strange child remained our only tie to civilization. We had long ago left the boat behind, and I could no longer even see the water. "How come you couldn't just burn the curse away?"

For a while, I thought Kel wouldn't answer on the grounds of giving away heavenly secrets.

At last he said, "It doesn't work like that. I have dominion over powers above and below . . . and certain personal gifts allow me to combat heaven's enemies in this world." Like inhuman strength and healing, not to mention high pain tolerance. "But magick like that hex belongs to human beings, who have free will."

"So it makes the spell untouchable for you because it's like interfering beyond a permissible point." I thought about that. "But you can kill people."

"Not just anyone," he said. "Only if I'm assigned the task."

"By God." I tried not to sound skeptical. It didn't make sense that I still would be, after all I'd seen, and yet I had a hard time imagining an omnipotent being selecting people for execution based on events that might come to pass. That obviated the notion of free will—and made me profoundly uncomfortable.

"I report to an archangel," he corrected.

That was little better: powerful entities—not God—deciding who got to live, based on suspect criteria. But it worried me that he was being so forthcoming. If I reflected long on the ramifications, I felt sure I wouldn't like what such confidences portended.

The kid turned then and gave us an impatient look. *"Rápido."*

We picked up the pace until we were nearly running. I ducked low-hanging branches and stepped around spiky plants growing up from the ground. Everything was impossibly green, and I didn't recognize any of the birds or insects. The strangeness made me uneasy.

At last we came to the top, where the ground leveled out. Here, someone had built a small hut out of driftwood and scrap tin. Vines lashed the wood together; the construction looked rickety, but the rust on the metal roof told me the structure had stood for several seasons at least. Instead of a door, a ragged white curtain hung in the opening, frayed strands blowing in the breeze like cobwebs.

In this clearing clay idols shaped into primitive gods peeked out from various bushes, and there was a shallow tray on the ground, full of water. Kel stood beside me, quietly taking everything in. I wondered what he made of this place, which owed so little to his god. Or maybe I didn't know as much as I thought I did. After all, I'd never heard him refer to any particular religion. So maybe the deity he served didn't care about such things. I'd always secretly suspected that would be the case in any powerful, self-respecting divinity.

The boy bowed to statuettes at what I took to be cardinal directions. I glanced askance at Kel, but he lifted his shoulders in a nearly imperceptible shrug. Then the kid went through the curtain, and I heard a rapid-fire exchange in Spanish, too soft and low for me to make out. By his intent expression, the guardian could understand it.

He interpreted my look correctly. "He's telling her she

has clients, and she's saying she has a bad feeling about helping us."

Well, that answered any lingering questions about her legitimacy.

The quiet argument continued for a couple more minutes before the kid came back. "Just you," he said, pointing at me.

Nodding, I held out my hand to Kel, who dug into his pocket for the white case. In exchange, I gave him Butch, who was still cowering at the bottom of my bag. I sympathized with him. The boat trip had not been as scenic or safe as one might hope.

Kel caught my gaze with his. "I'll be right out here. If you feel frightened or threatened at any time, say my name."

Why did that sound so suggestive? He was the last male who'd drop a double entendre into a conversation. Maybe I'd just read too many books that used the line with sexual context. Shaking my head, I followed the boy into the hut.

I'm not sure what I expected, but the woman inside, presumably Nalleli, was neither old nor cronelike. She was perhaps ten years older than I. Her hair shone black in the candlelight, and the sun had browned her skin even darker, dark enough that I thought she probably had some Huastec blood. The witch wore a brown-patterned skirt and a simple white blouse, further confounding my expectations. She didn't look like any *bruja* I had ever seen.

Her hands were graceful as she gestured for me to take a seat on the second rough-hewn stool. The hut was surprisingly snug, gaps packed with clay. In her shrine, she'd mixed Christian saints and the Virgin Mary, along with ancient gods like Quetzalcoatl, bearing out my guess about her heritage. Herbs burned in censers along the walls, giving the small space a smoky air.

"*Bienvenida*," she said. "We will tend to your business, but first . . ."

It was a shock to hear her speak English—accented, but better than most. Perhaps I shouldn't have been surprised the witch would be bilingual, though. It was in her best interest to talk with as many clients as possible, and English was a common second language.

She went on, oblivious to my speculation. "You must have a cleansing. All manner of ill luck clings to you. I have never seen anything like it."

Chance. It had to be: something else for which to thank him. My ex had uncanny luck, but the person closest to him received bad fortune to establish cosmic balance. *He wins the lottery, and I fall two stories through the floor in a burning building.* To make matters worse, he hadn't told me about the jinx or that his lover before me died of it. But I'd thought once I got away from him, it would ease off; I felt sure even he hadn't known the effects could be permanent.

I nodded my assent. If anyone needed a break from bad karma, I did.

While I watched, she prepared a mixture of herbs, oil, and water. She lit a white candle and placed it on the table before me. "Cup your hands over the flame, not close enough to harm, but where you can feel the warmth."

That was easy. I complied as she painted my pulse points. I recognized mint, lemon verbena, and a hint of vetiver, all woody and green. Once applied, the solution burned like camphor on my skin, though I could detect no trace of it in the actual composition. I took that as a manifestation of her power.

"Rise," she instructed, "but do not remove your hands from the flame."

Doing that proved a little trickier than anticipated but I managed, levering myself off the stool while keeping my palms cupped. Nalleli produced an egg, and I remembered Eva telling me how her grandmother had done this on nude people. *Aw, come on.* This was where I drew the line.

I stood still, waiting for an instruction that never came. The witch rubbed the egg over my exposed skin and only tugged clothing aside to hit a chakra. I guessed Eva's grandmother just liked making people get naked. Both she and

Chuch came from powerful lines; their unborn child would probably carry an incredible gift.

It took a long time, and Nalleli got a fresh egg twice, muttering blessings and incantations in a polyglot of Spanish and Teenek. For a final step, she pulled out a leafy branch and lashed me with it gently, as if brushing away any lingering traces.

At last she gave the signal to sit down. Just as well—my hands were bright pink, not damaged, but tender, as if I'd scoured them with sandpaper. "Did it work?"

In answer, she cracked the first egg. To my horror, the yolk had turned a slimy, viscous black, more ghastly in contrast with the white, which was now bloodred. The shell had been completely intact; this wasn't trickery. Silently, she showed me the other two. The second was paler, and the third showed barely any trace of corruption. I couldn't doubt the efficacy of her work and shuddered to think of all that filth sticking to me.

"Now that you are no longer defiling my space . . ." Her smile took some of the sting from the words. "Tell me why you've come."

"A friend in the city referred me to you."

She studied me for long moments in silence. "Tia."

My brows went up. "Yes."

"It is good to know she thrives, even in a world of concrete and steel."

"She sends her regards." That wasn't strictly true, but it might help our cause. I gave Nalleli the condensed version of events, leaving out only the bit about Ernesto and the massacre at Monkey Island. "So I need you to remove the curse from the saltshaker, and, if possible, the tracking spell as well."

"I can do this." Her manner remained serene. "But it carries a high price." Well, I'd been expecting that. I reached down for my purse. She stopped me with a hand on my arm. "Not from you. There is no coin sufficient for me to take this risk."

"What do you need, then?"

With some trepidation, I remembered that Twila, the voodoo priestess who owned Twilight and San Antonio, had wanted my dog at first, and then time alone with Chance once she realized he was the greater prize. I still didn't know what they had been doing all that time, and it wasn't likely my ex would ever tell me, not the way we'd parted.

"Call your companion."

Was this a trap? My heart raced. But this woman could hardly do my guardian real harm after all I'd seen him suffer. Hoping I was doing the right thing, I spoke his name. Kel bounded into the hut; he should have looked ridiculous with one arm raised to do battle, the other cradling a Chihuahua, but he didn't. His skull tats glowed faintly. I'd come to recognize that as a sign of him drawing power.

He assessed the scene at a glance. "You're fine."

"She won't help us without payment from you."

"Is this true, witch?" The word could've been a curse or condemnation, but spoken in that tone, it became an honorific.

Nalleli inclined her head. "It is."

"I have no monetary wealth."

Their eyes locked, questions asked and answered in a blink. My gaze ranged between them, sensing hidden currents. I hated being the only one in a room who didn't get the joke, and this was only a hundred times more serious. Restraining a growl, I plunked the white box on the table in case they decided they could do business—whatever that business might be.

I figured they must be communicating silently, and then Nalleli said, "That's not the payment I seek, as you well know."

"Step outside for a moment," Kel told me.

Dammit, not this again. Chance had done the exact same thing to me in San Antonio and I'd wound up attacked by a shade in a cemetery. If anything bad went down while Kel was otherwise occupied, I'd be a sitting duck. God knew, the kid couldn't protect me.

"No."

He didn't push the matter. "Your choice." The free-will thing again. I could get used to this. "Very well, I accept your terms," he told the witch.

Nalleli rose, a silver dagger in hand. It had runes etched into the blade, not that I could read them. She cut a thin slice in his arm and caught the ruby red blood in a bowl. If she drank it, I was so out of here. But no, that wasn't the master plan. Instead, she painted her fingertips and brow with a minuscule amount. The rest she poured into a glass vial and then capped it with a wax plug. Okay, I didn't want to know what she planned to do with it; I was a little worried on Kel's behalf.

"That's all," she said to him. "Go now."

The whole process leaned toward the wham-bam-thank-you-ma'am side of blood donation, but he didn't seem to mind. Butch whined as they left, and the curtain billowed inward as if warning of a coming storm.

"Why did you want his blood?"

Her brows lofted. "You truly do not know?"

Man, I hated this. I'd never been good at puzzles or guessing games. "Because he's God's Hand?"

"If he has not confided in you, then I must respect his privacy. But with such a potent source, I can work miracies." Her eyes shone with ambition.

Frustration surged. It didn't seem fair that she knew his origins, but she was right in that Kel should choose what he told me—and when. Accepting that, I muttered, "So we're square. You'll remove the curse and the tracking spell."

"I will," she said. "I'm protected so long as I wear his blood. They will not be able to scry for me, and by the time it fades, my magickal tell will long since have vanished in the ether."

Pretty slick, I had to admit. Plus, she got to use his left-over blood—whatever was so special about it—for her extracurricular spells later. I dug into my bag for the sketch Kel had drawn. "I'm not sure if this will help, but Tia gave us an idea what the practitioner looks like."

Nalleli nodded. "Thank you. Now I need for you to sit quietly. It's important you don't touch or attempt to communicate with me from this point."

"Would you prefer if I left?"

"No," she said. "Unless you spook easily."

I didn't think I did. So I settled on the stool opposite and watched her preparations. First she laid a white cloth across the makeshift table and then she set it with terra-cotta clay dishes. On each plate, she put a different item: corn tortillas, grilled fish, green plantains. Once she'd finished, Nalleli bent, rummaged through the crates stacked against the wall, and straightened with a carafe of red oil. *Palm oil*, I thought. I knew of no other that carried that precise hue. She drizzled the fluid over the top of the other offerings and then set out red candles in a circle. To some degree, it reminded me of the séance we'd conducted in Laredo, but this was altogether more elaborate.

"Everything is red," I said as she lit the candles.

I'd forgotten I wasn't supposed to interfere. She cut me a look, but answered, "Yes, it is the color of sacrifice."

I wasn't sure I liked the sound of that. "I thought there were two types of magick, white and black."

"There are three," she corrected. "White for purity, black for destruction—"

"And red for sacrifice."

She nodded, fixing me with a steely look. "I need you to be silent now, or you must leave."

Chastened, I fell quiet, promising myself that no matter what happened, I wouldn't react. Given the atmosphere rising in the hut, that might prove a bigger challenge than I anticipated. Though it was a warm day, since she started her ritual the air had cooled until I could see my breath. Goose bumps rose on my bare arms, but I didn't dare rub them.

Once she arranged the table to her satisfaction, Nalleli lit the candles and called, "Pedro, *los tambores*!"

"*¡Sí, mamá!*"

Outside the hut, I heard the sound of something being dragged over dry palm leaves and then a simple rhythm commenced. The sound was hypnotic; I could imagine the boy playing with his small, quick hands: three drums, one cadence. Before me, Nalleli swayed, listening to otherworldly whispers. Her eyelids grew heavy, but not, I thought, through any lack of concentration.

She sang out, *"YaYa, yayita, büey suelto / Oya viene alumbrando / como es / YaYa, yayita, büey suelto / Oya viene alumbrando / como es."*

Though I didn't understand all the words, in my bones I recognized a summoning chant when I heard one. My blood sparked and kindled, as if some long-dormant part of me sprang to life in welcome. In anxious reaction, I curled in on myself, wrapping my arms about my knees. Mist rolled in, peculiar and blood tinged; I had never seen anything remotely like it, except, perhaps, for fog burning in the wake of distant taillights.

Nalleli's movements became a dance as she shuffled, sang, and swayed. The air gained weight, as it had in the boat, but it did not carry the same stench, not sulfur and brimstone. Instead, it smelled of copper and yarrow, a fruity-grassy scent I remembered from my mother's kitchen, similar to sage. For a moment I could feel her around me, warmth discernible for the way it shielded me from the surrounding chill. Though it was impossible, I actually looked for her and found only that red mist.

Beneath my feet, beneath the spellbinding surge of the drums, the earth rumbled as though something ancient and powerful had awakened. Nalleli moved faster now, her hands trembling as she set the palm oil alight. It should have seared the cloth and begun a blaze inside the hut that we'd be hard-pressed to contain. Instead the flame burned with merry intelligence, devouring the food that had been set forth.

"Bienvenida," the witch crooned. *"Bienvenida, nuestra señora del relámpago."*

Welcome, our lady of the lightning. That, I understood.

"Acepta este sacrificio en tu nombre."

Accept this sacrifice in your name. The words sent a chill through me. Would I have agreed to this had I known? Ani-

mal sacrifice led to darker things. I touched the hard place
in my side where the murderer's weapon had plugged my
wound. Perhaps I ought to be asking whether I could have
countenanced this before—before Kilmer, before the demon,
before I died. I didn't like where those thoughts led.

Yet I did not protest. I had promised I would not, and
I feared the consequences of disrupting her work. Nalleli
withdrew a small bird from one of the crates behind her and
cut its throat with a slim, wicked knife. The fresh blood spattered atop the offerings already set forth. Somehow, I swallowed my moan, wishing I'd waited outside.

Say nothing. This was surely the reddest magic I'd ever
seen. The whole hut swam with the shade—and the bloody
mist threatened to choke me. I breathed through my nose,
mute witness to what transpired next.

To my utter shock, Nalleli set both palms in the burning
oil; she should have been maimed, but the blood on her
brow and the backs of her hands exuded a heavenly aroma,
a mix of cinnamon and raw brown sugar, and her flesh did
not singe. Instead the flames ran up her arms, coiling about
her head in snakes of smoke and ash. She screamed then,
but it was too late—or maybe it was exactly what she wanted;
I didn't know enough about her rituals to be sure.

The fire winked out and her dark eyes filmed white like
heat lightning. In that moment, I knew I was seeing something very old—not Nalleli at all. Whatever she'd summoned
studied me with a tilt of the head, and I could clearly see
that the spirit used her as a vessel. There was nothing of the
island witch left at all. The creature inhabiting her body
dismissed me as a nonentity—and I felt grateful. She turned
her attention to Eros, raised in the center of the offerings.
Energy crackled about its frame, such as would cause burns
and lesions without paranormal protection. With no meas-
urable fear or curiosity, the lady of the lightning took Eros
into her cupped palms, sniffed it, and then took the item
into her mouth. Her head fell back, and I would've thought
she was choking, except her chest rose and fell in normal

breaths. A rumble sounded both overhead and underfoot, thunder to accompany its lightning.

What. The. Hell.

Red thunderclouds formed and a sizzling arc slammed down from the top of the hut; as if that acted as the catalyst, Nalleli hunched forward, vomiting forth the saltshaker, along with a host of other things—dark sludge, what looked like congealed blood roiling with maggots. I just barely kept my breakfast down; in self-defense, I squeezed my eyes shut until her convulsions stopped. Blind, I listened to her blowing out the candles and cleaning the silver saltshaker before I trusted myself to look again. Somehow, I stumbled out of the hut without seeing the bird carcass or the mess left behind in removing the malignant spells.

In my absence, Butch had relaxed enough to venture off on his own, sniffing around to make sure things were safe. As he'd been borderline catatonic after the boat adventure, I took that as a good sign. I was still shaky, rubbing my hands up and down my thighs.

"Don't go far," I cautioned him.

Worrying about my pet distracted me from what I'd seen, at least. The dog threw me a look as if to say: *Do I look stupid?* Yeah, Butch was back.

"Everything all right?"

My gaze went to Kel's forearm, where the wound he'd inflicted on himself had already sealed into a thin purple line. "Not so much."

The shit I'd seen in that hut would stay with me. At last Nalleli emerged, but she looked markedly older, as if years had passed instead of minutes. Her hand trembled when she handed me the white box.

"Even shielded as I was"—she indicated the blood on her brow—"this was a nearly impossible task. Never have I seen anything woven with such mal intent."

"So the guy Montoya hired—he's good?" That didn't bode well for us.

"The best I have ever seen. The orisha *and* your companion's blood barely shielded me from his darkness. Go now. As it happens, you did not pay me enough." And Nalleli crumpled, the color draining from her face.

Kel caught her before she hit the ground. At the boy's instruction, he carried her into the hut and laid her on the pallet. She had, at least, cleaned up the evidence, though the smell lingered. I hovered, unsure of how best to help, and then I checked her vitals. It seemed she'd fallen into a swoon, nothing more serious. Her pulse was good, even if her skin was clammy.

"*¡Váyanse!*" her son spat.

We had no choice but to comply. Since it didn't look as if the kid would be guiding us out, I hoped Kel had been watching the route. I sure hadn't been.

He took point. I paid greater attention this time and saw there was, in fact, a faint path. It led downhill, but the soil was soft and moist, so I slipped as much as I walked, grabbing onto branches and leaves to break my clumsy descent. Green stained my palms by the time we hit the tiny, rocky beach, which wasn't sand but mud. Three puppies frolicked in the shallows, where the boat was still moored.

Thank God.

I assumed the dogs belonged to the witch and her boy, but the sight of them reassured me. Despite everything I'd been through today, dogs still chased their tails, growled playfully, nipped, and peed on trees. *How'd the world know I needed to see something normal right about now?*

Kel helped me aboard, untied the rope, and vaulted up himself. I sat down in the rear seats this time while he took Ernesto's place behind the wheel. The boat engine caught readily, and he reversed at low throttle, churning the water as we left the island behind. From a distance, it looked like any other isle in the lake: densely wooded, impossibly green, and full of mystery.

At length Butch felt safe to pop his head out of the bag and yap at birds. Then he fell to watching the water as if hypnotized. I could relate; the way it rose and fell beneath the boat was oddly compelling.

There was only one thing left to do. I didn't tell Kel I meant to test her work, but there was no way I could sell the thing without touching it to be sure. I opened the white box, ignored my guardian's sharp warning, and curled my left hand around Eros.

Reports of My Death Have Been Much Exaggerated

The customary burn hit my palm, but nothing more traumatic.

Heat carried the images that flowered in my brain. The scene came right from the fifties, including clothes and décor—a man presented the white case to a woman. An anniversary gift? Their silver, if I guessed correctly based on the present. Her face creased in a broad smile after she opened it, and her head swung around as she tried to decide where she should display Psyche and Eros. I caught the titles on the bookshelf; it seemed she loved reading about mythology.

Aw, what a sweet present. The scene faded, leaving me a little shaky. I put Eros back, still smiling. I suspected she must have passed on, which was the only way these would've left her possession. I hated that something she'd loved so much—and that had been given in love—had been used with murderous intent. Still, I could sell these to the Spanish professor with a clear conscience now . . . assuming we ever made it back to the shop.

"That was stupid," Kel bit out. "I cannot protect you from yourself."

"I had to be sure it was clean or I couldn't sell it."

He made an uncomplimentary frustrated noise and went back to driving the boat. When we reached the shallow cove where we'd docked before, the old washerwoman was gone. The day had reached that indefinite point between afternoon and twilight, and the trees cast long shadows in the water. This time, he let me make the jump on my own, which I took as a manifestation of his annoyance. Without his help I landed without grace and sloshed toward shore.

We crossed the small strip of land and climbed some crumbling stairs to the *malecón*. The market where Ernesto had bought the fruit was gone, tables and tents packed up and taken home for the day. After we walked a block or so, Butch wiggled in my bag. I put him down and he promptly peed on a strip of brownish green grass. I let him trot along sniffing stuff until we came to a more populated area, and then with a murmured apology I picked him up again. I didn't want the traffic squashing him.

"There's a *sitio*," I said, pointing.

The taxi stand lay half a block away and there were a couple of men lounging outside their vehicles. Kel quickened his pace. He handled the hiring of the cab; within moments, we were on our way back to La Finca. The car had no shocks to speak of, so I felt each rut in the road. Warm wind roared through the open windows, effectively preventing conversation. By that point I was starving, but it seemed indelicate, as if a person of sensibility would've had her appetite ruined by the day's events.

The driver made the last turn, and shortly thereafter we pulled into the shaded parking lot. I paid him, and we slid from the vehicle. After checking to make sure I wasn't leaving anything behind, I headed for the lobby. It was unlikely Shannon would still be poolside this late, but you never knew.

The pool area was empty; a maintenance man turned off the waterfall as we watched. I assumed they ran it only when there was sufficient demand to justify the expense.

I turned to Kel. "She must be in our room."

He followed me to the stairs, a shadow I couldn't shake. Despite our relative success today, this wasn't over. Montoya needed somebody to blame for his failure with Yi Min-chin. With her dying breath, the prostitute who aborted Montoya's child—with Min's help—had told him that Min had cursed his manhood and he'd never sire a living heir. Of course, there had never been a curse, but either age or intense superstition rendered Montoya impotent. Therefore, he couldn't rest until he got Min to "remove" the hex. Wisely, she'd used a dark ritual to prevent Montoya or any of his relations from going after her only living child—Chance— and she'd called the Knights of Hell to witness the deal. Talk about serious enforcement.

Since Chance was off-limits, Montoya had chosen me as a scapegoat. It wasn't just the loss of his warlock or his compound; he was also still grieving because he had no son and heir. Everything he'd built would crumble at his death. His lieutenants would quarrel over the cartel like dogs after juicy scraps, and nothing of his legacy, bloodstained and evil as it was, would survive. Somebody had to pay for that. In other words . . . me, because he'd doubtless thought I'd die easily and assuage the pain other women had caused him.

It wasn't in the cards.

I found Shannon watching TV, the remnants of room service on the table. Tension I hadn't noticed before eased from my neck and shoulders once I saw she was safe. But before I clued her in, I filled Butch's collapsible food and water bowls and set them down. He hopped out of my purse and crunched his kibble with gusto.

"Did you learn what you needed to know?" She clicked off the TV.

"Yes and no," I said.

While Butch ate, I provided the succinct version of our day. Shannon listened with full attention, and when I was through, she asked, "This witch wasn't able to tell you anything about the sorcerer?"

I raised a brow. "Why do you call him that?"

"I'm not ignorant," she told me with a roll of her eyes. "You fought a warlock before, right? Well, I've done some reading on Area 51 since we got wireless and found out that warlocks are defined in two ways. In the first, a warlock is a male witch turned oath breaker, revealing coven secrets for money."

"Like hiring out to the cartels," I said. "But Nathan Moon was related to Montoya by blood."

"Which made him the other kind. There's an older definition from the Old Norse: *varð-lokkur*, or 'caller of spirits.'"

That tracked with what I knew of Nathan Moon. He'd been the most powerful necromantic practitioner I'd ever heard of or encountered. "So what makes you think we're dealing with a sorcerer?"

"What you said about the demons. See, sorcerers use malevolent magic. The Templars were accused of sorcery and demon worship. So if this person is setting demons on you, it only tracks that—"

"Yeah, got it." If nothing else, a label might prove helpful. I wished we'd discovered more, but I had to be content with what we'd accomplished. Stomach growling, I went to the phone and paused, receiver in hand, angling a look at Kel. "You want something to eat? I'm ordering."

I was pretty sure he *could*; I just didn't know if he needed to. But he'd lost a fair amount of blood today between wounds and self-inflicted harm. Replenishing fluids sounded like a good idea either way.

"Sure," he said. "A burger and a beer."

That took me aback, but I asked for the same thing when the kitchen staff picked up. The spicy Veracruz pasta and shrimp tempted me, but it would be ill-advised to order an adventurous meal the day before a road trip. Mostly, I wanted to go home. The trouble was, I couldn't stay in Mexico City until I solved this problem. Montoya knew where I lived. He'd sent a package to my store and put a gunman on the roof.

So, on the surface, going back at all might seem foolish, but I had a plan. If we lured the next gunman into taking a crack at me, Kel could capture him. I had no doubt the guardian knew some effective interrogation techniques. So we'd return only long enough to put this plan into effect and then take the fight to Montoya.

"Shower," I said, snagging my backpack.

The bathroom possessed an austere charm, marbled but lacking in decorative touches. I turned the tap to hot and stepped into the tub as steam swirled in the room. After today, I had a lot to wash away. Plus, showers were great for thinking things through, and by the time I got out, I felt sure Kel was going to argue my scheme. That could prove problematic, as he had the car keys.

I dried quickly, spritzed my hair with leave-in conditioner, combed it out, and dressed. When I emerged from the bathroom, the food was waiting; it didn't take long to grill some meat and slap it on a bun. Kel opened the balcony door and pushed the small table outside. With someone else, I would've taken the move as a romantic overture. In this case, I couldn't imagine his intentions.

Nonetheless, I grabbed the tray and carried our food out while he brought the chairs. I took the one facing the playground, though the swings were quiet. The reason for this tête-à-tête became clear when he shut the door. Right, he wanted to talk about something in private. At that point I was too hungry to care what he had to say before I'd eaten, so I dug into my burger. He followed suit.

Sunset over Lake Catemaco defied description. The colors melted into the water, but the sunlight went fast. There was very little transition, and no city lights to stave off the dark. Gnats buzzed around the window; we wouldn't be able to stay out here long. This time of year, they flew in clouds.

When we had only fries left on our plates—and I was more picking at mine than really eating them—he broached the subject. "We can't go back to Mexico City."

So he already had an idea of what I had in mind, and he wasn't on board. That was less than ideal, since he played a vital role in capturing the next guy they sent to kill me. I couldn't manage that alone.

"Then what do you suggest? I have a girl and a dog depending on me for their livelihood. If we—"

"Stop," he said. "It would be best if you sent Shannon away until the dust settles. I'm sure her father would take her in."

Well, of course. Jim Cheney had moved out of Kilmer just a few weeks after we left. He hadn't even waited to sell the house. Now settled in Oklahoma City, he sent Shannon regular cards and e-mails; they spoke on the phone every Sunday night. He had a good-size two-bedroom rental house; I knew because he'd sent us pictures of the place. He'd put a daybed and a computer desk in the second bedroom, so he could also use it an as office. From Shannon's other comments, I knew he was doing handyman work and basic carpentry.

No wonder Kel had wanted to have this conversation out of earshot. She wouldn't be pleased, especially not when she'd just started to feel safe with me. We had a good thing going, and she fit in pretty well in our neighborhood, considering she was a white Goth girl living in Mexico.

I swirled a fry in catsup and then ate it to buy time, considering the pros and cons. It would be good to know she was safe. I wasn't sure if physical safety was worth the emotional damage, though. I didn't want Shannon to think I didn't trust her to pull her own weight or value her enough to believe she could help. After all, she wasn't a kid—and that made up my mind.

"Look, I appreciate your concern, but she's my worry, and I'm not sending her away. She's my friend . . . and besides, we might need her." At his doubtful look, I explained how she'd helped in Kilmer, what she could do, how she'd invented a portable personal protection charm—otherwise known as Tri-Ps—*and* repaired Chance's luck, at least while he held the clay tablet inscribed with runes similar to those found on the public library building where my phone had worked.

He considered my words with a somber look and then asked, "Did she bring the radio with her?"

The balcony door slid open in answer. Shannon stood in

the doorway, arms folded across her chest. "Of course I did."

So much for a secret discussion.

Kel glanced over at Shan and seemed to register her determination. "Then forget it. I'll do my best to protect both of you."

"Thanks," she said softly. But she was talking to me, not him, and the quiet pleasure in her face rewarded me far better than anything I'd known prior.

I grinned at her. "Let me guess. You're a champion eavesdropper."

"Yep." She shrugged. "There wasn't a lot to do in Kilmer."

Obviously there was no point in staying outside, and with the gnats swarming, it was smart to head in. I let Kel bring the furniture while I carried the tray; Shannon rang the kitchen to tell them we had dishes outside to be collected. Afterward, she and I sat cross-legged on our bed, facing him, with the TV running for background noise. I'd always found it comforting—like nothing bad could happen in a house protected by a laugh track.

"You want to go back to Mexico City so you can sell those," Kel said, indicating the salt and pepper shakers with a tilt of his head.

I laughed. Already he knew me better than I'd expected, but he couldn't read me like a book. Not like Chance. "Well, of course I'll give them to Señor Alvarez while we're there, but no, that's not my primary motivation."

"What is?" Shannon asked.

I laid out my plan, and Kel shook his head. "Montoya will send someone. Before we got Nalleli to remove the tracking spell, the sorcerer would have relayed our new location, at least in general terms."

"The tracking spell went out on the island," Shannon put in, "but you told me Nalleli said they wouldn't be able to scry her."

"So our last known location is here. Or nearby," I finished, annoyed with myself. People had hunted me often enough—through means both magickal and mundane—that I should be well able to predict their movements. "If we stay put, the next hitter on Montoya's list will come to us."

Fortunately, we had a killer of our own.

Kel nodded. "That seems likely."

"That's good, right?" I considered the interrogation aspect of my plan. "We'll have ample chance to question him."

The corners of his mouth curled. "You're a formidable woman."

"I don't like being threatened," I said. "I like it even less when people make good on those threats and try to kill me."

Most likely we could expect Montoya's man to burst into our room in the middle of the night. Instead of running, like sensible people, we hoped for that development as the best possible outcome. How fucked-up was that?

With a faint sigh, I picked Butch up. After dinner, he needed a bathroom break before we could retire for the night. The dog nestled into my arms as I opened the door. Kel followed me like he thought I might be in danger every waking moment, and based on events to date, I couldn't say he was wrong.

"Lock the door," he told Shannon.

Worry dawned on her pale face, as if up until this point, it had all seemed like a game. I didn't want her traumatized, but a healthy amount of fear offered a certain value. Though I'd come up with this plan, anxiety thrummed through my veins. Butch caught my mood and stood up in my arms, licking my cheek with his little tongue.

"It'll be all right," I told him.

He yapped twice, disagreeing with me. I let that go. You just couldn't win an argument with a Chihuahua.

When we reached the ground floor, I set him down just off the path and let him frolic in the manicured foliage. In the distance, I could hear drums and chanting; it came from the small clay house at the far end of the property. Smoke rose from the building, indicating that a tourist group was

participating in the *temascal* ritual, which involved smear-
ing mud all over your body and sitting in a steam bath with
a local shaman. With faith and preparation, you could experience visions and learn about your animal spirit guide as
well as purify your spirit. But after my time with Nalleli, I
didn't need a cleansing; nor did I imagine Kel had any dirt
clinging to his soul.

The lights lining the walk shone brightly enough for me
to keep an eye on Butch. I made sure *not* to look at Kel,
who carried sigils in his skin that rendered me wildly uneasy; I didn't want to recall what he'd said about my blood-
line or what it portended. He astonished me when he turned
my face toward him, forcing me to meet his gaze. In the
dark his eyes shone like mirrors, silvered and reflective.
Though he dropped his fingers right away, I could feel them
burning on my cheek.

"You cannot hide," he said softly. "Ignoring me does not
change what will be. Refusing to acknowledge truth does
not make it a lie. It only makes you a coward."

"You can't have it both ways," I told him angrily. "Either
I have free will or I have a destiny. It cannot be both."

Kel smiled, and his tats gleamed blue in the dark, a tiny
little ripple of power that I didn't like at all. "No?" he
asked, and I felt sure he already knew the answer, glimpsed
from some high precipice.

"Well, maybe you do know how it all turns out. I don't
want to."

And I didn't—because such knowledge would pare
away my humanity. As far as I knew, Kel couldn't receive
comfort from a touch or take pleasure in anything at all.
Long ago, he had pledged to a greater good, and now he
existed only to serve and follow orders. To me, that sounded
like slavery.

Perhaps he read a glimmer of my thoughts in my expression. The light died away, leaving his face in shadow, revealing only the edge of his brow and the slope of his nose.
He was magnificent and terrible in the dark.

"Some things about you, I cannot see." He leaned in, and

I froze, too astonished to breathe, until he plucked a struggling moth from my long hair.

Embarrassed and bewildered, I called Butch and fled back up the stairs as if all the hounds of hell followed at my heels, not a holy warrior sworn to guard me.

Dead Man Says What?

I woke to two silenced shots hitting the towels mounded to look like me. At Kel's insistence, Shannon and I had bedded down on the floor in between the two beds. Now I appreciated his caution.

Her breathing said she was awake, but we didn't speak. The slow grate of footsteps over glass, coming through the balcony door, suggested the gunman meant to check his work. He was competent; he'd just never run into targets like us before. Montoya should've briefed him better.

His shadow fell across the bed as he ripped the covers back. An oath escaped him when he saw he'd killed a number of dirty bath towels. Kel hit him from behind, wrapping a shoelace around the other man's neck. Their struggle was relatively quiet, as such things go, until at last the gunman went limp. Kel made sure he wasn't playing possum, and then he swung him over his shoulder, strode to the balcony, and jumped.

That was our cue. We weren't conducting the interrogation in here; blood in a hotel room would arouse too many questions. For a moment I paused, shocked at the coldness of the thought. Likely, such a consideration wouldn't have occurred to me before. I didn't even know whether the thought had come from me or some darkness lingering from the demon who saved me . . . or the murderer's weapon in my side. It was a pragmatic concern, however, and I could not deny its validity. Still, I shivered, a ripple of dread warning me that once I started down this path, there could be no return to innocence.

Yet I told myself I needed to find out what this hired gun knew. He couldn't be a good man, or he wouldn't be on Montoya's payroll. Good men didn't break into hotel rooms with a silencer and try to murder women sleeping in their beds. Determined, I threw off the blanket with Shannon hot on my heels. Since we were both fully dressed, I only needed to snatch Butch and hurry out the door. I took the stairs two at a time, an athletic feat that surprised me because I didn't fall. When I hit the ground floor, I broke into a jog.

They had security here, but they wouldn't say anything about registered guests exercising on the property in the middle of the night, so Shannon and I offered our best impressions of fitness nuts. The bored guard we passed just raised a hand in greeting; I could imagine his perplexity, but as long as he didn't catch us doing anything worse, we'd be fine.

I ran through the parking lot and down toward the lake before doubling back toward the *temascal* hut. As she was taller than me, Shannon kept up easily. A smoky scent lingered, though the fire had gone out. I set Butch on the ground.

"You're an important part of this plan," I told the dog. "If anybody comes within sniffing distance, bark twice. I mean it—you can't wander or be distracted by a bird."

He lowered his head. I could almost hear what he was thinking: *Not fair, that only happened one time.* But he gave a yap, indicating he understood his mission. He was crucial to our success; early warning would permit us to escape undetected.

We sank to hands and knees to crawl inside; it was dark and close and there were stones inside that could be heated to inflict excruciating pain. In short, the place was ideal for inflicting physical and psychological damage. I sat down, and Shannon brought out the candles she'd tucked into her pocket. Kel had made a supply run earlier in the evening, lifting some from the patio tables for our purposes now. She lit the candles and eerie little flames kicked up in a semicircle, lending our faces a demonic aspect against the clay backdrop.

The killer lay like a Christmas goose, bound with arms over his head and ankles securely fastened. At most, he could flop around like a dying flounder. No threat—and if he moved with too much enthusiasm to the left, he'd burn himself on the hot rocks. To the right, he ran into Kel and his blades.

"Bring him around," I said.

It might seem cruel to start with physical pain, but this man had tried to kill me, and it wasn't as if he'd go away if I asked him nicely. These men played hardball and I had to prove I understood the rules of the game if I wanted to survive it. Still, I looked away as the guardian produced a knife, made a shallow cut, and then sprinkled salt in it. Incredible: The man could create a torture kit out of items found on a room service tray. In the same motion, he clapped a hand over the gunman's mouth, anticipating the scream. The assassin gazed up at us, eyes wide.

Kel addressed him in Spanish. "You work for Montoya, yes?"

Not surprisingly, the killer kept quiet. He knew his life was worth less than nothing if he talked. He couldn't have been more than five-foot-eight, average build. Sweat damped his shoulder-length black hair, and his eyes gleamed like a frightened child's—probably because Kel's skull tats glowed faintly.

The guardian played with his knife, letting it hit the candlelight just so. "You jeopardize more than your life," he said quietly. "If you die unshriven, it also imperils your immortal soul."

Since Mexico was a predominantly Catholic country, he played that card well. I read soul-deep fear in the gunman's body. He was thinking about that, dying here without talking to a priest one last time. We could do worse than draw a few cuts, of course. We could unleash the spirits on him, but I was reluctant to go that far if we didn't have to. At this point, it was impossible to say what Shannon's ghosts might do, or what could happen if they broke free. I wasn't eager to relive that terrible night in the woods outside Kilmer.

Shannon added softly, "That wouldn't be so bad, if you'd led a good life. But you haven't. We know the things you've done for Montoya."

I was proud of how quick she'd picked up Spanish. Like me, she wasn't fully fluent, and she thought before she spoke— doing mental translations—but by the way the man whimpered, he took her meaning. Still, he wouldn't break.

Kel carved a fresh line on him. Blood spilled from the wound, trickling hot over the killer's forearm. With exquisite, awful artistry, he sprinkled more salt, and this time he added lemon juice and then ground it against the cut. I clapped my hand over the killer's mouth and tried not to pity him as he ate his own screams. Shannon pinched his nose shut, frightening him with the threat of asphyxiation.

This man tried to murder you. You will not *feel sorry for him.* But I did. I also loathed myself for doing this, and loathed Montoya for making it necessary, even as a colder part of me nodded in approval; that aspect felt like a terrifying stranger struggling beneath my skin. The cartel hit man thrashed beneath our hands, but Kel held him still. By the time we let go, he lay writhing on the clay tiles, oxygen deprivation shorting his logic. His breath came in ragged pants.

"Do you know this man?" I asked, producing the sketch. I had worked with Kel to refine the image, based on what I'd seen handling the other assassin's dagger, and the candlelight was sufficient for our suspect to get a good look.

His eyes widened until the rolling whites shone. Clearly he did, but he turned his face away and bit down on his tongue. I worried that he'd chew through it to keep himself from talking.

"Physical pain alone won't break him," Kel whispered. "He smells frightened, but he fears Montoya and his sorcerer more."

"For good reason," I muttered. "All we can do is kill him. The sorcerer can summon demons to eat his soul and use his body as a puppet." I recalled the monkeys, and a shudder worked through me.

Shannon said, "I've been thinking. Before, you said the warlock was working on his own, and you took him out. So I suspect Montoya will keep his caster close this time."

I considered. "Yeah. Likely. So if we find Montoya, we find the sorcerer. We can take them both."

Kel stared down at our gunman. "And *he* knows where to find them."

"We have to break him." I didn't like it, but some things had to be done. "If not physical pain, then we move to plan B."

Time to raise the stakes.

"Check." Shannon dug into her bag for the radio.

As soon as she clicked it on, the hissing started. This was no ordinary radio. Using it, Shannon could contact the other side and summon the dead to her. Moreover, we could hear what they had to say on the tinny old speakers. Inside this tiny clay hut, the results would be terrifying.

She had never attempted to attune to spirits with whom she hadn't been personally acquainted before, but this would only work if she called the killer's victims. Without meaning to, I reached for Kel. He glanced at me, brow furrowed, but his fingers folded around mine—apparently he was permitted to give reassurance.

Shannon closed her eyes while she fiddled with the dial and whispered in Spanish. For a while, the only sounds within came from the eerily crackling radio and her pale, parted lips. In the candlelight, she owned a fearsome, witchy aspect—and the gunman couldn't look away from her.

"What's happening?" he demanded. "What are you doing?"

Nobody answered him. That silence built even greater dread.

I knew the moment she made contact. The atmosphere chilled, and shadows grew where there was no light to cast them. They swarmed around the killer's prone body, crooning to him in Spanish. I understood snippets, and fear went livid in me too.

Traitor. You murdered me. I will eat your heart and build a house of your bones.

As they fed from his terror, the summoned shadows gained form. They went from amorphous clouds of darkness to wraiths with faces twisted into rictuses of hatred and hunger. *Shit, what have we done to you, Shan?* She did not falter. The cadence of her murmurs took on the aspect of a spell, keeping them in check.

"At any moment," Kel told Montoya's assassin, "she can unleash them. They will make good their promises. You will face the dead you wronged."

Time to play good cop. Doubtless I looked the part more than the other two.

"Pero no necesita ser así. Puedes cambiar tu destino. Solo dime dónde puedo encontrar Montoya."

I paused, aiming a glance at Shannon, who paused her chant for a few seconds. The angry ghosts surged, nearly reaching the assassin's skin. She stopped them with a murmur at the last second, and the gunman moaned in abject horror. Nothing like being confronted with your own sins.

"Sí, voy a hablar. No más, por favor. Montoya es—" He broke off, his face purpling.

While we watched, his face withered in the candlelight as if the spirits were, in fact, sucking the life out of him. Shannon shook her head, her denial discernible in the candlelight. His tongue swelled in his mouth, turning black and eventually rotting away in putrid chunks. It was like watching an accelerated film from the Discovery Channel, where they show you how decomposition works.

"Can you contain the ghosts?" I asked her.

But something else was already happening. The candles revealed a darkness rising from the ravaged mound of flesh. A jubilant, wordless cry sounded over the radio, and then, in a roil of black, they all went away. One last scream echoed in the tinny speakers, raising goose bumps on my arms.

And Butch barked twice.

"That's our cue," Kel said. "I'll pack up here and meet you back at the room."

Shannon and I scrambled for the exit. We couldn't do anything for the dead man, but here, at least, they could burn the scraps of remaining flesh, although they would have to wonder what the hell had happened. Hopefully they would assume some animal had crawled in to die. That'd be the best possible outcome; maybe it would be a while before the next ritual.

"We're going walkies," I told Butch loudly in English. "Aren't walkies fun?"

He looked none too convinced, but he did trot at my heels as I cut a path toward the lake. Maybe I could convince the security guards we were crazy tourists who didn't want to waste a moment of our magical vacation sleeping. We crossed paths halfway to the shore. I beamed at the man in uniform.

"*Bwa-noes noe-chays*," I offered in my worst American accent, and then added, "*Kay bone-eeta!*" while pointing toward the lake. I'd found the tourist persona helpful, as Mexican nationals assume you're too dumb to be up to something if you can't speak the language properly.

The security guard merely waved as he went by. For appearance's sake, I let Butch pick our path back to the hotel, which meant we stopped every four feet so he could smell something. No problem, he'd earned it. When we reached the parking lot, I picked him up again.

At a glance, I could tell Shannon needed to eat. Though she was a trooper and not complaining, summoning screwed her sugar levels. Which was weird, because using my gift had a different cost. Still, once we let ourselves back in the room, I dug in my purse for the Snickers bar I kept on hand for just such an occasion.

Her fingers trembled as she unwrapped it. As promised, Kel sat waiting for us. He'd put the blankets and pillows back on the bed, not that we'd sleep again. It was two hours before dawn; I figured we'd leave at first light.

I asked the unspoken question. "What happened back there?"

Kel shrugged. "My guess? A trigger spell. Powerful sorcerers can set a curse that will be set off only if certain conditions are met."

"Like a henchman about to betray *el jefe*," Shannon said around a mouthful of chocolate, peanuts, and nougat.

"Exactly," he answered.

"He definitely recognized the caster and he feared him." I sighed. "Unfortunately, it leaves us back at square one. In Laredo, we had a list of his properties, but he'll have sold them by now, and most likely plugged the leak Esteban exploited to get the info in the first place."

Shannon asked, "Who's Esteban?"

I gave her the short version of how I'd read a necklace for the guy—he worked for a rival cartel—and told him why his sister disappeared years before. Esteban had been so grateful he'd produced the information we needed to go after Montoya in his mountain fortress. That wouldn't be happening again—and as we'd realized earlier, when we found Montoya, he'd have this new sorcerer at his side. *Not. Good.*

She nodded, thoughtful. "We need help from somebody higher up the food chain this time."

Like that was going to happen; I didn't know any cartel bosses. In Mexico, it was bad news to evince curiosity about doings near the border. Living in the interior in a safe neighborhood was a different world from Juarez, Nuevo Laredo, or Tijuana.

We needed to move. . . . I just didn't know where to go.

Kel had been quiet. I glanced over and saw his eyes were closed. For all I knew, he was communing with his archangel, and was about to dump us for new orders. I didn't kid myself he'd care.

Sensing my regard, he sat forward in his chair. "There was a woman who helped you before. In Texas."

I shook my head. "Oh, no. I'm not dragging Eva into this. She's got to be eight months along."

"Not Eva."

For a moment I couldn't think of any other woman, and then it hit me. "You mean Twila?"

Right, he'd been shadowing me, so he had probably trailed me to her house. I knew that because he saved my life for the first time in the cemetery. Back then things were simpler, because I thought he wanted to kill me.

"Yes. She may have contacts we can use."

"To do as Shannon suggested?" Surely he wasn't endorsing the idea that we join forces with a rival cartel. That was like using a rabid dog to kill a few rats. The whole thing put me in mind of the old lady who swallowed the spider; this idea had a snowball-rolling-downhill feel to it.

"I have been watching the possible outcomes," he said softly. "And that may be your only hope."

The words dropped into the room like lead shoes, so when Shannon crumpled her candy wrapper and Butch whined, the sounds seemed extra loud. Even my breathing rasped in my ears. Kel alone appeared unmoved by the pronouncement. My little dog covered his muzzle with his paws and burrowed deeper into my arms.

"Why do you say that?" I asked.

In answer, he clicked on the television; I judged the move wholly out of character until the clicking remote stilled. Kel left it on a news channel. I didn't understand why, but we watched for five minutes in silence. And then the presenter answered my questions in the worst possible way.

I translated the Spanish mentally and came up with: *Firebomb in Mexico City. As yet no terrorist factions have claimed responsibility. Luckily there was only one fatality and the blaze did not spread to adjacent buildings. Police suspect it may have been cartel related. Gang and drug violence on the rise*—Kel muted the television before the man could complete the sentence.

"No," I breathed.

Stop, I mentally commanded the announcer. *I don't want to see—*

Oh. Before the images came up on-screen, I knew. It was *my* shop. Kel had known before the news came on; perhaps he had been receiving a bulletin in his head. From the beginning, he might have even known I'd never see the place again, and I hated him for his distance, his surety, and his calm.

Seeing the truth made it no easier to bear. Burned plaster and chunks of cement littered the street. As the camera swung around, they showed scavengers picking through the rubble. Once again, I was homeless, reduced to what I could carry. Chance had sent my belongings as promised, including my Travis McGee book collection. All gone. Those were my things, treasures Señor Alvarez had—

One fatality. It sunk in at last, above my own misfortune. *Oh God. Oh my God. He died because of me. First Ernesto, and now Señor Alvarez.* Sick, I wondered how many innocents would die so that I might live. At what point should I stop running and take the bullet?

"When did this happen?" I asked hoarsely.

Shannon didn't know, of course, but the question wasn't for her. Kel answered readily. "Shortly after the gunman died."

I thought about that, and came up with only one interpretation. "It was a warning. Montoya's sorcerer must've known his spell went off. So now he's telling me that no matter what I do to him, he will visit it upon me a hundredfold."

"Yes," Kel said. "You see why I counseled you to seek aid from one as powerful as Montoya."

"Because you can't just smite him," I said nastily. "What good are you?"

Nothing I said touched him. He was made of ice and silver. "There are limits to my power, as there should be."

The weight fell on me like my collapsed shop. When I turned to Shannon, I saw the echo of it in her eyes. She, too, had been displaced. She, too, had lost her home—for the second time in less than a year. I tried to bite back my tears, but when I saw her eyes swimming, I stopped fighting it. We went into each other's arms and wept for everything we'd lost. I couldn't tell her it would be okay; I had no platitudes, but I wouldn't ever leave her. That much I could promise.

Kel stood and gave us his back. It might've been embarrassment at our weakness or kindness in offering privacy. "Get ready. We're heading for Texas in an hour."

Vagabond Blues

It took us nearly a whole day to reach Texas.

I received four texts from Jesse during that time. *Something's wrong. What's up?* He also tried to call, but the mountains played hell with reception and the connection dropped before we could talk. I replied without revealing how bad things were; there was no point in worrying him. Instead, I texted: *I'm fine, try not to worry. I know you're soaking this up and I'm sorry. I'll explain when I see you.*

As we drove, I thought about the strange dream and his sadness over me. God, I didn't want to hurt him. Maybe it was backward of me to want to protect him, but I did. His life had been golden, with a family who loved him no matter what. I didn't want my darkness rubbing off on him; deep down, I hoped if I ever came out on the other side of this mess, he might be waiting and I could make a place in his world, even if I hadn't been born to it.

His reply came in slower. . . . I could sense his resignation. *You're safe?*

Yes, I typed, and then leaned my head against the window, watching the world go by. Eating or sleeping didn't seem important, given current events, so we committed to finishing this journey in one go. Since it was a seventeen-hour trip, it helped that we could all take turns driving.

We headed up the coast through Tampico and Tamaulipas, staying on the *cuotas*—toll roads—and *carreteras*—highways. I rode in back because I didn't want Shannon to see me crying and I teared up at odd moments. I hadn't felt so bereft since my mother died. Her grimoires had been upstairs, and I didn't know if they'd survived the explosion. Following her example, I'd kept them in a fireproof box, but someone would probably steal them from the wreckage before I got back.

Montoya intended me to run home, shocked and grieving, where he'd take another crack at me. That was the other purpose behind the bombing—to herd me. Well, I took the warning, but I wouldn't let him drive my decisions, however painful that resolve proved to be.

Kel was behind the wheel when we reached Avenida de las Americas and started seeing signs directing us toward International Boulevard. We crossed at Brownsville via the international bridge over the Rio Grande. For the first time since I'd known him, he donned a cap to cover his tats. Likely he knew law enforcement would look longer at somebody all inked up, and most people wouldn't recognize the patterns; an average cop would take them for gang symbols.

Once we were back in the U.S., we put two hours between the border and us. I felt a little safer on American soil, but not much. Montoya had a long reach, and even now, his sorcerer was probably working on a way to locate us. Fortunately, scrying spells proved nearly impossible to tune correctly so long as the target stayed on the move.

Though it had been my turn for several hours, Kel didn't pull over to let me get behind the wheel. The little car hurtled down I-37 as if he knew for a fact we had something chasing us. I didn't ask if that was true, because I feared he'd tell me. Shannon had dozed off a few minutes before, her head lolling against the smoky glass. I didn't blame her; according to the dashboard clock, it was pushing two a.m. At that point, he and I were both running on caffeine, sugar, and stubbornness.

"Feeling better?" he asked at length.

"Sure. A long-ass car trip with only minimal stops for food and hygiene could cheer anyone up."

To my surprise, the corners of his mouth tugged, as if he fought the urge to smile. It wasn't the first time I'd seen it, either, and this time—reflected in the rearview mirror—I was sure. His face revealed only microexpressions, but they did exist. Before I could question him, a black SUV came roaring up from behind us.

Even before it passed and cut us off in front, I had a bad feeling. A second SUV practically attached itself to our rear bumper—if Kel didn't keep the speed steady, we would find ourselves smashed between these two automotive beasts. I swallowed hard as a third zoomed up on the left and kept pace. *Shit.* They had us completely boxed in.

I slid over to the left side, directly behind Kel, and tried to get a look inside the other vehicle. So far they hadn't made contact or tried to force us off the road. That seemed unlike Montoya. Unfortunately, the windows were tinted too dark to make out anything about those within.

My phone pinged. The message had nothing to do with our current situation, but I flipped it open and looked anyway. My stomach clenched.

I read the text aloud. "'Pull off at the next rest area.'"

"Are you sure?" he asked, voice taut with tension.

"No. But I suspect they'll force the issue if you don't comply." That was the point of boxing us in, and our car couldn't take the damage three SUVs would inflict.

"Very well."

They'd chosen their spot with care. Two miles up the road there was a rest area; no cars came up from behind to challenge their blocking trifecta. Kel slowed as they did and guided the vehicle into the nearly empty lot. As in most such places, there was a twenty-four-hour building that offered a foyer full of tourism pamphlets and, beyond that, restrooms. Along the front nestled a bay of vending machines. At this hour, I saw only semis in the far parking lot—not many, either.

Fear roiled in my stomach, making a mess out of the

chips and chocolate. I curled my hands into fists and braced them on my knees. I didn't know whether to get out boldly and ask what they wanted, or sit here waiting to be summoned.

"They want to talk," he said quietly. "If they'd wanted you dead, one shot would've done it as we drove. Here, they have greater vulnerability."

That was certainly true. Kel was no longer handicapped by managing an automobile, so he could fight. Maybe they didn't know who—or what—he was. Another advantage they couldn't factor.

Thus bolstered, I climbed out of the vehicle. Slamming the door jolted Shannon awake, and I saw alarm when she registered the three black SUVs, but he stilled her with a hand on her arm.

Thank you, I thought. *Keep her safe for me.*

Everything looked pale and wan beneath the lights. I heard bugs whirring around the building, distant sounds of cars on the highway. I played cool and leaned against my car door like I wasn't expecting a shot through the forehead any second. Wait, no—they'd give me two to the back of the head, make it look like an execution to avoid questions.

For several long moments, nothing happened, and then a strange man—strange in the sense that I'd never seen him before—stepped out of the nearest SUV. They drove Denalis, I noted, less flashy than a fleet of Hummers. I was conscious of my wrinkled clothing, dark circles beneath my eyes, messy hair, and orange Cheetos dust on my chest, but I didn't move. If we were going to have a stare-down before he spoke, so be it.

Henchman One paused, a hand on the open door. "Corine Solomon?"

"Who's asking?"

In answer, he twirled two fingers in the air. Three more guys stepped out, grabbed me before I could do more than throw a wild punch, and chucked me headfirst into the Denali. My face skidded across fine gray leather and someone slammed the door behind me. In a squeal of tires, we were moving.

Oh, shit. I'd been kidnapped.

I lunged for the door, only to be brought up short by one of the thugs. He didn't hurt me, but he effectively blocked me from flinging myself out of the moving SUV. The sister vehicles stayed in the rest area, and as we sped away, two shots rang out. I screamed and pounded on the glass.

No, no, no, no. Kel can fight incredible numbers. He'd done it before. I had seen it. The guardian could live through damn near anything—maybe even a bullet in the brain—but Shannon . . . *No, not Shannon.* A scream built in my throat.

Shortly, the other two SUVs flanked us, providing protection, I supposed. Four men accompanied me in this one, and they all wore black and impassive expressions. They were mixed nationalities, so I couldn't be sure who'd taken me. Regardless, it meant nothing good. I tried again to get to the door, though we were on the highway and doing eighty. Dumb, sure, but no worse than believing gangsters wanted to talk.

"You're going to be difficult," a man said with faint exasperation. His accent was difficult to place, but it wasn't Mexican. Not Canadian either, more like—

Before I could make up my mind, a needle prickled my skin and I fell into a dark hole.

I woke in a sumptuously appointed room, all white—impossible to keep clean without an army of maids attending to every smudge and spill. Judging by the pristine carpet, whoever had taken me possessed such an army. I fought down a sick certainty that, like Señor Alvarez, Shannon had died because of me. My head felt thick from whatever they'd drugged me with, and my tongue tasted funny.

A disembodied voice sounded on the intercom, different from the man in the SUV. "You will find clean clothing in the armoire. Please avail yourself of the facilities. In half an hour, someone will escort you to my study."

Even if I had wanted to argue, I saw no button I could press to make my fear and fury known. I slid off the mattress and onto the thick, plush carpet, and then glanced down at myself. My jeans were stained; my shirt still carried orange smudges. God only knew what my hair was doing. It would serve this bastard right if I confronted him in all my stink, but I couldn't stand myself another minute.

In the wardrobe, I found a small array of attire: a pair of jeans, designer slacks, a couple of blouses and sweaters. More unnerving, they were all my size. I closed the door on such creepiness and went into the bathroom. If possible, that was worse.

Oh, it was a dream of a room, all gilt and marble; there was a Jacuzzi and a separate glass stall for when you wanted to rinse off. Since I didn't think it was right to lounge in a spa tub when my friends might be dead and I had been abducted, I glared at the offending opulence as I got in the shower. Even the toiletries bespoke an unnerving knowledge of me. The expensive shampoo and conditioner smelled of frangipani, my preferred scent.

Well beyond worried and now into creeped-the-fuck-out, I rushed as I would never ordinarily do. I only had thirty minutes anyway, if I didn't want some goon dragging me out of the bathroom naked and wet. Clean clothes would armor me for what was to come.

I dried off and couldn't resist the frangipani body cream. All this luxury had the effect of diffusing my fear, cutting it with anger instead. I could use the boost of looking more together than I felt. Worry gnawed at me underneath, mostly about Butch and Shannon. If they weren't okay—

I cut the thought and dressed quickly. Each article contained silk; I could tell by the way it slid against my skin. They had even provided shoes; I growled over the fact that they fit when I jammed my feet into them. Someone knew me better than I knew myself; they'd bought black slacks and a matching V-necked sweater. Add platform Mary Janes, and you had an outfit I'd buy on my own. This look leaned toward the conservative end of my spectrum, but still. I might've thrown myself out a window if the closet had contained long skirts and peasant blouses.

I checked the time and found I had enough remaining to

deal with my hair. Since it was wet, I could only plait it, but I went with a French braid so I didn't look schoolgirlish. I needed power for this confrontation.

A few moments later, a knock sounded. *Really? We're pretending I have a choice? Why not just drag me by my hair?* I wore a scowl when I flung open the door, hoping I didn't appear frightened. I didn't want them to think they'd succeeded in terrorizing me, although they totally had.

"Follow me." It was the same henchman who'd said, *You're going to be difficult,* right before he drugged me.

Because I wasn't looking for a repeat performance, I fell in behind him. He spoke not a single word as he led me down a long, luxurious corridor—I recognized some of the artists whose work hung in a display worthy of a gallery. Priceless objets d'art lined the walls, but it was simple and elegant, not as if the owner sought to boast of what his money could buy.

We passed a number of rooms, some of which I would be hard-pressed to name. Others I knew, like library, conservatory, dining room. My escort swung open an ornate, beautifully carved teak door. This room was unquestionably a man's study, from the gleaming desk to the matching wing-backed chairs. Even the carpet seemed manly, with its muted maroon pattern. Reflexively, I started pricing the furniture for what I could get for it in my shop—and then I remembered I had none.

"Wait here," the henchman told me.

"Of course." I didn't know whether he noticed the biting sarcasm. Probably not. Thugs were not known for their intellectual acuity.

He left, shutting the door behind him. I knew this tactic. They were watching me to see what I'd do alone. The waiting was meant to soften me up, so I'd agree to anything by the time my captor arrived.

I obliged them by wandering, a sign of nerves. In my circuit, I read the titles on the shelves. *The Prince* by Niccolò Machiavelli. *The Art of War* by Sun Tzu. *The Divine Comedy* by Dante Alighieri. *So he's a learned man and a strate-*

gist. There were titles in other languages as well; evidently this villain was multilingual, as he owned texts in Chinese, Russian, German, Italian, Spanish, and Portuguese. It was also possible he was a collector, which boded ill for me. Maybe he'd change his mind when he found out I wasn't a natural redhead.

A soft footfall from behind made me spin from my scrutiny of the shelves. A man in his late forties stood before me. He was tall and slim, almost painfully elegant in a white linen suit. His sharp, foxy face came to a point at his chin, balanced by the blade of a nose. Bronze skin contrasted pleasingly with a spill of iron gray hair. He gave the impression of careless grace, but I had the feeling he never made a move without orchestrating it. His eyes shone like black pearls, lustrous but containing terrible depth.

I didn't know exactly what Montoya looked like; in my vision where I saw Min with four men, he could've been any of them, so that offered no help. As my host padded forward, I noted he wore no shoes. Interesting dichotomy, that informality when measured against his crisp white clothing— perhaps it was meant to disarm me.

"I trust you found the accommodations to your liking," he said in a low, smooth voice. "Would you care for something to eat?"

"I have nothing to say until I know my friends are safe."

In my head, the shots echoed as we drove away, and I couldn't restrain a flinch.

"They are well," he assured me.

Relief left me light-headed, so much that I couldn't speak. *Thank you for Shannon.* He took my silence for skepticism.

"But I do not believe you'll take my word. Shall we call them?" He lofted my phone—the same one they'd texted. I had no idea how long it had been, how long I had been unconscious.

Sudden hope surged through me, but I managed not to snatch it from him. "Let me dial."

"Of course."

He passed the cell over and I punched in Shannon's number. It rang three times and then her wonderful voice came on the line. Caller ID told her who it was before she picked up. "Corine? Where *are* you? God, we've been so worried."

"I don't know. Are you okay? I heard gunfire." Even if I had a clue where I was, I wouldn't tell her. I didn't want Shan involved further, if I could help it.

"They shot the engine block." The disgust in her voice came across clearly. "You have any idea how long it takes to get a tow truck in the middle of the night? I had Skittles and Pepsi for breakfast."

"Where are you? Did Kel find a place for you to stay?"

I heard a rumble of background noise, a cocktail of male and female voices. "We went to Laredo." *Ah, shit.* Shannon confirmed my fear. "I'm staying with Chuch and Eva. He's funny, but she's *so* mad at you for not calling. They're really nice. I think Jesse's coming over tonight."

Great, when this was over, I was so going to hear about my failure to communicate. Assuming I survived. But I had to find a way to keep Shannon safe, a solution that didn't endanger her . . . or anyone else, for that matter. I'd never forgive myself if anything happened to Chuch and Eva, after they'd been so kind to me. I wouldn't be ringing again after this. Given sufficient warning, I wouldn't put it past Chuch to try to trace the call. The former weapons dealer had crazy connections. Like it or not, it looked like I was on my own.

"And Butch is all right?"

"He misses you."

Despite my wishing Kel had gone another route, there were few people I trusted more than Chuch and Eva. They'd look after Shannon, and he likely hadn't known where else to go. It wasn't like God's Hand had contacts of his own; he was too much of a rolling stone.

"I'll be in touch when I can."

"Wait. Where—"

Before she could finish the question, my host took the

phone from me and hit "end." Not content with those measures, he powered the device down and handed it back to me. "Feel better?"

"Some." If he'd meant to harm us, he could've done so already. Well, not Kel, not permanently, but Shannon was fragile. I wished I'd sent her to Oklahoma City.

"I merely wished to discourage your friend from following. He has a history of leaving wreckage in his wake."

I considered what we'd done at the warlock's compound and then later at Montoya's mountain hideout and had to agree. "Fair enough. You've gone to a lot of trouble to get a little private time with me. So what do you want?"

"You interest me," he said. "Montoya has gone off the deep end over you, señorita. Others have failed to provoke such a powerful reaction. Why is that?"

I shrugged. It was a long story, starting with my ex-boyfriend's mother, a dead prostitute, a fictional curse, and a bunch of bad luck. As ever, mine.

"The better question is why you care."

"I am Ramiro Escobar," he answered, as if that explained everything.

Horribly enough, it did.

Deals with the Devil

It all made sense now. Back in Laredo, a man named Esteban helped us out when we went up against Montoya for the first time. He'd told us he worked for Escobar, Montoya's biggest rival. I could only surmise I'd been taken by the same guy. Still, it seemed best to confirm the supposition.

"You sometimes find yourself in competition with Montoya?" I ventured.

He smiled. "I see you've heard of me."

Well, only because of Esteban. But I didn't want to hurt his feelings by letting him know his legend wasn't as big as he believed. No man wanted to hear that. I relaxed a little, though. Now I thought I knew why he'd scooped me up. Sure, since he had my cell number, a preliminary conversation would've been more polite, but handled this way, he proved he meant business. A benign kidnapping revealed certain panache, but I shouldn't lose sight of how dangerous this man was.

"Yeah. One of your . . ." What did you call a guy who worked for a drug dealer? *Henchman* sounded very 1960s Batman. I decided on, ". . . employees helped us out a while back."

"I am aware."

A micromanager, eh? "Look, I'm sure you didn't pull me out of my car for the pleasure of my company. Why don't we get down to business?"

Clearly he wanted something from me or I wouldn't be here, at least not with all my parts intact. Montoya might be a rabid dog, but Escobar had an equally brutal reputation. He just went about his work more quietly; the bodies he dumped didn't surface and wind up on the news.

"A meal first," he said with implacable politeness.

I managed a smile. "I can't remember when I last had a proper meal. That would be lovely."

A little voice shouted in the back of my head that this was crazy, but I crushed it. One didn't anger the wolf by refusing to share his meat. According to older rules of hospitality, if I ate his food and drank his wine, he shouldn't do violence against me. I'd just hang on to that hope.

"He hunts you like an animal," he noted as he turned to step into the hall. I heard him speaking to someone in a low voice. When he returned, he added, "Our repast will arrive shortly. Will you sit?"

I'd known enough dictatorial men to realize that wasn't an invitation; it was an order wrapped in a courteous coating, like the hard candy shell on M&M's kept the chocolate in line. Muting a sigh, I crossed to the pair of wing-backed chairs. They were angled for intimate discussion, and the gleaming cherry table between them could easily hold a tray. Despite myself, my stomach rumbled.

Since he didn't yet want to talk about why he'd brought me here, I made small talk—and I wasn't good at it in the best of times. This didn't qualify.

Still, I offered, "You have a lovely home."

Escobar scrutinized my movements and mannerisms. "Yes." Unlike most, he didn't thank me for stating the obvious. "As I said before, you intrigue me. Would you mind if I have one of my men examine you?"

"What would that entail?"

I wasn't about to offer myself for rectal probing or freelance vaginal spelunking. Like hell would I budge from this chair, unless he answered the question in a less-than-alarming fashion. Surreptitiously, I wrapped my fingers around the arms. I could do the passive-resistance thing.

"Nothing invasive."

Claims the kidnapping drug dealer.

"Maybe," I said. "It depends on how dinner goes."

From his expression, he took that as a flirtatious rejoinder. *Oh, crap.* While I was trying to figure out how to backpedal from that, someone rapped on the door. At Escobar's murmured assent, a servant clad in black and white entered with a tray of cold cuts, gourmet cheeses, and fresh fruit. While he laid out the repast, I sat quiet in my chair, battling back the fear that pounded like a pulse. Despite my bravado, I was in a precarious situation. I needed to make this man happy enough to let me go, but without selling my soul in the process.

"That will be all, Carlitos."

The employee nodded and he didn't quite back out of the room, but his look as he left offered that sort of deference. Since I was hungry, I served myself some rolled ham, a few slices of cheddar cheese, and a handful of grapes. He waited until I cleaned my plate, anxious to be a good host. I found that slightly distressing.

"So now we've eaten," I prompted.

"Let me cut to the chase, then. I believe you could prove useful to me."

Oh, man. That was the second-to-last thing I wanted to hear, right after, *I want to cut off your head and make a bowl from your skull.*

"How so?"

"Montoya has shown he will stop at nothing to get to you, and his anger makes him vulnerable. In the past weeks, he has taken great risks. Therefore, I want you to help . . . remove him as an obstacle to my business interests."

"Are you sure you have the right woman? I can't even fire a handgun."

"You surround yourself with dangerous, capable people," he said quietly. "The lack of martial physical skill is of no consequence to a good general. He must merely know when to deploy his men."

"I don't have 'men.'"

"You do." He spoke with the air of one who never argued; Ramiro Escobar didn't need to. "Under the right conditions, I will offer you my protection, which will incense Montoya all the more. In short, I intend to use you as bait. If you survive, I will reward you richly."

Who wouldn't leap at a deal couched in terms of *if you survive*? But with his blood money, I could rebuild my shop. I saw it renovated, better than ever. Temptation swirled in my head. I remembered the clips of the wreckage on the news; there was no way I'd manage without a windfall. Otherwise, I had to start over.

Maybe—no. I mentally shook my head at the offer, trying to resist. *On the other hand . . . I mean, it's not like he's asking me to do anything bad. I was going after Montoya anyway.* My conscience whimpered. *Yeah, that's how it* starts. I couldn't afford to alienate him inside his stronghold, however, so I maintained an impassive expression. Well, I tried, anyway.

"I have to deal with him," I admitted. "He's not walking away from this."

Not after Ernesto, Señor Alvarez, and my shop. If I'd considered running, that was no longer an option. He had made Shannon and me homeless and killed innocent people trying to get to me. If I didn't stop it, the body count would just keep rising.

I went on. "So, I'm listening."

He smiled. "I thought you were a reasonable woman. But before I cement an alliance with you, I want tangible evidence that you are, in fact, as tough and resourceful as I believe."

I'd seen *The Labors of Hercules* on his bookshelf, so I feared I knew what came next. "Let me guess. A test? I hope not twelve of them."

"We can learn a great deal about how our would-be allies perform under duress," he observed. "For you, I set forth three tasks. One challenges your physical endurance, another tests mental acuity, and the last feat, your courage."

"How am I supposed to survive long enough to run the gauntlet?"

"Where I will send you," Escobar said softly, "my enemy will never find you. If you return successful, I will extend my protection to you, and we will move forward in our joint efforts to destroy Diego Montoya."

My skin crawled at the idea of being beholden to Ramiro Escobar. Beneath the polite, urbane exterior lay a yawning emptiness that suggested he did not acknowledge anything beyond his own fingertips as sovereign or self-willed. Could I walk away from this, or had he just made me an offer I couldn't refuse?

"Assume I pass your trials. Assume we crush Montoya with me as bait and you as the steel trap."

"Highly desirable outcomes."

"What then? Will we have any obligation to each other thereafter?"

"No," he said. "Though as a courtesy I will not rescind my protection, so long as you do not cross me or interfere in my affairs."

That could be handy, if I didn't think about all the harm he caused, lives ruined, people murdered. You know, little things. I took a deep breath. This was worse than any course I'd considered to date, using evil to fight evil. If I allied with him, I had to accept this tarnish on my soul. I shuddered because I knew what kind of man Escobar was; drugs might even be the least of it.

"If I refuse your offer, what happens then?"

"I let you go." Escobar lifted his shoulders. "In all likelihood, Montoya will succeed in killing you, which will be unfortunate, but I cannot mourn someone who passed up such an opportunity."

Kel wanted to ask Twila for an introduction to this guy, or someone like him. He glimpsed my future and it didn't look bright. Even he can't keep up with the numbers Montoya can send—it only takes one stray bullet.

"You'd let me go," I said, trying to reason out his motives. "On the off chance I might do Montoya some harm before I died?"

"Precisely."

"But if I'm not willing to take your challenge, then I'm not worthy of your protection."

Which was pretty messed up, as I considered—he was saying I had to prove I was good enough for him to use as bait. Ramiro Escobar had a high opinion of himself. Then again, maybe he wanted to make sure I had the nerve to see the scheme through—that I wouldn't turn on him halfway through and try to make a deal with Montoya, using *him* as the lure. Since I had no beef with Escobar—apart from his pulling me out of the car and drugging me, he'd proven himself a pretty good guy, for a cartel boss—I'd never do such a thing. Regardless, I had to admire such twisty thinking.

"I see we understand each other."

I had a clear picture, all right. Now I just needed to decide what to do. To give myself time to think, I took two more pieces of ham, some cheese, and apple wedges. Escobar watched me eat, elegant in his white suit. I couldn't help but imagine the pale linen spattered with blood, but it would be mine spilling out if I walked away.

"Okay," I said at last. "I'm in. What am I supposed to do first?"

"You will be allowed to pick one person to help you. *Only* one. I will send men to secure this individual and deliver him or her to the starting point. There will be clues along the way as to what you need to be doing. Once you pass all three tests, I will return you to Texas."

"Where we'll take on Montoya together."

It sounded like he was describing *The Amazing Race.* Great news for me, he loved mythology, strategy, and challenges straight out of reality television.

Escobar rose and padded over to his desk, where he lofted a sheaf of paper. Contracts, maybe. "Upon confirmation of his death, I'll pay you one hundred K."

That was nothing to him, but it nearly made me choke on my cheddar. "Whatever you're having me do first, it must be worth something to you."

"Some things," he said, "are priceless."

I'd heard that tone before. "You want me to retrieve some lost artifact. Then, once I've got it, you're going to make me handle it, knowing it's charged with hellacious shit."

"I did say the final task would test your courage."

I knew the drill now. Mental acuity amounted to locating the damn thing. Physical challenge would be the actual acquisition—and courage? Well, who wanted to touch a magickal item that caused mayhem and destruction? He wasn't sending me to Calcutta to retrieve Mother Teresa's thimble.

"So you did. Are you going to call your guy to check me out now?"

"As long as you're willing."

Oh, sure. I had all the power in this partnership. "Go for it."

Escobar used the intercom this time, murmuring in Spanish. The gist was that he wanted Paolo to come to the study right away. I occupied myself with eating. There were tiny Belgian chocolates arranged artfully around the edge of the plate.

When Paolo appeared a few minutes later, I decided *man* was a stretch. The kid couldn't be more than eighteen, slim and pretty, with caramel skin. He had doe eyes and long lashes, and I stopped worrying that his examination would be awful and invasive.

"Señorita Solomon," he said, bowing over my hand.

When our fingers brushed, it threw a spark. My eyes met his in silent recognition. He was gifted, but it would be rude to inquire in case his boss didn't know. I held my tongue.

"Ah," Escobar said. He had noted it too, so apparently he was familiar with such things. "She is like you, it would seem."

"I have brought two objects for you," Paolo murmured. "One contains a charge that will tell you something about Señor Escobar that you could never otherwise know."

So it was a test more than an examination. I wished he'd said so in the first place. Though perhaps Escobar's English wasn't so precise as I'd thought—he might have used *examine* as a not-quite-accurate synonym for *test*. I did that kind of thing in Spanish all the time.

The boy opened his palms, which were long and narrow. In his left hand he held a silver key—in his right, a gold ring. Most likely they wanted a show. Well, I was in no mood for theatrics, so I merely brushed my fingertips over each item. The key contained nothing, though it presumably unlocked something. That established, closing my eyes, I took the ring and curled my hand about it, accepting pain as the price of my gift, and let the images come.

When I opened my eyes, I was smiling. "Your first name isn't Ramiro, and your mother loved you very much. That was her wedding ring."

"What is my name?" Escobar asked, his voice gone hoarse with some emotion I was afraid to identify. His lean jaw clenched in expectation of my answer.

"Efraín," I said softly. "Because you were second-born of twins, but your brother died when you were small, and you cannot bear to hear the name spoken because you miss him, even now."

I had seen her writing their names in a baby book, each letter lovingly inscribed with near-calligraphic quality. Somehow I doubted the woman I had seen would be proud of the life her son had chosen. Escobar knew it too.

"You have a real gift," Paolo declared.

As do you, I said with my eyes. But still, I would not ask. He should tell me, if he wanted to, but this was neither the place nor the time. Not with Escobar pacing like a tiger. When Paolo slipped out, I wanted to follow, but I hadn't been dismissed.

Escobar ran an agitated hand through his shoulder-length silver hair. "The hour grows late. In the morning, I will hear your choice as to your partner in the coming trial. Leave me now." He spun away to pace some more.

I hastened out of the study, where I found Paolo waiting for me. "I thought you might need a guide back to your room."

"Yeah. I wasn't paying attention before."

"Not surprising. You were doubtless worried."

I smiled. "To say the least."

"You were curious back there. About what I can do."

"Obviously. But it's up to you if you want to tell me."

We walked for a few moments in silence. The house seemed bigger now that it was full dark, endless corridors full of shadows. I felt very small and cut off from the people who cared about me. Tomorrow, who knew where the hell I was going—and to make matters worse, I had to pick one person—*only* one—to take with me, even though I didn't know what I was getting into or what kind of help I'd need.

"I don't mind," Paolo answered eventually.

I expected him to tell me, but he showed me instead. A single white rose sailed out of a nearby vase and floated toward my hand. Smiling faintly, I took the bloom. "Fantastic control. I expect you can do damage as well."

He dipped his head in acknowledgment. It made sense that Escobar would cultivate employees whose talents could be weaponized. This innocent-looking boy had probably killed with his gift—a sobering thought. I'd do well to remember that a pretty face and big eyes didn't equate to harmless.

"Well, thanks for the escort," I said. "This is my stop."

"My father will send someone for you at first light."

That revelation rocked me. Nothing in the older man's manner had hinted at a paternal relationship. To the best of my recollection, he'd treated Paolo like staff.

"You're his *son*?"

Slim shoulders rose and fell. "He has many. Most were discarded."

Oh, the irony. Montoya went mad because a prostitute aborted his child and he never sired another. Escobar appeared to have demon sperm, but he was also a cold, heartless bastard, and he had sons enough to abandon if they didn't measure up. No wonder Montoya hated him, quite apart from their business conflicts. It must seem like salt in the wound.

On another level, it reinforced my need to be cautious here. A man who could treat his flesh and blood like help was capable of damn near anything, and I would do well to remember that. I'd fallen into the shark tank for sure this time.

"Good night," I said then. "I have some thinking to do."

How could I ever choose? I had the funny feeling this decision might prove portentous in ways I couldn't yet imagine.

Corine's Choice

Dawn stole across the horizon. From the bed where I sat propped against the pillows, I could see tendrils of light. Montoya's men would arrive soon to ask for my decision. And really, it was no choice at all. Right then, there was only one person I could ask. Yet I found myself examining my reasons, just to be sure I'd made the right call.

Not Shannon. I was sure about that. As much as I cared, that was *why* I couldn't take her with me. I needed her to be safe.

And though Jesse might never forgive me, I couldn't envision any scenario involving him ending happily. After all, he worked as a cop. If Escobar scooped him up, his colleagues would either mount a manhunt or—after the debacle with his partner—assume he too was on the cartel's payroll. He had a family: Off and on for the past few months he had been bugging me to come to Laredo again to meet his parents. I thought it seemed precipitous, but unless I wanted them to hate me for ruining his life, I'd better not go that way. *So not Jesse, either.*

Chuch would never leave Eva, and she was pregnant. Plus, they functioned as a unit; I could hardly ask for one without the other.

Chance? With the way things ended between us, I had no right to drag him into this mess now. My heart ached at the thought of him. I hoped he was happy and safe, at least, but if I wanted him to stay that way, I needed to leave him alone. Additionally, Nalleli had just cleansed me of all the ill luck, and it made no sense to summon him when I didn't know what I'd be facing.

That left only one alternative, as I'd known all along.

Since I wasn't sure where they were taking me, I dressed in jeans and a plain pullover. It gave me the willies when I located fresh underwear. Escobar just knew too much about me for personal comfort.

Paolo came for me shortly thereafter. Doubtless that was meant as a kindness, since he was young and nonthreatening. I followed him through the silent, opulent halls. Instead of turning toward the study, we went all the way through the house to an enormous veranda. Beyond, a private plane sat waiting on a distant airstrip.

"I'm not seeing your father again?"

"You will not," he said, "until you've proven yourself. He is . . . reclusive."

This just kept getting better. "Okay. So do I tell you the name, then?"

He inclined his head. "Please."

"Kel—big guy, bald, tattooed—he was with me when they grabbed me. I'm sure your dad knows who he is."

"Undoubtedly." His tone implied Escobar knew everything worth knowing. "Farewell and good luck."

I made my way across the veranda, down the steps, and across the field. A man in black waited for me, arms folded, beside the stairs leading to the plane. I had no idea if we were even still in Texas; the landscape gave me no clue. We might've crossed the border while I was unconscious.

"*¿Lista?*" the thug asked as I approached.

Ready as I ever will be. Nodding, I preceded him up the steps. He gave the orders and we got under way. I didn't mind flying, except for takeoff and landing, but everything shook more in a small plane. This one couldn't hold more than ten people. That meant we couldn't be going far— well, not across an ocean, anyway.

Apart from my silent guard, I didn't see anyone besides the pilot, and unlike commercial planes, I could see right up the aisle into the cockpit. They exchanged a few muttered words in Spanish, and then the plane powered up. I buckled in. A little voice asked if I was crazy. As we zoomed toward the end of the airstrip, I decided the answer was yes.

We put down in what seemed like a sea of trees—from the air, everything was green. I closed my eyes rather than watch the pilot aim for the impossibly small runway that was more of a dirt track in a clearing. The man guarding me grunted at me to exit the plane. I was tired and sore by this time, so I stumbled down the metal steps and into sweltering heat.

It was a different kind than I had felt in the mountains of Mexico; this was jungle heat. Monkeys chattered in the distance, and I suppressed a shiver. The guard gestured me toward an old decommissioned military jeep. *They aren't big on the explanations.*

When I approached the vehicle, relief spilled through me. Kel sat in the backseat, and he didn't appear to have come to any harm. I swung up beside him, immediately feeling more centered. It had shaken me more than I wanted to let on, the easy way Escobar had taken me.

"You knew I was in no real danger, right?" I asked softly. "That's why you didn't fight?"

"It was a necessary risk." Which meant he hadn't been sure.

"Did they explain the point of this exercise?"

"You chose me." Somehow he made it sound like more than it was, a decision driven by necessity, as if I *wanted* him here, and, moreover, as if that meant something. "We'll see it through together."

The men conferred, and then two of them turned back toward the plane. One got in the driver's seat. He didn't speak to us, merely took off driving along a rutted road. A couple of times, I tried to ask a few questions, but he wouldn't give me anything, so we passed the miles in silence. The light faded over the trees, and at nightfall, we came to the out-skirts of a village.

Our driver cut the engine and addressed us in accented English. "This is as far as I take you. Instructions wait at house of Señora Juárez."

"Fantastic," I muttered. "Thanks for the ride."

Kel was already out of the jeep, so I got down too. He led the way down the narrow dirt track leading into the small cluster of houses. I had no idea where we were, but from the look of folks going about their business, I guessed somewhere in Central or South America. That covered a lot of territory.

He stopped a man at random. *"Perdone. Estamos buscando a la Señora Juárez. ¿Sabe dónde vive?"*

Though the villager treated us both to a look of justified suspicion, the guy pointed us in the right direction. Broken glass crunched underfoot as we walked. The few shops open were small, occupying the bottom floor of someone's home, and the brands of beer advertised rang no bells either. We definitely weren't in Mexico, where you couldn't go twenty feet without seeing a Sol sign.

"You don't mind that I called on you for this?" Based on his reaction earlier, he might even be pleased, but I needed to be sure.

"If you had not," he said, "I would have found you. I have my orders."

"I don't think Escobar would take kindly to our breaking his rules. He's crazy."

In a different way from Montoya, of course, but I didn't feel any safer, even with this prospective alliance on the table. This was so far outside my usual parameters as to be laughable. And stupidly enough, I missed my dog.

"But he is well-disposed toward you, and you need his resources."

"Right. Is Shannon okay? And Butch?"

"They're fine. Shannon was helping Eva put the finishing touches on the nursery when Escobar's men showed up."

Honestly, that news scared the shit out of me. If Escobar

knew that much, Montoya might be able to find out too. There was no guarantee I could keep trouble away from Chuch and Eva's front door, much as I wanted to. *If anything happens to them—*

But this was no time to get emotional. I had to be strong and resourceful and brave. Especially brave. As we approached the ochre adobe house, I steadied my breathing and tried to compose myself.

He rang the bell and no one came, so he rapped on the heavy wooden gate. From within I heard slow stirring and footsteps. An old woman answered; she peered at us with rheumy eyes and then waved us in, but no farther than the courtyard. She bade us wait, shuffling around the corner of the house. Five minutes later, another woman stepped through the front door, carrying two backpacks. She was not young, and she wore fear in the shadows beneath her eyes. When she held out the bags, her hands trembled. I tried to question her as well, but she shook her head.

"Tell him I did as he asked," she said in Spanish. "Tell him. Go now."

Other than refuse and be ejected forcefully, there was nothing for us to do but step back onto the street. It was dark now, and there were no streetlights. Only the distant shimmer of *taberna* lamps lent any illumination. From this angle they might have been stars blinking back at us, sad and melancholy, through the windows.

"Whatever we're meant to do first, we can't begin in the dark."

He agreed with a quiet nod. "Did you notice anywhere we could stay the night?"

I recollected seeing a simple sign for Hostal Ochoa a few blocks back. It had been slightly off our route and down a side street, but I thought I could find it. This time I led the way, retracing our steps. After making the last left, I saw the white sign once more.

"There," I said, pointing.

It was a tall, narrow building, part concrete and part adobe. We mounted the few steps to the dark wood door. I'd never gone backpacking in Europe—the tour with Chance had been more upscale—so I didn't know whether one knocked or simply entered. Kel answered the question by trying the handle; the knob turned, so we stepped into the foyer, furnished simply in rustic style. The wood gleamed in the faint light, warm and welcoming.

A round, middle-aged woman came down the hall toward us. Her hair had been oiled and braided in a complex, impressive corona about her head. Her welcoming expression faded toward uncertainty when she got a good look at Kel. I tried to assuage her worry with a smile.

"Necesitamos un cuarto, por favor." I didn't ask if he wanted his own room.

"Claro. How long will you be staying?" she asked in Spanish.

"Una noche? No estoy segura." I hoped not more than one night, anyway. It occurred to me to wonder whether we had cash in our backpacks. I didn't even know what country we were in.

"Está bien." She gazed at me, probably gauging how much she could ask. Since I was wearing jeans and a pullover, I didn't look affluent. The backpack made me look like a traveler on a budget. She decided on, *"Cuarenta."*

To my vast relief, Kel produced a couple of orange bills from one of the pockets in his pack; it wasn't as pretty as any of the Mexican banknotes. I read the currency as he passed it over. Holy crap, we were in Peru; I managed not to let my shock show. Looking as if she felt better already, the woman led us down the hallway to the stairs.

They were narrow and dark as we climbed, but the house smelled fresh and clean. Plain wood floors needed no other adornment. On the third floor, she paused and opened a door near the stairs. The room was spartan and contained nothing other than a chair and a full-size bed. I presumed the door in the wall was a closet.

"The bathroom is over there." She pointed down the hall. "Shared, but I have no other guests on this floor tonight."

Good to know.

After informing us where to find towels and that breakfast would be served at eight a.m., she hurried out. I closed the door and turned the bolt. Since our room faced the street, I headed over and closed the curtains as well. It made the room seem even smaller—and it wasn't large to start with—but I could deal. I told myself it was cozy, seated myself in the chair, and rummaged through the backpack.

I found five hundred *nuevos soles*, a map, and five pairs of clean underwear. *Ew.* How long did he expect this to take? If Escobar's estimate was accurate, I'd be wearing these same clothes for almost a week. I had socks too, and hiking boots. When I glanced up, I found Kel studying me.

After opening the map, with a fingertip I traced the black ink path that had been drawn. "It looks like we're supposed to head into the jungle from here."

"Up the river."

I checked the scale and swore. "That'll be a hell of a hike."

It was a good thing Escobar had provided me with boots, but breaking in new footwear by wearing it for miles at a time was a crappy idea. Not like I had anything else. Everything I owned had been blown to shit, along with Señor Alvarez, who hadn't wanted to look after the shop for me this time. I'd known he didn't, and instead of closing the place, I'd made him an offer too sweet to refuse—fifty percent commission on anything he sold. The paper crumpled in my hands.

"It wasn't your fault," he said quietly.

"I didn't set the bomb, but I put him there in my place." Much as I appreciated the effort, I wouldn't be letting myself off the hook anytime soon.

Doubtless sensing I wouldn't be swayed, he changed the subject. "Did you find a pendant in your bag?"

I dug into the pack once more and found the necklace wrapped in tissue in a side pocket. Kel was already wearing his. When my fingertips brushed the metal, they singed, but it was like catching the embers of a fallen star, unexpected and magical. Images whispered in my mind's eye, showing me glimpses of the pretty young woman who had woven a protective spell on this medallion as if she were twining summer roses in her hair. Watching her I couldn't help but smile, despite our circumstances, and I dropped the leather cord around my neck.

"Saint Christopher," I said.

"Patron saint of travelers." His eyes were gray and grave, quiet like clouds gathering the strength for snow.

"Is that all true? The saints and miracles."

"I don't know. I'm not Catholic."

Again, the hint that angels and divinity lay outside the purview of organized religion. Oh, how his secrets intrigued me.

"This is meant to hide us, isn't it? Keep us from Montoya's sorcerer." Pity no such spell lasted forever. I could quietly disappear. But crossing Escobar would be suicide, as that move would leave me with two cartel bosses on my back.

"It is." He turned from me abruptly. "You should sleep."

"I suppose you don't?"

If that was the case, I should get off the chair, because he'd be sitting on it all night. Pity it wasn't padded, but the room didn't lend itself to such extravagance. There were no rugs, nothing that could be stolen or broken. Fortunately, I found the sheets clean, if slightly threadbare, when I turned down the bed. The gold and brown spread echoed the warmth of the wood, so the room was charming in its simplicity.

I'd almost forgotten the question by the time he answered, "I sleep."

There was no reason to make this complicated; most of the time, he didn't even seem to like me, so it wasn't as if I had to worry about unwelcome advances.

"Then do. We're safe, and it's hard to know when we'll see a bed again."

In an economical motion, I peeled out of my jeans. I removed my bra in a tricksy maneuver without taking off my shirt and slid beneath the covers. I rolled over on my side, giving him the choice to take the chair or climb in behind me. He moved around for a little while, and then he switched off the light. Eventually the mattress dipped with his weight.

"Are you certain you're not frightened?"

I thought about that, lying in the dark. Impossible question. I was afraid of what I might do in order to survive. I was afraid of the thing Escobar had sent me to find and the pain of reading it. I feared harm coming to my friends as a result of my bad choices. Hell, if I was honest, the idea of going out into the jungle scared the shit out of me too.

"I am. Of course I am. But you're the least terrifying part of this."

"It has been . . . long since I heard such. I've not been tasked with protection for many years."

"You slay and move on," I guessed.

I felt him nod. The pillow rustled, and I braved a look over my shoulder at him. He lay on his back, hands beneath his head. "They called me that, too, once."

Slayer. Sword. Wrath. Those were old words. A shiver rolled through me. I admitted to myself that *Hand of God* sounded less fearful.

"If I asked how old you are, would you tell me?"

"*Are* you asking?"

I eased over onto my back, deciding it was rude to talk without looking at him. "I'm curious."

"Older than the sands . . . and new like fresh-minted coins."

"That's no answer," I muttered.

"Sleep now."

Perversely, I didn't want to, even though I knew it was sensible advice. The morning would come fast, and with it, unbelievable hardship. On a whim, I reached over and put my palm on his chest. He'd removed his button-down while I was facing away, leaving only the undershirt. Relief coiled through me when I felt the reassuring thump of a beating heart. I pulled my hand away, but not before he levered up on one elbow to stare at me, his tats kindling blue in the darkness.

I shrugged away his reaction. "I needed to know."

"What?"

"How real you are."

"Enough to think on things I can't have," he said softly. "Good night, Corine."

Welcome to the Jungle

As it turned out, we didn't have the same things in our packs. Kel had protein bars and other survival gear. Just as well—I wouldn't have known what to do with most of it. We bought water first thing and headed out. I remembered Escobar saying it would take mental acuity to locate the item he wanted—and had told me squat about—so it seemed unlikely the map would lead us straight to it.

We attracted some looks on our way out of town, but nobody interfered with us. Whispers followed as we went. I didn't look back.

A dirt track led toward the trees. I followed Kel, watching where I stepped, even though the real dangers began once we entered the long, green shadows. The air smelled mossy, rich with new growth. I felt particularly alien here, where the trees tangled together, and I didn't recognize them.

Kel led the way. Soon the path we followed devolved into a nearly impenetrable wall of green. He drew a machete and went to work hacking our way to the river. I heard the water before I saw it. From there we headed north.

Roots grew thick and bumpy beneath the thin earth, creating a tiered path beside the river. The soil sank with each step, and the bugs swarmed me, biting like mad. I applied repellent Kel had in his pack, but it did a limited amount of good. Overhead, the canopy was so thick I could barely tell what time of day it was, apart from thin trickles of light filtered sickly green through the leaves. Animals prowled around us. I could hear them and smell them, but they seldom came into view. My arm hurt, but I didn't whine about it; that never did any good.

Thus passed two of the worst days of my life. Between the bugs, heat, uncertainty, and exhaustion, it became everything I could do to keep putting one foot in front of the other. In the evenings, we camped in the open, made more miserable by the fact that it rained the second night. For countless moments, I lay listening to the jungle serenade, an endless drone, underscored with other insects whirring, chirping. The darkness amplified the noise, so that I could hear even the rain plinking on the leaves. Used to city sounds and tires on the street, I found it hard to sleep, and when I rolled over, damp and despondent in my light sleeping bag, Kel's gaze met mine.

"You're not used to this," he observed.

"Are you?"

He considered. "Not any longer. In years past, I knew much worse."

"You weren't always God's Hand?" It seemed unlikely he would answer, yet I couldn't deny my curiosity.

"I came from humble beginnings. . . . I was a foot soldier. It took me a long while to earn my current title."

I wondered what constituted *a long while* to him. Sometimes as we'd walked, I surprised a peculiar expression on his face. I didn't know what to make of him, and something told me he didn't know how to feel about me either. Maybe we were both guilty of prejudicial behavior.

"Do you think I have a chance?"

He was silent for too long. "I am tasked to see that you survive, and have chosen our course accordingly."

My misery increased; I didn't like being a job to him. Somehow it felt like hiring company for the night because nobody wanted to take you home. Further conversation could only upset me, and I didn't need that, so I rolled over. Kel surprised me with a touch on my shoulder.

"Corine," he whispered, beneath the rain, "I'd help you without orders now."

Those words left me smiling. Soon enough, I slept; in the morning, we ate a couple of protein bars and continued on our way. It had been half a day since we'd seen other human beings, not that Kel counted. He was a capable companion, but I found his silence wearing. Since he didn't complain, I was damned if I would. Instead I hugged his compliment to my chest and called myself ten kinds of fool.

As the day wore on, my muscles ached in places where I hadn't known I had them, and sleeping on the ground left me with a bizarre kink in my neck. The new boots rubbed blisters through my socks, exacerbated by the salty sweat. I was afraid of taking them off; I might not be able to jam them back on my feet again.

In late afternoon, I stumbled behind Kel into a clearing. This was allegedly our destination, but I couldn't see anything here that could be considered a clue. I spun in a slow circle. Dirt, rocks, vines. The trees rustled overhead, conjuring images of snakes slithering across the branches. Despite the heat, I shivered.

"We're safe enough here," he said, reading my body language.

Yeah, but for how long? These amulets functioned for a limited time, and then we'd flash back onto Montoya's radar. If we were still out here in the middle of nowhere . . . Well, I could imagine few things worse. Fear prickled through me. Maybe Montoya had hired Escobar to take care of me; maybe this was an elaborate trap planned by two criminal minds.

Too late for second thoughts. I'm here.

I knelt and started going over the ground close up. There had to be something. While he stood guard, I crawled around for a good ten minutes, trying to hide how much my feet were bothering me. Near the western edge of the trees, I uncovered a clay statue, nearly hidden in the bush. The icon had markings on its feet.

"Our first clue?" Kel asked.

"I'm thinking so." But I couldn't read the symbols, nor did I recognize them. "This mean anything to you?"

He dropped down beside me. "Native writing."

"Thanks," I said dryly. "Could be Quechua or Aymara, I guess, but there are a bunch of aboriginal languages." Some of them were even extinct, which would make our task complicated.

"Can you handle it?" he asked.

"That was going to be my next move." I laid my scarred left palm against the statue and it felt cool, quiet. Not so much as a ripple. "Nobody's touched it enough to make an impression. What now?"

I was sure that was our clue, but without our being able to read the markings, it was impossible to say where we should go. The map gave no hint—the trail stopped here.

"We may as well make camp. I'll look at your feet."

"I'm fine."

"You're not. I smell blood."

A reflexive flinch surprised me, but I didn't argue further. In the jungle, infection could set in if you weren't careful, and I hadn't been taking care of myself. I hoped if I ignored the problem, it would go away. No such luck.

Instead of arguing, I settled in the shadow of the trees, beside the clay statue, and unlaced my boots enough to slip them off. My heels stung like hell, and once I had the boots off, I saw the stains on my socks. I'd felt the warm trickle, of course, but I hoped it was the blisters popping. I took a deep breath to brace myself to remove the socks as well; it felt like I'd lost an inch of skin. I chanced a look, and damn. *What a mess.*

Instead of chiding me, Kel went to work cleaning my wounds. His hands were warm and sure. Such silent care summoned images of holy men who had been directed to go forth and tend to the lowest among them.

"Thank you," I said when he was finished, though it seemed inadequate—as if I should not have permitted the attention.

"I am here to bear your pain, my blood for yours." Sunlight filtering through the leaves shaded his face, but I thought I saw a glimmer of regret. For what, I couldn't say.

"I'm pretty sure that's a bad bargain. Nalleli seemed to think yours is valuable."

"It is." There was no false modesty in his tone, only intensity and purpose.

I wished I knew more about him.

I started to move away but he motioned me to stillness. Right, my feet were raw and they needed bandaging. He produced a knife and made a small cut across his palm. Too late I realized he'd meant it literally—*I am here to bear your pain, my blood for yours.* I tried to recoil, but he held me still, sealing the trickling wound against the worst of the damage.

A glorious heat filled me, as if I could fly, or simply float away. My whole body felt weightless and blasted with irresistible euphoria. Once, I'd done a little E, and this was a thousand times more powerful. I laughed—and the sound swirled into endless echoes. A distant roar came back, and I giggled over that too. Boneless, I didn't struggle when he treated my other foot. The fizzing in my brain increased until the whole world sparkled, as if through a diamond rain.

"I'll heal your arm too. Too much risk of infection out here."

"That's nice," I mumbled.

The roaring got louder, or maybe it was my heart. I could feel him inside me, seeping into my cells with that fierce heat. Kel turned his face away from me and then he sprang to his feet.

"Stay here. Don't move."

Well, where would I go? Disjointed noise spun all around me, and I tried to track his movement, but he slipped and slid in a dazzling display of pyrotechnics. I blinked, trying to force the colors to die down, but no matter how I looked at him, I saw his body edged in silver and gold, crowned in a white light. But he hid darkness in his core, a tiny little knot of sorrow.

Wait—is he fighting? It was an animal, but so smeared in red I couldn't see. Images overlaid my vision, transparent and only half realized. More light. More shadow. Every tree and rock gained new dimension, as if I could see in a spectrum of color to which I'd been blind before. My eyes hurt with it, so I closed them and dropped my head on my knees. The world needed to stop now.

I felt his hands on my shoulders and I jerked. Not in pain, but because the power of him swam inside me. Before, I had no idea how strange he was—how alien—and now he felt too big to be crouched beside me, a force of nature rather than a person. He glowed like a sun.

"It will wear off soon."

Blindly I reached out and fisted my hands in his shirt. There was no spark, reinforcing the fact that he wasn't just a gifted human. "What did you do to me?"

"Just breathe."

"You had wings," I whispered. "Two of those scars on your back—you had *wings* once, raven dark, inky blue. When you flew, people crossed themselves and hid in their homes."

Because I had hold of him, I felt the shudder that ran through him. "Now there is proof you are born of ancient kings. You saw too much. Such a small amount of my blood should not affect you so."

"There's no taking back what you've given me, Kelethiel."

A low growl slid from him. "That name must not be spoken."

"Keleth—"

He sealed his hand over my mouth, silencing me. "Name me not, unless you mean to bind or banish me."

Some devil prompted me. I did the one thing I was sure would make him recoil: I moved my mouth in the faintest whisper of a kiss. He tasted of salt and copper, the hint of the blood he'd sacrificed for me lingering on his skin. My lips burned, his power seeping in through the dry cracks.

He did not withdraw, merely stared at me through narrowed eyes, as if I had transformed into a dangerous creature. His shoulders tensed, but he appeared to be appraising me in a way I could not measure. And then he moved his hand in increments of millimeters. Maybe it wasn't his intention, but his withdrawal became a sweet torment of fingertips dragging over sensitive skin. I had never received a kiss that stirred me more than that furtive, forbidden caress.

It's the blood, I told myself. *Not him. He's like a powerful mushroom or an exotic toad. He can't help the effect.*

His mien grew stern. "Are you yourself again?"

Ah. So that was how we were going to play it. My mind must've been addled for me to take such liberties with God's Hand. More fool me, because my heart thumped at his proximity, kindled by the traces of fierce magick in the air. He crackled like a fire, all leashed power and restraint.

"I am. Your secret is safe with me," I assured him quietly.

He lowered himself to the ground beside me, beside the clay statue, and his head went down, hunched shoulders indicating weight I could not see. For those terrible moments where I'd glimpsed him from the inside out, I had seen countless wars. Never-ending wars. Wars on earth, in hell, and in heaven. He had seen far too much for me to comprehend all of it, and yet—

I cut the thought mercilessly. That tree could bear no fruit. *Ah, Corine. Always the emotionally unavailable men, but this one makes Chance seem like an open book.*

What are you, Kelethiel, whose name I must not speak? All the lore I had read made me think he was an angel, but surely not. Not squatting in the mud with me.

"No wonder Nalleli wanted your blood," I murmured. My mind was clearing, so maybe I had been addled when I kissed his palm. In the silence I wondered how it would be to have him focused on me with the intensity he devoted to divine orders. "For spells . . . and probably chemical diversion as well."

Christ, a trace of his blood got me high as a kite and made me see things I wished I hadn't. Infinity hid behind his eyes, like precious gems beneath a layer of ice. For a whisper of a moment I'd seen him as he was—and as he saw himself. I didn't know if I'd ever recover.

He merely nodded. "I've driven away the cat. A jaguar."

"You didn't kill it?" *Interesting.*

"It was roused by our intrusion into its territory. We'll be on our way shortly."

I nodded. "As soon as we figure out the meaning of those markings. And I think I know what I need to do."

"And that is?"

"Sleep."

Booke would have answers. After all, we'd solved a number of problems via dream consultation. If anyone could help me, the hermetic scholar in the U.K. could. I liked to picture him in an enormous library, surrounded by arcane tomes. But before I could tap that knowledge, I had to prepare. I got a piece of paper and went to work. By the time I copied the glyphs, the sun hung low in the sky, though I could see only glimpses of it through the canopy. I could tell it was sunset by the lengthening shadows.

I had no idea whether this would work, but I had to try. On those other occasions, Booke had found me in my natural sleep; this would be my first crack at tracking him down. Before my power shifted—expanded—I doubt I would've attempted it. I was too accustomed to seeing myself as crippled in this world. I didn't feel that way anymore.

"I'll keep you from harm," he said.

And I trusted him to do so.

Dreamwalker

Acknowledging Kel's promise with a nod, I lay down on top of my bedroll. Sleep scooped me up fast and carried me away. First, I dreamt of angels with fiery swords and night-dark wings, but I couldn't stay to watch the titanic clash. From there I wandered into a world of shades that whispered of death and tried to touch me with smoky fingers. It was cold in comparison to other worlds, so I shifted again.

This time, I found myself in my old apartment, watching Chance. As always, he was lean and gorgeous. His hair had gone wild in shaggy layers, falling into his tiger eyes. By the angle of the sunlight, it was early afternoon, and he held his cell phone, arguing with someone over a repayment schedule.

"No," he bit out. "You're two weeks overdue. I'll start doubling the daily vig if you don't get me my money tonight."

I couldn't hear the other half of the conversation, so I watched as he listened. A cruel smile curved his mouth. "You think so? Listen, asshole, you do *not* want that. If I become your new best friend, it'll be worse than if I had your legs broken."

Another pause.

He laughed softly. "Well, you're welcome to test it, but you'll be sorry."

That, I knew, was true. When we were together, he'd enforced his loans like that. Instead of inflicting injury on his delinquent debtors, he offered friendship—and that was about the worst thing he could do, particularly since the bad luck clung like barnacles, and without fail, it would crush the person closest to him.

This reminded me of when I'd dreamt of Jesse, another instance when I played the invisible ghost, watching what they did without me. But entertaining as my subconscious proved to be, I shouldn't linger here, yet I couldn't make the shift. Something locked me in place, despite my struggles to move on. I scanned for Booke, seeking his familiar air. His personal tell felt to me like a lonely, pebble-strewn beach, and so I cast for it, eyes closed, denying what I saw, denying Chance.

But he didn't go away.

Once he cut the call, he ran a hand through already disheveled hair in a gesture so familiar it tugged at my heartstrings. It gave him no pleasure to use his gift this way. I knew that, but he had been obsessed with making money as long as I'd known him, as if nothing could ever be enough. I didn't quite understand why.

After a moment, he rose and strode over to the bureau, where we'd once kept our keys and miscellaneous objects. I assumed he still did. Most people had one junk drawer—because of my pack-rat ways, we'd needed five. He pulled out a photo album, the red one I made our first year together.

He opened it and I followed to see what he was looking at: a picture of him and me, taken by his mother. We stood by the ocean, the sun setting behind us, and I looked so happy it hurt. I had been blond then, and relatively tan. I almost looked like a different person.

"Soon," he said softly.

I forgot I wasn't there—that it wasn't real. "Chance . . ."

He spun, his hands white-knuckled on the book. Did he hear me? Clearly he couldn't see me. I wondered whether I actually went somewhere when I dreamt, but before I could speak again, test my curiosity, the tug came; I recognized Booke latching onto me as the lonely beach of his soul abutted mine. *Not now. Not yet.* I slid away, speeding toward a new dreamscape.

Booke waited for me, as always, in a library that existed only in my imagination. It looked like an old-school gentleman's study, with burgundy carpet and matching leather chairs, all mahogany and tasteful draperies. My mental image of Booke summoned a man in his late thirties or early forties, with a sharp, clever face, nut brown hair, and eyes like slate. Where he lived—and what he really looked like—well, I didn't know, because I'd never met him. He existed only as a voice, but he was more real to me than that.

"Could you feel me?" I asked, as the world went three-dimensional.

He nodded, wearing an expression of abject intellectual intrigue. "It was rather like a knock. I wasn't asleep, but I felt you buzzing in the back of my head, like a fly."

"Don't you have trouble sleeping? How did you—"

"Took something," he said. "I do resort to the chemical solution now and then. I collect you have need of me?"

"Things have been . . . eventful since we last spoke." I sat down in the leather chair across from him, crossing long legs that existed only in this dream space. "My shop is gone, and Montoya's hunting me."

"Oh, Corine." He leaned forward as if he wanted to comfort me, but he caught himself at the last moment. If we touched, it would jolt us both awake. Lucid dreaming had few rules, but that one was ironclad. Since we weren't physically together, contact broke the shared illusion. "Were there any casualties?"

I nodded. It was tougher to say aloud than I'd expected. "Señor Alvarez. He worked for me, mostly in a contract capacity, but he ran the store when I had to travel. He was . . . a fine man. I believe he had family in Monterrey."

When this was all done, I would find out who they were and provide for them. Kel had said, long ago, *I do not understand why a good man like Alvarez chooses to work for you*, as if he saw integrity in him that I lacked. Now he was dead, and I'd made a deal with the devil to save my own skin. Guilt gnawed me from the inside out, but maybe, just maybe I wasn't wholly damned if Kel would choose to aid me of his own volition—and he'd said so, hadn't he? Perhaps my soul wasn't as black as it felt.

"I'm sorry," he said with such sincerity that it felt like the hug he could not give.

"Me too."

Booke cleared his throat, acknowledging there was a reason I'd come looking for him. "Care to tell me what's afoot?"

I summarized my situation in a few words. Since he'd been involved in our fight against Montoya and helped us locate Chance's mother, he knew everything but the most recent developments. In dreamtime, I had no way to tell how much time had passed in the real world, but Kel would guard me.

"And so," I concluded, "I must pass this test for Escobar to seal our alliance against Montoya."

" 'The enemy of my enemy is my friend,' " he said softly.

"Something like that."

"You can't use your cell phone to ask for the information you need, because that offers proof you used more than one partner to complete these challenges."

I appreciated how quickly and accurately he assessed a situation. "Exactly. We've come to the spot marked on the map, but there's only a statue here, apart from all the wild-life."

"Can you show me the markings?"

"Better."

His eyes brightened visibly. "Translocation?"

"Yep. I have a sketch for you. I made sure every line is accurate."

"It would be interesting to know whether you could take a photo with your cell phone and send me that," he mused. "Do you think a gadget could make the transition intact?

There has always been a certain disconnect between magick and tech—"

"Well, if it didn't, then you wouldn't have an image to examine, and I would have no cell phone." Sometimes I had to rein him in.

"Yes, of course. I didn't mean now, when your need is pressing, but perhaps it would make an interesting test another time?"

"Sure," I said. "I'll buy a throwaway phone and we can try it later."

Like, after the dust settled, and I'd taken care of Montoya. Once, I would've shied from making that claim—I would've been paralyzed by fear and indecision. For most of my life, I'd constantly sought someone to keep the darkness at bay, but I could work a flashlight, and I liked fighting my own battles.

"Then I suppose we need to replicate what we did before. Can you create the campsite for me?"

I could. While I had been drawing earlier, I was also capturing details in my mind's eye to make our shared space real enough to allow for translocation. I built each tree, each leaf, everything I remembered, down to Kel sitting quietly beside our supplies. The library shifted slowly to the jungle, and Booke watched with pleasure shading his features. I didn't know if he had succeeded in contacting anyone else this way, and I'd never inquire, because that would sound proprietary. You just can't ask: *Do you share your dreams with anyone else?* without the other person taking it wrong.

"I'm here," he breathed—and joy threaded his voice like silver ribbons.

From his own account, he had seen so little of the world. I didn't know why he was trapped in Stoke, only that he was. Booke carried all manner of mysteries, but he did not invite confidence. I wasn't even sure I could call him a friend. Such relationships must be reciprocal, and he shared nothing with me. Ever. Even during our virtual chats, he spoke only of books he'd read or programs watched, nothing personal. Nothing meaningful. To him, I was a voice to fill the silence, and someone who occasionally needed a bit of research done.

I let him explore the small clearing, pacing its length, before I bent and retrieved the paper upon which I had drawn the markings from the statue's base. If anyone could get us a translation, Booke could. If he didn't know, I was sure one of his online cronies could put him in touch with the right person. For a few moments more, I watched him drink in the feeling of standing in a jungle. When he faced me at last, his expression glowed with wonder.

"Anywhere you'd like me to," I said softly, "I'll go for you. And we'll share it."

He froze, like a child afraid of reaching for a treat. "Egypt?"

"Certainly."

"That would be so *brilliant*." His smile cut his cheeks so wide that I thought they'd crack with the strain.

Yes, he was my friend, after all. I'd hardly make such an offer if I didn't care. What the hell—I'd always wanted to travel. I could see a lot of sights on Escobar's money, as well as rebuild my shop—which would take time.

"I promise."

He reached for the paper. We took care not to brush fingers as we made the exchange. If everything went well, it would disappear from the camp in the real world. I wondered what Kel would make of that.

Booke hesitated, as if weighing the risk of what he might say against its possible value. "If we go to my house, I might be able to find the information right now. I know the place well enough to re-create it, including every book and scrap of paper." Bitterness colored his voice.

He hated his captivity with a ferocity I could only imagine. If nothing else, since I hitchhiked out of Kilmer when I was eighteen, I had at least been free. Frequently, I had been alone, frightened, hunted, and desperate—or some combination thereof—but I'd never been trapped the way he seemed to be. I wished there were something I could do, but right then I had problems of my own.

But research within the dream . . . Well, it would certainly be easier than trying to find him again. I wasn't sure how long it had taken this time. Even with Kel keeping watch, I couldn't sleep the days away. Escobar had made it clear we had a deadline.

"Do I need to do anything?" Both times we'd worked the translocation, I'd taken care of constructing the new environment.

He shook his head. "Just keep your mind clear, please."

"Okay, tell me when you're done."

To make that easier, I sat down and closed my eyes. I blanked my brain, which was harder than it sounded. Though Booke seemed capable of watching me build the new environment without exerting any influence, I didn't think I had that much mental control. Better to let him finish.

Despite my pressing need to wrap up here and move on with my challenge, anticipation spiked through my veins. He was going to show me where he lived. I wondered whether he would show me his true appearance as well.

"All set."

When I opened my eyes, the world had changed. Though I expected as much, I was rocked by how wrong I'd been. I sat on a plain hardwood floor. From the exposed stonework and the weathered beams, I guessed the cottage was a couple of centuries old, at least. Directly across from me a fireplace heated the property. The furniture—a chair and a settee—was faded and threadbare; it might've been fashionable in the thirties or forties. Books and papers surrounded me in piles, the sort of disarray born of a restless but brilliant mind.

"May I look around?" I asked quietly.

The question was far more significant than it seemed, and we both knew it. If he said no, I'd never try to get to know him any better. Since I'd promised, I would still go to Egypt, but he could keep his secrets. Booke studied me, his

stance wary. After a moment, he nodded. He looked the
same as I imagined, so I wouldn't be receiving further reve-
lations tonight.

It didn't take long to explore the cottage. He had a sitting room, a bedroom, a kitchen, and a bathroom—hopelessly
dated, tiles crumbling, and an old-fashioned slipper tub. The
enamel showed scratches, but he kept everything clean.

In the bedroom, I found his computer, the only new item
in the place. Whatever money he earned, he clearly spent
it on technology. He had so many gadgets and gizmos attached to it that I didn't know what they all did. This room,
too, was buried in books and documents, some of which
looked to be ancient, as if they should be on display in some
museum and might crumble at a touch. His kitchen was tiny
and likewise outdated. The whole cottage held a wretched,
melancholy air, as if it had slipped through a crack in time.
Even the pictures on the walls looked tired, depicting dated
scenes and people long dead.

Once I thoroughly scoped out the place, I returned to the
sitting room, where a fire crackled in the hearth. I could
even smell the wood smoke; oh, but he was *good*. I sat in
the chair because on the settee we risked an accidental touch.

"Now you know," he said quietly. "I am not distinguished
or a man of means. As you can see, it is all rather wretched."

I shrugged. "You saw where I stayed in Kilmer. Growing
up, I lived in places that were much worse."

"With an important distinction. You left. Because you
could."

"Did you want to discuss the why of that?"

His face closed. "No."

"Then you should begin the research. There's no guarantee how long I'll sleep before Kel feels compelled to wake
me."

"Of course." He opened a book and read a bit before
adding, "It appears to be Aymara, very old. Just give me a
while."

Once he started, it was simply a matter of waiting. I pe-
rused a few of his tomes, not that I expected to be much

help. As it turned out, I laid hands on the one he needed and placed it beside him so he could make notes on the paper. I couldn't be certain how long the translation took, but I felt a tug, as if I might soon rouse naturally.

"Hurry," I murmured.

"And that's got it."

Intellectual diversion burnt away his bitterness, so he was smiling when he handed me the sketch with the notes on the back. This time, the endeavor felt more natural, less an act of will and more a function of our shared reality. Because we were sure this worked, we were sure we had the power, it grew easier with each execution.

"Thank you."

"Corine," he said, as I felt a stronger tug. I had only seconds before I woke. "I *will* tell you. Someday."

And then I opened my eyes to find myself on the ground, damp with morning dew. Kel had not slept. I could see it in the shadows beneath his eyes and the weary slope of his shoulders. Despite his great ability, his resources were not infinite. Tonight, I would keep watch over him.

Smiling, I sat up and examined the paper I held—translation on the back, as I'd known it would be. I read the words aloud. "'Follow the serpent until fire eats the sky. In the hollow of the lady, unearth her bones.'"

"Directions," he said.

"Can you walk?"

He cut me a scathing look, his gaze on my feet. "Can you?"

I dug up a clean pair of socks. As I'd noted prior, there were no clothes in my pack, just socks and underwear. Escobar's test qualified as cruel and unusual in my book. Not that I wanted to haul a wardrobe through the jungle, so maybe his intentions were good. He was lean enough to have spent some time hiking around out here.

"You healed me, remember?" I could hardly forget.

My feet were filthy now, but they weren't bleeding or blistered, and my boots had softened up enough that they shouldn't inflict more damage. I put them on and laced them up. Maybe lucid dreaming was better than common sleep, because I felt stronger today, less sore and beaten down, even though our predicament was every bit as dire, and the day threatened the same swelter. I tightened up my braid, trying not to consider how badly I needed to wash my hair, and pushed to my feet.

Kel leveled an assessing look on me. "Don't you want breakfast?"

"Not really."

"Eat," he insisted. "And take some water."

God save me. Well, since he had to know more about this stuff than I did, I obeyed, downing a protein bar and some water from the canteen. "How are our supplies holding out?"

Finding clean water was going to be a concern if we went much deeper. Already I had no clue where we were, other than surrounded by wild animals and heavy green trees. I trusted Kel to guide us in, and he'd have to get us out again. If I focused on how isolated we were, how much danger stalked our every move, I'd freeze into a woman-shaped lump.

"We have one more day, if we're careful."

Shit. I sweated like mad in this wet heat, which led to dehydration. "There are plants you can cut open, right? I've seen a few survival shows."

He nodded. "I'll look as we go."

"Have you had anything today?"

"I can go without." His tone made it clear the point was not up for discussion, and as I didn't know his personal limits, he could judge that for himself. He wasn't human. *Not* human. I couldn't afford to forget that, no matter how his secrets drew me.

"I'm guessing the river is the serpent. I think we should follow it for a day. 'Fire eating the sky' sounds like sunset to me, and I'd say the hollow is a valley."

"The *lady's* hollow."

"We'll have to watch for a marker of some kind once we leave the river. Maybe you can go up and take a look around."

God, this was so far outside my usual purview it wasn't even funny.

He gazed up at the canopy. "I can free-climb."

"Then let's go."

And we headed deeper into the jungle.

Where Fire Eats the Sky

The river wound in slow undulations like a snake, bearing out my hypothesis about our path. Scarlet macaws and wild yellow-ridged toucans watched from the trees. As we walked, I kept an eye on the rippling water, watching for anacondas. It could also be alligators, I supposed, though that didn't improve the situation.

Shannon liked to watch the nature channels, so after she moved in, I got cable TV. While I was okay living in the Dark Ages, I wanted more for her, knowing she'd grown up in Kilmer; I understood all too well what that was like. We'd seen a show one afternoon last month about how alligators stalked their prey, watching from beneath the murky water and learning their habits. Sometimes they would take days about it and then strike when the hapless campers were bathing or drawing water. I never dreamt I'd find myself in a situation like this one, where facts gleaned on Animal Planet could be useful. Unfortunately, it was also terrifying.

A few times I started at some small amphibian hopping in or out of the river.

Pygmy marmosets chattered in the trees. As long as they were around, I knew we didn't have to worry about hunting cats . . . jaguars and ocelots mostly. If the monkeys scrambled away, we needed to worry. Along the route, I saw a capybara rump in distant undergrowth, but it lumbered away from us as only a giant rodent could. By clinging to the river's edge, we avoided a lot of the need to cut our way through the jungle. Still, Kel had to swing the machete now and then. It would be easier if we had a boat, but that offered other risks.

By midday—or what I guessed was midday—my clothes stuck to my skin, sodden with sweat, and my whole body felt like fungus grew out of every pore. We paused for food and drink. Wading in the water would cool me off, but walking in wet clothes afterward sounded hellish, and I didn't feel sanguine about stripping.

As I weighed the pros and cons, a weird cry rang out and then a creature launched from the branches above. I caught only a glimpse of striped, spotted dun fur, and I scrambled backward. My arms windmilled and I tumbled into the river. Kel called out, but the current snagged me and knocked me off my feet. Fear of what lurked beneath the surface had me thrashing wildly before reason reasserted itself. Sailing along, I assessed my predicament.

I'd managed to get farther from land with the flailing, so I oriented myself and tried not to think about piranhas. On Animal Planet, I'd also watched a special about how struggling, injured prey incited their feeding frenzy. *Smooth, strong movements. Show no fear, no weakness.* That mantra in mind, I angled toward shore, though I sped along faster than I liked. The river pulled against me, but I swam until my arms burned and my thighs hurt, concentrating on keeping my head above water. I passed a fallen tree and skinned my hands grabbing onto it. Using it as leverage I pulled myself into the shallows, where I could crawl back onto the banks. The ground was slippery with mud and moss, but I just lay down and flopped over onto my back. My breath came in heavy gulps. Christ, I'd *never* liked swimming in lakes or rivers, where the water was dark and muddy. I preferred the ocean.

I heard footsteps, and then Kel loomed over me. "I was right behind you."

"Good to know." But I was proud; I'd handled the situation without screaming, no helplessness. This success set a strong precedent for the challenges to come.

"You might want to rinse your hair."

Well, yeah. It had all kinds of crud in it—dead leaves, bugs, moss, fungus, and mud—from my sojourn on the bank. By comparison even river water sounded fantastic. I took his proffered hand and felt a pinch as I stood; there was something on my stomach. Now that the terror had subsided to manageable levels, I felt the pressure. A shudder rolled through me.

Don't look, don't look, don't look, don't look—

I raised my shirt and looked. A flat gray-black blob stuck to my skin. "Please tell me that's not what I think it is."

"It's a leech. You likely stirred it when you crawled past the dead tree."

With some effort, I spoke through clenched teeth. "Get it off."

Get it off, get it off, get it off. Some people feared insects; spiders and snakes topped the list for others. For me, it was any water-dwelling critter that lacked arms, legs, or fins, which encompassed a large spectrum of creepy crawlies.

His tone was so soothing that I wanted to punch him. "If we attempt to remove it, there's some risk it'll vomit into the wound and you'll get an infection. Since we don't have many medical supplies, it's better to let it eat." He put a hand on my shoulder. "Come. Stand by the water. When it's done, it'll drop off."

In movies, they put salt or fire on it and the thing shriveled up. But we didn't have either one, and I didn't want him taking a knife to me. I let him lead me, but tears slid down my cheeks. Escobar hadn't been kidding when he said my courage would be tested. I stood still, teetering on the edge of a complete meltdown.

With a gentleness I didn't expect, at least not for *me*, Kel took down my braids and used a long leaf to scoop up water to rinse my hair. In time, his methodical movements took my mind off the thing drinking my blood. His care reminded me of the way monkeys groomed one another; I'd watched that on Animal Planet with Shannon too. I wondered how she was, whether she was helping Eva, and if they were petting Butch enough.

"This too shall pass." My mother had murmured that to comfort me when times got bad.

His hands stilled. "Do you know the story behind those words?"

"I don't think so."

"King Solomon wanted to humble one of his ministers, so he sent him to find a magic ring, giving him six months to do so. Solomon told the man it held the power to fill a happy man with sorrow and cheer a woeful man. The king knew the man would never find it, because it didn't exist, but failure would temper his arrogance. The adviser searched everywhere, and on the day before he must concede the loss, he passed through the poorest part of Jerusalem. On impulse, he asked a merchant if he had heard of such an item. In answer, the old man gave him a ring engraved with the simple phrase in Hebrew, 'This too shall pass.'"

By the time he finished, so had the leech. It fell off my body and splooshed into the river, presumably returning to the dead tree. I had a small wound on my stomach, trickling blood, but it wasn't as big as I expected. I exhaled unsteadily.

Another King Solomon story. I was too tired to protest that it was a common saying. After everything that had happened, I had no energy to spare wondering about my bloodlines or my destiny; no matter what else, I liked the cleverness of the fable. A happy man, reading such, remembered that pleasure was fleeting; a sorrowful man recalled that no pain lasted forever. I needed that reminder.

Since I was wet from head to toe, walking would be a misery henceforth, because the humid air wouldn't allow me to dry out. I had to smell disgusting. But he wasn't done with me. He stripped off his shirt, dipped the clean end in the river, and used it to wash my face. Beneath his care, I felt vulnerable.

Wordlessly, I braided my hair into a single plait. He froze then. For the first time, his expression told me clearly what he felt. Fear. Likely I didn't want to know what could scare him.

I asked anyway. "What?"

In answer he indicated my throat; my palm rose to investigate. No pendant. No protection. The next time Montoya's sorcerer sought, he'd find me. Wonderful, so it really would be like *The Amazing Race*. But we were far enough out here that his men would have a hell of a time catching up. Sendings and summonings were different, and I didn't have a Tri-P—one of Shannon's portable protection packs—on me, but even if I'd had the foresight to make one in the village, the river dunking would've rendered it ineffectual. I was so screwed.

"That just raised the stakes," Kel said.

No longer could we consider this a challenge without outside antagonists.

"We'll just have to push harder." Which meant running through our dwindling supplies faster. "You know how to survive in hostile conditions, right?"

His expression said I probably should've asked him that before I chose him for this job. As if I'd had an opportunity. "Try not to worry. Just keep moving."

Apart from that one ocelot, the wildlife mostly left us alone, as if Kel emitted a low-grade signal that warned them away. Partway, rain blasted through the leaves like a watery blanket. It was a sudden, fierce shower that left us drenched but did nothing to cool the air. We walked until fire ate the sky. At that point, the river bent right, which I thought was east, but I wasn't sure anymore.

"I think this is where you head up."

He nodded. "Watch the packs."

It wasn't until he started climbing that I got nervous. As long as I'd been moving and not thinking—and frankly, I was almost too tired to do more than put one foot in front of the other—I could quiet my mind. Now that it was just the jungle sounds and me, fear strolled in, hand in hand with visceral exhaustion. I slumped against the tree trunk while keeping an eye out for reptiles and unfriendly amphibians. I retained the good sense not to call out, though it was tough.

An eternity later, he dropped from the lowest branches. "We need to cut west, away from the river. A tall pile of stones marks the way."

"One that looks like a lady?"

He nodded. "Undoubtedly. Just beyond there, the jungle thins. I think there's a valley, just as you predicted."

"How far? Should we risk it tonight?" The light was fading fast.

"I don't think it's more than an hour or two. Stay close."

He didn't have to tell me twice. In the dark, the jungle was a hundred times as frightening. Each noise seemed magnified. Each time a branch rustled or the leaves stirred, my muscles clenched, bracing for an attack. Kel used the machete more in that last hour than he had all the days prior. There was no path; we might have been the first people to walk this way in hundreds of years.

I was stumbling, borderline falling on my face, when the trees gave way to rolling hillside. For the first time in days, I saw the sky and it was magnificent. Out here, no city lights dimmed the display, and the stars shimmered like heavenly crystal on dark silk. I had never in my life seen anything so lovely or so welcome.

"We'll camp at the lady tonight," Kel said. "She's just over this rise."

I didn't argue with him, though I was none too sure my legs would hold me. In the past days, I had gone well beyond my imagined limits and I was still going. He led the way, and I trudged on, weakness quivering in my muscles.

When we crested the hill, I saw her, and she was awe-inspiring in the moonlight, a work of art to make one wonder at the ingenuity of indigenous people. Four enormous stones had been stacked and shaped—how, I could only guess—but this was, unquestionably, the lady's hollow. They had given her a feminine silhouette and a swollen belly, but she lacked a head. Maybe she'd had one in days past and it had yielded to the elements.

My pace increased until I was leading the way. The ground was relatively level near the monument, so I sat down. My skin bore countless insect bites; I was sore, chafed, and so grateful to be still I couldn't articulate it. A burn in my shoulders punished me for carrying a backpack for days at a time when I was used to sitting at a counter, but at least out of the jungle, we might pass a dry night.

"So you think we need to dig?" I asked.

Unearth her bones, the translation said. I hoped to all gods and goddesses we were not actually being asked to rob a grave. I didn't think I could do it, not even to save my own skin. With Montoya's assassins, I could tell myself they were paid to kill me and feel better about their lost lives. I could even rationalize the alliance with Escobar for the sake of my own survival, even though accepting his patronage would taint me in ways I might not discover right away.

But to desecrate a grave to pass Escobar's test? The coffin contained a peaceful soul who never did me any harm. I knew how *I'd* feel if someone dug up my mother's remains to steal from her body. I couldn't do that to an innocent, grieving family, even to save my own life—and surely Kel wouldn't want me to. Yeah, I'd done some bad things along this road, but corpse defilers were universally loathed.

"Hard to say. We'll find out in the morning."

With some effort, I put the macabre possibility from my mind. While I was at my physical limit, I had a little brain juice left. "You need sleep. I'll take first watch."

To my surprise, he unrolled his ultralight sleeping bag and lay down without argument. Which meant he had to be dead on his feet. I pulled my knees up to my chest and wrapped my arms around them. It was too warm a night to need a fire, even if I'd wanted to go wandering in the dark to find wood. I didn't.

After a while, the faint breeze cut through my damp clothes.

I shivered and wrapped my own bag around my shoulders, but I couldn't close my eyes. With my back against the comforting stone of the lady, I felt reasonably sure I could get through the night—or at least a few hours. Thoughts of Chance filled my mind, unsurprisingly. I could go months pretending I didn't miss him, but in the darkness and the silence, I remembered how it felt to touch him, how he smelled, and the way his hair felt slipping through my fingers. Seeing him in the dream world brought it all back. *Go away*, I told the dream Chance. *You made it clear where we stood when you didn't call or write.*

Time passed slowly, and I struggled to stay awake. With no watch and my cell phone off, I had no way of knowing how long I had let Kel sleep. He roused with a jerk, somersaulting to his feet and reaching for a weapon that wasn't strapped to his back. His muscles tensed and twitched; in those moments, I had no doubt he didn't know where—or possibly when—he was. I didn't dare move.

"The night's been quiet." I hoped my voice would be enough to orient him, and some of the strain eased from his stance. "Bad dream?"

He turned and braced his forearm on the stone, then dropped his head onto it. His breath came in fast, shallow shudders. *Damn.* I'd never seen him like this. I had no idea what to do about it. Tortured muscles groaned as I pulled myself up. Approaching as I would a wild animal, I hesitated. He didn't move. I set my hands lightly, tentatively, on his shoulders. Kel trembled, not at my touch, but from whatever he'd been reliving.

"It's okay," I whispered, hoping it was.

What would I do if he went batshit on me? I had little sense of direction, couldn't hunt, and wouldn't be able to find clean water unless it came from a drinking fountain. Hell, maybe not even then.

He turned then. His head dropped toward mine and he rested his cheek against my hair, the lightest pressure, so brief I might've imagined it, and then he stepped back. Once, he would've withdrawn completely, hidden his pain, but we'd shared so much in a short time, bonded in blood. We were not the same as we'd been when he first walked through my door.

"Yes," he said, ignoring my reassurance. "Bad."

"Tell me?"

He closed his eyes, sinking down against the stone. It scraped the amputation scars I had identified when he shared his blood. Copper scented the air, but he would heal, though that did not stop the pain.

"I dreamt of lost days," he said at length. "Of when the Romans took my wings. It was a time of martyrs, when it pleased the archangels to see holy blood spilled to unite the faithful. In the hidden chamber deep within the coliseum, I told Emperor Commodus I would not kneel to him, and thereafter, they made a spectacle of me."

"You fought?" I knew little of those days. My mother hadn't believed in religious education, and what I'd learned in school had been sketchy at best. I doubted it would have prepared me for him in any case; he seemed so weary in the moonlight . . . and utterly alone.

Kel nodded, his expression distant. "When they saw I could not die, they hunted me for sport, and the archangels saw fit I should be punished. But once my persecutors fell to dust, I stood in the broken stones of that coliseum, saw how the mosaics are ruined and faded. The timeless work of mankind means nothing."

" 'Look on my works, ye mighty, and despair,' " I quoted, mostly because I couldn't think what else to say. I had no context for comforting someone so old. I must seem like a veritable speck of dust.

As if voicing my thoughts, he went on. "To me, eternity means only time that does not end, but runs on and on like a dark river that feeds the sea. As they did then, witches and warlocks still crave my blood, so I hide my nature. Time has ground me down. . . . I am less than I was, and yet the work must be done."

"Is there anything I can do to help?" Stupid question. If nothing else, I'd make him laugh at my presumption.

But he didn't. Instead, he pushed out a slow breath, and when he spoke, he offered a faint, cryptic smile. "It helps that you asked. Rest a little before the sun comes up. I will not sleep again this night."

I listened to him breathing for the longest time, and even though I should be sleeping now that he was awake, I couldn't still my mind. Considering what he'd shared, I didn't think I'd drift off, but I must have.

At first light he roused me. His face offered no evidence of the night before, quiet and composed as ever. He took off his shirt and wound it around his head like an Arab head-dress. We ate in silence and shared the last of the water. If we didn't find some soon, we'd be in trouble. Well, more than we were already.

The sky shone blue as the sun rose, and I followed him down into the valley. From this point, I didn't know what we were looking for. *Unearth her bones* wasn't as specific as one might prefer for relic hunting. My gait reflected the soreness in my muscles, but I kept moving over uneven ground.

Eventually I glimpsed a goat path and I hurried toward it. Surely that meant something. If nothing else, it was the first sign of civilization we'd seen in days. I could take learning we were offtrack, if it also meant a bath and clean clothes.

The trail led down into a village, smaller even than the one near where Escobar's men had dropped us off. Squat adobe brick houses clustered together in the greensward. There were few vehicles and nothing like what I'd call a road. From the looks of those eyeing Kel, indigenous people lived here. I saw little Spanish blood reflected in the faces we passed on our way to the market in the center square, a glorified widening of the dirt.

We passed chickens and goats rummaging outside the houses. In every respect but one, this was a humble settlement. I paused outside the church. The crumbling stonework showed it to be ancient, older than anything else in this place; it dated to the time of the conquistadores and it carried Aymara symbols similar to those we'd found on the clay statue. Graven letters on the cornerstone told me its name: *Nuestra Señora de la Peña.* Our Lady of the Sorrows.

Right then, the way I felt, the name seemed ominous. Even Kel paused, gazing up at the relic of times dead and gone. I could hear people passing behind us, speculating, but I didn't turn. I continued around the side of the church-yard littered with fallen stones and weeds. Behind it lay a cemetery.

Unearth her bones.

No, it couldn't be literal. Could it? Dead man's hands slid down my spine, icy cold and full of whispers of dark-ness to come.

Unearthing Her Bones

There were no hostels in the unnamed village, nor even a proper store. In the market, we bought fresh fruit. To my vast relief, one stall sold clothing. I doubted the vendor made much from the other villagers, so I didn't haggle. By standards set elsewhere in the world, I still got a bargain, even if she'd refashioned old garments into new: fifty for the set, a yellow peasant blouse and a gaily patterned skirt.

I knew we looked disreputable and dirty. It wasn't just Kel's tats or the color of our skin that made people give us a wide berth. We also reeked of the jungle and hard living. It was time to do something about that, or nobody would talk to us.

"Disculpe, por favor . . ." More than one person ignored my polite overture.

At last, I offered a woman a couple of coins to answer a few questions and she pointed me to an old man willing to rent the use of his bathroom. Lines seamed his brown face, his snowy hair in contrast, and he didn't say much, other than *gracias* when Kel paid him. But he stepped out of his four-room home to let us bathe in relative privacy. God's Hand stood guard outside the bathroom.

The water came from a cistern outside and the shower was primitive, but it did the job. I washed quickly, knowing Kel still needed to take his turn and we shouldn't use all the water the elderly gentleman had stored. We thanked the señor again for the privilege and for his generosity, then said farewell. He didn't budge from his chair, merely watched our progress with raisin-dark eyes.

Clean and wearing fresh clothes, I felt better, though I had only battered walking boots and my sneakers. I wore the latter because they were lighter and cooler, at least. I'd worn those boots enough to last a lifetime and put countless miles on the soles.

In the village center, with the market closing up around us, we made a picnic out of the fruit: mangoes, prickly pears, guanabana, bananas, passion fruit, and papaya. After endless days of protein bars, this tasted wonderful. Some of it was messy, but I wiped my fingers on the grass. Nobody would object if we camped here for the night.

This must be the last leg of the journey. Whatever we were looking for *had* to be here.

Glancing at Kel, who was skinning a mango with juice dripping from his fingers, I thought aloud. "There's nothing unusual about this place except the church. It's old, old as that statue looked . . . and I saw Aymara markings."

"As did I."

"Then that's where we should start."

Since we'd purchased only a little food, we left the remnants—skin and sweet pulp—for the birds. I pushed to my feet and walked back down the dirt track. The church doors stood open as we approached, but I couldn't see within, where shadows pooled. Bolstering my strength because I always felt weird in consecrated places—the whole witch's-daughter thing—I led the way.

Kel followed, a comforting presence at my back. It was funny how used to him I'd become. He was like a well-placed rock; you could climb on it to escape floodwaters, use it for self-defense, to prop something up, or simply to rest against when you were weary. But unlike that rock, he had feelings. I suspected it had been a long-ass time since anyone asked him how he felt, or what he wanted.

Letting my eyes adjust, I took stock of the place. There

were no pews. If one knelt here, it was on the floor. Flowers had been left at various shrines along the wall. The silence felt cool and soothing, like a weight had lifted when I stepped inside. Whitewashed walls bore traces of rust; likely the roof leaked and there was no money for repairs. Except for one, I didn't know the names of the saints depicted on the walls, but I recognized Saint Martin de Perres from his dark skin. The altar was a heavy block of stone, etched with ornate patterns that didn't always look wholly Christian to my eyes.

As we stood there, a thin man in black stepped out of the back room. *"Buenas tardes. ¿Puedo ayudarles?"*

To his credit, he didn't react to the picture we made. On his own, Kel offered a hundred reasons to be wary, and I was obviously a redheaded *güera*. But if we were to unearth any bones, the priest might be able to tell us about a woman buried in the graveyard. It wasn't enormous, so I hoped for luck. If cleansing the bad karma offered any benefit, I was due a break.

"Sí. Estamos buscando . . ." What *were* we looking for? I couldn't say *a woman's bones*—and maybe it wasn't so literal anyway. So perhaps I should start with the man who'd sent us here: *". . . información acerca de la familia Escobar."*

Surprise slipped across his face before he schooled himself. He answered in Spanish, "I have not heard that name in a long time."

I had been shooting blind, so elation raced through me. *"¿Qué?"*

"Escobar. Come," he said, gesturing to us. "You will be historians, yes, or writers, maybe?"

Nodding, because his conclusion sounded more credible than the truth, I trailed behind him through the cool, dim church and into his private rooms accessible through a narrow corridor. He had a small sitting room with a niche for his cot. We took our seats while he fetched three brown glass bottles with gold and red labels that read CUZQUEÑA; it looked like beer. The priest cracked them open and the cold air smoked a little in the heat. As soon as I took the bottle, it tried to feed me images of what it had been doing, nothing traumatic, but I shut it down. I took a sip and judged it delicious, a nice, light lager.

"Thank you," I murmured.

He indulged in a long drink and then said, "Forgive me; I have been rude. I am Father de León."

"Mucho gusto." I extended my hand, since I had to be on my best behavior.

He returned my greeting with the limp grip of a man more devoted to heavenly pursuits than earthly ones. But his manner remained friendly enough. Maybe we offered a welcome break in the killing boredom of his daily routine.

"The story," Kel prompted.

Clearly there was one, or the man wouldn't have escorted us back here. He would've simply said, *I don't know*, and shown us out. I seconded with an inclination of my head, Cuzqueña in hand. God's Hand didn't touch his drink.

"The Church sent him to found the mission here. He was the only Spaniard for a very long time, but he related well to the people, and gradually, they came to his ways."

"But something went wrong," I guessed.

De León wore a grave mien. "Yes. A girl accused Father Escobar of rape. Since she was, as they say, touched by angels, no one believed her. She saw things that weren't there, and she often cried for no reason. But when her belly swelled, the villagers decided she must have been telling the truth. They would have killed him, but he fled into the jungle. I do not know what happened to him, but the villagers were superstitious. They thought either he must be innocent, and God had taken him, or he was guilty, and the devil had come to drag him to hell."

With Kel sitting beside me, neither proposition seemed as far-fetched as it might have once. "What do you think?"

The priest lifted his shoulders. "It is an old story, nothing more. Those who came before me recorded the interesting tales. I will do the same."

"And have you?"

"So far, no."

I hoped we wouldn't bring "interesting times" to this quiet place. "What happened to the girl?"

"I don't know," he said. "The other priests did not find her plight intriguing enough to write about her fate."

That rankled. I knew he wasn't responsible for his predecessors' decisions, but the Church had too often either dismissed women as insignificant or persecuted them as sinful. They were either madonnas or whores, no middle ground.

Regardless, dead end there, then. So perhaps I wouldn't be digging up some woman's bones. *Thank all the gods and goddesses.* If Father Escobar had any connection with the man who'd sent me, however distant, then I was sniffing in the right spot. This was a long shot, but: "Did he leave anything behind?"

He angled his head. "That, perhaps. In the journals, the priest who came after him said Father Escobar left all of his things behind."

Kel and I followed the trajectory of his gaze. On the wall hung a tarnished crucifix—silver, but it needed polishing. I remembered there were silver mines in Peru and that the country had conflicted with Mexico over it, long ago. The object was crudely cast, not made by a master, but I saw the signs of handwork on it.

"May I see it?"

This was going to be tricky. If this was the object I was meant to retrieve, how could I get it out of the church? First things first, however: I leaned forward in anticipation as de León stood and crossed to the wall, where he took down the crucifix with reverent hands. He passed it to me with an expectant look, as if I ought to comment on its obvious age or weight.

I glanced at Kel, who took his cue. He began to question de León, drawing his eyes away from me. The sound faded to a low buzz as I curled my hand around it. Old things always carried layers, so I took the burn and watched the slow procession of years. Most came from faith and devotion, so I saw priests praying in procession. Such memories, though powerful, carried only the heat of a summer day.

At last I hit bottom, a charge so powerful it stayed in the silver, even as others added their own experiences. I saw a whisper of Ramiro Escobar in this priest's lean build, though the resemblance came from stance and attitude. He had a proud face, even as he prayed, both hands wrapped around the cross. I fell into the reading as if the bottom had dropped out of my world.

Surprise surged through me. I had not expected to see her again so soon, though she had spent a great deal of time here in recent days. I noted her prettiness in an abstract way, as I strove to keep my manner paternal with every female parishioner. Bitterness laced the observation. First I had been sacrificed to the Church, and then I had been exiled from my home. I could not pronounce her name; it was something savage, so I called her Juana.

I showed none of that emotional turmoil as she genuflected. I had yet to explain the difference between kneeling to God and kneeling to me, and so the natives continued to do both. They seemed to think I merited such obeisance as part of my position, and it pleased me to receive it.

Thus, I smiled at her approach and bade her rise. Belatedly I noted the fear in her eyes. She wore bruises on her thin arms like matching bracelets. I started to ask what had happened, but she threw herself at me. I caught her because I thought she was about to faint, and then she pressed her mouth to mine fiercely, desperately. The kiss lasted only a few seconds, and then I put her away from me.

That life was not for me. My father had chosen my path, and I could not let the wiles of a half-mad native girl sway me. She fell to her knees and kissed the hem of my robe, my feet, and I cringed in horror and discomfort. Her weeping filled my ears with its shrill tenor. Soon her cries rose to a crescendo; they would draw others.

I begged her to be silent.

And then the villagers came.

I fell into my own body with a sense of queasy disorientation. My gift was not the same as it had always been. Ever since I'd touched the necklace that contained my mother's power—and gods only knew what else—readings were ir-regular. In Kilmer, the power burned a piece of paper to ash. Before, I saw only what they saw, but this time I *became* the priest, thinking his thoughts while they soaked into the crucifix in his hand. I trembled a little, eyes closed.

A hand lit on my shoulder. Kel, I felt sure. The drone of conversation had ceased. *Shit.* I hated this part, where every-one treated me like a freak. When I opened my eyes, they were both staring at me.

"*Estoy bien. No se preocupe,*" I said, trying to convince all three of us.

"What were you doing?" the priest asked.

My hand shook when I reached for my beer to buy some time. I brought it to my lips and took a long swallow. Father de León watched me all the while.

Kel spoke for me. "Like the girl, she is angel-touched. She can see secrets left behind."

Hm. Perhaps that was what the message meant. Unearth her bones. Learn her secrets. I didn't know that I'd call what I did *angel-touched,* but that reply seemed more politic than the alternative when keeping company with a priest.

"Did it belong to him, then?"

I finished my beer and nodded. "Yes. And others too." But his charge had been strongest, such shock and shame at the accusations. "I'd like to buy it."

Ridiculous—we didn't have the cash to pay for such a relic. Though our expenditures had been low, we had only seven hundred *nuevos soles* left. Yet I had to try. I didn't want to sneak here in the dark to steal the crucifix. Surely Kel wouldn't go along with that, even if I was "important."

"It is part of the history of this mission," Father de León said. "One cannot put a price on such things."

As a former pawnshop owner, I noticed one thing straight-away: He hadn't said no. That meant he was open to hag-gling, and *that* was my forte. He started out by naming an absurd price, ten thousand.

"*Ridículo,*" I said, laughing. I half rose, as if to leave.

"*Espere. Quizás . . .*"

Kel touched my arm lightly and whispered in my ear. The news made me smile. In the end, we dickered for a quarter of an hour before I got de León to accept six hundred cash and a matching pair of silver salt and pepper shakers: Eros and Psyche, of course. He could tell they were valuable and would buy a much nicer, newer crucifix, as well as other things for the church, but he hid his satisfaction well. Instead he wore a grave expression, as if he let the old one go only with great reluctance.

"It was a pleasure," he said as I stood. "But why do you want it?"

"I work for a man descended from Father Escobar. He desires it for sentimental reasons."

The priest nodded as if that made perfect sense. "What did you see when you touched the cross? What happened?"

I smiled slightly. "He didn't hurt that girl. And I don't know where he went, once he left it behind."

"Not heaven, I think."

No, probably not. I figured he'd headed north. If he was related to Escobar, he'd fathered children, just not on the poor girl who had wanted him to claim her baby as his own. I guessed she didn't understand the concept of celibacy—only that he was powerful and could shield her from shame, if he so chose.

"*Gracias por todo*," I told de León.

He waved as I tucked the crucifix into my bag and Kel followed me out. It was getting on toward evening. Everyone had gone home, so there were few people about, but still chickens and goats. The former squawked as we passed by, pecking at grubs I couldn't see. We followed the track back to the village center, unrolled our sleeping bags, and I sat down, facing him.

"How did I do?"

He shrugged. "If that is the right object, then very well."

I laughed. "Faint praise, indeed."

In the dark, his tats glowed faintly, signaling power or strong emotion. With Kel I'd never been able to differentiate the two, and perhaps in him they were inextricably bound.

That fact explained at least half of what rendered him so fascinating—and utterly off-limits.

"I don't mean to slight you," he said gravely. "I expected you to falter on the way. You have more fortitude than I knew."

"More than I knew, frankly. There were a few times, out there"—I gestured toward the horizon, where the jungle we couldn't see teemed with fearsome creatures—"when I wanted to give up."

"I know." His tone was gentle, but also impersonal, like a nurse offering reassurance to a patient when he'd had seen so many that they had become numbers and diseases instead of names and faces. Rarely, he displayed real emotion, but I had the sense it was painful for him—he needed the impassivity to function in a world where he comprised the only constant.

"You've been fantastic. I couldn't have done it without you."

He tipped his head forward, acknowledging the praise. Only a faint curve at the edges of his mouth showed his pleasure, but I saw. His archangel probably never said, *Good job*, or, *Thanks for killing that infidel*. I had no idea why he wasn't crazy; too much isolation could drive a person out of his mind.

"Should you call Escobar?"

"I don't know if the phone has any charge left." But I powered it on and found I had half a bar, just a flicker of juice. Unfortunately, we were far out of range of any cell towers, and there were no pay phones. I sighed. "We'll have to find a way to a bigger town. We can ask around in the morning."

"There's no road," he observed, "so that means no buses."

I groaned. *Not more walking.* "Maybe we can go by donkey cart."

"Better than camels." From his expression, he meant it as a judgment drawn from personal experience.

With some effort, I killed my curiosity and lay down. We needed rest. In the morning, we could discover how people traveled from place to place; I hoped it wouldn't be expensive.

At some point after dark, I woke with fear choking me. The air tasted thick and heavy and foul, like I remembered from Catemaco. It carried a familiar taste as I sucked in a breath, openmouthed.

No. Oh, shit, no.

They'd found me.

Demon in the Dark

The ground trembled like the precursor to an earthquake. I scrambled away as the air thickened, gaining volume. And then it *tore*, something I'd never heard of or even imagined. I thought demons were evil spirits, some powerful, certainly, but lacking form in our realm.

I had never been so wrong.

Darklight swelled through the hole in the world, and then a powerful black-scaled shoulder wedged its way through, followed by a long arm topped in razor-sharp talons. It was like watching a hideous, unwholesome birth, and every inch of the demon was worse than what came before. The thing had a ridged skull and deep-set eyes that glimmered in the dark; it wore a spiked leather-and-metal harness emblazoned with infernal sigils. If only I could read demonic script, but I had never studied such things. One of the symbols looked faintly familiar, as if I had seen it before. Possibilities flickered through my mind, but horror and fright warred against coherent thought.

My guardian rolled to his feet. The monster pushed all the way through, nostrils flared as it cocked its head as if listening to unheard orders. Instinct shouted at me to flee, but like a mouse mesmerized by a snake, I couldn't make my muscles respond. Violence clung to this creature like oil on its back, tainting the air around it. The beast shook off the disorientation and charged.

In one hand, Kel wielded the kukri-style machete; in the other, he held the slim, silver blade I'd seen him fight with in Laredo. He didn't look my way as he placed his body between the beast and me.

"Run."

"Can you kill it?" My fingers closed on my backpack, and then I realized it was fruitless. I owned nothing that could hurt it. "Will your flash do it?"

The demon lashed out with an enormous claw. Kel blocked with the machete, still taking a deep slash along his forearm. His tats blazed nearly incandescent, kindling a halo about him. His beacon probably wouldn't do anything against an otherworldly monster like this; the Klothod had been spirits inside the monkeys, and the destruction of the demons inside burned up their bodies too. This thing unquestionably came from *elsewhere*.

"He cannot. It will not." The deep rumble of a voice sounded as though it came through a fissure in the earth created by the slow grate of obsidian and basalt. "I am here for you, and I cannot be slain or unsummoned until I have tasted your blood. But I do not mind at all playing first with this little fallen angel."

"This what?" Maybe I could stall. Distract it. Give Kel a chance to kill it, even if the fiend claimed invincibility. Demons lied; there had to be a way.

"How rich. How *delightful*. You don't even know who he really is, do you?"

Kel landed a blow that should have decapitated the thing. But it didn't.

"So tell me," I begged.

"He is Nephilim," the monster roared. "Half-blood offspring of an angel and a human female, born of lust. Small wonder the archangels punished him. The flesh must be mortified and made humble."

"That is *not* why," Kel growled, whirling into motion

with his blades. "There are no strictures against such a joining. Prince of lies, tell her all of it, if you must."

"Prince?" Its teeth gleamed in the dark. "You flatter me. Not for paternal lust, then, but his human mother did drive the celestial hate. The host can be so intolerant . . . and you made it worse with your defiance. Disobedience. You would not learn your place. Poor half-breed . . . so reviled. It will be a mercy when I devour you."

"Perhaps," he answered, "but every cut will cost you."

Their movements quickened until I couldn't follow the slashing, snarling blows. I smelled sweet, coppery blood in the air as I scrambled to my feet. Terror clouded my thoughts. I didn't want to leave him. It seemed like treachery, cowardice, and abandonment. Kel's kukri showered sparks anytime he connected; only the silver dagger seemed to do the devil any damage, but not enough. Not *nearly* enough. In fact, the wounds made it stronger; it gloried in fear and pain, drinking them down like osmotic ambrosia.

The demon was too strong. Already I could see that Kel, who had seemed so fast, so tireless, was slower than the monster. He took more hits than he blocked, and his fair skin ran red with blood, illuminated by the shine of his tattoos. He had no breath to tell me again to run, but I saw the command in his eyes. It hurt me to see his wounds.

His words echoed in my mind. *I am here to bear your pain, my blood for yours.*

At last self-preservation kicked in, and I sprang away. Though there was nowhere for me to run, my legs pounded against the dirt. I had my pack still in hand, but it availed me nothing. No weapon. No sanctuary.

As I rounded the corner that led toward the church, I glanced back. Horror froze me. The demon impaled God's hand on its talons, lifted him high, and twisted. Kel made no sound, and the monster's laugh rang out. "Kelethiel, my old enemy, son of Uriel and Vashti, in the name of the Morningstar, I turn and banish thee."

Darklight swelled again. After it dimmed, there was only

the demon, the dark—and me. Nobody would care if this village vanished. When the greater world noticed its destruction, they would attribute the carnage to natural disaster, disease, famine, or some minor guerrilla war. My champion was gone.

There was no reason to hide. Even if the church lay on hallowed ground, the demon would prowl around outside and murder everyone in their beds until it starved me out. I wouldn't buy my own life at that price. So I spun and faced it.

"Are you not afraid to die, little one?" The fiend slowed as it came toward me.

It could likely see I was no threat, trembling like a bird, a backpack dangling uselessly from one hand. I didn't answer. Thoughts flashed through my brain, almost too quick for me to track them, and then I had an idea. Before the fiend reached me, I dug into the bag and produced the crucifix.

"Stay back." My voice shook.

"That only works if you have faith." Its low, rumbling voice became caressing. "And you don't. Not since your mother died."

I didn't understand why it wasn't engaging. If it had been sent to kill me, well, I was helpless. Then it shredded my blouse with its talons—and I knew. My skirt fell in tatters beneath razor claws. *No. Not that. Just kill me. Please.*

It slammed me to the ground and came down over me. The scaly hide bit into my skin, echoed by the painful prick of the metal spikes on its harness. I tried to keep my thighs together, but it ripped them wide-open with a casual gesture. I ground my teeth. It couldn't end like this: raped and murdered in a village whose name I didn't even know.

Think.

The demon ran a claw tip down my neck. I felt almost no pain, but then hot blood trickled down my neck. Its long, forked tongue flickered over my skin, snakelike, and it shuddered in pleasure. I lay still, trying not to provoke it. *Take your time. I'm no threat.* The crucifix had fallen to my side when the demon knocked me down. I fumbled for it, a new idea kindling. If only I could—

Got it. I curled my fingers around it and dropped my mental blocks. As I'd hoped, the years of priestly faith remained, there for the taking. I let their surety and peace swell through me. *I* didn't believe, but four hundred years of devotion offered significant power, and I owned it now.

To distract the creature, I softened beneath it. I couldn't bring myself to arch or moan, but it noticed. The fiend paused in licking up my blood. "Do you attempt to bargain for a painless death?"

In answer I curled my free hand through its harness. It couldn't know my gift, what had been my one little useless gift. Though I was more now, the touch would save me. Bolstered by the gentle strength and piety of long-dead holy men, I rode the anguish that blazed through me. For countless, infinite moments, I waded through the degradation, terror, and agony it lived to inflict. I lived a thousand nightmares before it carried me to the heart of what I must know.

When I came to myself again, rich in new knowledge, it lay atop me, poised to enter. In some hideous sibilant tongue it crooned to me, opening my legs wide.

I smiled and struck.

My time in the jungle had given me greater strength, or perhaps priestly shades lent theirs as well—whatever the power, the crucifix sank into the side of the monster's neck. It screamed and rolled, talons scrabbling at the holy object. The cross sizzled in the wound, sending foul ichor bubbling forth. A vile smell filled the air, like burnt, rancid meat.

"You have not slain me," it snarled, ripping the cross out of its flesh and flipping upright. "Only roused my wrath. Now I shall devour you while I fuck you, accursed meat-girl."

As it leapt, I dove. Elation flamed through me. It had tasted my blood; therefore, it could be unsummoned, no matter what safeguards the sorcerer had put in place. Now that I knew its name, I owned this thing; the power of ancient kings sang in my veins, and for that moment, I believed.

"In the name of north, south, east, and west, in the name of the once and future queen, in the name of the smoke and the earth, and the wind and the water, I name you Caim, Knight of Hell, who was banished from light of the daystar and may not walk this earth without my leave. I turn and bind you back from whence you came. *Tsurikshikn!*"

Darklight swarmed around it. If I expected fury or outrage, I was disappointed. Instead, the thing displayed reverence. It fell to its knees as the world ripped wide once more. "My queen," it breathed. "You are she, born of Solomon the Binder's line. Master did not tell me, I swear. I did not know."

And then it crawled backward from whence it had come. Distant screams came to me as if filtered through a layer of water. I heard the pain and the anguish, and then that too fell silent. The air lost its viscosity, holding now only the hint of sulfur and brimstone.

Kel. If that was where the fiend had sent him, I had to get him out of there. My hands shook as I fought to recall precisely what the demon had said to him. If I could find the right words, words that were precisely opposite, I could call him. I knew his name. I crawled across the trampled grass to the crucifix; I would use it as my focus. Once more, the energy surged through me.

"Kelethiel, my friend and guardian, son of Uriel and Vashti, in the name of the smoke and the earth, and the wind and the water, I call and command thee."

Nothing. No flash of light. No otherworldly pyrotechnics. *No, no, no.* I wasn't leaving this up to divine minions, who might not get around to liberating him for a hundred years. Maybe I hadn't gotten the verbiage quite right.

I wrapped both hands around the crucifix, feeling the burn start on my branded palm. Power built, like lightning in the air before a storm. "Kelethiel, my true friend, son of Uriel and Vashti, on the strength of your sacred vow, I call thee!"

Everything shifted and slowed. It wasn't like before, but more like the world split in two and then merged. In the old one, I was alone. In the new version, Kel tumbled to the ground before me.

He looked dead, so many wounds. Blood smeared his skin, obscuring his tattoos; they held no light at all. Visible bite marks scored his skin, as if a horde of demons had chewed his flesh. The hole in his chest hadn't healed, either, not even a little. He had no power in hell, or whatever dimension contained the demons. They'd stripped him, as if his clothes contained his strength or his power. Or maybe they just hadn't wanted his garments getting in the way of good torture.

Movement in my peripheral vision caught my eye; a few villagers had come out of their homes to investigate the weird lights and noises. I shooed them off with a fierce scowl and a bark of, "¡Lárguense!" I'm sure the sight of a bloody, naked woman and a dead-seeming man did more to frighten them than my voice.

Shielding his body with mine as they hurried off, I remembered how he'd pressed his hands over the wound in his belly in my bathroom; that seemed like ages ago now. Uncertainly, I sealed both his palms atop the gaping wound, using mine to hold his in place. If the fiend had pierced his heart, perhaps he couldn't heal from this. In all the lore I'd ever read, destruction of the heart guaranteed true death.

For the longest time, I maintained the pose. I didn't know how the magic functioned, and I'd give ten years of my life for my mother's grimoires. For the first time, I thought they might work.

His blood bubbled up through my fingers, dark and rich. If I had open wounds on my hands, I'd be insane with the rush. Fortunately, I'd also gone past revulsion; I found it hard to credit that I'd once been squeamish. I'd changed so much since I left Chance. There was no way I could doubt it; I wasn't the same woman I had been. I shouldn't be able to call upon the power of dead priests to bolster my own strength. Once, handling only offered pain and heat and information. Now I had stepped through a veil, and the world reacted to me in a different way.

Since you took your mother's power, and you died, a little voice whispered.

"Wake up," I said shakily. "I don't think I can get back to civilization on my own. Please don't leave me here by myself."

Tears filled my eyes, spilling down my cheeks. They dropped onto his pale, still face. When I'd touched him in the hostel room, he'd had a heartbeat. He didn't now. Which meant he was dead. It didn't mean he couldn't come back, if I helped him.

So breathe for him.

I'd taken CPR years ago. Did I remember it? *Fingers on nose and chin . . .* When I moved my hands, his stayed on the wound. I bent down and opened his mouth, tilting his head, and then gave him two breaths. I could remember very little other than that. I counted and exhaled for endless moments, need and worry tangled up inside me. Listening, I couldn't tell if it had any effect.

The tenth—or twentieth—time my lips touched his, a tremor went through him. His tats kindled with a pale glow, telling me systems had come back online. From here he should heal on his own, though it would hurt like a bitch and kick him into a long sleep afterward. Eyes still shut, he flung me onto my back. Despite his injuries, he was incredibly strong.

I wouldn't risk fighting and hurting him worse. His blood covered me as it was. But this wasn't an attack. His eyes opened; silver filmed them. I knew he didn't see me. Not wearing a smile like that. It almost stopped my heart.

"Asherah," he whispered. "Asherah."

The name rang distant bells, but he lowered his head and obliterated my long-term memory. His mouth took mine, full of possessive need and hot with devotion. Gods and goddesses, how I wished I *were* Asherah.

If I'd ever wondered whether he was a fully functional man, he put my curiosity to rest with slow hip movements. At some point he had been some woman's lover. The name sounded old—why didn't I stop this? I shouldn't—

Oh.

His lips traced over the side of my throat, tasting the blood the demon had drawn. "Who hurt you, *dādu*? I will bring you his heart." He nuzzled my ear, whispering in a language I didn't recognize. *"Ana dadika."*

Even knowing he held another woman in his mind, I couldn't pull free. I told myself I didn't want to fight him; there was no telling what new hallucination resistance would summon. Slowly I grew conscious of my nakedness and that there could be people watching us. He wouldn't thank me if I let him sweep me into the delusion.

"Kel," I whispered.

His hands wandered, exploring me from shoulder to hip and back again. His tats blazed until they burned against my skin. He bit down on the curve of my ear. "Say it again."

"Kel."

"It's been so long. *So* long since I touched you."

I exhaled slowly. If he moved or I did, protest would be moot. Already I could barely remember why I didn't want to do this.

"Look at me. I'm not Asherah."

Finally, the silver shine faded from his eyes. I could tell the moment he recognized me. But his desire didn't vanish; since we were naked, I would've been humiliated if it had. Instead his longing gained layers. His gaze carried eternity, the weight of loneliness, and something unfamiliar. I only knew that I had never seen that expression in anyone before.

"Binder," he breathed. Dimly, I remembered Caim using that word. "You called me back. You gave me your breath."

"You needed it."

"I need *this*." He shifted his hips as if asking a question.

I didn't ask why. In truth, I needed it too. No promises, just relief and the keen, knife-edged moment. I needed to wipe away the horror handling the demon's harness had left behind.

He lowered his head, and this time he kissed *me*. His lips felt fevered against mine, faintly flavored with my blood. It did not revolt me, only offered a coppery tinge, and then it was more, a kiss that took my breath and gave it back. Heat rose from his body like sunlight on crystal and quartz.

"This creates energy," he whispered into my throat. "I can use it to drive off that cursed sleep. I can't leave you unguarded now."

I didn't care about his reasons. I just wanted him. It was enough that he knew who I was. In answer, I wound my legs around his hips. I didn't care how many people might be watching from the shadows. Let them think we were pagans or devils.

He filled me with divine heat in one smooth motion, and I arched. His fingers curled around the rope of my braided hair, tugging my mouth to his. We kissed endlessly, our bodies rocking as one. As the heat amplified and his motions quickened, his tats shone brighter. I could feel them on my skin like starbursts.

"Corine," he murmured. "Binder. Thank you."

Kelethiel, son of Uriel and Vashti, I whispered back soundlessly. *Thank you.*

His face struck me as reverent, as if we shared more than our bodies, as if for him, this counted as both prayer and ritual. I responded, letting the sweet glow carry me higher. Sheer intensity ratcheted my need to ferocious levels, and I lost myself in him, bucking and whimpering against his lips. When he came, the sigils on his skin lit in unison, bright and pure and powerful. Answering energy burned out of me like a meteor and fell into his skin. When the glow dimmed and died, there were no new marks on him. No dried blood. Just the old scars. With my fingertips, I found the place where once wings had grown. He shuddered beneath my light touch.

"Will you get in trouble?" I asked.

His head rested in the curve of my shoulder. He did not move. "For what?"

"I just assumed . . ."

His lips lifted against my skin; he was smiling. "I'm not celibate by vow. . . . The rules of your religions do not come from us. We are older than your writings."

I felt impossibly young and inexperienced beside him, yet safer than I ever had. "Oh. Well, I'm sure you—"

He put a finger on my lips. "I needed to share that with you . . . for many reasons. To fuel my healing, as I said . . . but that's not the only reason."

"There's more?" *Please, let it be something good.* I needed to hear it, even if there were no promises. I didn't ask for those . . . just a memory of his voice in the dark.

"You called me back from the pit and asked *nothing* in return. I know of no other way to express . . . no deeper—" Words failed him then.

"I get it."

Maybe it seemed strange, but I believed we'd performed some ancient rite, and it also served as a way for him to say, *Thank you*, and *I care*. We said with our bodies what we could never speak out loud.

He went on. "Ordinarily . . . I abstain. It is unfair to share such intimacy when I can never stay. And I have spoken too many good-byes."

That addressed his longevity, but it was more too. The moment they ordered him elsewhere, he would go. That much I knew. It hurt, but it wasn't an impossible pain. Instead I felt lucky to have this moment; despite everything, I felt perfectly balanced.

"Who was Asherah?"

Behind his eyes, oceans of sorrow rose and fell in moon-touched waves. "Someone I loved and lost, long ago."

That was no answer, but I didn't press. I hadn't earned his secrets, even if he was crushing me into the ground, draped over me like a blanket. I hesitated to complain; once he moved away, the moment would become a memory. So I asked something else.

"What does *ana dadika* mean?" I butchered the pronunciation, but he recognized the phrase.

"Where did you hear that?"

"You whispered it to me."

"Ah," he said. "It is Babylonian, and it means, *I am made for your love.*"

Melancholy washed through me. What wouldn't I give to have someone say that to me for real? "I'm sorry I'm here instead of her."

One big hand curved against my cheek. "I'm not."

My breath caught. Fresh yearning rose and he didn't try to hide it from me. This time we had no excuse, not even a thin one. We did it again because we wanted to.

The End Is the Beginning
Is the End

At daybreak we dressed in clean underwear, filthy clothes, and our hiking boots. The village remained unnaturally quiet. I sensed people watching us through their windows and sometimes I caught movement in my peripheral vision, but when I turned, I saw only closing doors. A few children were bold enough to stare out the windows, but their parents swiftly pulled them away and closed the curtains against us.

The silent message was clear: They weren't coming out until we were gone. Based on the events of the night before, I understood their caution. Only the churned earth and faint, lingering smell gave a hint what had happened here. Maybe in a few days' time, this would seem like a collective hallucination, and they'd start to forget. Today, the silent treatment proved a pain in the ass, and I didn't look forward to more walking, but we wouldn't receive further assistance. I was glad, however, that none of the villagers had come to harm because of me; I didn't think I could stand more innocent blood on my conscience.

I ate the last of the protein bars and drew some water from the public well. With a philosophical shrug, I filled my bottle, and Kel did the same. The parasites might bother me, but we needed to keep moving. If we lingered here too long, Montoya's sorcerer might send something else, something worse, though that defied imagination. Since I hadn't known demons could be summoned in corporeal form, there was no telling what gruesome surprises lay in store.

In silence, I led the way toward the church, intending to ask the priest for directions, but the doors were closed, and he didn't respond to my tentative knock. I glanced up at Kel, who said, "The best thing we can do is move along."

Since I agreed, I didn't argue. Logistics posed a problem, however. "But where?"

He canted his head while the day brightened around us, as if listening to silent voices. Then he pointed. "That way."

"Did your archangel tell you how far it is too?"

Kel almost smiled. "No. I don't call him—he calls me."

"Oh." I fell into step beside him. The dirt track led toward gently rising hills. "So what did you do just now?"

Once, I never would've bothered asking, but there was something between us now, even if impossible, ephemeral, and fragile as spider silk. He waited to answer until we had left the village some distance behind. I concentrated on walking.

"I can . . . ask questions," he said eventually. "Mine information."

"Kind of like a divine Internet?" The concept amused me.

"A little. But it's not as comprehensive." He looked as if he wanted to explain further, but in the end, he chose not to, and I didn't press.

The path led toward the mountains in the distance, hulking and dark, wreathed in mist at their peaks, but the way before them lay green and bright. My steps followed a route that looked as though it had been worn by horses and donkey carts. I didn't think cars had ever been out this way. It would take a helicopter to reach this hidden valley.

For this last leg of our journey, we had water, but no food. I regulated my sips and kept walking. In the distance eucalyptus groves rose, slim and straight, but far enough that we wouldn't pass through unless the path turned. Instead we trudged through pampas grass, interspersed with the brightness of coral trees, orchids, dusty ferns, and lady's slipper. Other plants defied my ability to name them, blooming in a profusion of yellow, scarlet, and shades of pink. The landscape was a study in contrasts: here brown, there green, prickly and delicate by turns. I particularly admired a plant with veined oval leaves and red bell-shaped flowers that hung in a graceful cluster.

Now and then, Kel slipped off to forage; he found breadfruit, wild potatoes, and a couple of custard apples. The first two needed to be cooked, but we could eat the latter now. As if in response to my thought, he broke one of the apples in half and I took the offering. Inside, the green tuberculated fruit was pale, dotted with dark seeds. I pried those out and tossed them away; then I ate greedily, finding the taste a perfect blend of pineapple, strawberry, and mango. I'd never had anything so good. Using my fingers, I scraped out the last bit and then dropped the skin.

"There's another one," he said, "but we should save it for later."

I nodded. After taking a little more water, I had the energy to go on. My muscles burned, and I had bruises and cuts from the confrontation with Caim; I didn't mention them. Kel might feel compelled to heal me again, and my crazy reaction to his blood sounded worse than bearing the pain.

Come nightfall, he built a fire and roasted the breadfruit and potatoes on sticks. By that point, I was ravenous, and could hardly wait for the food to cook, let alone cool. I burned my tongue as I ate and didn't care at all. Insects and birds serenaded through the meal, though the smoke kept the worst of the former away. Kel broke the last custard apple and I devoured it as dessert. The temperature dropped enough for me to be grateful for the sleeping bag after we finished the meal.

It's a good thing he didn't go comatose, I reflected. I would've had no way to get out of the village, no way to move him, and the villagers' animosity would've manifested, if Kel had been unconscious. One lone woman wouldn't seem like a threat with her protector down. If the Peruvian villagers weren't worrisome enough, failure to move on would've earned Montoya's sorcerer another shot at us. Without him, I wouldn't know which way to travel or how to find food.

Even now, he protected me, per his orders, but it was more too. He set his sleeping bag no more than five inches from my own. Part of me wanted a repeat of the night before by crackling firelight, beneath this star-studded sky, though the rest of me knew it would be ludicrously unwise.

"Will you remember?" I asked into the silence.

Maybe time fades it. Maybe he won't. But, I told myself, *he recalls Asherah.* And there was no telling how long ago he'd lost her. While I awaited his reply, lyrics from an old Sarah McLachlan song ran through my head.

But Kel knew what I meant, and his answer pierced my heart. "Yes. Always."

That was comfort of a sort. Even when I died, as I inevitably must, last night guaranteed me some form of immortality. Silence fell and I closed my eyes.

In the morning, we had the rest of the breadfruit and potatoes. We walked on.

Eventually the track widened and went from dirt to rough pavement. Miles farther, I heard the roar of a distant engine. *Civilization at last.*

I waved my arms frantically as the rattletrap truck barreled toward us. A raised thumb might not convey the urgency. At first, the driver passed us, and my heart sank, but he slowed and pulled to the shoulder. Without looking at Kel, I summoned the last of my energy and sprinted toward the vehicle.

A quick conversation and the last of the cash convinced the driver to take us to the nearest city, where he was headed anyway. At his request, we got in back. I didn't blame him; we smelled pretty rank.

The trip took most of the day, and the wind whipped my

face like mad, but the weather was clear, and by dark, we arrived in Huánuco. This city was big enough that our appearance drew attention in a different way from in the village.

The streets were narrow, cobbled in places. Many of the homes were adobe, as in Mexico, but there was a faintly Mediterranean influence as well in the open terraces and breezy arches. Stone walls marched up gentle inclines to the market; this was a proper *zócalo* filled with merchants, artists, and artisans in a beautifully landscaped garden. We didn't linger there.

People gave us a wide berth. Not that I cared. I wanted this madness to be over, so I could see my friends again, and then take the next step toward handling Montoya. He'd killed a man I admired and respected, along with Ernesto, who was in the wrong place at the wrong time. Montoya had nearly slain me twice. I felt hard as I never had before, coolly determined. As long as I had Kel beside me, I feared nothing; I'd come to rely on him more than I cared to admit.

Outside a tiny convenience store, I found an outdoor outlet for my cell phone. We worked quickly to disable the deterrent measures; then I plugged in and powered it on. It wouldn't be long before someone caught me and shooed me away. My tired eyes located the street sign—oh, God, it was littered with "Q"s, "L"s, and "A"s, not Spanish. I'd never pronounce it, assuming I could get hold of Escobar.

He'd put his number in my directory as Efraín. I hit the green button on my keypad and lifted the phone to my ear. It rang three times and then: *"Bueno.* I trust you have good news for me," he continued in Spanish.

I answered in kind, though my mind was slower at translations than I would've liked. *So damned tired.* "I have it. I'm in Huánuco, on . . ." I spelled the street for him and then glanced at the store for the number.

At that point, the owner stepped onto the walk and started cursing me for stealing his power. The socket had been secured; Kel had snapped the padlock and I'd pried the cap off it, so I couldn't argue with his outrage, and I had little currency to soothe his distress. My partner in crime overheard.

"Give him the phone," Escobar ordered.

I did as instructed.

Five minutes later, the owner handed it back with downcast eyes and he hurried back into his shop. I honestly didn't want to know what Escobar had said or promised. "*¿Ahora qué?*" I asked. *Now what?* It was a good question.

"Wait there for my men," he answered. "The proprietor has been instructed to offer you food and drink. He will be recompensed."

"*Hecho,*" I said. Which meant, roughly and in short, *You have a deal.*

Since, after that, I had permission to use the outlet, I sent texts to both Jesse and Shannon. I didn't feel up to long phone conversations with either of them. Doubtless Chuch and Eva would want to hear my story too, so apart from my low-ebbing energy, I was also being practical.

Kel stepped into the shop, and when he returned, he carried a small bag. He produced *tortas* wrapped in waxed paper, and two icy orange sodas. A few moments later, the owner brought us a couple of rickety chairs. Clearly he wanted us gone but he also didn't want trouble. He set them down with a muttered imprecation, well outside the store. I sat down gratefully as the day died around us.

We ate in silence, but I could finish only half of my sandwich. I gave the rest to Kel, and downed the Fanta in a thirsty rush. I ached from head to toe. By the time we finished and balled up our trash, a dark town car was pulling up to the curb. Two men in black got out. Since it was nearly dark, they didn't wear shades, but their impassive expressions matched what I had come to expect in minions.

One of them went into the store to settle our account; the other waved us into the backseat of the vehicle. They drove us to an airfield an hour outside the city, and soon, we were in the air. Thank all gods and goddesses this was nearly done.

I'd had enough of playing this man's game, and I badly wanted some return on my time and trouble.

The flight was long, and we stopped once to refuel—I didn't know where. Kel and I stayed on the plane. He was so quiet it troubled me, but I could find no way to inquire. At the second takeoff, he surprised me by curling his fingers through mine.

"You don't like to fly?" I guessed.

His mouth turned down ever so slightly. "Not like this."

Ah. I understood. I wished I didn't. In my mind's eye, I saw scars, not wounds he'd taken fighting, but those inflicted while he knelt bound and unable to resist. The amputation of his wings had been a punishment for some transgression; I knew that much. The demon had hinted that the archangels abused him both because of his human mother and his own disobedience. How much of that was true? He hadn't denied anything, as I recalled, except the idea that desire required penance.

At length, we slept, and I held his hand until we landed. When I opened my eyes next, I recognized this airstrip, and the house in the distance. We were back on Escobar's property, wherever that might be.

Goon A escorted me from the plane while Goon B took charge of Kel. "You will be permitted to bathe and change before you see *el Señor*."

I found the honorific amusing because that was also what some people called God around here. Or maybe I just was too tired to know what was funny. *"Gracias."*

Paolo stood waiting for me on the veranda. When I turned, I couldn't see Kel anywhere. I started to protest but he held up a hand. "Your companion will not be harmed. He is simply not part of your business with my father." He spoke kindly, gently, but his eyes reflected the same implacable core I'd glimpsed in Escobar.

Divide and conquer. I recognized the tactic, but I couldn't think of a reason to fight it. Kel could take care of himself.

"Okay," I said wearily. "I'll take that shower."

The boy led the way to the suite I'd occupied before,

what seemed like ages ago. I cringed a little, catching hints of my filth in reflective surfaces along the way. Even so, I wasn't prepared for the wreckage that greeted me when I stepped into that palatial bathroom.

My hair stood in a wild nimbus on top, a straggling, messy braid down my back as if those feral demonic monkeys had styled it for me. I had a long scratch down my throat from where the demon marked me, and various bruises darkened my skin. More shocking, my face was thin and sharp, browner than I could ever remember seeing it. The blue of my eyes gleamed brighter by comparison. I got my biggest surprise when I peeled out of my filthy clothes. I ran my palms down my stomach. Ribs. I could feel my ribs. I had no idea how much weight I'd lost out there, but I could see the difference. The muscles—and apparently I had some— showed much closer to the skin now.

Well, whatever. It wouldn't do to keep Escobar waiting— any longer than necessary, anyhow, because I didn't mean to rush this shower. Given free rein, I'd spend days getting clean.

A long while later, I stepped out of the stall. I took advantage of the nourishing creams and then wandered into the bedroom, steam trailing me like wistful air elementals. I tried not to be outraged when I saw he'd replaced the clothing in the wardrobe with smaller sizes. I was even more agitated when they fit. I hated the idea that Escobar could foresee every eventuality, as if he were privy to a celestial chessboard nobody else could see.

"If that were true," I said aloud, "then he wouldn't need me to help him take out Diego Montoya."

I told myself I wasn't putting on the white dream of a dress to impress anyone, but part of me wanted Kel to see me wearing such a lovely thing. It was a pure slice of feminine vanity, but it suited me, and I would've never dared to wear a halter top before. I made sure it was tied tight before I went to work on my hair. It took longer than I liked to dry it, but after so many days of braids, I wanted to wear it loose.

Paolo knocked on the door as I finished up. He paused for a moment, taking in the picture I presented, though I was too old for him. Still, it was a kind flattery, one seen often in Latin men. "Come. It is time."

His escort was unnecessary. Along the way, he showed off for me a little, spinning another white rose in the air. I caught it and found it had already been stripped of thorns. So when I stepped into Escobar's sanctum sanctorum, I carried a white bloom. White dress, red hair, brown skin, blue eyes—I didn't think I'd ever been so exotic before. I hoped Escobar didn't expect a virgin sacrifice to seal the deal. That ship sailed long ago.

I wasn't surprised at all to find him standing before the windows, back to me. That sort of pose offered all kinds of power advantages, especially if I sat. I didn't. I was patient; I could wait him out.

The backpack that contained the crucifix sat on a striped damask chair nearby. To confound his expectations, I crossed the room and stood beside him. This side of the room had a majestic view, and for the first time I realized the house had been built into the mountainside. Below lay only open space.

He turned then, assessing me in a glance. "Show me what you found."

Obedient, I snagged the backpack and dug inside it. Happily, someone had already disposed of the other noisome items it'd contained, leaving only the tarnished silver cross. Making sure of my shields—because I assuredly did not want to read this thing, as I had likely imprinted it with my struggles—I lifted the icon into the light.

"Here it is."

"Tell me the story."

After offering it to him, I summed up what I'd learned. "You placed the clay statue there," I finished. "You must have, like a marker for me to follow."

"Not me," he said. "One of my men."

"Why didn't you have him fetch that thing home? Or do it yourself?"

His lips quirked. "Do I look as if I would enjoy trekking through the jungle?" *As a matter of fact, no.* "I admit to being curious as to how you deciphered the markings. Your phone indicates no outside help. Does your companion speak Aymara?"

I merely smiled. *Let him wonder.*

Accepting my silence as reply, he went on. "And the relic would have done me no good without someone to give me the answer I sought."

"Which was?"

"Whether the story was true."

"Why did you care? It was so long ago."

"Blood matters," he said gravely. "Would you not wish to know whether you came from a line of liars and rapists?"

I found his concern for family honor peculiar and off-kilter, given how he had built his own empire. Still . . . "Yes. I'd want to know. But why did you think it would be so bad, that handling?" In truth, my courage had been tested more in other ways over the course of the trial.

"Wouldn't it have been, if it had been true?"

Ugh. Yes. The priest might've clutched it, reliving his awful deeds, and his salacious sadism would've filled me as if I were a drunkard's barf bucket.

"I've done it," I said then. "Passed your challenge. May I go now? I need to reassure my friends and get some rest before we begin."

Get your live bait, right here. Sweet Georgian bait. That would go over *big* with the folks in Texas.

"You're worthy. Our initial agreement stands." Escobar lifted the crucifix as if weighing the silver content, and his nostrils flared. "What's this on the bottom of it? It reeks."

"Demon blood."

"And yet you're here. You made no mention of demons before."

"I guess I didn't." There seemed to be no point in doing so now.

"The journey did you well."

I raised a brow. "How do you figure?"

"Some metal, *inferior* metal, will break if you attempt to smelt and refine it. Quality steel only becomes finer and sharper."

"That might make sense, if I were a weapon."

He smiled then. "But, *querida* . . . you are."

I ignored that, despite the shiver of dread it raised on my spine. I'd wondered before if the blade in my side was shaping my decisions, turning me into a killer suited to its use. "Am I free to go? Can you get me to the border and give me bus fare?"

"I treat my allies far better than that," he said gently. "But I see you've lost your protective charm. That's probably why you had demons. I'll give you another—please try to be more careful with it, and don't remove it until I tell you."

"Until we've laid the trap."

"Yes. It will drive Montoya mad when his sorcerer fails . . . and fails and fails. He'll contact you, if I know him at all. He'll try to draw you into the open."

"And I'll go," I said softly.

"But of course. You'll insist on a face-to-face to settle things. He'll see it as very Wild West. He likes that. If you live, I'll pay you handsomely." When he finished, he gave me his back.

Clearly dismissed, I strode toward the door. Paolo opened it. In one hand he held an amulet similar to the one I'd worn before. This one whispered of a different caster; I listened to its secrets with half an ear as I looped it around my neck.

"Aren't you worried that the time I've spent in this house will lead Montoya right here?"

Paolo shook his head, smiling with patient amusement. "The whole place is warded. I'm surprised you can't feel it."

Now that he mentioned it, I could. Little tingles of energy struck my feet as I walked, as if the floor itself had been laid with magickal energy. Though I cringed at the notion of getting on another plane, I was so eager to get to

Shannon, Jesse, Eva, Butch, and Chuch that I'd run all the way to Texas.

"Where's Kel?"

"Your companion is waiting for you in the kitchen. I have instructions to feed you both and then have our pilot take you to Laredo."

I didn't want food. I wanted to leave. But since I needed Kel before making my escape, I followed Paolo through the winding halls.

Kel sat with a plate untouched before him, and he glanced up as I came through the swinging door. The kitchen was as large as one might expect, but emptier. The space echoed, and there were no servants to be seen. For a nonsensical moment, I wondered if this mansion was like that haunted castle, where common household furnishings came to life to tend the beast.

"Are you ready?" I asked him.

He stared at Paolo until the boy shifted uncomfortably. "Give us a moment."

With alacrity astonishing in one who had surely grown immune to intimidation, Paolo disappeared the way we'd come. I stood still, not knowing what to expect. He rose and crossed the floor to me. They'd given him black to wear; doubtless the outfit belonged to one of the burly henchmen.

"You look lovely." And he seemed surprised to hear the words, as if he had meant to say something else. Kel stopped just short of touching me.

"Thanks." That was why I'd worn the dress, after all, but I felt stupid, trying to please him as if he were the kind of man who could be swayed by such things.

"He's sworn to protect you?"

"Mission accomplished," I answered, lifting the amulet. "I have a new one. It's supposed to last until we're ready to deal with Montoya."

"Ah," he said, and a whisper of regret salted the syllable.

My breath hitched. "No."

"The risk fades to acceptable levels once you secure the alliance with Escobar. You've done so. My mission is ended."

He was so terribly gentle. "I will not be going with you any farther."

"New orders?"

"Yes."

Maybe they'd demanded he depart already. He had places to go and people to kill. I appreciated him sticking around to say good-bye; that might even be borderline disobedience, the sort of thing that earned him castigation before. I wouldn't make it worse for him, even if tears clotted my throat.

I managed a light tone. "Maybe our paths will cross again someday."

"Perhaps. You *do* attract trouble." He hesitated, then took my hand. "I can't promise. I may never be sent to you again."

The faintest stress on the word *sent* made me furrow my brow as I gazed up at him. My mind was tired or I would've caught on right away. A smile built when it dawned on me. Both Kel and Caim had named me Binder. If I'd called him once, I could do so again. Only one thing must I remember: I could call and call and call him, but he could never stay.

"I'll keep that in mind."

"I must go."

The request burst from me before I knew I meant to make it. "One kiss?"

Keepsake, memento, something. Please. Ease my way into this good-bye.

In answer, he dipped his head and brushed my mouth with his. I felt as though the heat of him would melt my bones with the aching. And then he stepped away. I closed my eyes so I wouldn't see him go. A word drifted back to me, lower than a whisper—a sigh. I thought I'd heard it the night before, but he hadn't spoken it to me then, not when he knew me, at least, and even now I wasn't sure.

Hours later, I sat in an impersonal motel room in Laredo. Since it was late, I wouldn't call the others to come get me yet. Not until I had a chance to sort these feelings and seal them away.

With keyboard in my lap, I sat cross-legged on the bed at three a.m., Googling old Babylonian words on the in-room television. Apparently, *dādu* meant *beloved*, and Asherah had been the Assyrian goddess of desire.

I wept.

The Day After

First thing in the morning, my phone rang. I'd almost forgotten Escobar had given it back to me. I glanced at the number and, with a flicker of relief, identified my caller.

"Jesse."

When he was worried, his drawl became more pronounced, and he sounded like pure Texas just now. "I'd love to know what's goin' on with you, sugar."

Good—he didn't know about what had happened at the shop. I hoped Shannon wouldn't say anything before tonight; I'd feel better telling him in person. "Things are . . . complicated."

"Are you safe?" His cop mind sorted the probabilities faster than I wanted. "Does this have to do with Montoya?"

That was like asking a mouse in the gullet of a cobra how its day was going, but he didn't need to know that. "Yeah . . . and yeah. I'll see you tonight at Chuch and Eva's if you're not doing anything. We'll talk about everything then."

He laughed. "The woman I want to see hits town and you ask if I can make room in my schedule? I think I'm offended."

Jesse wanted me to move to Texas and rejoin the America he called home. He wanted me to get an apartment and

meet his family. I know he foresaw Fourth of July barbe-
cues and Thanksgiving dinners, wherein he could show me
what I'd missed.

I knew I had trust issues, but part of me wasn't sure he
could accept what I was doing to ensure my own survival.
His sense of morality wasn't fluid; he came from a bedrock-
solid foundation, and he'd never slept in a bus station. It'd
be better if I could look into his eyes and explain what I'd
done, along with the choices I'd made. If he cared about me
as much as he claimed, he'd understand the necessity.

"Well, I didn't want to assume." There were no promises
between us, so he might've had plans. He had a way with
the ladies, and I didn't expect him to change his life unless
I showed up in Laredo, ready to open a shop and commit to
a relationship.

"You caught me on a free night," he admitted then. "I'll
be there."

Once we disconnected, I checked out and went out front
to wait for Shannon. She arrived twenty minutes later.

"Where's Kel?" Shan asked as I got in the car.

Chuch had sent her to pick me up in one of his spares.
This one was a half-restored but functional 1972 Dodge
Charger. She looked fine, healthy, and her black hair sported
new pink tips on the bottom. God, I hoped she had my
purse. I hadn't seen it—or Butch—since Escobar took me.

I swallowed hard. "Gone."

"He bailed on you?" Her expression darkened.

"He saw me through what he needed to. Please don't
blame him. He reports to a higher authority." Whatever else
had come of this, I believed in his orders.

The Charger peeled out of the parking lot. It wasn't the
same shitty La Quinta I'd stayed in when I was here with
Chance, but all cheap motels more or less looked the same.
Escobar's men had given me a small wad of bills, payment
for my time, and dropped me off at one they knew accepted
cash. Since I didn't have any ID on me, it had to be a place
like that.

"Someone in the backseat wants to say hi."

I slid my knee up on the seat so I could twist at the waist. Butch popped out of my purse, which was lying on the backseat, and gave a happy little bark with his tail wagging in excitement. I reached for him and cuddled him to my chest. He licked my face and hands, vibrating doggy Morse code for, *Dude, I missed you; where you have you been?* For long moments I just petted him and tried to let go of the surreal quality of the past days.

Maybe that was the best attitude to take. It wasn't real. *None* of it was real. Therefore, I couldn't miss him.

Shannon drove while I cuddled an ecstatic Butch. Her familiarity impressed me. Clearly she hadn't spent her time sitting around Chuch's house all day. "I've been helping Eva," she explained. "Running errands. Grocery shopping. You wouldn't believe how cranky and tired she is."

By my reckoning, she must be more than eight months along by now, so I would. "I'm glad you're both okay." I included Butch in the word *both* by rubbing my chin against his head. *Wag, wag, wag.* His tail thumped against my arm.

"They're great," she said, smiling. "I mean, I felt weird at first, but Chuch said, 'Any friend of Corine's,' and they just took me in, no questions asked."

"That sounds like him." My throat felt choky. It wasn't like me to get tearful so fast; life had given me a harder shell than that, but I'd seen and suffered too much in the past few days, so my emotions bobbed near the surface. "Would you rather stay? I mean, Eva will need help after the baby comes."

At this point, I didn't know where I was going, if I would survive the encounter with Montoya. I touched the pendant I wore, ostensibly to protect me from being located by Montoya's sorcerer. For all I knew, it could also compel my loyalty or give me plantar warts.

My mother would've known.

There was no guarantee I'd ever be able to repair the shop. No guarantee of anything, really, and part of me thought Shannon should stay with Chuch and Eva, where she'd be safe. They offered the family warmth she needed.

"Are you kidding?" She cut me a quick look before she went back to watching the road. "I want to see the world, not settle down in some Texas town. Seems to me that sticking with you is the best way to accomplish that."

"Well, that much is true."

Butch yapped, leaving me in no doubt about his opinion. Holding him made me feel better, despite the uncertainty. The rest of the ride passed in silence.

The Ortiz family home hadn't changed much since my last visit. It was still a good-size stone ranch house, but I did notice a couple of improvements. Instead of having half-fixed cars in the driveway, which drove Eva crazy, Chuch had paved some ground to the right of the garage, out of sight. Since they had substantial property, it didn't lessen their lot size, only increased the appeal of the place.

Shannon pulled the Charger onto the cement pad. Two other cars kept ours company, an Impala with its guts hanging out, and a sweet little Ford Opal. The latter looked like it was nearly finished.

I reached over the seat, snagged my purse, and slid out of the car, Butch nestled in the crook of my arm.

Shannon's eyes widened as she took her first good look since I hopped into the car. "Holy shit."

Despite the heaviness of my heart, I couldn't help but smile. "Yeah, I'm planning my own infomercial: the Jungle Diet."

She laughed as I meant her to and led the way to the front door, where Eva stood waiting. I ran to hug her. It had been months since I'd seen her, and the belly didn't permit the kind of embrace she preferred. We managed.

"Look at this," she said, holding me at arm's length. "I'm big as a whale, and *you're* skinny."

I wasn't sure I'd go that far, but it was nice to hear. I knew I'd dropped some weight. I'd sweated and walked and eaten little and fallen in a river and then fallen—

No. Not that. Never that. If nothing else, I was a realist. While I might indulge secret pipe dreams, I understood the difference between desirable and attainable.

"How're you feeling?" I asked, following her inside.

"Huge. The baby keeps kicking me in the kidneys, and I have to pee *all* the time."

I filed that away for future reference. It seemed unlikely I'd ever have children of my own, but one never knew. "Where's Chuch?"

"He ran to the store to get me some pistachios. I'm going to crush them up and put them on cherry-swirl ice cream."

As weird pregnancy cravings went, I'd heard worse. "Look, I'll tell you guys the whole story, as I promised, but I'd rather wait for Jesse to get here. That way, I only have to tell it once."

"Fine with me," Shannon said.

Eva nodded. "*Nena*, the only thing that matters is that you're here and you're safe. You know we've got your back."

That was the problem; I did know. And I didn't want to lead trouble to their door. I was here only because of Escobar's pendant, and maybe I trusted him *too* much. He was a bad guy, after all, but I thought he possessed a rigid sense of personal honor, apart from what he did for a living. But if I were wrong about him, if he was using me as bait right *now*, I endangered Chuch, Eva, and their unborn child. Just thinking about the potential consequences filled me with horror.

On second thought—

"You know," I said, striving not to show my sudden fear, "I only have the clothes I'm standing in. Do you feel up to going shopping?"

Eva shook her head. "I wish I did."

I'd known as much when I asked. I could see that her ankles were swollen and she needed to get off her feet. But I didn't want her worrying in her condition, and shopping provided the most believable reason for me to scram as soon as I arrived. *Dammit, why didn't I consider the danger before I brought my problems to their front door?*

Shannon started to protest, and I knew she was about to say she still had the bag I'd taken to Catemaco. I quelled her with a look. *Not now. We need to go.*

"Would you mind if Shannon took me to the mall in the Charger? Chuch will be home soon, right?"

"Yeah, he just popped down to the mini-mart. He's going to be sorry he missed you. Are you sure you have to run off again?"

"I'll be back," I promised in Arnold tones. "But I do need to get some things, and we might as well take care of it before we rally the troops."

Kel had mentioned something along those lines, I remembered. *You muster your allies,* he'd said. *And plan for war.* Escobar had compared me to a general, and I didn't like where that comparison ended. Me, sending people to fight and die on my behalf. Yet there was no question I had changed; perhaps one day soon I would be cold enough not to care. The prospect unsettled me.

"You're going to Del Norte?" Eva asked Shannon.

The girl nodded. "I know the way; don't worry."

Eva grinned. "I wasn't worrying. I was going to ask you to get those Disney decals we looked at last time we were there."

"No problem."

When she tried to lever off the sofa to get her purse, I said, "Don't get up. It's my treat. A small thank-you for taking care of Shannon while I was gone."

"*Claro,*" Eva said. "She's family now."

Though she tried to hide it, I could see the pleasure rising in Shannon's pale face. Like me, she had been cut off from forming bonds with people. "Oh, goody," she muttered. "We're going shopping."

Butch in bag, I climbed back into the car. On the way, I explained to Shannon why I didn't want to linger at Chuch and Eva's place. "And I don't have anyone here I can ask to verify this amulet—that it does hide me and nothing more. I'm not taking any chances with their safety."

Her lips firmed. "But you'll risk ours?"

I hid a wince. Yeah, the game plan for taking out Montoya permanently wasn't going to make anyone happy tonight. Unfortunately, I was committed.

As we approached the mall, I said, "Keep going on San Dario."

If memory served, there was a Goodwill store farther down. I did need to augment my meager belongings, but I didn't see why I should pay mall prices. I hadn't grown up roaming consumer megaplexes as a kid, so there was no nostalgia in it for me, only expensive merchandise. And while I had a small wad of money from Escobar that added up to nearly a thousand bucks, along with the fifteen hundred pesos in my purse, I didn't know how long that would have to last. I'd been broke and starving before; I didn't intend to let it happen again.

I saw the sign ahead. "Turn there."

For the first time since we'd gotten the car, Shannon smiled. "Okay, I'll stop being mad at you. This is very cool."

Whoa, she was more like me than I'd realized. We parked and got out; the lot was nearly empty. I wore a bemused expression as I followed her toward the building. Most people thought thrift stores were all seedy and disorganized, but I'd been in some that were better maintained than Wal-Mart. This was a nice one with the racks of clothing sorted by sex and size. I liked these places because you never knew what you might find; the treasure hunt appealed to the pawnshop owner in me.

I quickly located a couple of pairs of jeans, some tank tops, and a few pretty Mexican peasant blouses. Shopping in Texas meant I could satisfy my quirky sense of style. I found a retro blue cardigan to replace my old green one. I'd miss that sweater. Like nearly everything else I owned—and a few items were irreplaceable—it had been destroyed in the blast.

They had a small fitting room where I could make sure everything worked. While I was in there, Shannon convinced me to add a wide leather belt with some interesting stitchery on it. "I've seen the look in magazines. It's kind of like yours, only—no, not like that."

I stood patient while she untucked my blouse and fastened the belt on top of the fabric. Okay, I liked it. With a

nod, I handed it to her and she put it in our basket. Pretty
soon I had a basic wardrobe. Nothing fancy, but for fancy
occasions I already had the white dress. I just didn't know
if I could wear it without remembering the look of admira-
tion in Kel's eyes. He'd lived so damn long and seen so
many women. If he saw something in me to appreciate,
then it carried weight.

She also brought me a plain black vest. I was convinced
it would make me look like a valet or a waitress, but she
paired it with old ratty jeans and a white tank. With a strand
of chunky beads, I found the look suited me.

"Wow, you're good at this. You should go into business."

Enthusiasm lit her expression. "You know, while you were
gone, I was thinking . . . we should go into business together. Like partners? You could sell your treasures, and I
could do vintage clothing."

"You mean a thrift shop, instead of a pawnshop. We'd
buy on consignment instead of paying cash." That would
mean looking at lots of old clothes, of course, but from Shannon's expression, she'd be happy to handle that part.

If I lived, if Escobar paid out, I'd have enough to rebuild.
I owned the property where my shop stood through a *fideicomiso*, which meant through the good offices of the Mexican
bank acting as trustee on my behalf. I had all the benefits of
being a direct title holder, and the contract lasted for fifty
years, renewable for another fifty, and I could transfer own-
ership anytime I wanted.

Belatedly I realized I'd kept Shannon waiting too long;
the light started to die in her eyes. I answered quickly, "That
sounds great. Kind of a spooky vintage place."

"I know how we can attract the college crowd too." As
we walked, she outlined her ideas, and they were good,
though I wasn't sure we should display our gifts.

"No," she insisted. "They'll think it's fake. That's the
cool part. But they'll want to hear the stories of whatever
we're selling too. They'll come for the entertainment and
you'll be able to tell which ones should buy what."

That was true enough. "I like it. Start thinking about a name, okay?"

I had to think positive: new beginnings and happy endings. Since I had only my small gray duffel, the rest of these clothes needed somewhere to live. A little while later, I found the perfect suitcase, probably from the sixties or seventies. When I picked it up, it wanted to show me where it had been . . . and I let it. There came a minor burn, but no trauma in this bag—only the happy excitement of a girl going away to college. She used it in the early seventies and then tucked it away, forgot about it as the loud flowered fabric fell out of style. But I loved the crazy floral print and the red plastic handle with matched binding. The thing carried a price tag of three dollars.

Shannon sighed when she saw what I had. "You are so not decorating our new place by yourself."

I grinned at her, leading the way up front. A few knick-knacks distracted me, but I didn't let them keep me long. I had no business buying anything until I knew where I was setting up home base. I didn't let myself consider the alternative: that I had no future and Montoya won.

Another reason I loved thrift stores? My total purchases when the cashier rang me out came to less than fifty bucks. I paid with one of Escobar's hundreds, and the clerk narrowed her eyes at me. Damn, I hoped it was clean. The way I was dressed, she doubtless thought I was up to something, shopping at Goodwill and dropping big bills.

"I got mugged," I offered. *By a firebomb.* It was almost true. "So a friend wired me some money. I need clothes but I didn't want to spend a fortune."

Her distrust softened into sympathy as she saw the few pesos in my wallet. "Oh, honey, stay away from the border. They're mean as snakes around there."

"Do you mind if I change out of this dress into something casual?" I lifted the bag and tilted my head toward the fitting room.

"Not at all."

Because it made Shannon happy, I put on the jeans, white tank, and black vest, along with the necklace—the exact outfit she'd recommended. The good leather sandals Escobar had bought me were stamped, MADE IN SPAIN, and they went with anything.

Shan popped the trunk and I folded my clothes in my obnoxiously floral suitcase. There was room for the stuff I'd taken to Catemaco too, and I could probably roll up my duffel bag. It would fit in the corner there. Staring down, I saw the remnants of my broken life, and it saddened me.

"It'll be okay," Shannon said quietly.

I gave her an impulsive hug around the shoulders. "I know. I got you, babe."

"Please tell me you're not gonna sing."

"How do you even know that one, anyway?"

"Oldies radio," she said with an exaggerated shudder.

"Sonny and Cher were before my time too." I got in the Charger. "Let's go to Target. There's one a mile and a half up the road."

"What else can you possibly need?"

I sighed. One thing I never bought used. "Underwear."

"Right."

We didn't linger. I hated big stores with fluorescent lighting and people wandering around who seemed angry to answer your questions. Sometimes dealing with customers could be nightmarish, but I loved helping people find stuff.

My phone rang on the way out of the store. I peered at the caller ID—unknown number. With some trepidation, I answered, "Hello?"

"¿Bueno?" I'd recognize Tia's voice anywhere.

"Sí, bueno. ¿Como está usted?"

"No hay mucho tiempo, pero estoy feliz que estás a salvo." Not much time, but I'm glad you're safe, I translated mentally. She went on in Spanish. "I've called before, but I got voice mail. I have a metal box from your house. It was all I could save from the thieves looting the place."

Oh, my God. My mother's grimoires. Even if I couldn't use them, it would mean everything to touch them again.

"*¿Puede enviarmela por* FedEx?" I asked.

I agreed to wire her some money via Western Union. There was a place she could pick up the cash near her home. Shan and I took care of that, and then I called back with Chuch and Eva's address; Tia agreed to send the books overnight. I thanked her profusely and hung up, relieved beyond words.

The day was half gone by that point, so we stopped for barbecue at a little dive on Lafayette that Chuch liked. I fed Butch tidbits from my plate, and he showed his appreciation by licking my fingers. I gave him a drink in the ladies' room and then we paused for him to do business on the scrubby trees that landscaped the place.

I sent a text message to Booke, letting him know I was all right and in Texas. Shannon started the car and backed out of the restaurant lot. I was glad we'd been able to eat our sandwiches without the car exploding, like it had with Chance and me the last time I was in Texas. I didn't know about going back to Chuch and Eva's place, but maybe I could use the grimoires to set rune wards, not just herbal ones.

"We should get the decals now," Shannon said.

I nodded agreement.

After that, I had only one thing left to do now: explain the devil's bargain I had made with Escobar. I wasn't looking forward to that conversation.

Dark Tides Rising

By the time we got back, everyone sat waiting for us, including Jesse. Chuch swept me into a big bear hug, nearly crushing Butch, who gave an indignant yap. The mechanic held me at arm's length to get a better look at me, but there was no masculine awareness in his gaze; for Chuch, the sun rose and set with Eva. He was like a big brother, and God knew I could use his uncomplicated affection right then. Then he hugged me a second time for good measure.

"You're a sight for sore eyes, *prima*. Heard from Chance?" That was Chuch at his most subtle.

"Not since we left Kilmer." At first, I'd been crushed that he wouldn't even try to prove himself, that he offered only empty words. But I'd had months of silence to come to terms with it. Kel had proved a remarkable help in that regard. At least now I had someone new to miss—depressing thought.

"Well, he's working on it. Trust me on that."

On what? Before I could ask, Shannon handed Eva the Disney decals, and then she got shanghaied into hanging them in the baby's room, where she was sleeping. Since the Ortizes had a three-bedroom house—and one had been turned into an office—it meant the nursery had to do double duty. They'd put in a daybed, along with the crib, when they swapped out the full bed. Since he was a smart guy, Chuch glanced between the cop and me, and then decided he had business in the office.

Jesse's sun-streaked hair was disheveled, his jaw unshaven. In faded Levi's and a blue-and-white-striped dress shirt, he looked weary and rumpled. I didn't know whether I'd contributed to that, or if it had just been a bad day at work. God knew his job wasn't easy on the best of days.

"I didn't want to get into it on the phone," he said, "but I lost you."

"What do you mean?"

"I can't feel you anymore. Last week, you went quiet."

Strange. In the jungle, I remembered telling myself I needed to block better and not broadcast my feelings. *Looks like it worked.* That meant I didn't have him reading my moods anymore, no special advantage on his part. I had to admit that made him more attractive to me.

"You must've been worried."

He closed his eyes, and his lashes curled up against his cheeks, shining gold in the lamplight. "Until you answered the phone this morning, I thought you were dead."

"I'm sorry." The words seemed pitiful and inadequate.

Only then did he move, sweeping me up into a bonecrushing embrace. Jesse buried his face in my hair, and I could feel him shaking. This wasn't my need or my desire influencing him. I wrapped my arms around his waist and rubbed his back.

"God, I'm glad to see you." The low fervency in his voice touched me.

Before, I'd always possessed a kernel of doubt about him, suspecting he wouldn't be attracted to me if we hadn't shared a weak moment where my sex drive got the better of me. I'd always secretly supposed he'd lose interest in me without my emotions for feedback. More telling, he didn't even comment on the fact that I was thinner. I'm not sure he even noticed.

Despite my distrust, this was real. And I could build a life with Jesse Saldana. Maybe he didn't have to give up everything to prove he wanted to be with me. I doubted I would've moved of my own volition, but since I had no shop in Mexico, Shannon and I could rebuild here. She'd said she didn't want to settle down in Texas, but once we got the thrift store going, we could travel.

I knew the score. I could spend my life alone, pining for the impossible. Nothing would ever change as long as I clung to unattainable dreams and distant memories. It was ridiculous to think my life would alter in any meaningful way when I kept making the same mistakes. I was familiar enough with my own weaknesses to realize that if I let myself, I'd fall in love with Kel, given the least encouragement. Or I could wise up, face the facts, and make a different choice—a conscious one this time, not left to messy, desperate impulses.

You've been saying you want a normal life, a normal guy. Here he is. Time to put your money where your mouth is. Love wasn't magickal; I could finally accept that. There would be no Prince Charming to sweep me off my feet. Deep down, I always hoped for perfection to balance the terrible decisions I'd made when I was younger. But the best I could hope for was a man who offered a reasonable fit, one who cared. Jesse did. It wasn't contingent on my gift, what I did for him, or even how I looked.

"I'm glad to see you too," I managed to say.

"I feel like I've gone blind," he said softly. "I don't know whether you want me to kiss you or let you go."

Part of me still mourned what I'd lost in the jungle, while the rest of me accepted the impossibility of it. I had to stop myself from wanting what I couldn't have. I wondered if that made Jesse "good enough"? Somebody I could have without wishing for the moon. Maybe that was all anyone could hope.

"Maybe you'd better wait to hear what I have to say before we start kissing." *You may not want to afterward*, went unspoken but he got the message and stepped back.

As if they had been waiting for the cue—and they probably had been—Chuch, Eva, and Shannon came back into the living room. Chuch settled in his armchair, and the sight hurt, because in my mind's eye I saw Kel there, watching TV Azteca and petting Butch. I hadn't known him at all then.

Once everyone settled, I summarized my situation. I expected the outcry that followed. To my shock, Shannon and Eva were most vociferous in telling me why I couldn't use myself as bait. Chuch shared Escobar's opinion that it was the most efficient way to draw Montoya out. Jesse sat silent with his jaw clenched.

"I'm having my mother's grimoires sent here," I went on. "For obvious reasons, I can't stay until I put some proper wards on the place."

Eva raised a brow. "I thought they didn't work for you."

"They didn't before. They might now." I didn't elaborate. "I've probably been here too long as it is. I'm putting too much faith in Escobar's amulet, when I really don't know the man. He might think nothing of having a shoot-out here—without warning me first. Which means I need to keep moving." I turned to Shannon. "Could you run me over to—"

"Get your bag. And your dog." Jesse pushed to his feet. "As I'm sure you understand, Corine and I have things to discuss. I'll take her home with me tonight."

I'd never heard that tone before; he was worrying me a little. He seemed like an easygoing guy, but like most, he had limits. It appeared I'd found them.

"Will you be okay?" I asked Shannon.

She grinned at me. "I should be asking *you* that. But yeah, I'm fine."

While Shannon gathered up Butch's food and water dish, along with enough kibble to last a couple of days, I grabbed my suitcase. Jesse's bitter chocolate eyes narrowed as he watched me, and then with a muttered farewell, he towed me by hand out to the Forester. He bodily boosted me inside and then peeled out of Chuch's driveway in a squeal of tires.

We drove at least halfway back to town in seething silence before he spoke through gritted teeth. "You're working for Ramiro Escobar."

So maybe I wouldn't put it like that, but in essence, yes.

"Who else was I gonna call, Ghostbusters?"

He didn't take the sarcasm well. "Christ almighty, Corine, bad as Montoya is, Escobar is worse, because he's *not* crazy. If he decides to have someone killed, he's weighed the P and L of it. Doesn't that bother you at all?"

Of course it did. But he didn't have the right to judge me. "You can never understand," I said softly. "Your history makes you strong and centered and certain you're always on the side of right."

"Not always. But I damn well know you don't dine with the devil to kill a demon." He slammed his fist against the dash. "Vigilante justice is against the law. I crossed the line once. Since it happened in Mexico, I tell myself it doesn't count, but it does, and anything else is self-deception. How many times are you going to ask me to look the other way? When you know where Montoya will be, let the law handle him. I can contact federal agents who would *love* to lock him up."

"You think that will stop it? Even if Montoya's lawyers didn't get him out on a loophole, he could still send people after me from prison. You know that. This only ends Wild West style—him or me."

A fulminating silence followed my words, and it lasted until he slammed his car into the parking lot where he presumably lived. I'd been to Laredo twice, and Jesse had always just picked me up at Chuch and Eva's, or we met somewhere else. Which meant I'd never seen his home.

He lived in a three-story brick building. It wasn't part of a complex, but there was a small lot attached with a security camera on a light pole. I put Butch down in case our fighting had given him a nervous bladder; it had. Jesse let himself in the front door with a key, and jogged up two flights. It was a testament to his anger that he let me carry my own suitcase. I went up with less alacrity. I had a feeling the scrap wasn't over; this was just the intermission.

His apartment was different than I expected; probably

I could credit his mother for the décor. The place was a homey jumble of plaids and stripes that harmonized because of the colors. White walls, of course—it was a rental—but everything else had red and yellow running through the pattern. Overstuffed furniture with throw pillows added real warmth. The place had one bedroom, living and dining combo room, kitchen, and bath. Not much to see, but it was cute and clean. I should've guessed as much from his uncluttered desk at work.

Jesse disappeared into the bedroom. Once I set my bag down, Butch hopped out and went around sniffing. If there was anything out of the ordinary here, he'd find it. The little dog had an uncanny ability to scent supernatural skullduggery.

I put my flowered bag down and dropped onto the couch. Likely I'd be sleeping here, so good thing the fabric felt soft and smooth beneath my fingertips. Leaning my head back, I closed my eyes. If it wasn't for the fact that if something went wrong, Jesse could have Laredo SWAT here in a few minutes, I wouldn't be here. Chuch and Eva would *not* be caught in the cross fire this time.

A few minutes later, Butch pawed at my leg. I bent down and picked him up. He snuggled into my lap with complete confidence, which told me the place was secure for now. It drove me nuts worrying about Montoya's resources, whether he knew about Chuch and Eva, if Shannon was safe with them. I fought the urge to call, like an overprotective parent, and toyed with the charm around my neck instead.

When Jesse emerged a bit later, his hair was damp. He must've taken a shower to cool off. I almost smiled at that. He propped himself against the wall just inside the living room.

"Is it always going to be like this with you?"

"What?" But I knew what he meant.

"Is it always going to come down to a choice between upholding the law and protecting you?"

"I don't know," I said quietly. "But it might. I'm not

Heather." I named a pyro ex of his who had gone to prison for arson. "But I'm not the girl your mother always wanted you to bring home either."

He exhaled in an unsteady rush. "There's something I never told you about Heather."

"And that is?"

"I'm the one who put her away."

Ah, damn. I understood his raw reaction to my working outside the law. He'd been forced to make this choice before. Any other time, I might've made some joke about how bad girls proved irresistible to him. But his obvious torment made me feel tender and protective toward him. Sure, he had a white-knight complex a mile wide; he always wanted to save the damsel in distress, but I'd discovered I preferred slaying my own dragons. If he couldn't accept that, then our relationship would be stillborn, even if he offered the best chance at a normal life.

"Look, in the usual course, don't worry about me breaking the law. I wouldn't have chosen Escobar as my partner, but I don't want to die either." I sat forward, elbows on my knees. "That's the one thing you need to know about me. I'm a survivor, and I'll do whatever it takes."

In fact, it was worse than he knew. If I died, I went straight to hell, because I had a demon debt weighing on my soul. Back in Kilmer, I'd been fatally stabbed, and the demon saved my life by using the murderer's knife to plug the wound. Oh, I could've objected, but if I had, I would've expired on the spot. If I failed to satisfy the compact, both my life and soul were forfeit. Nervously, my fingers went to the metal in my side. Not repaying Maury before eternity punched my card . . . well. It didn't bear consideration. I'd gotten a glimpse of the place when Caim crawled back home, and I had no interest in making a personal visit. So I had to stay alive, no matter what it took, until Maury called his marker due.

The alliance with Escobar also carried a heavenly blessing, but I wouldn't tell Jesse that. Sometimes I found it hard to credit, as if those days with Kel had been a vivid dream.

"I can't condemn you for that. It makes you strong, and I admire that about you." Jesse pushed away from the wall then and sauntered toward me with deceptively lazy strides. "You're wrong about one thing, though."

"What's that?"

"My mama wants me with somebody who makes me happy. That's all."

"And *I* mostly make you mad."

His dark eyes crinkled with a smile. "Yeah, you do. But only because I care."

"You sure you don't see me as some fixer-upper project?"

Jesse sat down beside me. "Not anymore. At first, sure, because that's the way I'm wired, but there's no changing you. You're stubborn as hell, and I either love you like you are, or I don't."

His easy use of that word tightened my stomach. I didn't know if I wanted to know, if I was ready to hear it. I damn sure didn't know how *I* felt. Instead of time clearing up my confusion, now I had more, because I secretly wanted something I could never have, and if that wasn't self-destructive behavior, then I'd never encountered it.

I heard myself say, "And?"

He threaded his hands into my hair, delicate as fireflies at dusk, and leaned his brow against mine. "I do. I'm not sure I even knew myself before last week, but when you went quiet on me, I don't know when I ever felt so grim. Thinking I'd never see you . . ." Jesse trailed off and shook his head, dusting a kiss against my temple. "I don't want that feeling again."

Sweet, powerful emotions stirred in response to his declaration. I couldn't tell him I loved him. Not yet. So I did the next-best thing, and for me, it constituted a hell of a leap. "You know how you've been saying you want me to meet your family?"

"Yeah."

"Think maybe your mom could set an extra place some night this week?"

He wrapped his arms around me. "She'd love to. For about the last month or so, she's been pestering me about the secret girl I'm seeing. I didn't have the heart to tell her it was virtual dating. I don't think she'd understand."

Despite my nerves, I smiled. "Most people wouldn't."

Hell, I didn't myself. I wasn't sure if this was right; I knew only that if I claimed to want a normal life, opening myself up to Jesse made the most sense of anything I'd ever done. Kel couldn't give me that. Neither could Chance, even if he'd wanted to, and clearly he didn't. He talked a good game, but when I demanded a good-faith payment, he disappeared. So this was a logical step, a commitment to my future. With Jesse's empathy blind to me, it might be the beginning of something special.

"So that's it?" he asked. "You're my girl?"

I told myself he was the only one who cared enough to stay, and I nodded. "I am."

"I have a couple of ladies to let down easy, then." He wore a sheepish look.

If anything, I admired his honesty. I didn't begrudge him a good time while we were doing the long-distance thing, but if we intended to take a real run at this, we had to go all the way with promises and monogamy. I was ready.

Butch stirred between us. At first I thought it was Jesse's proximity, but he hopped down with a little whine. He trotted toward the door and then glanced back at us with an imploring, bug-eyed look. With any other dog, I'd guess he needed to pee again.

With Butch, it meant something bad was on the way up. No question. God, I wished I knew how to fight, but this was exactly why I hadn't wanted to stay long at Chuch and Eva's place. *Please don't let anything happen to them. Please, please, please, please.* I saw Eva's face, glowing when she talked about the baby, and Chuch's complete pride and adoration.

And then, of course, there was Shannon. I loved her like a little sister, and we had plans together. As soon as this was all over, we were going to open a new shop together.

Spooky Vintage. The name had resonance. I'd ask Shan if she liked it, if I lived.

Jesse summed up the situation in a glance; he knew to take the dog seriously too. "Behind the couch," he growled at me, and then spun—he went toward the bedroom at a dead run. When he came back, he held a cocked gun; he took a tactical position beside the door.

From my place crouched behind the sofa, I heard footsteps. Butch must've detected them as soon as they came into the foyer downstairs. Those oversize ears of his worked like satellite dishes. Butch trotted up beside me, but he had sense enough not to make any noise. I pulled him into my arms and curled my body over the top of him.

Belatedly it occurred to me that Jesse was one human being. He might be well trained, and he might be a cop in good shape, but at base, he was an empath. He couldn't survive multiple stab wounds like Kel. He couldn't live through a demon shoving a claw through his chest. *Oh, Christ, what have I done?* But it was too late for self-recrimination.

Montoya's men burst into the apartment and filled the air with hot lead.

Mundane Mayhem

I didn't see how it all went down, but I heard the gunplay and cries of pain. Butch hid his face in my arms; I made myself remain still and quiet and until Jesse said, "You can come out now."

There were three. Two had been shot and the other one lay cuffed on the ground. I didn't recognize them, but that meant nothing. Montoya had a practically never-ending supply of foot soldiers.

"You all right?"

"Yeah."

But he kept a hand against his side. If that meant what I thought it did, this was the second time he'd been shot defending me. As I watched, a slow trickle of blood bubbled through his fingertips. I ran toward him and helped him to a chair. Somehow he managed to keep his gun trained on the injured shooter.

"Backup will be here any minute, along with the paramedics." Jesse waved me away when I offered to get bandages.

"It don't matter. He'll just keep sending men until the *puta* is dead." The handcuffed killer glared at me. "In fact, we got a team heading for another location as we speak. Choke on that, bitch."

Shit. Oh, shit. He knew about Chuch and Eva. With shaking hands, I got out my cell phone and hit my speed dial. *Pick up, pick up, pick up.*

"What's up, *prima*?" I had never been so happy to hear the mechanic's voice.

"Get out now," I told him, nearly frantic. "Montoya's sending a squad over to your place. Do you have anywhere you can go?"

"Well, sure, but—"

"No *but*. Go. Go *now*."

"Hang on a sec." I heard him call out: "Eva, pack a bag." And then: "Okay, we're on it. Thanks for the warning." He paused. "Oh, shit. I gotta go. They're here."

And the phone went dead, but not before I heard gunshots. "Jesse, can you report a crime faster than nine-one-one?"

His color wasn't good, and his hand shook as he got out his phone. "Yeah. Chuch's place?" At my nod, he called a patrolman he knew. He summarized the situation in pained gasps, then added, "You'll need more than one car. Get there fast."

The guy on the floor laughed. Shortly thereafter the paramedics arrived and took care of the two injured shooters. By the damage, it was obvious who had done what, so once they stabilized, they'd be sent to the station for processing. Other cops arrived within a few seconds, and my skin started to crawl.

They all snapped alert when a tall, gray-haired man stepped into the apartment. "Saldana, you all right?"

"I'm fine, Lieutenant. Surprised to see you."

His boss smiled. "I was in the neighborhood, felt like stopping by. You want to tell me what happened?"

"I suspect this was a reprisal related to the death of Nathan Moon and the destruction of a key human-trafficking facility belonging to the Montoya cartel."

So that was how he spun it. Well, it fit the facts, more or less. He just wasn't the intended target. But I had my answer, didn't I? Even with a bullet in his side, Jesse Saldana chose to protect me, even if it meant lying to his boss.

"Are you telling me the cartel's put a price on your head, son?"

Jesse looked his boss square in the eye and lied. "Yes, sir."

"Then after you leave the hospital, you're heading for a safe house."

Alarm flashed in his dark brown eyes. I knew exactly what he was thinking—that if he got locked up for his own protection, I'd be on my own. "That won't be necessary. I can handle this."

"The hell you can. They shot up your apartment, and it was damn lucky they didn't catch you sleeping. No, we'll take it from here. Sooner or later, one of Montoya's men will roll, tell us when he's gonna be in the country next, and then we'll have him."

I didn't think that was likely, but it was also better I didn't draw attention to myself. As the paramedics helped Jesse from the couch onto the gurney, the lieutenant walking alongside, Jesse cast a desperate look over his shoulder. I smiled at him, telling him wordlessly that it was okay. Since he belonged to a brotherhood, this development didn't surprise me.

A cop came over to take my statement. I stuck with Jesse's story, since it made sense. No, I hadn't seen anything. I was hiding behind the couch the whole time—and how that rankled. Demons I could deal with, but I could do nothing about men with guns. I *so* needed to learn how to use a weapon.

"We're all set here," the cop said at last. "If we need anything else, we'll call you."

I'd given him my cell number, since I didn't have a physical address. "Will it be okay if I take Jesse's Forester to see how he's doing? I don't have my car here." Or anywhere—I didn't own one. "What hospital did they take him to?"

"Let me find out." He got on the phone and a minute later he said, "Doctors Hospital. Need the address?"

"Please."

Silently, I chafed with the need to find out what had happened at Chuch's place as well, but I scrawled the address

with a murmur of thanks. I snagged Jesse's keys from the
hook beside the door. A crime-scene crew was setting up
their gear as I left. Blood spattered the place and bullet holes
dotted the wall, testifying to the fact that the bad guys had
come in with guns blazing.

If not for Butch, they might've caught us on the couch,
as we'd been moments before. Easy pickings. Jesse had time
to get his weapon and take a strategic position, thanks to
the dog's early warning. I rubbed his head and he nuzzled
my hand. Butch seemed just as upset about Jesse and maybe
even worried about Chuch, Eva, and Shannon. There was
no telling how much he knew or understood. Sometimes I
had the feeling it might surprise me.

With lead in my stomach, I punched the address into the
GPS. Though I wasn't supposed to drive and dial, I called
Chuch's cell. No answer—it went straight to voice mail. I
fought down the fear. If anything happened to them, it'd be
my fault. Escobar had claimed he would protect me, but I
didn't see much evidence of it, apart from the amulet, which
offered no aid against mundane attack.

And then I remembered what he'd said: *It will drive Montoya mad when his sorcerer fails . . . and fails and fails.
He'll contact you, if I know him at all.* I really was bait. Not
once or when I removed the amulet. Escobar had fully expected this, so in a way, he was still testing me. If I survived long enough to drive Montoya over the edge, he'd use
me—if not, no big loss. I shouldn't be surprised; Escobar
was the coldest son of a bitch I'd ever met.

It didn't take long to reach the hospital, a blocky gold
building designed in modern style. I parked, ran through the
parking lot and into the lobby. At the information desk, I
asked, "Do you know where they took Jesse Saldana?"

"Are you family?"

"No."

"Then I'm afraid I can't give you any information."

I set my jaw. "I was *with* him when he was shot. If you
don't tell me what I want to know, I'll create the grand-
daddy of all scenes. Want to find out how loud I scream?"

"Girlfriend, then. That's close enough." Her worried smile said she thought I might start yelling anyway. "Ah, yes. He's being prepped for surgery."

That couldn't be as ominous as it sounded. I went up to the waiting room nonetheless and tried Chuch again. He picked up this time.

"Is everyone okay?"

"They didn't stay." He sounded weird, subdued. "Just fired a few warning shots. I got the fire department out here now."

Fire department—

"Oh, no," I breathed.

"I gotta go. Eva's crying." The stark simplicity of his grief hit me like a fist.

They'd burned his house down. A Molotov cocktail would do the job. I could see the scene all too clearly, and it filled me with white-hot rage: everything they'd achieved in their lives, gone, and all the work on the nursery, destroyed.

I could handle being hunted. In one form or another, I was used to it, but when they targeted women and unborn babies, they went too far. I was staring at my hands, trying to figure out my next move, when someone cleared his throat.

Glancing up, I saw Jesse's lieutenant standing before me. "No organ damage but they have to go in, remove the bullet, and do a little repair work." He sat down beside me. "I'm his boss, Lieutenant Glencannon. Try not to worry about him."

I kept my hands laced in my lap, hiding the scars and brands. People always viewed my palms as evidence that there was something wrong with me. And there was, just not in the way they thought.

"Thanks." I didn't know what he wanted, but when cops paid attention to me, apart from Jesse, it seldom ended well.

"So you're the girlfriend?" he asked in a musing tone.

"I guess." The relationship was too new for me to feel comfortable discussing it with his superior. God, we'd barely agreed to try when Jesse wound up taking a bullet for me. Shit, if I'd ever doubted it, I was poison. Maybe I should aim myself at Kel, because he could survive me.

"You haven't visited him at the station . . . and he doesn't have any pictures of you in his office."

Now I felt like he was leading up to an interrogation. "I travel a lot . . . and we haven't been together long." Massive understatement.

"Well, don't let tonight put you off," he said. "While there's always a certain risk in dating a cop, it's usually not quite like this."

No shit. But I finally got it. He was being paternal and protective because he thought my bowed head and silence hinted at shock or traumatic stress.

"I'm just afraid for him," I said quietly. "You'll make sure nobody can get to him, won't you?"

"My word on it. I'll post guards on his hospital room, and when he's recovered enough, I'll oversee his transfer myself." He hesitated. "You understand, for security reasons, you won't be permitted any contact with him while he's in protective custody."

If he expected me to pitch a fit, he was mistaken. "I understand."

Whatever else he might have said was forestalled by the arrival of a woman who could only be Jesse's mother. She looked exactly as he'd described her: small, brown, and round like a partridge. Her dark hair stood on end, and her makeup had smeared from the tears. A tall, lean man trailed in her wake; I saw more resemblance to Jesse in him. I stood as they approached the waiting area.

"Mike," Jesse's dad greeted Lieutenant Glencannon. "What news?"

"He'll be fine."

"Oh, thank God." Mrs. Saldana burst into tears and her husband pulled her into his arms as easy as breathing. He stroked her back while talking quietly to Jesse's boss.

I felt like an interloper and I had just decided to slip

away when Mrs. Saldana raised her head. "You must be the girl Jesse wouldn't tell me about. I'm glad to meet you, but sorry it's under these circumstances."

Ironic, I had just agreed to have dinner with them, and here they were. I mustered a smile. I felt vaguely surprised he'd mentioned me to his parents. Jesse was so different from any man I'd ever dated; he made no secret of his emotions or his intentions.

"Me too. I'm Corine, by the way."

I extended a hand, only to have her tug me into a motherly embrace. She patted my back gently, as if she thought I might break down . . . because normal women didn't handle gunshots with such aplomb. As I'd known all along, I wasn't the girl she expected. But I returned the hug, absorbing the warmth. Jesse's dad put a hand on my shoulder—just that, only that, and it was both awful and enlightening. I'd forgotten what family felt like.

"If you folks will excuse me, I have some arrangements to make." Glencannon strode away.

A few seconds later, his parents let me go. I'd intended to leave, but it didn't seem right, now. I sat as Mrs. Saldana asked, "Can you tell us what happened? The officer who came to the house only said he'd been shot."

To keep Jesse's story straight, I had to lie. Self-loathing spilled through me. "A while back, Jesse crossed a powerful cartel boss. His partner was dirty, and Jesse found out. Now Montoya wants revenge." At her intake of breath, I hastened to add: "But Glencannon is pulling him off the street. They're going to do a sting or something to arrest the guy. Jesse won't be hurt further."

Lie after lie after lie. But I found I wanted to protect her faith in a world that worked according to certain laws, where the guilty were punished and good men didn't die for no reason. Relief etched her features. Mr. Saldana rubbed her back gently; he looked so much like Jesse, just older and more weathered, that it hurt me to look at him. I could have this, if I was brave enough. *If I survive.*

We waited about an hour before a nurse came to give us an update. "He's in stable condition. He has some healing to do, but there's no permanent harm."

"When can we see him?" Mrs. Saldana demanded.

"You can look in on him now, if you like, but he won't be awake for hours yet."

Feeling like an impostor the whole time, I followed the Saldanas down the hall to Jesse's room. Against the pale sheets, his skin glowed tawny, but it didn't make up for the lack of life in his face. Attached to machines and tubes, he struck me as fragile for the first time since I'd met him.

I'd made a mistake in turning to my friends in this mess. When I allied with Escobar, I had the right idea. If this vendetta caused him casualties, I didn't care. I simply couldn't risk further harm to people who mattered.

"I'm going to sit with him awhile," Mrs. Saldana said, eyes again wet with tears.

Murmuring a noncommittal nothing, I fled.

As Montoya had known, these attacks closed all the usual doors to me. Part of me wanted to summon Kel, but he had other orders. I'd never ask him to choose between his mission and me.

I hurried out of the hospital and ran toward the Forester. I couldn't use this vehicle much longer. Montoya's men knew what Jesse drove; they'd known where he lived too. He might have people watching the hospital as well.

In the dark between parking lot lights, the shadows swarmed. Maybe the sorcerer couldn't get to me as long as I wore this pendant, but a bullet could. At each sound, each movement, I flinched, and my hands shook by the time I got to the vehicle. The Forester beeped as I turned off the alarm and slid inside. When I started the engine, I half expected the SUV to blow up.

Instead, as I took off, my phone rang. I answered without checking the number. "Yeah?"

"Can you come get me?" Even through the static, Shannon sounded shaky. "Chuch and Eva are going to her mom's, but I don't feel like I can tag along." I heard Chuch arguing that she should go and Shannon's stubborn refusal.

Never mind that I didn't know where I was going, or that I shouldn't be driving this car around. She needed me. "Where are you?"

"I'll have them drop me off." She named an all-night restaurant near the mall.

"I'll be there in fifteen minutes."

In fact, I cut the trip to ten. She was inside nursing a Coke when I arrived. Her face lit with relief when she saw me. I dropped a few bills on the table and assessed her physical state. In the fluorescent light, I could see smears of soot on her pale skin. She'd washed her face, but the backs of her hands showed signs of the fire.

"How bad is it?" I asked, sitting down beside her instead of across the booth.

"Bad. They took out most of the front room and couple of Chuch's cars."

"The Opal and the Impala?" I guessed.

She nodded. "He's really pissed." That made me wince. "No, not at you. I'm afraid of what he's going to do once he gets Eva settled."

Shit, that sounded like Chuch. He'd once made it clear what would happen if anyone went after his family. Montoya had rattled a dangerous cage by targeting his wife and unborn child. God knew I didn't want to wind up on the wrong side of him, but he might bite off more than he could chew, alone.

I gave her a hug and she returned it fiercely. For just a moment I closed my eyes and whispered in my head: *Please let me keep her safe.*

"We'll deal with that when the time comes," I said, regarding Chuch. "So can I put you on a bus? It's a long way to Oklahoma City, and you'll be safer with your dad."

She grinned, visibly recovering from her shock and fright. "I wouldn't know what to do with 'safer.' Hanging around with you is the most fun I ever had."

A little whuff of a laugh escaped me. "You're crazy."

"Maybe. But so're you." She made a *duh* face. "And you get me. You know where I come from. That's why we're best friends."

I'd never thought of it in so many words, but we were—of *course* we were. And unlike Sara, who had been my best pal in Tampa, I could never leave Shannon behind. At this point, she was the most important person in my life. Though men might come and go, our friendship was forever.

"Okay, then. We have to keep moving." I led the way to the Forester.

Right now, Montoya's men were looking for us in places where we'd gone before. I'd miscalculated in coming to Laredo. That meant I had to break my patterns and develop new habits.

"Do you know where we're going?"

"First, La Rosa Negra." It was a little dive I'd visited once before with Chuch, full of Escobar's men. I hoped I remembered how to get there. If the bastard wouldn't send soldiers to guard me, I'd find them. If luck played a part, I might even find Esteban there. "After that, we'll see."

Shannon wrapped her arms around Butch, who had crawled out of my purse and into her lap. "I trust you have a plan?"

"In fact, I do."

I couldn't fight. My skills with a gun were indifferent. But I had a good brain, and I wouldn't let anyone else get hurt because of me. If they wanted a chase, I'd lead them a merry one. I knew how to be prey, and when they caught me, I'd show them I'd grown teeth.

I just needed one night to prepare first.

The Black Rose

I didn't find La Rosa Negra on the first try. Not surprisingly, it wasn't listed in the GPS, and I drove around the back-streets of Laredo before stumbling into an adjacent avenue that I recognized. Bangers and wannabes stared after us, assessing the likelihood of jacking our ride. If only they knew.

After a couple more turns, we arrived at the same crumbling green stucco building, same Corona sign in the window as the last time I'd visited; a line of restored classic cars ran from the front door around the block. A few men stood outside, smoking, the haze curling up toward the sky. Distant city lights dimmed the stars, making it seem as though a gray veil lay over the world.

I recognized Ricardo Arjona playing inside, *"Sin Ti . . . Sin Mi."* I loved his voice, mellow, soulful, and full of longing. As I stepped inside, I remembered how Chance had shown me a side of him I didn't know existed. Yearning and melancholy twisted up inside me; a small part of me wished he hadn't run from the idea of making a real effort instead of offering empty words, but I'd made up my mind to move on. No more of that. Jesse Saldana defended me with his life; that meant everything.

My gaze touched the familiar features of the cantina: scarred wood floor, mismatched tables and chairs, amber paper lanterns, and neon *cerveza* signs. Only the oil panting of the lady with the black rose distinguished this dive from any other. Like last time, hard-eyed men studied us with watchful suspicion, and I didn't see Esteban anywhere.

"You sure about this?" Shannon whispered.

In fact, I wasn't, but it was the only idea I had. Kel had said, *Muster your allies and prepare for war.* Not friends. He hadn't meant Chuch and Eva or even Jesse; I just hadn't glimpsed enough of the future yet to realize it. In retrospect, I realized he'd told me as much as he could—without risking spoilers. I had to make the decisions on my own, not through his direct intervention.

Knowing I couldn't show fear or hesitation, I strode to the center of the bar. *"Apague la música."*

"¿Por qué?" one of the dancers demanded, even as the bartender complied.

I pulled my pendant outside my shirt and held it up, then spoke in English. "This is why. Who recognizes this?"

As I'd hoped, a little gasp went through the room as I spun, giving them a better look. I'd gambled everything on Escobar's being too much the egoist not to use his own personal mark on a protective amulet. The mood shifted, and the danger passed.

A tall, dark-haired man with gray at his temples stood up and invited us to join him. From his expression, he was high man present, so I'd do business with him. His skin held the weathered bronze of one who had worked a great deal outdoors, making it hard to judge his age.

"I am Francisco Zaragoza." He extended a hand to both Shannon and me. No spark, which meant he was a normal human.

"Mucho gusto," I murmured. "I'm Corine Solomon and this is my friend Shannon Cheney."

Zaragoza inclined his head. "What does Señor Escobar wish of us?"

I knew only what *I* wanted. "I'm waging a war against Montoya. I need four of your best men."

"Best in what sense? The men in this room possess a wide variety of skills."

My gaze met his. "Destruction of property and, if it comes down to it, killing. Montoya hit a couple of sites today, quite against my interests."

"I understand." He surveyed the room with assessing eyes. "Then I will give you García, Petrel, Santos, and Morales. You understand, however, that I must verify your authority?"

"Of course," I said quietly. "I could've stolen the amulet."

Zaragoza's eyes flickered. "That would be most . . . unwise."

"Go ahead. Call it in."

Beside me, Shannon practically vibrated with tension. It went without saying what would happen to us if Escobar denied me. As Zaragoza went outside with his cell phone, the waitress stopped at the table.

"Something to drink?" she asked.

Given my current endeavor, only one drink would do. "Shady Lady."

In a place like this, she wouldn't be carded, but Shannon still ordered a Coke. "Gotta keep my head clear. I'll be your designated driver."

She had a point. I handed the server a bill to cover our drinks and murmured, "Keep it."

The waitress brightened and went to give our order to the bartender. It didn't take long for her to serve us. Mine was pretty, made with melon liqueur, tequila, and grapefruit juice, garnished with cherry and lime, and it tasted better than it looked. I'd be the first to admit that I needed a drink, after the turn my life had taken.

Shortly, Zaragoza returned, phone in hand. "He wants to speak with you."

I took the cell and said, "Hello?"

"So you make your first move." Escobar sounded amused. "I wondered how long it would take."

"You said I should stay alive. You never said how or using what resources."

"I know," he answered. "Which is why I am giving you the soldiers you ask for. This should prove quite entertaining."

"I'm so glad." I gave the phone back to Zaragoza, who spoke a few more words in Spanish and then terminated the call.

"It seems you speak the truth," he said, sitting down once more. "It took four phone calls to reach Señor Escobar, but he knew who you were at once."

"Excellent. In addition to the men, I need a safe house in the area, something you don't think Montoya would know about. A recent purchase would be best."

Zaragoza thought for a moment. "We have a place down in the industrial area. It's not a good neighborhood, but people are unlikely to notice any strange occurrences there and even less likely to answer the police, if they ask."

I paused. "You're not even going to ask how I know him?"

"I have learned the hard way to restrain my curiosity," he said with a faint trace of irony. "But if I had to guess, I would say you're his latest *brujas*."

Shannon smirked at me. With her black clothing, dyed hair, and heavily outlined eyes, she fit the profile. I neither confirmed nor denied his supposition, but merely smiled. If fear laced their obedience, even better—they'd be less likely to cross us.

"Give me the address."

He scrawled it on a napkin. God, I could get used to this kind of power. No wonder people worked for Escobar. His name carried serious weight.

"Anything else, *patrona*?"

"Find me a property owned by Montoya, something it will hurt him to lose. Something . . . expensive."

Zaragoza grinned, showing a slight gap between his two front teeth. "This mission, I could get to like it a whole lot."

"Can you get me the info?" I remembered it took a day or two for Esteban to get his hands on a list of properties, but I suspected Zaragoza could get faster results with Escobar's name lending weight.

"Let me make a few calls."

Shannon leaned over and whispered, "You can be scary, you know that?"

I allowed a sharp smile. "Good. We'll need that."

For a few moments, I watched the couples dancing. Now Paulina sang "*Causa y Efecto*"—a more up-tempo song than one would expect to hear in here. It hurt a little watching them twirl and spin. Despite Shannon's presence beside me, I felt lonely and unsure, but at the same time, a core of pride grew—that I was handling this myself, just like the fall into the river. I'd make Montoya wish he'd never been born for killing two innocent men, hurting Jesse, burning Chuch and Eva's house, and rendering me homeless.

By the time Shan finished her second Coke, Zaragoza returned. "He's got a place in Sonterra, far north side of San Antonio."

"Perfect. I have a sketch here. . . ." I dug it out of my bag; it was very battered, but at least it hadn't gone into the jungle with us. "Do you recognize this man?"

Zaragoza froze and then crossed himself. "*Madre de Dios.*"

"I take it you do," Shannon said.

The breath slipped out of him in a pained sound. "That's Diego Montoya's younger brother, Vicente."

Holy shit. I hadn't been prepared for that. "Tell me what you know about him."

"Not much. He's been out of Mexico for a long time."

I nodded. "Anything you could share would be helpful."

Zaragoza thought for a moment and then conferred with some of his men. "He's always been a hedge wizard, little training. And for a while, he managed their business in Colombia, but lately the word is Diego sent him to the islands after his warlock died to learn the dark magick."

"What islands?" Shannon asked.

I gave her a nod; I would've asked that myself. Leaning forward, I sipped my drink, listening, and considered what this meant. If he had some magickal talent even then, Vicente would have been present for the ritual Min conducted, and he would've known it for a true summoning. The Knights of Hell couldn't be faked. But he must have been sent back to Colombia when she was stalling there at the end, claiming the astrological elements weren't aligned for curse removal. Otherwise he'd have certainly told Diego that she was full of it. Therefore, the dynamics had shifted, and there was no telling what he'd learned since then. The scope of his power must be considerable since he'd sent Caim after me.

"Haiti, Jamaica," Zaragoza said with a shrug. "After he mastered his craft—and I'm telling street stories now, nothing more—Montoya sent Vicente to put the fear of God in his Colombian partners."

"But he called him back," I guessed. "When he realized he needed help dealing with me."

"Tell me about it. Two *brujas* are way too much for one normal man to handle." Zaragoza flashed us a sly grin edged in mischief.

I tucked the sketch into my bag, shaking my head. "His brother. He'll definitely keep him close, after what happened to his warlock, Moon."

"What?" he asked.

"My people killed him," I said softly. "I'll take the men with me now."

He nodded. After he spoke with Escobar and then us, Zaragoza's manner became deferential. Evidently he saw in my demeanor a woman worthy of respect. I'd never known the like.

"García, Petrel, Santos, and Morales!" He beckoned to them.

The four men, who had been playing cards, stood up and headed over to our table. García was mid-thirties, short and stocky, with unexpectedly graceful hands. Petrel was a tall, lanky youth who I would've taken for French or Belgian, if I'd seen him anywhere but here. Santos had the look of a grizzled war veteran, gone gray, and acne scarred, whereas Morales was the best-looking—smooth brown skin, dark liquid eyes, and the handsome features of a man who was used to getting what he wanted from women. I suspected that if anybody gave us trouble, it'd be him.

"*¿Sí, jefe?*" Santos asked.

"*¡Inglés, cabrón!*" Zaragoza switched to English himself. "Escobar has given you to these ladies. I expect you to obey their orders as if I gave them. *¿Comprenden?*"

Morales said, "Yeah, we got it."

I finished my drink in a long swallow. Though one cocktail wasn't enough to impair me, I tossed the keys to Shan. I'd rather be in the passenger seat with this crew, where I could keep an eye on them.

"Let's go," I said.

Santos nodded. "*Claro.*"

The men filed out behind us. Since Santos was the oldest, I judged him the senior member of the crew. "*¿Tienes un carro aquí?*" *You have a car here?*

A flicker of approval in dark, deep-set eyes said he'd rather take orders from a *güera* who spoke passable Spanish. "*Sí, patrona.*"

"*Entonces sígame con . . .*" I glanced at the rest of the crew and decided aloud, "Morales. Petrel *y* García *conmigo.*" *Then follow me with Morales. Petrel and Garcia with me.*

Shannon swung into the driver's seat while I rode shotgun. As she took off, I punched the address Zaragoza had given me into the GPS. I kept one eye on the men, using the side mirrors, but Petrel and Garcia seemed content to wait until we rejoined the others. Just as well—I wouldn't answer questions. I needed time to put on my game face, convince them I was tough, scary, and I meant business.

In the dark, the neighborhoods grew progressively worse. We passed the railroad tracks and the streets became more industrial: warehouses, crumbling apartments with broken windows. Shannon parked the Forester in front of a run-down building. It had once been white, but graffiti had nearly obscured the paint on the front.

"Around back," Garcia said. "Don't leave your ride on the street."

Petrel jumped out and went to open the gate. He fiddled with the combination lock and then swung it open for us. Shannon put the SUV in gear and passed through. He waited for the other car to slip in behind us, then locked up and followed at a lope.

Santos led us in the back way. The inside was surprisingly nice. Clean. Worn tile covered the hallway, leading up to the ground-floor apartment. Inside, it had been decorated in tasteful rustic style. Heavy blackout shades beneath the bars on the windows prevented anyone on the street from seeing what went on in here.

Perfect.

"Here's the job," I said, once we all settled in. "You drive to San Antonio. Once there, you hit this address." I passed it to Santos. "I want it blown the *fuck* up. Montoya spent a lot of money in Sonterra, and when you're finished, it should be nothing but soot and smoke. If anyone gets in your way, end 'em. I mean Montoya's guys, of course. Try to stay away from the five-oh. Any questions?"

Shannon's soft intake of breath said I'd surprised her. She sank down on the plain brown sofa with dismay written on her face. Before we were through, she might want to go live with her dad after all.

Morales leveled a slow smile on me. "Naw, *jefa*. You want us to go in hard and quiet and slip out like ghosts."

"Exactly. And make it quick. After you get some sleep, I'll have more work."

"*No hay problema*," Petrel said. "There's a reason Zaragoza tapped us."

Santos gestured and the soldiers rolled out. Once we were alone, I went back out to the SUV and brought our things in: Shannon's battered bag and my new flowered suitcase. It was hard to believe that earlier today, we had been shopping. I had been with Jesse and he'd said he loved me. Everything was different now.

I wasn't just allied with Escobar with the vague agreement that I would serve as bait. I'd given orders to his men, like his lieutenant. Part of me felt sick, while the rest knew I'd do whatever it took to end this. I refused to consider what the final cost might be.

This was my breaking point—even a cornered rat would

fight, sometimes with more ferocity than folks believed possible. While I hated the necessity, I wouldn't shrink from it. They had gone too far. I didn't want this. I hadn't started it. But from this point on, I would make an implacable adversary; I would protect the people I loved.

I set the bags down and scoped out the place thoroughly—two bedrooms, living room, kitchen, and bath. One bedroom had a full-size bed; the other offered bunk beds. I guessed this was where they stashed their women and children. The furniture was clean, despite the neighborhood, and the door had a heavy steel core. Seven dead bolts, plus a chain and crossbar reinforced it. Clearly they didn't mean for anyone to get in who didn't belong.

"You know he might have family there," she said softly. "People who haven't done anything. There might be staff who don't know what he does for a living, only that he pays well."

"I considered all of that."

"And you're still going through with it?" I hated the disillusionment in her voice. She rested her elbows on her knees and wouldn't look me in the eyes.

"Escobar made it clear I need to drive Montoya crazy. I have to push him over the edge if he's going to contact me, so I can arrange a meet." *Where he'll be shot like a dog.* "And I don't know how to accomplish it other than to pay him with his own coin. There may be casualties. I accept the risk."

"I see your point," she said dully. "But I'm glad it's not on my conscience."

There was nothing I could say. I had already let slip the dogs of war, so I merely got out my cell phone. I called the FedEx customer-service line and spent twenty minutes being transferred around, while I gave people the tracking number of the package Tia had sent from Mexico. In the end, I managed to get the grimoires rerouted. The perky rep promised I'd have my package in the morning.

"We should get some sleep," I told Shannon.

"I guess."

I hesitated, wishing I could make up for disappointing her like this. "You can have the big bed if you want."

"Whatever. I'm going to check my e-mail."

Her attitude hurt, but I couldn't rouse any anger. It was a good thing I wasn't officially a witch, part of some coven, or this path would get me booted for violating the "do as ye will, an it harm none" tenet. I took the lower bunk bed as a sort of penance, and my dreams that night were uneasy.

In the morning, I awoke to pounding on the apartment door. I'd slept in my clothes, so I rolled out of bed fully dressed with my heart hammering. *Nobody should know we're here.* Still, I stopped off at the kitchen for a knife. Stupid as it seemed, I felt better with a weapon in hand, even if I couldn't use it expertly. Anything that could break down the door would likely eat me in one bite. Nonetheless, I braced myself.

I peered out the peephole, and I recognized Petrel first. His height made him memorable. Relief blazed through me. After undoing all the locks, I let them in. They carried the smell of fire and smoke with them, and they all wore wolfish smiles. No visible injuries.

I asked nonetheless, "How'd it go?"

"No major hitches," Morales said.

"Do you have a phone?"

He nodded, so I extended a hand for it and programmed my number in. "If you need to get in touch with me, that's how."

Hesitantly, Santos offered me a package. "Are you expecting this? Should we dunk it? We pulled up just as the delivery guy was about to leave."

"No, don't." I snagged it from him, recognizing Tia's spidery writing on the label. "It's definitely for me."

Shit, I'd forgotten there was no way into the building from the front. Those doors were boarded up, as if the place had been condemned. They must've intimidated the driver into handing the parcel over. I couldn't worry about a FedEx driver's bad day, however.

"García wanted to chuck it," Petrel said.

"Well, *you* wanted to open it, *cabrón*."

They were like children, fighting to impress the schoolteacher. I stifled a sigh.

"Good work, all of you. Head home and get some sleep. I want you all back here tonight for round two, because that was only the beginning." I made a point of patting Morales on the shoulder, because he was young and cocky, and he'd least suspect a casual touch. Sure enough, he smirked as he made his way to the door.

As the soldiers left, Shannon stumbled into the living room, where I sat opening the package. Tia had wrapped the grimoires in newspaper, so it smudged off on my fingers. I washed my hands after I threw the paper away; I didn't want to stain the pages. These books were incredibly old, and they summoned a mental image of my mother as soon as I took the first one in my lap.

"Oh, wow," Shannon breathed. From her tone, she'd either forgotten she was mad at me or the grimoires trumped her anger. "Can I see?"

"Sure, but don't read any of the incantations aloud."

I handed her the blue one—with runes etched in silver, it was the smallest and contained the most advanced spells. I wouldn't try those for a long time, assuming I could make the magic work at all.

"Okay. I'll be careful." She touched the engraved cover with reverent hands.

The one I held was oversize and bound in vermilion leather; before she died, my mother had let me practice some charms. I couldn't remember whether I'd ever gotten one to function properly. I just knew I'd enjoyed spending time with her, measuring the herbs and saying the words. These were blessings, mostly, and mild spells. With these, I could make someone crave strawberries or give them a gentle run of luck; it was suitable for children.

Taking a deep breath, I opened a spell book for the first time in many years. Even the smell—old paper and ink—filled me with nostalgia. I could almost hear my mother murmuring, *Be careful with that, Corine.*

I flipped through the book until I found the spell I wanted. Nothing heavy, nothing difficult or sophisticated. Eyes fixed on the page, I memorized the chant. This was it—the big test.

Taking a deep breath, I went to the kitchen and rummaged for a plain white ceramic dish and a book of matches. I set both items on the table. Across the saucer, I laid a strand of Morales's hair, the one I'd stolen. Thus fueled, if I couldn't make this spell work, I never would. It was that simple.

With my eyes closed, I created a mental image of Morales: his black hair with a hint of a wave, his liquid brown eyes and caramel skin. I added the cocksure smile and the glint in his eyes, the hint of a swagger in his step. Then I sent the heat of my gift to fuel the compulsion; the same fire that burned me when I read an object would touch him, just a whisper.

Once I held his visage firmly in mind, I whispered, "By fire, earth, wind, and rain, you will not rest until you hear my voice again. As I will, so mote it be." In speaking the last words, I struck the match and burned his hair until there was nothing left but the lingering smell.

Shannon came to the doorway of the kitchen, watching with a raised brow. "What did you do? Did it work?"

I don't know, I started to say.

And then my cell phone rang.

Swerve

After assuring Morales we were fine, I disconnected.

Shannon stared at me with a touch of amazement. "You made him call you."

"I think so, yeah."

"What else can you do?"

"I can make breakfast." Sadly, I found only instant oatmeal in the kitchen. In sealed cartons, it kept better than milk or eggs.

But it was sustenance, so I made it and doctored the bowls with packets of sweetener and instant milk. The time in the jungle with Kel had reduced my standards on what constituted a meal. We ate in silence.

"Are we just hanging around here all day until they get back?"

I was torn. "If I'm going to practice, I need supplies."

"Like what?"

"An athame and a chalice, for starters." I paused, sighing a little. "If my mom had lived, or if they had managed to save more of her things, I'd have hers."

"I'm sorry," Shannon said softly.

"For what?"

"Judging you."

"It's understandable." I didn't like the path I'd chosen

any more than she did, and sometimes only the fact that Kel had endorsed it made it bearable. Which spoke volumes—once, I'd thought him crazy as bedbug; now I considered him a moral compass. Surely his archangel wouldn't give him orders that resulted in a gross loss of innocent life. Would he? No. I shook my head, trying to reassure myself.

"Not really," she said. "I mean, I have my own regrettable shit. I left my dad, knowing he felt guilty, when it would've meant everything to him if I'd given him some hint I didn't blame him for the Kilmer clusterfuck." She bent her head, so that black hair hid her face. "But the truth is, he was supposed to protect me, you know? And I don't know if I'll ever trust him again."

Wow. I didn't know how to respond since I tended to hold a grudge. It took a fair amount to get me riled, but once somebody landed on my list, I almost never changed my mind. Yet I didn't feel comfortable preaching the Dead to Me philosophy when Jim Cheney was Shannon's closest relative.

"I guess you give it time. When missing him outweighs the anger, then you go see him."

She pushed her bangs back, blue gaze steady on mine. "What if it never does?"

"Honestly, I try not to think about the future when it's hard enough to get through a single day."

"Carpe diem."

"Exactly. Do you have your laptop?"

In answer, she got it out of her backpack. I waved her over to the desk, where there appeared to be a cable. I plugged in, booted up, and found we had Internet. Shannon must've discovered that last night; I remembered her saying she was going to check e-mail.

"What're you doing?"

While Shan watched, I pulled up Area 51, a hidden bulletin board that pretended to be full of conspiracy theorists, when gifted humans—those with weird abilities, like Shannon and me—actually populated it. I skimmed the general posts, more curiosity than anything else. *Telepath looking for love in Atlanta. White witch new to Chicago seeks coven. Palm reading and tarot, first session free—Newport Beach.* Then I moved to the business listings, which was why I'd pulled up the site. Seeing her curiosity, I decided to make this a teaching moment. I was supposed to be her mentor, even if I hadn't offered her much worth learning lately.

"In most cities," I explained, "the true witch stores run quietly. They don't advertise in the Yellow Pages or put their information on the Net for the general public. So if you find a 'New Age' place that way, chances are they sell fakery stuff, gewgaws and worthless inventory. Nothing you could really use to cast a spell."

"So you're looking for a real one."

"Yep. Looks like there's a place downtown." I finished reading the description and then added, "Between Popeyes and a store that sells knockoff designer handbags."

"I'll get dressed."

After taking staggered showers, we headed out. I had to risk removing the amulet during my three-minute toilette; otherwise a thorough drenching might ruin it. Escobar hadn't included a care manual. It was unlikely that the sorcerer would be able to get a lock on us in the time I had it off. Even so, I didn't like driving the Forester in broad daylight, but Laredo was a decent-size city. Since they didn't know where we were right now, the gain should be worth the risk.

It was no trouble to find the store. Parking proved a little more difficult. I circled the block twice before sliding in when a van left. We walked two blocks to where the storefront advertised, ORIENTAL HOME FURNISHINGS. A bell tinkled as we came in, and a small shock sizzled through me.

To my astonishment, as I spun, I saw runes laid on the doorframe. They pulsed a pale, sickly green; I'd never been able to detect that kind of thing before. It was just a discouragement spell, old and faint, making random patrons feel like there was nothing they wanted in here.

A true practitioner would shrug it off, if he even felt it

through his shields. I wasn't sure I had any, though Jesse said he couldn't feel me anymore. I'd either developed rudimentary shields or what happened with Kel severed our tenuous emotional connection. Damn, I had so much to learn—and fast.

The store offered a few rugs and fans, enough to satisfy a cursory glance, but I glimpsed a back room, where the real merchandise must be kept. A grandmotherly woman stepped out through a wispy lace curtain, clad in black. She stood just under five feet tall, willow slim, with a surprisingly unlined complexion.

"Since you're still here," she said, "I must conclude you ought to be. Come along."

I followed her into the back room, a wonderland of fantastic items. Shannon split off to poke around on her own. A rack on the far wall held hand-carved wands in cherry, rowan, willow, and oak. I passed those by in favor of the daggers displayed in a glass case. Some had curvy blades, others serrated edges. Some were silver, edged in black leather, and graven with arachnids and runes, while others carried pictures of serpents or dragons. They all possessed different glyphs.

"Your first?" the old woman asked.

I nodded, still studying the collection. Intuition told me I needed to touch them all to learn which one was destined for me; at least, my foretelling gift *should* still function even with me as the prospective buyer. I'd never tried to use it this way before. But I didn't look forward to the pain.

Maybe I could start with the ones that spoke to me aesthetically. "Would you get those three out for me to look at?" I indicated the spider knife, the dragon one, and the one with the serpent coiled around the bone handle.

"Excellent choices." She told me a little about them, but I didn't need the histories. I'd see it all soon enough.

I curled my hand around the first knife, accepting the pain as price of knowledge. It had never been used; a smith in Ireland had crafted it. It told me nothing about its prospective buyer, which I took to mean nobody would be coming for it anytime soon. Including me. With some regret, as I liked it best, I put it back down.

"An untaught witch with the touch," she said with a raised brow. "Oh, but you *are* a rare one."

"Apparently." I took up the dragon blade. It felt unbalanced in my hand because of the jagged edge, and it burned like a low fire with old magic.

Closing my eyes, I read this one too. The pain lanced all the way up to my elbow as I saw a young woman casting the same spell over and over again: a would-be love charm. My mother had warned me that there was nothing so desperate or so hopeless. If it succeeded, the spell twisted the target and filled him with mindless obsession, not love. Never love. True love could not be compelled.

Panting with the pain, I let the knife go. Not this one either.

That left the serpent athame with the bone handle and the wavy blade. Mustering my nerve, I curled my branded palm around it, sealing the flower pentacle against the runes. A burst of lightning ran through me, as if a series of doors on a shared timer had all opened at once. In a bizarre reflection, I saw myself handing over the money for this one, and the old woman smiling.

"This is it. I'll leave it here while I finish shopping."

"Take your time, my dear." Her tone gave me the creeps, and I remembered what Jesse had said, so long ago: *Be careful when you meet a gifted person you encountered online. Ability doesn't make them trustworthy.*

If I didn't need this stuff, I'd throw the money at her and make a run for it. But as long as I watched her, she couldn't call anyone. So I kept one eye on her when I went to look at the chalices. This was less important than the athame, at least according to my mother. A chalice was merely a vessel, whereas the athame functioned as an extension of your will. I grabbed a simple silver one and then went to the counter to pay.

"Since it's your first time, I'll throw in a starter pack of herbs for you, the good ones. I know you'll be back once you see how well they work."

"Great, thanks."

Shannon put an amulet on the glass case, a leather cord with a silver pentacle, but unlike most Goth accessories, the item bore the unmistakable stamp of real magick. "What does this do?"

"Oh, that's a nice one. I made it myself, a simple protective charm. The world is a dangerous place." Was I going crazy, or did her words contain a warning?

"We'll take that too," I said.

Despite the fact that she freaked me out, her prices seemed reasonable, so I didn't try to haggle. We didn't have time anyhow. It worried me to be out in the open like this, no backup, but I could hardly deal with Vicente if I didn't try to wrangle my mother's power—mine now, I supposed—into submission.

She bagged up the athame and chalice, a weird smile playing on her lips. Her gray eyes turned an awful citrine not normally found in human irises. "Run along now, darling child."

The endearment froze me in place. ". . . Maury?"

That wasn't his true name, of course. If I knew it, I could bind him. He'd been careful to prevent that, even before I earned the honorific *Binder*. Since he wasn't physically present in this realm, like Caim had been, I couldn't touch him and learn his name, either. So I had to deal.

"Not at first," the demon said. "But this old she-witch has had *far* too much truck with the netherworld over the years. There's practically a swinging door in her head."

His appearance could mean only one thing, and it wasn't good. "You're calling payment due."

"You owe me a favor."

"What do you want?" Hell, I needed another chain saw to juggle.

"Is this the thing from Kilmer?" Shannon asked. "What did you do? Did you make a *deal* with it?"

Aw, crap. Well, no. Not intentionally. That technicality

wasn't going to make her like my answer any better. I motioned her to silence, because I didn't want Maury paying attention to her.

"Nothing too difficult," said the demon dressed in old-woman skin.

"I'm listening." I found it hard to imagine what I could do that *it* couldn't. Of course, the human mind balked at certain boundaries.

"You will sacrifice your firstborn child to me."

Shannon's breath came and went in a shaky hiss. She put a hand on my arm, as if imploring me not to agree. Jesus, her opinion of me had really gone down the shitter in the past few days.

"Relax," I said. "He's fucking with me. Aren't you, Maury?"

"Alas, you know me too well already. But look on the bright side—whatever I do ask for won't seem so bad by comparison, will it?"

"You're stalling."

"I had almost forgotten how tiresome you can be."

"I'm a real demon downer, all right. Spill it or I consider this conversation repayment in full, because you're wasting my time."

"Very well, no more games. Which is a great pity because I love them so. You, Corine Solomon, will summon my mate for me."

I said, "You'll have to give me his or her true name."

"I am aware of how it works," he said dryly. "You will, of course, pledge on your mother's immortal soul that you will never use it to my bind my love to your will."

Since I wasn't sure anything of my mother had survived to see the afterlife, I didn't consider that a powerful vow. Best not to tell the demon.

"And if I refuse?"

"I consider our bargain broken and you will die."

Kel could not have foreseen this. He wouldn't have left me to face this if he'd known it was coming. In a horrible way, that knowledge gladdened me. He had no dominion over the dark spaces, whereas I lived there. *Shit*. I didn't want to do this, but I could, if Maury told me the particulars. If I did this, everything would change. From tales told at my mother's knee, I understood that no white witch would help a dark practitioner; therefore I could find only training in the dark arts henceforth. And this act would leave a scar in the astral, so anyone who viewed me there would know I summoned demons.

"That's not a cake-or-death choice," Shan said softly. "It's more of a disembowelment-or-death choice."

Was I prepared to dwell in darkness in exchange for my life? Yet the alternative was worse—fall now and spend my afterlife in the demon realm. A bad choice and worse coming: At this point, that seemed like a too-familiar tune. Maybe this choice didn't mean I was damned; perhaps I could do enough good, somehow, to make it up, no matter what other practitioners thought of me. Really, there was only one call; otherwise Shannon must watch me die. I couldn't do that to her. *Couldn't*.

"Before I give my answer, can I ask a question?" It was best to make sure of such things, though I knew the outcome was inevitable.

"Indeed," Maury said. "But let that be the only one, lest I accuse you of, as you put it, stalling."

"Recently I ran into a Knight of Hell." Out of respect for the demon I'd bested, I didn't name him. No telling what Maury could do with such information. "He'd been summoned by a sorcerer, but not in spirit. He crossed over *fully*. Is that what you want me to do for your mate?"

I read real surprise in the old woman's face. "Truly, a corporeal manifestation? It takes an incredible amount of energy to create such a gate."

"I figured." Binding and banishing were different because when you returned a summoned creature to its natural place, the universe wanted to help restore order. Pulling things where they didn't belong—that took juice.

"No, of course that's not what I require. I merely want her here, as I am. It will be great fun for us to find a couple of hosts and . . . play for a while."

I shuddered to envision what Maury considered "play." "Like a vacation."

"Precisely."

"If I consent to this, we're square. No more favors. No more debt." A glorious new life, down a very dark road. I suspected I couldn't see how bad it would get from here, and that was probably best.

"Agreed."

I couldn't help but haggle, though he held all the cards. It was the pawnshop owner in me. "I'll do it under one condition."

"You're hardly in a bargaining position, but I'm willing to listen."

"You promise not to take unwilling hosts. Find a couple of coma victims or something. Stage a miraculous recovery and go about your business."

Whatever that might be. Don't think about it. Don't.

"Done. Such hosts are typically easier to control anyway. Most of them have no brain function to interfere with my driving."

Gross.

"Will she remember what we've talked about?" I nodded at the old lady. Her skin had turned a sickly shade, as if his presence made her queasy.

"No. They never do."

"Good." Before I could change my mind, I recited the address where we could be found. "Find a proper body and then come to us tonight. I'll need some time to study my grimoires. I want to make sure I do this right."

Because I'm sure as hell not doing it again, no matter what other witches think. One scar doesn't mean I'm evil. It doesn't.

"Until tonight, my darling child."

The old woman slumped to the counter, and it took a couple of minutes for her to rouse. We stuck around to make sure Maury hadn't cooked her brain. Other than being groggy, the witch didn't seem to have taken permanent harm.

"Are we finished here?" she asked in bewilderment. "I seem to have lost track of time."

"Yeah, we paid up. But we're still waiting for you to get that starter pack of herbs you mentioned."

"Oh, yes, of course. I'll be right back."

She gave me a pretty wooden box with ten compartments inside. Each one held a different herb, wrapped in fabric. I didn't know what any of this stuff did, but my mother could tell me, through the grimoires. I waved as we went past the curtain and out the front door.

Shannon broke the silence halfway to the SUV. "What didn't you tell me about what happened in those woods?"

Remembered pain rendered my words staccato, choppy. "Cooper killed me. Or the wound would have. The demon plugged the hole." Knowing it sounded incredible, I took her hand and pressed it to my side. Since I was thinner, the metal felt more obvious, a hard spot where the blade went in.

"I can feel it. That used to be a knife?"

I nodded, leading the way to the SUV. My gaze cut back and forth and over our shoulders. Nobody seemed to be paying us any particular attention, but I wouldn't feel safe until I had Shannon behind locked doors again.

"I have a murderer's weapon inside me," I said, hearing the despair in my voice. "It's no wonder I can give such orders. I'm afraid of what I'm becoming."

That was the first time I'd articulated the fear aloud: that I was filthy and demon touched. I had allowed whispers and doubts along the way, as I went farther and farther from the light. God, the one in the village had called me its queen. Maybe I was wretched and damned, and it would be better if Montoya exterminated me. I increased the pace, trying to escape the doubt. In no time at all, we reached the Forester.

Shannon touched me on the arm. "I may not know much,

but it seems like if you're worried about it, then you're okay. Evil people don't question right or wrong. They just do what they want."

I sighed as I got behind the wheel. "That helps a little. Or it *might*, if we weren't heading off to summon a demon."

"Cool," she said. "I'll wear my new necklace."

Despite myself, I laughed. God help me if I ever lost Shan.

Raising Hell

On the way back, I took a circuitous route and made a number of unnecessary turns. Shannon watched but she didn't see anybody tailing us. Maybe I was being paranoid, but I didn't intend to let Montoya find me before I was good and ready.

Once locked behind all the dead bolts, I skipped ahead in the grimoire. I paged all the way through the red one and realized the spell I needed must be in the blue one. I located the summoning ritual about midway in. In fact, I was surprised my mother had such incantations in her books. I couldn't imagine when summoning a demon could be considered white magic, and she'd told me more than once she only practiced beneficial craft.

Around noon, I made a call. I had Morales's number handy, since he'd dialed my cell. "Before you guys report in, I need some things. Got a pen?" I read him the list. "Send the bill to Escobar."

Strictly speaking this didn't relate to our shared persecution of Montoya, but if I wanted to stay alive, which was part of the deal, I required these items. He wouldn't even notice the expenditure. If he did, I'd account for it somehow.

"*Sí, jefa.* We'll be there later."

"No sooner than dusk. Your work is best done in the dark."

"I might have that slogan tattooed on me somewhere."

"The ladies might think you mean you're too ugly for daytime sex."

"*Nunca*. They got eyes, don't they?" With a little chuckle, he disconnected.

For most of the day, I practiced drawing pentangles. Most witches grew up with such coursework as a part of their normal school curriculum. With any luck, this crash course would suffice. I wished I could take baby steps; I wasn't prepared to jump from a mild *call me* spell to a major summoning, but in my case it was do or die.

"Ready or not, here I come," I muttered.

Shannon glanced up from the laptop. It amused me that she could read Web comics at a time like this. She was also IMing somebody. When I went over, I saw she'd been talking to Booke.

"Is he okay?"

"As much as he ever is. He asked about you."

"What did you tell him?"

"That you're working for one drug dealer to drive another drug dealer crazy."

Put that way, it sounded quite reprehensible. "In my defense, Montoya doesn't have far to go."

"I call 'em like I see 'em."

"Funny."

"Are you ready to do your thing tonight?"

"We'll find out, won't we?"

I occupied the rest of the day reading spells that would help if something went wrong. Even so, when the boys arrived with my shopping, I didn't feel confident. They filed in, looking pleased with themselves.

"You had us buy some *hudu* shit," García muttered in greeting. By the curl of his lip, he didn't approve.

I pushed to my feet and folded my arms, trying to look intimidating. "Zaragoza pegged us as Escobar's newest *brujas*." I turned to the girl beside me, and to Shan's credit, the sneer she'd perfected looked menacing. "What do you think? Should we show them?"

"No," Santos said quickly. "We'll take our orders and go. We don't want to interfere with your . . . other work."

So he's both the oldest and the smartest. I stifled amusement at guys like this fearing us. Certainly part of that fright came from our association with Escobar, but not all. They feared the powerful woman chanting in the dark, her gleaming eyes and streaming hair, her unnatural influence.

"Very well," I said. "Tonight, you will find one of Montoya's businesses—a crib, a crack house, a meth lab, a warehouse where he stores the expensive imported stuff— and you will destroy it. Choose your target according to what will hurt him most."

"*¿Estás segura?*" Petrel asked. "If we hit his goods, it could start an all-out war."

"That's kind of the point." I considered. "How likely is this to spill into the streets? Will there be shootings all over Laredo, innocent bystanders injured?"

García shrugged. "Maybe. If we're at war and his guys see us, they open fire. We shoot back. People will get hurt."

"All right. Change of plans." I didn't need to look at Shannon to know she was relieved. "Keep it personal. I don't want him to realize you work for Escobar until the end. Ask Zaragoza for your new target: another lovely home, something expensive. Cross the border if you must, but don't get caught."

"Just like last night," Morales said. "It's gonna be a party."

"Once you finish, leave this where he'll find it. I suggest attaching it to a stake and planting it at the edge of the property."

Santos took the lock of red synthetic hair with a confused look. This strategy qualified as both cruel and playful. Montoya would get excited, thinking I was dumb enough to leave real hair for his sorcerer. Then he'd realize it was fake; if Escobar knew his enemy's psyche, this gambit would enrage him. I had no doubt he would associate me with the token, a quiet signature that meant nothing to anybody else.

Just to fuck with Santos, I murmured, "You might want to put that away. It's not good to hold such things for too long."

He shuddered, stuffed the long strand of hair into a plastic bag, and then wiped his fingers against his brown pants. The others smirked a little, but I had no doubt they would react the same way, even though rationally, I couldn't have done anything to the item. They'd picked up the hair extension for me. But when the lizard brain spewed fear, logic disconnected.

"Anything else?" Morales asked.

"No. You have your orders. Call me once it's done."

The boys went out into the world to wreak havoc in my name.

Darkness had fallen by this time, which meant the demon would arrive soon to demand his due. I pored over the grimoires some more, trying to get ready, but how the hell did anyone prepare themselves for this? I had no answer.

Eventually, a knock sounded. No point in asking how Maury got over the fencing, complete with barbed wire. For all I knew, he could hurdle it. I glanced out the peephole, and I didn't recognize the man standing there.

"Maury?"

"None other."

I unfastened all the locks but didn't invite him in. "We'll have to do this outside." I turned to Shannon. "Will you bring the supplies?"

"Sure."

The body Maury had selected offered no attraction. He was thin and reedy, balding on top. But maybe nondescript was a bonus to a demon, making it easier to go about his business. Butch growled as if to warn me that this guy wasn't what he seemed.

I patted the dog. "Don't worry—I know that already."

He whined at me, none too convinced I understood what I was doing. But when I went toward the door anyway, he washed his paws of me and trotted back to the pillow we'd put on the floor for his comfort. A glance over my shoulder showed him turning repeatedly on the cushion to find the perfect place for his butt.

I chose a spot in the far left corner of the parking lot, away from the building, but screened completely by scrubby trees and chain-link fence. Here, the pavement appeared smooth enough for me to lay the pentacle, at least. In other spots, it lay broken and riddled with holes.

My hands trembled a little as I drew the pentagram. The chalk felt dusty on my fingertips, but when I finished I saw the shape was accurate enough to do the job. I followed up with a circle, and as I drew this time, I willed heat from my hands. Because of those long years when the touch comprised my only gift, I could not conceive of magic feeling any other way. By the time I closed the circle, my hand burned as if I had immersed it in a fire.

I dropped the chalk with a little moan and saw that my fingertips glowed orange like live coals. I had no doubt I could hurt someone with my bare hands. Perhaps not a fatal injury, but I could bestow a brand—sobering thought.

Seeing that, Shannon backed away. "Whoa, is that normal?"

"For most witches, no." I had handicaps, but considering I'd never thought to work my mother's spells at all, I could bear the pain. I was used to it, after all.

"What are you waiting for?" Maury demanded, as I trickled salt atop my chalk circle. This demon wasn't going anywhere unless I willed it.

"Almost finished. But I need her name now."

He pronounced each syllable with great care, as if caressing his absent lover. I found it oddly endearing. "Dumah Porai Valyonatha."

"It's been a long time since you've seen her."

"Only by your standards," he muttered. "But I have been away longer than I expected. She will be missing me."

I tried to sound casual as I finished spreading the salt. "You could go back. I could send you."

"I think not. Your people call my world hell for a reason."

"Very well." Using my athame, I cut a narrow slice in

my palm and let the blood drip inside the pentagram. I was careful not to break the circle, however. "By fire, earth, wind, and rain, I call you forth, Dumah Porai Valyonatha. I offer sacrifice in your name. As I will, so mote it be. In the name of Solomon the Binder, whose blood I carry, you must obey."

Unlike the spell I had used on Morales, this one required focus and repetition. My mother had once said: *There are no true magic words, only your will behind them.* Power sizzled through me, far more than I'd ever held before— more than it took to read a house or a patch of dirt. It felt as though my heart must cook inside my chest. I sent it to the circle and the salt ate it, blackening beneath the heat.

I don't know how long I chanted, but the air churned inside the pentacle. Not like Caim's manifestation, but it grew dark with smoke that writhed with signs of life. I saw a glimmer of eyes, a suggestion of a face.

"She's here," the demon breathed beside me.

Maury started to go to her, only to be brought up short by the power of my wards. I smiled. "My part of the bargain is fulfilled, and you are repaid."

"That wasn't the deal!"

"In fact, it was. You specified I had to *summon* her, not set her free."

"No, I wouldn't consent to that. The last part was implicit in the agreement."

And now I gambled everything. "If you have the power, if I have invalidated our deal, kill me now. Take the knife from my wound. I'm willing to risk it."

Long moments passed while Dumah twisted inside the circle. I hoped the confinement didn't hurt her, but surely it couldn't be any worse than hell. Sometimes I got a clear enough glimpse at her features in the smoke to know she longed for the creature I called Maury. I hadn't known demons could love.

"I cannot," it said at last. "You have satisfied the letter of our agreement if not the spirit, and so I have no power over you."

"Since she's here"—and I already had the darkness in my magick for other practitioners to see—"I'm willing to renegotiate."

Maury raised both brows. "What makes you think I'd trust you now?"

"Then I'll just banish her. I promised, as you recall, not to *bind* her." Which included forcing her to obey me. It didn't include sending her home. Maybe Solomon's blood ran in my veins after all; I'd used the claim to power a spell, and I seemed to own a knack for dealing with demons.

"Wait," he said. "Present your offer."

"You swear on her name that you will do no real harm while you linger here. Mischief and misfortune I can abide, but no death. No permanent damage."

"Can we cost a rich man his gold?"

I didn't need to think very long on that. "Absolutely. Limit your pranks to people who deserve it, and you'll have no quarrel with me."

"Oh, priceless," he said. "You would use two *demons* as angels of vengeance."

"Weren't you angels once?" Shannon asked timidly.

"No, my dear. That is yet one more inaccuracy in your history."

"It's not history," I felt compelled to point out, "so much as religious myth."

"Whatever. It's wrong. Will you let Dumah go now?"

I grinned. "Nice try. You agreed, but you haven't yet sworn on her name. I won't be defeated by loopholes to-night."

"Fine," he grumbled. "I swear by Dumah Porai Valyona-tha and my love for her that we will restrict our attention to those who deserve it and cause no death while we're here." Maury stalked away and gave me his back, doubtless telling me he was pissed I'd gotten the best of him this time.

"Then we have a deal." I rubbed my foot across the lines of salt and chalk, blurring it so the demon could escape.

The subsequent rupture surprised me and blew us back a

good ten feet. I lay there, dazed and bruised, with my head on the pavement. *Holy shit, what was that?* A dark force, smelling of cinder and smoke, writhed above me. Was Dumah *laughing*?

Maury certainly was. "Oh, poor fledgling witch. I forgot nobody ever told you to drain the power from the wards before you break a field."

Head throbbing, I crawled over to where Shannon lay. She looked impossibly pale, and a bruise was already forming on the side of her face. For a moment, she didn't seem to be breathing, and I went from worried to frantic in 3.4 seconds.

"Shan?" I felt for a pulse and found one.

Thank all gods and goddesses.

"Did you get the number of that truck?" she mumbled, opening her eyes.

"It's my fault. I got cocky. A few hours with the grimoires and I thought I knew something. God, I'm sorry. How much does it hurt?" I felt her head gingerly and discovered a lump the size of an egg.

"A lot. But I can deal. I'm thinking we should hose off the parking lot and get back inside, though."

I should've thought of that. The ending of the ritual had scrambled my brains. I couldn't leave my blood out here undiluted. Though it was a long shot anybody who meant me ill would stumble across it, it was possible Montoya's sorcerer could use it to pinpoint my location somehow. I had no idea what he might've learned in the islands; what I'd seen from him so far was powerful and terrifying. After I pulled Shannon to her feet, we stumbled toward the building.

We looked for a hose and didn't find one, so we wound up ferrying buckets of water to toss over the messy mixture of salt, chalk dust, and blood. Once we'd wet it all down, I swept it into a paste and then dumped another batch of water on it. More sweeping. If anyone could tell in the morning what we'd been doing here, I'd be greatly surprised. More important, the mixture rendered my blood unusable.

"That should do it. Let's get you an ice pack and some

Aleve." I'd started carrying the stuff in my bag because sometimes—after I'd handled my mother's necklace and my power changed—the burns hurt too much to bear, even though they no longer left new scars.

"I'll live," she said.

"This time." I had to stop putting her at risk. Maybe I should put her on a bus, even if she didn't want to go. Before it was too late. "Look, Shan, I really think—"

"*No.*" She slammed the first door open and stomped to the apartment. "If you want to get rid of me, I'll go. But you're *not* sending me to my dad. I'm not a little kid. . . . I can get a job. Maybe I'll try Cali. I hear it's pretty there." She glared, as if daring me to object. "*You* did fine on your own."

"Not really," I said softly. I'd never told anyone this. I didn't like thinking about it. "I landed well at first. I found a job in a used bookstore and I had a room in a boarding-house. But when the store went under, I couldn't find anything else. Pretty soon, I had no money, and I had no place to stay. I don't make friends easily, so I had nobody to turn to. I moved on with only enough money in my pocket to get to the next town. I found myself sleeping in the bus station. I did things I'm not proud of."

I'd taken insane risks, and it was lucky I wasn't diseased or dead. It would break my heart if I drove Shannon to that with my good intentions.

"Like what?"

She wouldn't be satisfied unless I told her. I wouldn't reveal my past to anyone else for any other reason—only to keep Shan from repeating my mistakes. I was over it, mostly. I'd learned to deal. But she needed to know how much I trusted her.

So while I wrapped an ice pack, fixed a glass of water, and set out two pills, I revealed the whole story. *Nobody* knew this much about me—I'd picked up men for food and shelter, using serial monogamy as a means of survival. Those relationships never lasted long, because I chose men who wouldn't reject me: ones who'd take me home and were lonely enough not to complain if I stayed. But I always moved on, feeling worse each time, because I lived with them out of desperation, not desire.

My past left me with such low self-esteem that I didn't demand to be an equal partner with Chance, when he came along. I didn't feel worthy of him, and I did anything to please him; I suborned my old identity because it was awful and tawdry, and I wanted to forget that woman, the sad, desperate Corine. It would kill me if Shan ever thought she wasn't equal to any man who wanted her.

I went on. "By the time I met Chance, I had gotten myself together. I had a place of my own and a job at a dry cleaner's. But you know how hard it is get work if you don't have an address? How hard it is to keep clean in public restrooms so people's eyes don't slide away from you? It's easier if you're young. But if you're old and homeless, it's the next thing to an invisibility spell. I knew people who died on the street, people who froze to death and nobody noticed. Nobody *cared*. The city just removed the bodies like they were leaves in the street." I bit my lip against the burn of tears and the throbbing in my head. "So if you think I'm letting you leave with nothing, you're out of your mind. I want better than that for you."

And that was part of why I couldn't turn down Escobar's money. I wanted her to have a future brighter than I could provide alone. Having a place of our own mattered desperately, and now maybe she'd understand why. If Chance knew, he might get why my pawnshop had meant everything to me, and, with it blown to shit, why I felt as if someone I loved had died. I needed a home, dammit.

"I had no idea," she whispered.

"Nobody does." I exhaled shakily and got my own Aleve and *agua*.

Her expression said she understood; we didn't need to speak of this again. *Thank God.* Though I'd come to terms with my mistakes, I didn't enjoy reliving them, even for Shan's benefit.

But she had her own point to make as well. "Look, I'll

stop threatening to leave if you stop talking about sending me away. I know it's dangerous; I'm not an idiot. But for the first time I feel like I belong and I'm not giving that up. Okay?"

I downed my water like it was a shot of something stronger. "Fair enough."

Devil and the Deep Blue Sea

In the morning, Chuch called. "Where are you, *prima*?"

"I think you're better off not knowing." I hesitated. "I'm so sorry. I brought this down on you."

"You don't know that. If Montoya knew we got involved in the raid on his place, then maybe he was already gunning for us. If you hadn't warned us, it might've been a lot worse. Maybe we wouldn't have gotten out the back."

I suspected he was trying to make me feel better. "I'd prefer it if you stayed with Eva."

He swore softly. "Who you think made me call you?"

I smiled because it sounded like her, nearly at her due date and thinking about revenge. She was going to be the most unusual mom on her block. "Don't you have other stuff to do, like, say, see about having your house rebuilt?"

"My cousin Ramon's already on it."

"The one who gave your *tía* Rosita such a cheap funeral?"

"Yeah, well. He learned his lesson."

"Eva really wants you to do this?"

The phone rustled; then his wife came on the line. "Seriously, *chica*. I'll call if I think the baby's coming. I don't feel right about you facing this on your own."

"I'm not, actually. I have Shannon. And Escobar's men."

"Pfft," she said. "You need friends too. I'd be there if I could."

A little pang went through me. "Even now? I cost you your house."

"Bullshit. It's like Chuch said."

"Okay. Here's the address." I recited it to her.

"Gotcha. Take care."

"You too."

Shannon stepped into the living room. Her bruises glowed almost purple, and her cheek had swollen overnight. She looked like I'd backhanded her for giving me lip. "Chuch is in, I take it?"

"Yeah. I just need to decide how he can help."

"Let me know if you need me. I'll be surfing."

With a nod, she went back to her laptop while I fretted over Jesse. Not knowing got the best of me, so I dialed the police station and asked for Glencannon. It was a long shot they'd put me through. The officer on the other end asked for my name and then put me on hold. I listened to bad Muzak for five minutes before anyone answered.

The lieutenant picked up eventually. "Ms. Solomon, what can I do for you?"

"I was hoping you could tell me how he's doing. Physically."

"I'm surprised you didn't call his parents."

"To be honest, sir, I spoke to you longer than I did with them. That was our first meeting."

"Ah," he said. "Not the best time for it. Well, he came out of surgery just fine, no complications. I posted guards and it's been quiet."

"Could you tell me what room? I'd like to call before he's sequestered or whatever you call it."

If he found it strange I didn't already know, Glencannon didn't mention it. "He's in four oh five. They should put you right through." He hesitated, and then added, "Tomorrow or the next day, he'll be transferred to a city-owned safe house."

"I understand." He was telling me to say what I needed

to because I wouldn't be speaking to Jesse for a while. "You'll make sure nobody else has access to that information, right?"

"I hope you're not telling me how to do my job."

I winced. *Smooth.* "Of course not. It's only that . . . well—"

"We had Nathan Moon on our payroll. I'll be careful, Ms. Solomon. I'm pretty sure the department's clean, but I won't bet Saldana's life on it."

"Thank you, sir."

After hanging up, I realized I'd called this man "sir," an unprecedented level of respect toward law enforcement. That had to mean something. Perhaps I could trust him. Whether he could trust me? Hm. I had a bad track record with cops, but I could cook up a charm to nudge him in that regard.

Shannon glanced up from her computer and grinned at me. "One more? Make it a trifecta."

Most likely, Jesse hadn't called because they'd kept him too doped up to dial. Still, I had to speak to him before he left the hospital. That was a girlfriend thing to do.

The phone rang several times before Mrs. Saldana picked up. I'd expected to find her there. She was the kind of mother everybody wanted and damn few people got. I had a great one of my own, but I didn't get to keep her long.

"Oh, hello," she said when she recognized my voice. "I know Jesse will want to speak with you. He's been very fretful when his meds wear off."

Well, yeah. He had to be worried. Even with a bullet hole in him and shot up with meds, he still had room in his heart for me. Maybe I'd fought the idea of falling for him because he stood for everything good and decent—and, well, I didn't. If the past left a mark on one's soul, mine resembled an old road map covered with dirty footprints, ashes, and spilled wine that looked like blood.

Yet maybe it was time to let the guilt go for good.

"Corine?" He sounded fucking stoned. "You okay? I keep telling them they hafta let me out."

"And they're not going to listen," I heard his mother say firmly. "Not until the doctors release you, and then you're going straight into protective custody."

"I'm fine. Just do as Glencannon asks. . . . I'll be all right. This once, let the damsel save herself."

The phone clattered, and then Mrs. Saldana spoke. "He's a bit out of it still. Are you working?" Her tone implied that was the only acceptable reason for my not being at her son's bedside. The truth would likely make her head explode.

"I'm sorry, yes." It wasn't a complete lie, and I couldn't explain that hanging around his room guaranteed more harm to come.

If I stayed away and caused trouble elsewhere, Montoya and his men should be too busy beating the bushes for me to think about the cop who got away. That was the plan, anyway. I made an excuse about getting back to my job and hung up. Lying to Jesse's mom made me feel lower than a worm's belly, but nothing could alter my circumstances.

To get my mind off Jesse, I e-mailed Chuch. He showed up within the hour, sooner than Escobar's boys. I ushered him into the safe house and he assessed the place with an approving eye.

"This is a great setup. Would take a small army or high-powered explosives to get in here. A Molotov won't do the job. It'd just burn the paint off the cement."

"Good to know," I muttered.

He spread his hands with a cheerful grin. "We all have areas of expertise, right? What's the plan?"

I filled him in on what I had Escobar's crew doing. "And so I'm waiting for them to report back. Two houses, two nights running, and I had them leave a calling card."

"You're doing that for me and Eva, huh? Hitting him where he lives and all."

"Yeah. Jesse too." *And Ernesto and Señor Alvarez. For the fact that Shannon and I are now homeless.* Oh, yeah, Montoya had given me many, many reasons to fight.

"You got a good head for battle, *prima*."

"I want him shaken." I sighed softly. "I'm not thrilled with hiding while I send other people to do my dirty work, but—"

"It's better than dying," Shannon finished.

Chuch nodded. "Nothing wrong with delegation. Speaking of which, you never did tell me how you swung an alliance with Escobar. He never sees anybody. Dude's crazy cautious."

"He tested me and found me worthy." I refused to say more.

The time I'd spent with Kel was too personal to share, even with my friends. I couldn't let myself think about him right then, where he was, whether he was lonely or loathed his orders. I would later, no question. Kelethiel, son of Uriel and Vashti, had forged a path in my heart that nobody else could tread.

"*Claro*," he said, as if that were the natural outcome. "So what's my part?"

We didn't have Chance to dowse this time, even if we got a list of properties from Escobar. After our last raid, I doubted we'd have it so easy if we attempted a frontal assault, and with his son or daughter about to be born, I wasn't sending Chuch into battle anyway. The current plan must stand.

"I need you to use your contacts to get a message to Montoya's people. I don't want you carrying it yourself. But you know people who can."

"That's *it*?" His offense was obvious.

"It's crucial. Now that I've done some damage, I need to talk some shit and up the stakes. But I can't come into the open prematurely."

"What do you have in mind?"

"For the message? I'm a ghost; he'll never catch me—I'm unkillable. Maybe even that I've made a deal with the devil." Considering what I'd done for Maury, that statement was closer to the truth than I liked. "Oh, and that anytime he wants to surrender in person, he should drop me a line."

Chuch laughed softly. "Damn, cuz. That's gonna burn right into his brain. He'll probably kill the *chingado* who brings him word."

"It's a risk you take working for crazy-ass cartel bosses," Shannon noted.

"So can you find someone to carry the message?"

Chuch considered. "Yeah, but you'll have to write it down and seal it. Otherwise, nobody'd be dumb enough to take that shit to Montoya."

"I can do that. And I'll send this along as my calling card." I held up the red hair extension. In this light, it was so obviously fake it wasn't funny.

Rummaging turned up a pad of paper, and I always had a pen in my purse. I scrawled my comments in particularly taunting cursive, and I didn't sign it. The red hair would do that for me.

Shannon watched, half-horrified, half-amused. "I hope to God Escobar knows what he's doing."

"Me too." I abhorred bullbaiting, but we were doing exactly that to Montoya. Only I didn't feel sorry for him at all. However this ended, he had it coming.

Chuch stood. "Do you want me to come back after I get this done?"

I considered. The less traffic here, the better, so I shook my head. "Just e-mail me a simple confirmation."

After he'd gone, I realized I'd treated him like one of Escobar's men. Find a Chuch-shaped task and aim him at it. I almost called him back to hug him or something. I didn't want to start seeing people as useful. Christ, that would make me just like Escobar—worse, even, because I knew better. I'd been a better person once.

"What can I do?" Shannon asked. *Not her too.* But the truth was, I had an idea, and she read it in my expression. "Spill!"

"Since I don't know much about Montoya and nothing about his sorcerous brother, I can't target them. The spells my mother left me rely on personal experience or sympathetic magic."

She nodded. "Right. You need hair, blood, or nail clippings. I'm familiar with the process."

"Without those components, I need to know where they are and what they look like. So even if I was an experienced, well-trained witch—and I'm not"—frankly, I wasn't sure what

I was, and right then it didn't matter—"it would be unlikely I could get a spell to work."

"I get that. How can I help?"

"The pants I wore the night Jesse was shot are bloodstained. Two of the shooters died at the hospital." Surely she'd see where I was heading with this.

"And you want me to try to use that to call one of those ghosts."

"Not if you don't want to. But we might be able to use his spirit in lieu of scrying. Find out how Montoya is handling the stress, which would offer insight on where to strike next. I want to break him, so he's ready to act on Chuch's message when it arrives. I want him frothing at the mouth at the prospect of killing me himself."

"What if he *does*?"

"Kill me? He can't. Heaven doesn't want me and hell can't handle me."

She smiled at the stupid line. As I'd known she would, she said, "I can try."

"You have your radio, right?"

"It's in my bag. I never leave it behind."

She'd carried it away from the ashes of her old life in Kilmer; it had belonged to an elderly man who spent his life fixing broken things. Too bad he'd died before he could take a crack at me.

"Then I'll leave it up to you. If you're scared . . . or even a little nervous, we don't have to do this."

"Check the cupboards for me."

I went into the kitchen, since I knew why she'd asked. If this went wrong, she needed a quick fix to offset the damage. I found some sugar cubes and tea bags. Not a Snickers bar, her preferred prescription for a nasty spirit suck, but it would do the job. I put the kettle on, just in case.

"You set?" I asked, coming back into the living room.

"I'm good. Get the focus item."

Gross. I went into the bedroom and rummaged in the flowered suitcase. I'd stashed my bloody clothes in a plastic bag. The stain didn't amount to much, just what I'd stepped in, helping Jesse to the sofa. Hopefully, Shannon could work with it.

I rejoined her and gave her the jeans. "On the hem, there."

"What did he look like?"

"I don't know. Want me to try to find a picture?" There might be photos in the newspaper. Sometimes they put convicted criminals in the headlines, along with old mug shots, but I didn't know whose blood it was for certain.

"I'll see what I can do without it." She put one hand on the radio and the other hand on the denim. Immediately, the room chilled and the antique device crackled with an unearthly sound. A shiver ran through me. No matter how many times I saw her do this, it always caught me in the gut.

"Restless dead, I call you," she whispered. "You're lost, and I can help you find the way home."

That might be a lie. I didn't know what happened to the spirits when Shannon finished with them. The room temperature dropped further, so that I could see my breath when I exhaled. Her voice softened, becoming crooning and tender.

My knees gave way and I sat on the edge of the couch, trying not to get in her way. When the shade manifested fully, it passed through me. Reaction hit in stages, like the sudden shock of ice crackling beneath your feet, followed by the inevitable fall. The preternatural chill lingered.

She tinkered with the tuning dial, looking for this spirit's frequency. "Are you there?" she asked yet again. The radio read 1490 AM.

"I'm here," came the tinny response.

With some effort, I corralled my visceral terror. The ghost wouldn't hurt me. No ordinary specter ever noticed me, so long as Shannon beckoned like a lodestone. I wondered how she looked to its otherworldly eyes.

"You worked for a very bad guy," she said softly. "And you died for him. Now I need you to do something for me."

"Montoya," the dead man whispered. "I remember him."

Shannon's voice took on the weight of a command. "Haunt him. And in the morning, tell me what you saw."

"Yes. I will. And then you'll send me home?"

"Certainly."

Her power astonished and humbled me. The ghost bled away in a trail of icy tendrils, leaving us both shivering. Without being asked I hurried to the kitchen to fix twin cups of tea. I laced hers with sugar cubes and carried the mug to her.

"They'll do anything for you," I said, sitting down.

She played with the spoon, eyeing me somberly. "Within their power."

"The ghosts in the Kilmer wood were uncommonly potent?" They'd killed for her, as I recalled.

"I think, because of the demon, they were different. They fed on the grief, fear, and pain there, just as it did."

Yeah, the one I'd unleashed on the world with a partner in crime. "That makes sense. So this one can't kill Montoya for us."

"Not unless he takes fright and falls down the stairs." She shrugged. "But not everyone can perceive the spirit world. The shade may spend its time following Montoya in impotent silence."

"Since the guy tried to kill Jesse and me, I don't feel sorry for him." I paused, hands cupped around my mug. "Thank you."

"Anytime," she said, and her smile made her look younger. "We're besties."

'Cause, yeah, the way to prove a friendship is to raise the dead. But hell, I'd do it for her. If she needed me to, I'd summon another demon and not even ask why.

"Yeah. We are."

"You wanna order pizza while we wait for the goons?"

"Secret safe house in allegedly abandoned building. I'm thinking no pizza."

"Oh, right. This sucks."

"You said it, sister. I'm going to lay some wards. Just for practice. You want to help?"

"Sweet."

"I figured I'd start with the door. In the blue grimoire,

there's an exploding rune that'll go off if anyone enters with ill intent."

"Do we even have the components?"

"It's energy work, actually. The more advanced stuff is."

"Then I revise my objection—should you try that? I thought you wanted to start with the easy spells first."

"These times do not lend themselves to simplicity. If someone comes to shoot us in the face, I'd rather not square off with Conchita's Unstoppable Tickle."

"You totally just made that up."

I grinned. "Maybe. But I can try an easier spell first, if you want."

"What did you have in mind?"

I explained my ongoing problem with law enforcement and how I thought a *trust me* charm might come in handy. Since it required far less energy and came from the simple grimoire, Shannon seemed more at ease with my attempting that one. She finished her tea while I set up.

After reading the spell six times, I said, "I need a token, something to invest."

"Maybe a coin you could keep in your pocket," she suggested.

"Great idea." I dug in my purse and came up with a "lucky" penny.

Curling my fingers around it, I whispered the words and called the heat. It singed my fingers against the metal; this was *far* worse than using the touch. The magic poured out of me until the penny blazed like a live coal in my palm. Gradually, the pain became almost unbearable, but I didn't stop until I'd finished, and then it cooled. When I opened my hand, the copper was misshapen, as if it had been run over by a train, and I wore a new mark. That was new; I didn't gain scars from the touch, but certain spells would inflict them. Good to know.

"Did it work?"

"I don't see how we can tell until we run across someone to influence. I mean, you trust me already. Right?"

She hesitated a little too long. "Right."

Before I could address that pause, a thump from behind the sofa distracted me. With Shannon close behind, I went to investigate and found Butch. He'd toppled a Scrabble game off the shelf and was busily pawing at the letters.

I sighed. "Feeling ignored, little man?"

He barked twice and kept worrying the tiles. Brow raised, I knelt. He was *spelling* something. No shit. In a freaky world, things just kept getting weirder. Instead of picking up the mess, I watched the sentence take shape:

The bad man is coming.

Storm Warning

"It has to be a coincidence," Shannon said.

"Like a hundred monkeys writing Shakespeare?"

Butch cocked his head, disappointed in us. He scrabbled at the tiles until the letters made no sense. Then he barked twice. *No.* Not a coincidence.

She studied him for a minute. "You know, we could ask him actual questions. And see if he answers."

Feeling like an idiot, I sat down on the floor. Shannon dropped down beside me. "What bad man?"

Butch went to work on the tiles. *Wants to kill you.*

"You mean Montoya?"

One yap offered the answer; he didn't need to spell it out. But, Jesus, this couldn't be happening. "How do you know?"

More tile work. *U didnt see, but ghost came back.*

"The one Shannon sent out? When?"

He rearranged them again. *While U did spell.*

I wondered how the hell the dog could see and hear ghosts, but it seemed like the most normal part of current events. "And he said Montoya's closing in on us?"

Another affirmative bark.

Anybody else would think I was crazy, but I took Butch's warnings serious as a heart attack.

I glanced at Shan. "We need to move. Get your stuff."

Next I grabbed the dog, plus the Scrabble tiles. We might

need them later. I had more questions, but this wasn't the
time. Within five minutes we'd packed and run for it. Laden
with Butch, my purse, a plastic bag containing my grimoires,
along with my suitcase, I didn't move as fast as I needed to.
Shannon fared no better. Her backpack, the antique radio,
and laptop bag weighed her down. We made it halfway to
the Forester before the weather hit.

Black storm clouds swelled overhead, and thunder boomed.
The torrent came out of nowhere, pouring buckets so we
could hardly see. Lightning split the sky, touching down per-
ilously close to our location. I ran full-out, my stuff bouncing. This was a solid nature spell, and if we let the weather
slow us down long enough for Montoya's men to get here,
we were so boned. Apparently, the sorcerer could do more
than major sendings and summon demons. He was a damn
jack-of-all-trades, this Vicente—and I wanted him dead almost as much as his brother.

It also meant someone had sold me out, either Chuch or
one of Escobar's men. I didn't want to believe that of my
friend, but if they'd taken him during his attempt to find a
messenger for me, I wouldn't blame him for giving me up
to save his wife and unborn child. In fact, I'd be mad if he
didn't.

The wind made it hard to move; it pushed us toward the
building like giant invisible hands. Head down, I shoved back,
but each step felt like a mile. Blinded by wind and rain, I
reached for Shannon's arm. Then the hail began, the rain turning to ice. Big as golf balls, it pelted our skin and left giant
welts.

Together, we fought to the SUV and managed to slide inside, but visibility was nil. Worse than that, the fence meant
to protect us would have to be unlocked manually. I knew
the combination, but that meant more time wasted. Still, it
wasn't like I had a choice. At least since it was magickal in
origin, this storm couldn't follow us. My amulet, tucked away
beneath my shirt, should still be functioning fine, so we just
needed to get out of here.

I jammed the keys in the ignition and whipped us toward

the fence. In the dark and wind and rain, I couldn't see it until I got right up on it, and then our outlook worsened. An SUV barreled toward us, head-on, from the street. We didn't have any weapons, and my spell casting wasn't good enough to help in a fight. Not yet. I kind of doubted they had any objects they wanted me to read. No, they had been sent with heavy weapons and orders to kill.

"Tell me you're buckled in," I growled at Shannon.

"Yep."

"Good. Keep your head down."

In answer, she pulled the shoulder belt behind her and tucked her body beneath the dash. Sucking in a deep breath, I slammed my foot on the gas and went for it. The vehicles hit hard, the gate broken between us. Jesse's car crumpled, but we had better position, coming down the slight incline. Momentum gave us oomph, and the black SUV slid down. I didn't need much, just enough clearance—

There.

I whipped the wheel hard to the right, spun over the ice onto the sidewalk. We slammed into the other truck side to side. They opened fire, and I nearly pissed myself. This SUV wasn't bulletproof or armor plated. Bullets sprayed the windows, but since we'd hunched low, they went clear through.

Fishtailing wildly, the Forester smashed a free-community-news box, and narrowly missed a light pole. They tried to trap us against the building but their tires spun in the ice and rain, and I bounced us around the corner, then laid on the gas pedal, peeling away onto dry pavement. Those seconds counted.

"Where's the highway?" I demanded.

Shannon sat up and went to work on the GPS. "Left here. Two blocks, another left." She risked a glance in the side mirror. "They're gaining."

"Okay, new plan." I wasn't up to a long high-speed chase that would end only in incarceration or death. Probably death. "Got your cell phone?"

"Yep." She whipped it out of her bag as only a teenager could.

"Call nine-one-one."

Shannon was already hitting the buttons. "And say what?"

"Attempted carjacking in progress, automatic weapons fired. We're fleeing the felons and in fear for our lives."

I stepped on the gas and made the turns she recommended. On the highway, I could get greater speed and hopefully attract a patrolman's attention. If I stopped, we were dead: two bullets, back of the head, *bang-bang*. That was if they didn't decapitate us as proof of a job well-done. Beheadings seemed to be high cartel style these days.

The police wouldn't understand, of course; they'd ask why we didn't just surrender the vehicle. Hopefully I could convince them my flight response was on steroids. At any rate, I'd much rather try to bamboozle a cop than eat lead. We'd find out if my *trust me* charm had any juice. *Come on, lucky penny.*

The Forester zoomed onto the on-ramp for I-35. I swung over to the far left lane with an expertise I'd learned in Mexico City. Though I didn't own a car there, Tia had an old one, but she couldn't see well enough to drive it anymore. So I often took her to the mall. That hellacious traffic in DF had prepared me fairly well for getting away from murderous gunmen.

I listened with half an ear as Shannon dealt with the 911 operator. "Yes, we're on I-35." She named the mile marker. "I'm afraid if we stop, they'll shoot us. Please tell me there's a policeman nearby. I'm *so* scared." Oh, she did the young-and-tearful thing very well. The quaver was a masterful touch. Or maybe she *was* tearful; she was certainly young. "We're in a green Forester. They're driving some kind of black SUV, and they're coming right up behind us."

Shit. That was my cue. I floored it and whipped around a white hoopty that shouldn't be in the fast lane. More staccato gunshots, but they sprayed the other ride, not us; it sounded as if they'd hit a tire. I couldn't spare an eye to look, but from the squealing of brakes, there must be wreckage behind us.

"Yes, we're northbound. Okay, thank you." Shannon flipped

the phone closed. "Keep us alive for five more minutes, if you can. There's a state highwayman on his way."

I exhaled in a low shudder. This baby had no more to give; the needle was already buried. When I glanced in the rearview, I saw the black SUV had steered through the crash—only the white car and a red one had collided—and the black thugmobile had more power than our ride.

"Hope he calls for backup," I muttered, because one state trooper wasn't going to take out a truck full of paid killers.

I zoomed past an off-ramp. I almost took it, hoping the black SUV would flip if I made them hit the exit too fast, but if they didn't, then the trooper wouldn't be able to find us. I watched them in the mirror, and a guy stuck his head out the left window to take aim.

I swerved right, yelling at Shannon, "Get *down!*"

Time for some evasive action. As long as I kept changing lanes, their bullets didn't hit their intended targets. My hands shook on the wheel, and my stomach cramped until I thought I might barf, both from motion sickness and terror. The Forester couldn't take much more damage before the shooters got lucky.

Finally, I saw blue and red lights flying in the rearview mirror, four of them. They went to work boxing the SUV in, aiming at tires, and doing shit you expect to see only in action movies.

I knew they'd want to talk with us about the incident, but I couldn't stop here. If Montoya's men saw a shot at me, they'd take it. This way, maybe they wouldn't resist arrest. Montoya would get them out on bond before it became more than an inconvenience. I didn't want the cops who had saved my ass—and man, I never thought I'd say *that*—to die for me. Clearly, the paperwork could wait.

I slowed way down and settled my driving as best I could with reaction shaking me like a 5.2 on the Richter scale. At the next exit, I pulled off and parked in the first lot I saw. It was a Circle K and the neighborhood wasn't the best, but given how our ride had already been shot to shit, I didn't see what bangers could do to us. I rested my forehead on the steering wheel for several long moments before I got myself together.

"You want a Slush Puppie? My treat."

I sat up with a desperate little laugh. "Clearly I do."

Butch crawled from beneath the seat and hopped onto my lap. "Thanks for the warning, bud. I don't know what I'd do without you."

In answer he licked my cheek. Yeah, I didn't want to find out either.

I tucked him under my arm as I got out to see the extent of the damage to Jesse's SUV. *Oh, Christ on a cracker.* I winced: front end smashed, long dent on my side, bullet holes all over the place, and that didn't speak to all the broken windows.

Once, I'd accused Jesse of having a white-knight complex. Only half joking, I'd said: *You go for the bad girl, the one with problems that blow up your car, trash your house, and steal your wallet. It's not her fault, of course. If she only had someone to love and understand her, that shit wouldn't happen.* I only needed to lift his wallet, and then I'd be three for three. Apparently, I *was* that girl.

Shannon came out a few minutes later, holding two drinks. She set them in the cup holders between us and I pulled myself back into the vehicle. Since the keys were still in the ignition, I started it up.

"Where do we go now?" she asked.

It was an excellent question. I presumed our safety had been compromised with Escobar's men. Weighing the odds, I figured one of them had taken a bribe from Montoya, and I had no way to be sure which. That meant I couldn't contact them again. Chuch's house was burned out, and assuming he was okay and hadn't given me up, I couldn't seek asylum with him either.

I had to hand it to Montoya. He might be crazy, but step by step, he'd closed off all my avenues of help or rescue. If he didn't crack first, he was going to kill me. For the first time, I believed it. Not even Kel could prevent it, if he was here. It was simply a matter of time and resources. And only the fact that the guardian claimed the risk of my demise went down after I cemented the alliance with Escobar gave me any hope at all. The situation seemed pretty fucking grim.

And then I recalled an untapped resource.

"The police station." I remembered the way, mostly, but maybe not from here, so I brought up the route on the GPS, just in case. "We need to come in and tell them our side of the story before they start hunting for this vehicle."

"In its current state, it won't take long for them to find it."

"Exactly."

After passing Butch off to her, I put the SUV in gear and we headed off to face the music. Certainly, I was guilty of reckless driving, maybe public endangerment. If they printed me, they'd find a number of other charges, but no convictions. Chance's luck had always taken care of that.

We drove in silence, apart from Butch's occasional woof or whine. He didn't like our prospects any more than I did. On the bright side, maybe if they locked me up, I'd be safe for a while, at least until Montoya tapped a guy in county.

Jesse's place of employment looked more or less as I recalled, newer than some government buildings. I checked my reflection to make sure I didn't look wild or crazy-eyed. I was thankful I hadn't been drinking. Shannon touched up her eyeliner and put on a little more lipstick.

When she caught me staring with a raised brow, she shrugged. "What? You never know—a local reporter might be bored and looking for the nightly news."

Oh, that'd be fantastic. I had a number of people hunting for me who shouldn't find me. TV would simplify their efforts.

Still, I squared my shoulders and marched toward the front doors. Inside, I tried to explain myself to the guy at the desk, but he was harried and he told me to take a seat. We sat there for a good fifteen minutes, and Butch started to whine. Poor dog. I couldn't remember when we'd let him out last.

"I can't leave," I said to Shannon.

She nodded and took him out front. When she got back, she filled his water dish from the drinking fountain. He lapped in sync with the flickering of the fluorescent lights overhead. By that point I'd lost patience. Too bad the *trust me* charm had no influence in the sphere of waiting to be served.

I went back to the window. "Look, we're here trying to do our civic duty. If nobody wants to talk to us—"

"Ms. Solomon?" Even before I turned, I knew the voice. Sure enough, Lieutenant Glencannon stood in the doorway that led into the private offices. "What are you doing here?"

This is it. Showtime. I curled my hand around the penny in my pocket and hoped for the best. "I'm sure you've heard about the chase on I-35."

Belatedly, I realized I should've gone to a state police outpost. *Crap.* Well, if my brain wasn't firing at full capacity, I could hardly be blamed—and maybe this would work out better. The state police didn't know me, but the Laredo police didn't hate my guts, and the lieutenant seemed to have taken a liking to me.

Come on, charm. Do your thing.

"Well, sure. Ugly business. Drug dealers hassling a couple of young ladies, I hear from radio chatter." His gaze softened then. "Don't tell me you were involved?" His tone invited me to confide, rich with wanting to believe whatever story I offered.

Thanks, Mom.

"Maybe you could take a walk with me, sir?"

"I have a minute."

"Thanks."

Without explaining further, I just showed him Jesse's ride. He could read the story in the dings, dents, and bullet holes. "What do you think about all this?" he asked.

"Well, sir, I was driving Jesse's Forester. He said it was all right. Near as I can figure, they must have recognized the plates. I think maybe they thought if they could get to me, I'd tell them where you're keeping him." It helped to leave your lies simple, I'd found. The more elaborate ones tended to break down under scrutiny.

He was already nodding. A plausible story, added to the spell, and I might walk away from this without too much trouble. "That makes sense. And they probably wouldn't believe it if you said you didn't know."

"I was afraid of that. It's why I didn't stop when they wanted me to."

"And that's when they shot at you, which proves you were right to be scared." He leveled a serious look on me. "Those men are no joke. At this point, I have no choice but to hide you along with Saldana until we get Montoya."

Oh, no, no, no, no. I oversold it, or made the charm too strong. Stupid penny. A reasonable person wouldn't fight that offer, given the circumstances. But it would lock me up and take me out of Escobar's sphere. He might even see it as a deal breaker, so then I'd have *two* cartel bosses after me. I had to get word to him somehow, and I had to be free to participate in the last stage of the plan . . . when Montoya snapped. This screwed everything up—I might be a witch now, but clearly I wasn't a good one.

My smile felt sickly. "That sounds wonderful."

"Do you need to stop somewhere to pick up some things?"

"No, sir. We had all our stuff in the SUV."

"Then I'll drive you out there myself. Don't worry. We'll get Montoya soon, and you'll be able to get back to your life."

Right. What life?

"Can Shannon come?"

"Ordinarily I'd say no, but since she was in the vehicle with you, that makes her a target as well. They might recognize her. I'll have to take your cell phones, and if you have a computer, I need that too. I can't risk your calling somebody and letting slip something crucial about where we're keeping you." He gave us what I'm sure was meant to be a reassuring look. "I know it sounds scary to be cut off like that, but you'll be under twenty-four-hour protection, and there are books and magazines and DVDs in the house. Maybe you could look on it as a vacation."

"I sure appreciate this." There was simply no way out. I'd talked myself right into protective custody. *Damn it all.* "Here are Jesse's keys."

"Let me just tell the desk sergeant I'm leaving, and then we'll be on our way. Come on back in for a few minutes. I'll feel better if you stay inside."

"Me too," Shannon muttered. The turn of her mouth reflected disappointment that instead of fifteen minutes of fame, we were getting hidden.

"Can you hide your cell phone anywhere?" I whispered. Mine was too big, or I'd shove it someplace unspeakable.

"Maybe." And that was the only hope we had.

Miserably, I followed Glencannon.

Safe as Houses

We drove out to a defunct ranch in the middle of nowhere. The place was a little run-down, and there were no cows or horses. It was dark by the time Glencannon delivered us to the officers in charge of keeping Jesse out of trouble. Now they'd added us to their burdens, and neither of them looked particularly happy about it. Still, they didn't argue with the lieutenant.

The first cop was a big buzz-cut-wearing bruiser named Clemsen. He looked like he had been military before going into local law enforcement; it almost always showed in stance and bearing. A guy named Rudd completed the detail; he was shorter and more easygoing. In some cases the duty cops rotated, but since Glencannon wanted as few as possible to know Jesse's location, Clemsen and Rudd would be here for the duration of our protective custody.

I took careful note of everything as we passed through the kitchen: old red and white linoleum floor, worn countertops. The windows were all covered, but not with blackout shades like at the cartel safe house, which I found slightly amusing. These were standard venetian blinds. The worn shag carpet started in the hall and continued into the living room, which held sagging yellow furniture.

The two cops went back into the kitchen to talk to Glencannon. Low murmurs reached us, the unmistakable cadence of argument. I paid them no mind. Until this moment, I hadn't realized how worried I had been. But Jesse was sitting up in an easy chair, watching network TV on an old set using a pair of rabbit ears.

Shannon went on into the bathroom. I didn't blame her. After what we'd been through, a shower sounded heavenly. But I had other business first.

"Corine," Jesse breathed.

He started to get up and then clamped a hand to his side. Still, he was stubborn enough to bust his stitches, so I went to him instead. Perching on the arm of his chair, I gave him a careful hug and rested my head against the top of his head; his hair smelled clean and lemony. He wound his arms around my waist, and a tremor shook through him.

"You're looking better," I said softly.

He raised his face, bitter-chocolate eyes searching mine. "I don't much like wondering what's happening with you. This emotional-silence thing sucks."

"I'm sorry. I didn't do it on purpose."

Well, maybe I did. We'd fought about it in Kilmer, how I didn't like him to be able to have insight about me that I hadn't shared. How I needed privacy. And now we stood on equal ground. I couldn't pretend to be sorry about that, only that he'd been hurt trying to protect me. I couldn't let that happen again, no matter what.

"I know." Lacing his hands in my hair, he tugged my head down for a kiss. I fell into it, appreciating his warmth and gentleness. I might not love him yet, but there was something sweet and delicious like hot homemade apple pie. "So you met my mama and my dad. What do you think?"

"About what?"

"Well, I'm going to look an awful lot like him in thirty years. You've just glimpsed the future."

"He was weathered and handsome. Just like you'll be."

It was certainly true. Some men got doughy as they aged; others acquired a distinguished patina of interesting lines that only made them more appealing. Jesse Saldana would fall into the latter category.

"Hearing that, I could almost forgive what you've put me through."

"Almost." I stood up and paced a couple steps away.

Glencannon left; I heard the unmistakable slam of the back door. The other two cops remained in the kitchen, talking in low voices. Maybe I was just paranoid but I didn't like the whisper of collusion.

He smiled at me. "Joking. I'm happy you're all right, though I'm wondering how you got the lieutenant to bring you here."

"It wasn't on purpose," I muttered. "And that's the thing. . . ." In one quick rush, I explained the events leading up to our inclusion in his protective-custody detail. I finished with, "Jesse, I'm so sorry about your ride. The apartment was bad enough, but damn, I wreck everything of yours I touch."

"Come here."

A touch reluctant, I resumed my seat on the arm of his chair. "Okay."

He tilted my chin down with his fingertips so he could look me in the eyes. "The only thing that matters—the *only* thing—is that you're safe, sugar. But I wish I could've seen some of your fancy driving. You must've been magnificent."

Right then, it caught up with me, and a shiver of reaction set in. "I don't know about that. I just had to protect Shannon and Butch."

"You did great. And you did right in going to Glencannon."

"Well, I didn't want *this*."

"This is probably best," Jesse said. "The police department will handle Montoya."

If they did, at the very least, Escobar would refuse to pay me, despite all my time and trouble, and Montoya wouldn't spend long enough in prison to end this mess. He'd just get out, madder and more determined than ever. Men like him almost never did hard time; they found some sucker to sacrifice and walked away clean. So if Jesse thought I planned to stay here quietly, he didn't understand me.

Because I knew we'd never agree, I said nothing. Instead

I stroked his hair and luxuriated in his heat. He wasn't a perfect fit; I had too much lawlessness in me. But with anybody, there would be sacrifices and compromises. I was ready to grow up.

When Shannon got out of the bathroom, I took my turn. I made it quick. The bathroom was tiny and full of ugly, crumbling tile; the plumbing groaned throughout my shower. I got out, wrapped myself in a towel, and padded down the hall. Our things had been stacked in the last bedroom. I supposed we were expected to share, and that was fine. We wouldn't be here long enough for it to matter.

Unfortunately, we hadn't been able to hide a cell phone. Glencannon didn't give us the privacy, and they conducted a thorough search of our bodies and belongings. The spell books comprised my sole asset at this point. I'd passed them off as historical journals, and they left them with me. After curling up on the bed, I immediately went to work paging through my grimoires. There had to be a spell that could get me out of here. I hesitated to use sleep, because that would leave Jesse vulnerable. Likewise, I couldn't confuse Clemsen and Rudd.

Shannon paused in the doorway. "Are you doing what I think you are?"

"No," I said automatically. "Do me a favor. Keep Jesse occupied."

"If he could move without pain, he'd already be in here checking on you. He knows you better than you think."

"Shit. Go distract him."

"How am I supposed to do that? Sit on his lap and call him Daddy?"

Now, there was a disturbing image. "No, but feminine distress should work. Can you summon some tears?"

"You owe me," she muttered, stomping back toward the living room.

"Any advice?" I asked Butch.

The little dog sat perched at the top of the vermilion grimoire, watching me turn the illuminated pages. He yapped once, tail wagging.

"Really?" Intrigued, I got out the Scrabble tiles and laid them on the bed.

He bounced into motion and pawed them like crazy. When he finished, they read: *Stay here dont die.*

I laughed softly. "One of these days, you've got to explain to me *how* you can do this stuff."

Butch gazed at me like that should be obvious, but right then I had other concerns. I returned to the grimoire and kept trying. I found spells to bring back a lover, for luck and health, charms to keep milk sweet and to drive away gophers.

I sighed. "*Really*, Mom? Gophers?"

"What're you doing?" Rudd stood outside the bedroom door, peering at me.

"Reading."

"We're making frozen pizza. Would you like some?" So this was the good cop. I could easily see Clemsen playing the other role.

"No, I'm fine." I couldn't remember the last time I'd eaten, but it seemed irrelevant.

"Okay. Let me know if you change your mind."

Mutely I nodded and moved on to the blue spell book. The ones in here were complex, and required will and power, not special ingredients. At last I located one but it would affect everyone equally, everyone but me.

Is this a good idea? Given how I'd overpowered the *trust me* spell, there was a good chance I'd screw it up. I had no training, and this was an advanced charm. Yet I didn't see a better option. *If I don't get out of here, if I don't end this, then more people will be hurt. So I'll accept the consequences, however dire.*

Making my choice, I closed the bedroom door and spent countless moments memorizing the spell. I drew a circle around myself, infusing it with heat. This felt more natural each time I did it, though no less painful. Considering the way I'd come into my power—my *mother's* power—I wasn't surprised. A lifetime of bearing such penance prepared me for the full-body agony of casting. Once I sealed myself in,

I locked the desired outcome in mind. I poured everything into the working. It *had* to take.

"'Forget me—forget me, my face, and my name. I was never here; we never were. Let this place feel as if I never came.'" As I spoke the last word, a white mist rolled outward from the circle, trickling beneath the door.

I needed to give it time to permeate everywhere. A forget fog—it shouldn't be permanent, but if I'd cast it correctly, none of them would remember I ought to be in the house for a while. They wouldn't come looking for me. Since Shannon wouldn't go to her dad's house, then I'd hide her here with Jesse; that was best. Despite her love and loyalty, she couldn't be with me when I faced Montoya. I wasn't *that* criminally irresponsible.

My new clothes, along with the flowered suitcase, I left behind. They would weigh me down. I put a few crucial items in my purse, including the grimoires. Now that I could use them, I'd never let them out of my sight again. Butch yapped as I unlocked the window. Sure, the locks were securely fastened, but this house had been proofed against intruders, not people inside who wanted to escape.

"It doesn't work on dogs, huh?"

He barked a negative.

"Of course not. I guess if I don't take you, you'll set up such a racket that it'll bring someone to investigate while I'm making my getaway."

And that would be bad news, given they wouldn't know what the hell I was doing here. They'd call Glencannon to have me arrested—and the only way I could explain it to him would be to make him think everyone here had gone crazy. While my lucky penny might lend credence to the tale, I preferred to avoid that scenario.

So I set Butch on top of the stuff in my purse, shouldered it, hunched down, and slid over the windowsill. Pulling it down after me, I hoped Clemsen would make the rounds soon and find the window unlocked. I hated leaving them vulnerable, even so briefly, but I had to get away.

Time to finish this.

I trudged five miles. If not for my time in the jungle, the walk would've defeated me. In the car with Glencannon, I'd tracked the way I needed to go, but it didn't seem as long, riding. After dark, in the middle of nowhere, without food or water, and a small, scared dog in my bag, this trip sucked. To his credit, Butch didn't complain. He got down and walked part of the way, sniffing ahead of me like a wee safety patrol.

When I saw the lights, I almost wept with relief. It was a gas station in the middle of nowhere, glowing against the dark with halogen brightness. I took note of the number painted on the building. The only car in the lot belonged to the clerk, well and good. Staying to the shadows, I crept around back; I didn't want the cashier to see me, though I felt near-starved. I made my way to the pay phone and dialed Chuch's cell. *Thank God I know it by heart. But he might not answer if he doesn't recognize this number. He might not be there. If Montoya has him—*

On the third ring, he picked up, rewarding my gamble. "Who's this?"

"Corine."

"Thank God, *prima*. Eva has been driving me crazy."

It wasn't Chuch. He's still solid. He couldn't sound so normal if he'd rolled on me. If Montoya forced him to a terrible choice, he'd warn me; he was that kind of guy.

"Can you come get me?"

He didn't waste time with questions. "*Claro*. Tell me where."

I did. "Pull along the left side of the building. I'll come to you."

"Be there in twenty minutes. I trust you got quite a story to tell me." With that, he disconnected.

Did I ever. Butch and I huddled together in the field behind the Supermart. Each gust of wind made me jump. More than once, I checked the amulet and found it safe and dry around my neck. Good, the pendant should still be proof against detection by supernatural means. I just had to stay out of sight.

Shadows thrown by the occasional passing car wore my nerves raw. A few people stopped at the convenience store to buy gas or smokes or whatever else they needed, milk or ice cream. For the folks who lived out here, this would be the closest store for miles.

At last I recognized the distinctive lines of his Maverick. As requested, he pulled to the left of the store, and I used the Dumpsters as cover to slide into the passenger side. With any luck, the clerk would think Chuch had stopped to check a map or something.

"Good to see you, *prima*. Saw you on the news, but it's just not the same." He flashed me a grin full of good-natured humor. "You talk. I'll drive."

I shook my head at the wonder of his unconditional friendship. "How can you not hate me, after all I've cost you?"

"You didn't do that. Montoya did. And he'll get his." The ice in his voice sent a chill through me.

It seemed best to let the subject go for now; I'd find a way to make it up to them.

The Maverick cut through the dark while I summed up the situation. I left out the part about my casting the forget spell, but he had to know I was a fugitive from police protective custody. If he wanted to aid me thereafter, it was his choice.

"Anyway, that's where I am. If you prefer to drop me off somewhere—"

"Forget it," he said with a frown.

"Okay. If you're still in, then I need a new cell phone, something cheap."

"We'll stop and get you hooked up."

We passed from the country and into the city; Chuch took me to a warren of low-slung buildings where the streets narrowed and people stood outside drinking. Salsa music thumped from somebody's speakers. If I hadn't been with him, I'd have been nervous. Then again, at this point, I felt mostly numb.

He approached a guy sitting on the trunk of a blue Dodge

Dart. I wasn't sure about the year, but I guessed late sixties
to early seventies. Unlike Chuch's cherry vehicles, this one
could use some work. It showed primer and a few dings.

The dude jumped down and clasped Chuch's hand with
an appearance of genuine welcome. Chuch had contacts all
over the place, and I was grateful. I stood quiet, conscious
of Butch's interest.

"¿Qué pasa, Ramos?"

Ramos opened up a plastic red and white cooler, lofting
a Negro Modelo. "Nada. ¿Quieres una cerveza?"

"No, gracias. I'm here on business."

That actually brightened Ramos's smile. He cracked the
beer open on the fender of his car and then popped the
trunk. Inside, he had a wondrous rainbow assortment of elec-
tronics. I chose a shiny blue phone, and Ramos dug a charger
out of the side netting. Everything was tangled, so it took a
while.

"Good solid tech," he told me, as if I wasn't already
sold. "You can find out your new number by calling Chuch.
You, um, may get some hang-ups and wrong numbers for a
while."

I didn't inquire if it was stolen. I did ask, "This isn't a
contract phone, is it?"

"No," Ramos said. "These are prepaid. Traded or bought
from people who wanted a different model. You can dial
this code to check your talk time, and if you get low, just
stop at a gas station and get a new card."

"Yeah, I know how it works. How much?"

"Forty bucks. This is a good deal. Still charged up, and it
has plenty of minutes left." He proved it by calling up the
automated line and letting me listen.

"Does it have e-mail?"

"Yeah. You can configure the mailbox when you mess
with the settings."

"I'll take it." I paid Ramos and then followed Chuch
back to the Maverick.

We left Ramos sitting on the trunk of his car, sipping
beer, glazed by the amber of distant streetlights. The dealer

looked like he had nothing to do and nowhere else he'd rather be. As we drove away, I envied him.

Chuch broke the silence a few blocks away. "Escobar's *vatos* sold you out, huh?"

"Yeah. I don't know which one."

"They all need killing," he said flatly.

I cut him a look; his face was rough and hard in the glare of oncoming headlights. "Not tonight."

The silence built. We drove a little longer, aimless now. I just needed to stay alive. Jesse was safe; so was Shannon. Eva was with her mother, and Chuch had made his choice. I didn't deserve his help, but I didn't know what I'd do without him tonight.

Eventually, he advised me, "Your message is on its way to Montoya . . . and he's going to lose his shit soon. Wish I could see it. Watching you on the news, shaming his guys . . . That's gotta sting."

"I can only hope."

"So what's the plan now?"

That was what I liked most about Chuch: Despite having all kinds of expertise and experience—stuff I couldn't even conceive, most likely—he never flaunted it, or went overt alpha dog. He flowed right into any capacity in which he was needed.

"I call Escobar and tell him he has a traitor in his ranks."

"And *Dios* have mercy on them all."

"Maybe." That couldn't be my primary concern. "But it's time to end this."

When Montoya broke, when he sent me the e-mail asking for a meet, I had to be ready to move. I got out my phone and dialed.

Once Upon a Time in Mexico

Chuch made a few calls and we wound up at a trailer owned by a friend of his cousin Ramon. We drove past mounds of trash, rusted carburetors and engines up on blocks. Our hidey-hole sat at the back of the RV park, where most residents didn't have a phone and weren't about to get involved in someone else's business. The trailer across the way had an impressive array of license plates, and the one catty-cornered appeared to collect hubcaps.

There were few trees, but plenty of dry grass and broken pavement littered with glass and plastic wrappers. Chuch stopped in front of a single-wide, and after he parked, I slid out; in the distance, I heard cars on the highway, barking dogs, and a woman screaming at her kid. Squaring my shoulders, I surveyed the cracked vinyl underpinning as I came up to the front door. The gaps meant that scurrying sounds could be rats nesting underneath. As long as they hadn't chewed their way in, I could handle it.

The trailer was to let, but since it smelled of old pot and cat piss, so far there hadn't been any takers. Imagine my surprise. Inside, I encountered stained brown carpet, spilled coffee grounds, an upside-down trash can, and a dilapidated couch in blinding purple plaid. I couldn't fathom why the prior tenants left it behind.

Chuch staked out bedroom territory. Since it stank even worse in there—of stale sweat, old cigarette smoke, and rancid massage oil—I didn't dispute his claim. He carried in basic provisions, nothing fancy: bread, peanut butter, crackers, chips, and soda.

I sank down on the sofa and made a call. An unfamiliar male voice answered, one of Escobar's thugs, most likely. "Tell your boss he's got a leak," I said in Spanish. "He might want to plug it."

"¿Quién es?" Who's this?

"Corine Solomon. And if I'd relied on his men to keep my whereabouts a secret, I'd be dead now. Tell him to handle it."

After I cut the connection, Chuch shook his head at me. "You like living dangerously, don't you?"

"Not so much, but sometimes it's necessary."

Too often for comfort, I found.

We spent the next forty-eight hours sleeping, waiting, and playing cards. It was a great place to lie low; nobody bothered us. Butch, at least, enjoyed the respite from car chases, flying bullets, and unquiet spirits. As time wore on, Chuch called Eva periodically to make sure she was all right.

"Told you I'm fine," I heard his wife say, ending the conversation. "I swear I'll let you know if that changes. I'm not going through this alone."

That night, I had a hard time falling asleep; it wasn't the lumpy couch or the undesirable location. I'd crashed in worse places. No, it was worry and regret tying me up in knots. I hoped Jesse and Shannon were all right. From there, my thoughts wandered to Kel, and I was still thinking about him— fallen angel, Nephilim, man who held me in the dark—when I drifted off.

But I didn't dream of him. I wish I had.

Instead I stood in Min's shop on the boardwalk in John's Pass Village. I'd spent hours here with Chance. With a twinge of pain, I recollected the photo studio where they'd taken our first picture together, the restaurant where we'd eaten, and afterward, we walked down to the ice-cream parlor to share dessert. We'd passed a jewelry store and, looking in the window, I'd wondered if he would ever buy me a ring.

I don't want to be here, I thought. *I don't have the mental energy for a stroll down memory lane.*

The quaint location attracted a lot of foot traffic from the beach, but Min had loyal local clientele as well. I knew this place like the back of my hand, its shelves stocked with wicker baskets, each containing a unique tincture or poultice. She also sold fresh dry herbs and oil extracts, candles and soaps, all handmade and carefully formulated to promote holistic healing. Even the tourists took home something, which I'd always thought meant she had laid a mild prosperity charm on the place. Not that Min would ever admit it.

The store smelled of peppermint today, probably due to the candles flickering on the countertop. Sachets filled with healing herbs were arranged around the cash register. I stood and drank the place in. When I'd left, I didn't think I would ever see it again, not even in my dreams. Here, I fell in love with customer service, working with Min. When I hadn't been traveling with Chance, I helped out; her shop had been like a second home to me. It all looked so real, from the glass storefront to the wicker chairs in the corner where Min did consultations.

By the darkness, it was late, though. The CLOSED sign showed in the window, and so I went through into the back room that served as her office. Min had decorated it with her customary panache: delicate screens and several water fountains, no metal file cabinets or ugly desk for her. Chance sat beside his mother over a pot of green tea and *maejakgwa*, the ginger cookies he loved. It looked as if he hadn't cut his hair in six months, the most disheveled I'd ever seen him.

"You should go before it's too late." She sighed and shook her head. Her expression was heart-wrenchingly familiar to me. . . . Min had never been one to take her son's part blindly. "Might be already. Stubborn, foolish boy."

I had the sense I'd entered a conversation at the midway point, but if I lingered, I might make sense of it. But the naked grief in his face astonished me.

"It's not. I won't let it be."

"Some things, dear son, are not yours to control. That was always part of the problem, you know. You're too like your father."

His father? My ears perked, but they spoke no more of him. Chance bowed his head and she put her hand on it, as if in blessing.

"You'll be all right?" he asked.

"Dae Hyun will watch out for me. Go with a clear conscience."

"Very well. I'm leaving tonight." Chance rose and kissed her cheek, and then strode out of her office.

Before I could follow, however, Chuch woke me with a friendly nudge. *Dammit. Just when things started to get interesting.* Then I got annoyed with myself for giving a damn what Chance was doing. I'd moved on. Jesse was my future. With some effort, I forced the unnerving dream from my mind.

"Wanna play some cards?"

With a moan, I sat up and invited him to deal me in. Five hands of Texas Hold 'Em later, I checked my e-mail. As Ramos had promised, my phone let me do so if I didn't take too long about it, as Net access burned twice as many minutes. Unlike the other times, I found a curt message in my box. *I'll kill you myself.* There was no signature, just a phone number, but my enemy had finally taken the bait.

Euphoria bubbled through me. Before I could rethink it, I dialed; I didn't wait for the other party to speak. "You really brave enough to face me?"

Challenge his manhood. Finish the job.

"Tomorrow." No preliminary chatter, no questions. Montoya named a set of coordinates and a time. "Across the border, past Nuevo Laredo."

I'd driven through there, lonely stretch of road between Nuevo Laredo and Monterrey. No chance anyone would stumble into our business. Good enough.

"I'll be there. And you'd *better* be, Diego, or I'll keep burning your pretty houses down. I only had the one, see, and now it's gone, so I'd like to level the playing field." Without Escobar, I didn't have the resources to do so, of course—I wouldn't be taking any more chances on his men— but Montoya didn't know that.

He sucked in an angry breath. *"Buena suerte, bruja roja. La necesitarás."*

I disconnected before Montoya could.

Chuch sat watching me. He shook his head. "You're really gonna do it."

"It's the best way."

"If you say so."

Setting his misgivings aside, I rang Escobar.

To my surprise, the big man himself answered this time. "What a pleasure to hear from you. I took care of the leak. Ordinarily, the allegiance of such a one would not merit my personal attention, but I ordered them to look after you. I cannot permit such lapses." He paused. "It was Petrel, if you're curious. He'll trouble you no more."

I should feel something now. The tall, lanky young man breathed no more, and I made it happen. But I could only muster impatience to finish this.

"Good to know. I've got a meeting with Montoya set for tomorrow." Quickly I told him where and when. "Can you come up with a strategy so soon?"

"Of course," he said, as if the question were ridiculous. "I'll send Paolo to you."

Montoya would likely show up with five trucks full of armed gunmen, Vicente the sorcerer, and God knew who else. He intended to send me in with a seventeen-year-old boy for backup? Dear God. Maybe Escobar wanted me dead.

I tried to point out as much. "I may need more help."

"He is adequate to the task, I promise you."

"Why?" I'd feel safer with a crew of gunmen at my back.

"He wants to prove himself to me. Therefore, he will fight with more dedication than any hundred hired soldiers. His skills are not in question."

Arguing with him would offer the same benefit as banging my head against the trailer wall, so I just listened as

Escobar told me where to meet Paolo. From there, we would travel together to the appointed location.

More waiting. I took Butch for a short walk around the trailer, and at midnight, Chuch got a call from Eva. He listened, spoke little, and hung up quickly.

"I'm sorry, *prima*. I meant to see this through with you— and she wanted me to, but the baby's got other ideas."

"She—or he—is coming?"

He already had one foot out the door. "*Sí*. Gotta go. Ramon will stop by in the morning and leave you something to drive. He just knows that you're a friend I'm helping out."

"My best to your family. Thanks, so . . ." But I was talking to empty air.

The night crept by. I lay on the couch because the bed still smelled sour, and I wouldn't sleep much anyway. At dawn I showered, though I had nothing clean to wear, and ate the last of the peanut-butter crackers, the only thing left from our bare-bones grocery run.

A few hours later, Ramon dropped off a Chevelle, total piece of crap; I hoped it ran better than it looked. Another car pulled up behind him, his ride, I guessed. They didn't knock. He left the keys in the ignition and I left the trailer as soon as they drove off.

Last leg of this mess. My hands shook a little as I went to meet Paolo. He was sitting in Denny's—a mundane place for this meeting—just as Escobar had promised. In this setting, he looked even younger than he had at his father's house. It was a wonder nobody had asked him why he wasn't in school.

"Breakfast?" He rose as I approached, well mannered in a way I found odd, given what I knew of his father.

"We have time." And I was hungry.

While we ate, we made small talk. Nobody could've guessed what we'd be doing later that night. Hell, *I* didn't even know.

Though pancakes and eggs had sounded delicious, I couldn't finish them. I fed the sausage to Butch in discreet nibbles.

He took care of the bacon too. Afterward, I paid the bill, and we headed out to the Chevelle.

Paolo had a black duffel; I had only my purse. It seemed we both traveled light. He got in the passenger side, his face serene. Perhaps he was just too young to worry about the future, but I didn't think so, and his serenity calmed my nerves. I trusted that Escobar wouldn't risk a gifted heir without a strong conviction that he could prevail.

"Does he have you do stuff like this a lot?" I asked, putting the car in gear.

"No. This is a test."

My heart nearly stopped. "Of what?"

"My skill. My loyalty. If I pass, he will reward me with more responsibility in the organization."

"Rite of manhood?" Talk about hard-core. Escobar sure loved his trials.

"*Sí*, near enough."

Throughout the day, I got a number of phone calls for a woman named Juanita. Apparently she'd traded her phone to Ramos without informing her creditors. I blew them off, and at noon, we headed for the border.

Crossing into Mexico never took very long. While the United States cared a great deal who got in, Mexico just wanted people to spend money. The agent checked our documents with cursory interest and waved us through.

Across the border lay a shantytown bearing the unlikely name of Blanca Navidad. The residents who founded the place claimed it snowed in the desert when they started building their homes: tin roofs, scrap wood and metal, chunks of scavenged cement. As far as I could tell, they had no electricity, and from the smell, no sewage disposal either. Most of the Navidadians worked in the *maquiladoras*, which were duty-free export assembly plants. The place made me sad as we drove past.

"I would live in a place like this," Paolo said softly, "if my father had not taken me in."

As far as I was concerned, Escobar owed the kid more

than a living, but it never did any good to get between child and parent. "Lucky he did."

"Not really. He kept only the gifted. My mother was nothing, a native whore."

My fingers clenched on the steering wheel. "She gave you life. I'm sure she loved you."

Paolo raised a brow. "Did she? Is that why she sold me to *el Señor* for eight hundred pesos and twenty-one grams of skag?"

Shit. Maybe you're better off with Escobar. Since I didn't know what to say, I drove on in silence. We passed through Nuevo Laredo and kept going. I remembered accompanying Chance to the *zona*, and how he'd fought for me there. *No. Not Chance. Think about Jesse. Wonder if he's healing.*

The surrounding land was dry, a long, low valley. According to the GPS, we had arrived at the correct coordinates—and several hours early. We'd long since left the main highway, off the beaten path on a dirt road. I wanted to check the place out, so I parked the car and got out to look around.

Montoya had chosen well; there was no cover for miles. Mountains in the distance on either side rendered this spot remote in ways few modern locations could match. There was just endless brown scrub sloping to unspoiled peaks.

Now we just had to wait. Butch didn't seem to mind; he could nap anywhere. I fidgeted and shifted and considered all the potential worst-case scenarios. In self-defense, I studied my grimoires and tried to commit a couple of spells to memory that might work, if I could cast them quick enough. I sat on the hood of the car and watched the road behind us. I pondered my options.

After arguing a little with Paolo about the viability, I went to work with salt and chalk dust, placing them carefully to the left of the driver's door. Against the dirt road, it didn't show, but the energy I used in crafting the circle mattered more than my tools; when my enemy arrived, I'd be ready.

At last the bass roar of a powerful engine signaled an arrival, and the dust trail rising confirmed what we heard. I got my athame out and hid it behind my back. As he parked, Montoya had to be thinking, *Look at her . . . she's helpless. Dead meat.*

A stocky man in late middle years, Montoya eased out of the driver's seat, an enormous gun dangling from one hand. He hadn't brought an army of thugs, as I expected. Instead, only Vicente emerged. Even numbers? That decision suggested Montoya had complete confidence in his brother's ability to deal with me up close, and I hated to think what led to that surety.

"You're dumber than you look," Montoya growled, leveling his gun on me. "You brought a boy with you? Only a boy?"

Before I could reply, Vicente lobbed a spell, crackling blue energy. I dove behind the Chevelle and it hit the hood with a hiss, dissipating with the smell of a lightning strike. *Fuck. He called it before and held it ready. I don't even know to do that. There's no fucking way I can beat him in a straight-up duel.*

Paolo crouched beside me as Montoya opened fire. They sprayed the dirt and pelted the old Chevy; I hoped like hell they wouldn't break my summoning circle. I needed to get close enough to pull my ace in the hole, but with the two of them out there, it would take some quick thinking to push those five feet.

"I thought you can't die," Montoya taunted in heavily accented English. "Made a deal with the devil, no? Yet you cower like a little bitch, not the fearsome red witch. So beg me, and I make your death quick instead of giving you to Vicente, like I plan."

His brother rumbled a low, awful laugh, full of such anticipation as to make my skin crawl. "Don't beg," the sorcerer said.

More bullets sprayed the ground, slamming into the Chevelle; we were pinned down. If only I'd been faster, if only I hadn't hesitated. Dammit, we needed to get to the circle. Fear slammed in my veins, creating adrenaline, and to compound my desperation, Vicente started a new spell.

"Is there anything you can use nearby?" I whispered to Paolo.

In answer, he leaned out and scanned the ground. "Nothing but rocks and dust."

That was an old schoolyard trick, but given our situation, it couldn't hurt. "Try to distract them, but don't get shot."

I shuddered to think what Escobar would do if I survived but his son did not. By the sound of their footsteps, our enemies were pushing closer. Montoya laughed, the son of a bitch. I rolled beneath the car and squirmed on my belly as a minor dust devil sprang to life. They cursed and spit, trying to clear their eyes and mouths. The sorcerer's concentration faltered, and Paolo taunted him with gutter Spanish; I understood only about half the words, but judging by Vicente's roar, the boy had flair.

Once I had line of sight, I started my own spell. Drawing down the power, I used one of the two I'd memorized from the blue grimoire. My mother's books contained no lethal spells, but this—if I cast it correctly—would cause some pain. My palms burned as I whispered, "Things that buzz and fly and crawl, heed me, heed my call. Come, come, you fearsome, darken swarm. Oh, feed and eat! Upon my enemies ye shall feast. As I will, so mote it be." Even on my belly, I could complete the gesture, flaring my palms outward in a "V," fingers fluttering like insect wings.

An orange glow burst forth and struck the dirt in front of Vicente. His scornful laugh rang out. "You missed."

On the other side of the Chevelle, Montoya shot at Paolo, who countered with a mix of quick reflexes and telekinetics. Then a droning sound began, increasing as the dark cloud drew closer. Vicente turned, and a muffled sound of horror escaped him when the bugs enveloped him: stinging, biting, trying to crawl down his throat and into his mouth. He screamed and Montoya whirled, going to his aid.

In that respite, I asked Paolo, "Can you kill them with your TK?"

"I don't think so. They're both wearing body armor, and there's no wall to slam them against. I could try to break their backs on the hood of the car, but I've never done that before, and I won't have the energy left for defense. Do you want me to go for it?"

Stumbling and slapping all the way to the trunk of his car, Montoya got a fire extinguisher and shot a white cloud on Vicente, driving off the bugs. They were both furious, bloodlust burning in their eyes. I had to decide fast—Paolo or me. *Who's going for the home-run swing?*

Before I realized I'd made a decision, I whipped my athame out and slashed my palm. *Me. It has to be me. I'll end this.*

"Guard our backs," I told Paolo.

With my bloody palm curled toward me, I crawled the distance to the circle they hadn't noticed, drawn as it was in the pale dust. I whispered, "By fire, earth, wind, and rain, I call you forth, Dumah Porai Valyonatha. I offer sacrifice in your name. As I will, so mote it be. In the name of Solomon the Binder, whose blood I carry, you must obey."

Now free of my swarm and enraged beyond sanity, Vicente raised a hand to unleash a spell. I felt the magick gathering in the air, swelling like summer lightning. He used a mish-mash pidgin for his casting, no doubt learned in the islands, and I didn't understand the words. I didn't know what he was doing, nor how to counter it, but something terrible would happen if he finished the incantation. He was done fucking around, letting us dodge and hide.

Because I'd summoned her before—and she was already in this realm in a human host—Dumah appeared in a swirl of inky smoke. I spoke quickly, racing Vicente to the finish. "For this single moment, my enemies are yours. In return for your help I offer you their souls and their power. You will not harm me or mine."

Annoyance flashed on her ephemeral face and then she registered those outside the circle. Greed and hunger replaced her displeasure. I wasn't binding her to me permanently and forcing her to serve; this was a simple summoning—catch and release. I hadn't broken the letter of our agreement . . . but it bothered me just how good I had become at negotiating in such degrees.

As Vicente released his spell, the demoness whispered in my head: *Done*. This time, I knew to drain the energy from the circle before breaking it, and Dumah flowed in inky darkness toward the two men. She ate the magickal energy en route—it strengthened her—and then she continued toward them.

Montoya responded by unloading his whole magazine, the last of his ammo. I had no defense against that; Dumah was a creature of spirit, and could not stop a bullet. Maybe this was it. Butch whined as I dove; I tried to save him from the impact.

There was no need.

Bullets hung in the air like black hailstones, mere inches from my body. Paolo trembled, his face pale and damp. Sweat rolled off him from the strain of such fine control, and then they all fell, bouncing against the ground. I couldn't believe his father had asked this of him—and I was glad I hadn't asked him to kill for me. Better I should bear another astral scar; it was worth the price to see this nightmare ended at last.

The two Montoyas screamed as Dumah pressed against their eyes, testing their defenses. She devoured Montoya first; like the old witch in the supply store, his shields were soft and weak. In a black trickle she slithered in through his eyes, and he clawed at them, screaming. His nails left bloody runnels on his face until his whole body went slack. Horror seeped through me.

She'd eaten him, just as I promised she could.

Vicente lifted his hand, preparing another spell, but Dumah went for him next. His brother's soul had made her stronger, so she had the power to fight him. His shields were stronger, but while he resisted her attack, he couldn't cast. Paolo dived for Montoya's weapon.

"No," Dumah said. "This one's mine. Promised."

I stilled the boy with a hand on his arm. "We must let her have him or she'll be free to turn on us."

I could banish her, perhaps, using the incantation I had used on Caim—assuming my shields were good enough to stave her off—but maybe, like Vicente, I wouldn't be able to remember the words while struggling with her for control. I would rather not risk it. What was more, that call, if I succeeded, would seriously piss Maury off. I didn't want to get on his bad side.

At last, she took Vicente and swept through him like a dark tide. His body crumpled, still living, but empty. I stared at the two Montoyas, chilled at the decision I'd made and what it meant. Paolo raised the gun and glanced at me for confirmation.

"Our bargain is done," Dumah whispered. "I give you leave to call me anytime, Corine Solomon. This was . . . fun."

Worse and worse. I didn't banish her; she simply threaded away—back to the body she'd left behind, I assumed. I imagined the scene there: Woman fainting on the sidewalk. Maury telling people she was pregnant, not to worry, she'd be fine in a few minutes.

"I should finish this," the boy said. "As my father requires."

Gods knew I didn't want to, so I merely nodded and turned my face away. Two shots rang out. *Simple. Elegant. Awful.* I'd fed the eternal part of them to a demon. Even if they were awful men, there was no denying it; I was a bad woman.

The devil shone in Paolo's eyes as he examined the bodies. "Ah, Montoya. A son is *always* more powerful than a brother." He gave me a look. "You will wish to turn around now."

I didn't ask why. I complied. When I glanced down again, the heads were missing. In response to a gesture, the two corpses bounced away, obedient to his will, until they landed in the drainage ditch on the side of the dirt road. I knew now what the black duffel was for. I didn't imagine we'd be smuggling those back into the States.

"I need proof," he said in a faintly apologetic tone. "Shall we call him?"

We did. Escobar instructed us to meet his men at an airfield three hours away. Numb, I drove on with two heads in a bag in my backseat and a killer beside me. Paolo scared me now because he seemed so gentle, and yet I saw nothing in his eyes that indicated conflict over his actions, whereas I felt like a hot mess of roiling regret and uncertainty. But a good robot never doubted its programming.

A plane sat waiting for us. Two hours in the air, and we arrived at a new location. Three goons conveyed us to yet another Escobar property. I hadn't seen this house before; it was almost a cottage compared to the other. Beachfront property—the ocean glimmered silver in the moonlight.

Escobar greeted us on the terrace, a glass of wine in hand. Once more, he was barefoot, clad in white, and wearing a most disarming smile. Before he spoke, he took the black bag from Paolo. He looked inside with a ghoulish expression of anticipation. A quiet inhalation bespoke pleasure, and I shuddered as he handed the duffel off to one of his henchmen.

Christ, I couldn't get away from these people fast enough. I might never wash myself clean. And, of course, there was the matter of what I'd done to survive.

"I am proud of you, *hijo*." I couldn't help but wonder if he'd ever called him that before. Escobar clasped Paolo on the shoulder. "There are only two Montoyas left, and they will not fight me. One is stupid, and the other is lazy. He will take what money he can and find someplace to retire."

"Pleased I could help," the boy said, as if he'd gone to the store for milk.

I closed my eyes. I wanted to be away from here. But I feared insulting my host. Now that he needed me no longer, I'd become acutely aware of my isolation and my vulnerability. He might decide I knew too much or something equally clichéd.

"You may go now," he said, and Paolo passed along the terrace without another word to me.

Eventually I opened my eyes and studied the view. Staring out over the sea, I didn't move when Escobar joined me. His tone was musing when he spoke. "You have proven useful. I believe I owe you payment for your time and effort."

"That was the bargain."

At a gesture, one of the goons brought him a fine leather briefcase. He opened it, and I got to see what 100K looked like in cash. "I will have my people take you wherever you like, one last time. I trust we will not bother each other again."

"Never," I promised.

Escobar was a man of his word, fortunately. Perhaps he had more of that stern priest in him than I'd realized. No question, he was an evil man who did terrible things, but like all demons he abided by his agreements.

"Where to, then?"

"Back to Laredo, please." I needed to see how Eva and Chuch and the baby were doing. I *wanted* to see Shannon and Jesse. "Will you make sure law enforcement learns that Montoya is dead? I need to get a friend out of protective custody."

"What would you have me do, order my men to toss those heads into a cantina, as you hear of imbeciles doing on the news?"

"Could you? This once?" I smiled as if that might persuade him. Escobar had ice water in his veins.

He considered. "Yes, but only because it amuses me. Someone else will surely take the blame, because that is not my style."

I knew that. Escobar was the quiet knife waiting in the dark, not the burst of automatic weapon fire. "Thanks."

"Rodrigo, deliver Señorita Solomon safely to Texas." He turned, glass of bloodred wine still in hand, and dismissed me.

Once we were up in the air, I realized I'd abandoned the Chevelle in Mexico. Fortunately, it hadn't been a nice ride, and maybe nobody would mind much. With the baby and all, it might go unnoticed.

At my request, the goons deposited me at a used-car lot, where I spent a small portion of my blood money. For a thousand bucks, I drove away in a maroon El Camino and the satisfaction of knowing I didn't have to give it back or explain if something happened to it. Butch yapped in approval as he sniffed the clean black cloth seats. The rest of the interior was ugly maroon vinyl, but it was *mine*. This would be great for hauling stuff, once we got the thrift store going. I couldn't wait to show Shannon.

Since I hadn't eaten since that morning, I found a drive-up and munched a burger in the parking lot. Butch ate half of a kid-size one on his own and he whined because it wasn't Carl's Jr. quality. I shrugged. "Better than starving, right?"

The dog looked unconvinced.

Once we finished, I called Chuch. "Hey, how are you guys?"

I wished I could ring Jesse, but he didn't have a cell phone at the safe house. But as soon as news hit about Montoya's demise, Glencannon would spring him, and we could talk. We had a lot of things to settle; Shan and I needed to go apartment hunting. Maybe starting over in Laredo wouldn't be so bad.

"Great." I could hear the glow. "I got a little girl."

"I'll swing by. What hospital?"

He told me, and then belatedly realized aloud, "Shit, if you're here, then—"

"Yeah. It's done."

Chuch whooped and then somebody shushed him, probably a nurse. "Gotta get back. Eva's dying to see you."

Circle of life, and all that. I was dying to see her too. I started up the El Camino and drove over to the hospital. I knew where it was: same one where Jesse had been laid up recently. I hated hospitals, but for this, I'd go in smiling. I hid Butch as we went through the automatic doors.

It wasn't hard to find the maternity ward, even less difficult to locate Eva's room. Between her mother and all the Ortiz cousins, they were driving the staff crazy. I figured one more person didn't matter, though there was barely room for me to step inside. Watching, I felt more alone than I ever had, because they shared a support network that I'd never possess.

But maybe, maybe with Jesse.

Eva waved at me from bed, offering a half smile, and the feeling passed. "Glad you could make it."

"Better late than never." I stopped in the doorway, not wanting to fight the crowd to get closer.

She looked exhausted and blissful, long black hair sticking to her forehead. Dark circles under her eyes didn't diminish her beauty at all. The baby was so tiny, red faced, wrinkly, and wearing a wee pink hat. She had a bracelet on her wrist, and she seemed like she might start wailing at any minute. Relatives milled around me, murmuring in Spanish. Rather than making me feel out of place, it felt homey and familiar. I'd gotten to the point where I had to remember to speak English in the States.

"What's her name?" I asked a random Ortiz.

Chuch materialized behind me. "Camelia Corine."

Everything I'd been through lately—and *that* did me in. So I was crying when I spotted Chance. He perched on the window ledge, foot propped on the arm of the chair. Some woman sat beside him, gazing up at him dreamily.

"What's he doing here?" I demanded, low.

Chuch followed my gaze. "He's her godfather. Figure it out."

Oh. I was *not* disappointed; for me, it was Jesse Saldana from this point on. But I couldn't help the wild dread that Chance could undermine my resolve when my ex cut through the crowd toward me.

Blue Night

After assuring Chuch I wouldn't miss the baptism in a couple of days, I made a quick exit. Today was Eva's—and Camelia's—day to shine. Only a total drama slut would get into it with her ex in front of her friend's family. Better for me to leave quietly and avoid taking the focus away from the glowing mom. Sure, we could participate in the ceremony later and be polite in front of the family, but otherwise, there was no need for us to socialize.

The grimoires weighed heavy on my shoulder. I increased my pace until I was running, my Converse sneaks making no sound on the tile floor. The lights seemed too bright, and I needed to get away. Butch whimpered in protest; I murmured an apology and kept going. I caught a stern look from the nurses' station, but I didn't slow until I got out the doors, where I stood in the night air, drinking in great, gasping breaths.

My fingers shook as I got out my cell phone. God, I needed to hear Jesse's voice right now. I wanted his arms around me, but I'd settle. Hell, I'd leave a message if Glencannon hadn't heard about Montoya yet.

To my vast relief, he answered, his voice weary and tight. "Yeah?"

Looks like Escobar moves fast.

"Hi, it's me."

"Me who?"

Was he being funny? "It's Corine. I just wanted to make sure you're okay. Did the lieutenant spring you and Shannon?"

Frost turned his tone icicle sharp. "If this is a prank, it's not funny. You have information on an investigation that you shouldn't possess. As for Shannon, you leave her the hell alone. She's a good kid, and she's been through enough."

No. Oh, no. Dread built inside me. I'd never worked that spell before. Just like the lucky penny, I gave it too much power. *Stupid untaught witch.*

"Can I speak to her?"

Surely Shan remembers me. We're besties.

He muted the call for a few seconds, and then came back on the line. "She doesn't know any Corine. Look, lady, I've got your number now. If you bother either of us again, I'll take it badly."

And he hung up. I was left standing in the dark with a dead phone in my hand. Shaking set in. *Maybe it's not permanent. Maybe they'll remember me in time. It'll wear off. Other people will talk about me and prompt their recollections. I hope.* Tears filled my eyes, even easier this time since the baby had opened the floodgates. *I didn't get to tell her the name of our shop. Spooky Vintage.* I leaned against the solid wall just outside the doors and squeezed my eyes shut, trying to contain the reaction. Stupidly, I felt as if they'd both died.

But maybe I deserved this. Maybe it was a punishment for what I'd done to survive. If I lived, I had to pay for it, so the universe removed the truly good people from my sphere of influence. The wound swelled within me in a scream I couldn't let out. Salt stung my cheeks and my nose started to run.

Not Jesse. Not Shannon. I dug the heels of my hands into my eyes, hoping the external pain would balance the devastation within. As I fought for composure, the nearby hospital doors swished open and footfalls pounded toward the parking lot. It wasn't until they slowed and then angled my way that I opened my eyes.

Chance. Well, of course he wouldn't be able to resist an opportunity to tell me how well he was doing. By comparison, I'd lost my best friend, seen murder done, and been wearing the same clothes for three days. The breaks always swung his way. Maybe he'd even show me a picture of his new woman, and ask if we could be friends. I braced for salt in the wound.

Instead of such a gambit, he stopped before me and stood silent. Gazing. Even in the poor light, he was unearthly in his beauty: angular features, sculpted mouth, and almond eyes shining cat-gold. He never had five-o'clock shadow, not even at midnight. Why had I never noticed that before, or the faint sheen of his skin? In the moonlight, he didn't look quite human. I'd always just felt grubby by comparison and never wondered why.

"You look tired," he said. "Lovely, but tired."

I didn't. Not lovely. I could believe tired.

I spoke in staccato bursts, forcing the words past the lump in my throat. "You got here quick. The baby's beautiful."

"I was already on the way."

I raised a brow. "Did you have a premonition?"

The dream I'd had in the trailer came back to me, an odd echo. Maybe that was something my mother could do, those true dreams. I wondered if she could control them. Not for the first time, I wished I could ask her—so many things.

"No. Look, can we go somewhere? Talk?"

"I passed a park on the way here." Even if I had a hotel room, I wouldn't take him there. I probably lacked the energy for this, but at least it was a distraction from my latest fuckup. What a cherry-topped disaster that forget spell turned out to be.

You lost your best friend, and *your boyfriend. Had him for less than a week. That must be some kind of record.*

"Which one's yours?" Chance asked.

"The El Camino. You still driving the Mustang?"

He nodded. "I'll stay close."

"I'll watch the stoplights between here and there. It's not far."

That said it all. At least the exchange had dried up my tears; I didn't want Chance thinking I was pathetic. I drove with an eye on my rearview mirror, making sure I didn't lose him. My heart twisted, because I knew what he wanted—some job done or a reading as a favor. In the latter part of our relationship, that comprised the sum total of our emotional exchanges. This time, though, *this* time I'd say no. I owed him nothing, and he was square with me. I wanted it to stay that way.

But I'd hear him out for old times' sake, mostly because I couldn't face being alone just yet. Otherwise, I'd have to think about all I'd lost: my home, Señor Alvarez, Shannon, Jesse, Kel. The damage was incalculable. Impossible. Unbearable.

No. I'd handle it. I always did.

It was a small park, well kept, with benches, a water fountain, and a playground. More important, it had security lights. We should be safe enough here. But I could stop looking over my shoulder, more or less. Or at least dial the paranoia down to normal levels. I'd walked through fire and come out different, darker, on the other side.

I parked beneath a lamp and set Butch down. Using a nearby water fountain, I filled the dog's collapsible dish and gave him a drink. He expressed his appreciation with a wag of his tail and then set off to explore.

Chance pulled in only a minute behind me, and strode up the walk toward where I sat idly swinging. The wind smelled of distant mesquite, as if someone in a nearby neighborhood might be barbecueing in his backyard. The simple goodness made me ache. He took the swing beside me, but didn't push off. His fingers were long and elegant wrapped around the chains.

"The reason I'm here so fast is because I was already on my way to see you."

I smiled. "Sure. What's the job?"

"No job."

"What do you want me to handle?"

If I hadn't been watching so closely, I would've missed his faint flinch. "Nothing. For the first couple of weeks after I left Kilmer, I was so mad at you. Here I'd broken my back begging for a second chance and it wasn't enough."

"I got that by the way you drove off without saying good-bye." And by the way he'd FedExed all my Travis McGee books back to me without even a note. Those were nothing but ash now.

"But gradually, I started thinking about what you'd said and it sank in. My mom helped to explain it," he admitted.

"How is she?"

"She's fine. Thinking about opening a second store."

"It's doing that well?"

"Homeopathy is hot. People are reluctant to go to a doctor these days because it starts never-ending appointments and expenses. Times are tough."

"I know. You were saying?" I prompted.

"I realized it's not fair to expect you to give up everything for me. If we try again, it has to be about what *we* want. And if you don't care to live in Tampa, if that brings back too many bad memories or makes you feel like you're doing all the giving, then I have to make a change." He flattened his hands on his knees and gazed out over the grass, where Butch had cornered something small and furry. "I called in all my loans. Everything owed me has now been paid. I also hired a guy to help my mom with the store. She doesn't know it, but he's also protection for her, since . . . Well, you know. Just in case."

The certainty in his voice hit me like a fist. He was driving across country, intending to join me in Mexico City, when Chuch told him about the baby? Talk about a leap of faith.

I exhaled shakily. "Why didn't you call me? Not once. Not in six months."

Funny. Chance never wondered how I'd feel about his

grand gesture. He just assumed I'd welcome him with open arms after a long silence and a bitter parting. No need to discuss anything with me, because I'd always be his for the taking. He still didn't understand that I needed a full partnership . . . but this was forward progress, at least.

Now I had to decide if it was enough.

"I didn't want you thinking this was more of my bullshit promises," he said quietly. "You wanted action, right? Here it is."

Low, almost desperate laughter burst out of me. "We're like that couple in the story. At Christmas, she cuts off her long hair and sells it to buy him a chain for his pocket watch. He sells his watch to buy her pretty gold combs for her hair."

"'The Gift of the Magi,'" he said, frowning. "The moral of that story was that it didn't matter because they had love. Somehow I don't think that's what you're getting at."

"Not exactly. See, my shop's gone, Chance, and now so's your business. Neither of us has anything."

He froze, studying my face. "I thought you were here because of the baby, but . . . you're not. At least, not entirely."

"Hardly. Montoya kept me busy."

Chance swore in a mixture of English and Korean and then slid off the swing to kneel before me. "What happened? What can I do?"

"Nothing. I took care of it." With Paolo's help I had. Yeah, I served as bait in Escobar's trap, but I'd proven myself more dangerous than anyone expected, using Dumah as my finishing move. "He won't bother Min—or anyone—again."

Something like fear flickered in Chance's face, as if he didn't quite recognize me. But he didn't back off. Instead he took my hands in his; as always they felt warm in comparison to mine. Not fever-hot like Kel, nor with Jesse's safe heat. But familiar and precious, nonetheless.

I expected him to ask why I hadn't called him for help. He didn't.

"I suppose there's no point in asking. Done is done. I

want you to know, I understand now. . . . I did you a disservice by not realizing you aren't the same woman, and if I want to be with you, then I need to—borrowing my mother's expression—court you properly. There are no guarantees, but you wanted proof that I'm not all talk. Here it is."

The enormity of it humbled me. "And you'll go anywhere I want?"

"I've no ties anymore, Corine. You take the lead this time. I'll follow. And I'll do my best to open up." Chance lifted my palms and kissed them with a tenderness that acted as the sweetest balm. "I'll tell you about Lily. I know it *has* to be different this time, because I won't get another shot with you."

Lily had to be the lover who had died because of him. I didn't remember him ever mentioning her name before. That had to mean something.

There was no telling how much cash he had in the Mustang. If he'd called in all his loans, it must be a lot. We could go anywhere. Seductive thought. Or I could take him to Mexico City, where we could rebuild together. Hard to say how much temptation to try again came from not wanting to be alone, how much I wanted to say yes because I'd lost so fucking much tonight. Was Chance my consolation prize?

His fingers tightened on mine, giving away his tension.

"We take it slow," I said at last. "Dating, no promises. Not yet. You need to get to know me again—and vice versa."

I wasn't the same woman. Not even a little bit. This Corine might surprise him; he might not want her when he realized how deep the shift ran. He believed he loved me, but he didn't know me, not anymore. Chance remembered the woman who gave up everything for him, followed him blindly, and let him make all the decisions; he loved that complete and selfless devotion. I couldn't offer that again.

"Absolutely." The relief in his voice nearly floored me.

Plus, we still had the problem of his luck, but maybe we could manage it this time. Maybe if I got regular cleansings, we could deal with it and minimize the effects. I'd be proactive and seek solutions instead of wishing for miracles.

"We won't be living together right away," I cautioned.

"If we rebuild on your property, we could have two flats put in up top," he offered softly. "That way I'll be close by, but you can always send me home."

It was a reasonable suggestion, but I hadn't seen the extent of the damage. Maybe it would prove an impossible task, or I'd have trouble with the *fideicomiso*. I was too numb to make plans, and it felt wrong to leave Shannon so quickly. I wanted *our* future, *our* shop. It remained to be seen whether Chance could be part of that.

As he rested his head on my knees, I put my hands in his silky hair and breathed in the smoky, sweet scent of burning wood. Somewhere, somebody was singing a Spanish love song, and it curled through me like a ribbon of light, banishing some of the darkness and desperation.

Chance couldn't know about Chuch's house yet; he must've come straight to the hospital. He didn't know how close to dying I'd come or that I could cast spells and bind demons or had whispered kisses into a fallen angel's skin while his tattoos glowed blue against a deep jungle night. I had my own secrets now—and not just shameful ones. At base, I no longer felt unworthy of Chance. Maybe this time we could make it work because we'd be equals.

Time would tell.

Read on for an exciting excerpt from
Ann Aguirre's next Sirantha Jax novel,

Aftermath

Coming September 2011 from Ace Books

Dying isn't like living; it requires no effort at all.

I just have to sit quietly and let it happen. But I can't. Like a fish with a barbed hook caught in its mouth I twist and pull, desperately fighting my way back to the anguished meat I left in the cockpit with Hit. She has no way home without me, and if I don't succeed in this, the consequences will be far worse than two lost females. Despite the siren call of grimspace and the scintillating colors, I *must* live; it's never mattered so much before.

I have to get back. I have to warn them, or every ship that tries to jump will never come out again.

As I draw closer, the pain ramps up. At least I have the assurance that the nanites will repair the damage, so whatever I've done to myself, I won't wind up trapped in my own body. If March were here, he'd help anchor me, but Hit lacks his Psi ability, which means I'm on my own. Instead of the door in the far horizon—that place of passing through—I focus on my body. Past the silent screaming I can hear my heartbeat, faint and sluggish, right now no more than a reflexive physical response. Yet it might be enough.

With each thud, I pull myself closer, as if that tenuous thread is a rope I can grasp with ghostly hands. Each pound of my pulse brings me a little closer, and then, with a wrench almost as agonizing as the one that tore me loose, I fall back in. My hands move, and I feel Hit beside me. *You back, Jax?*

Sickness boils in my veins. I don't feel right in my own head, as if I've come back smaller somehow, but I block it off from her. She's done enough. The consequences from this point on are mine alone.

Yeah, I reply, *time to go home.*

I don't know whether I've been gone minutes or hours, but we've tarried too long regardless. Grimspace is a bitch mistress that will drain you dry and leave the husk without a second glance—and without my implants, this suicide run would've killed me, no question. Weakness racks me, but I can get us out; I have that much left. Though it might break me, I'm determined to bring my pilot home safely. The colors glow brighter as grimspace swells within me, and it feels as if a door opens in my head. Thanks to the neural blockers, I can't feel the associated pain; the ship shudders and sails through.

We emerge in straight space, high over Venice Minor. Such a long, impossible journey, when we didn't go anywhere at all. Not really. Not in the sense of distance, but this is the nature of paradox. My hands tremble as I unplug, and then the scene unfolds before me.

Lights twinkle in the dark, but they are not stars. *Mary, no.* We weren't fast enough. So many Morgut ships made it through; they dim the constellations. Their shapes are alien to my eyes, like creatures that came out of the sea, finned and spiny, with odd appendages and strange designs. Because we're so small—a two-person vessel—we haven't registered on their sensors yet; there are too many energy signatures clustered in a small area for our numbers to leap out at anyone. But it's only a matter of time, and we have no weapons.

Sweat cools on my forehead as I study the scene. My mother died to give us a chance, and with some relief, I note there are no more dreadnaughts. If we can get ships up here, we have a chance in this final battle. It looks as if they're positioning to bombard the planet. The flagship is enormous, with jutting guns powerful enough to take out entire city quadrants. As yet, I don't see any movement from the armada; they must still be forming up and executing repairs down below.

I hope they weren't sending reinforcements here when I changed the beacons. But I refuse to let fear govern my actions. That's not me, and it never will be. First off, I must bounce a message about what I did, but we're close enough to the Morgut fleet that they'll definitely catch the transmission and then blow us to hell. I weigh the risks and decide the warning can wait until we land; if I die here, then I've set humanity back a hundred turns in terms of using the beacons to navigate. Still, I don't feel good about the call. At this point, every second counts.

"Do we make a run for the surface?" Hit asks.

"We can't do anything here."

No weapons, no shields. So that's the answer. She offers a brief nod in reply, and then we start the insane journey home. As we approach the atmosphere, the enemy fleet notices us, and Hit dodges shots coming in hot on our stern. One successful strike and we're done. But she flies like other people dance, and even negotiating the burn as we fall planetside, she manages to skew us away from the incoming barrage. I can only watch; I've done my part, and the rest is up to Hit. Her constant maneuvering makes for a rocky reentry; she can't calculate the best angle and take care with the ship hardware, so I watch the ground sail toward me at an insane speed and fight the urge to close my eyes. The flagship shoots wide, its missiles zooming past us toward the ground. *Ha. Missed.*

The clouds whip past, and the tiny dots on the ground resolve into lines and then trees; the green and brown patchwork sharpens into the lines of my mother's garden. In the distance I glimpse the blue shine of the sea, but several alarms flash red, and a low whine fills the cockpit. The small ship rattles as if it might break apart entirely. I do shut my eyes then.

Our vessel goes into a low roll as we near the ground; impact flings me forward, but the harness catches me. I'll have bruises to show for this most recent bit of insanity. I risk a look and find we're upside down, but more or less in one piece, outside the hangar at my mother's villa. I don't know who's more surprised, me or Hit. She flashes me a triumphant grin and a high sign.

"Pretty fragging good, right?"

"Maybe the best I've ever seen," I admit.

She winks. "I won't tell March."

We've burned out the stabilizers, but otherwise we did remarkably well. Maybe *only* a tiny ship like this one could've gotten past the vanguard of the Morgut fleet. I imagine the rest of them lost in grimspace, trying to interpret the new signal and failing. They'll die there, no matter how powerful they are or how indestructible their dreadnaughts.

"Does the comm still work?"

"It should."

I set it to Tarn's personal code and then bounce a message at the highest priority. "Don't let any Conglomerate ships jump. They won't be able to interpret the new beacon frequency without instruction. Give coordinates for a central meeting point and instruct them to make their way via long haul. Doesn't matter how long it takes—it's better than being lost. I'll explain everything fully when I see you."

Not content with toppling the closest thing we had to a stable government, I've now crippled interstellar travel. But it was for a good cause. I'm still positive I did the right thing, no matter what they do to me later. If it means prison time or an execution, I'm not sorry. Someone had to make the tough call, and I was there.

The doors are jammed from the rough landing and don't respond to the computerized controls, so Hit and I kick our way out. My limbs still feel weak as I pull myself up; I'm not prepared for the wreckage that greets us. Oh, not from our ship. All around us, the jungle burns, black smoke swirling toward the sky. Stone rubble constitutes all that's left of the villa, just a bombed shell with broken walls rising no more than two meters. Cracks web the foundation, charred black, and I can smell death in the air. It's not a scent you forget.

"They weren't shooting at us," I realize aloud.

As we rocketed toward the ground, the bombardment began. The wrongness hits me then. Because we left, we lived. From a certain angle, it feels like cowardice.

"No," Hit says on an exhale.

But there's no denying it. I can't see the point in destroying such a beautiful, defenseless place, but I'm not Morgut. Maybe this devastation serves their master plan, or it's simple retaliation for our defiance. Millions of innocent civilians will die on Venice Minor, innocuously enjoying their vacations; they might've saved for the trip their whole lives, as such consummate luxury doesn't come cheap.

I see the smoldering wreck of the *Triumph*, recognizable only from the charred metal piece bearing its Conglomerate registration number. The rest of it lies scattered around the hangar in bits no bigger than the span of my arms. God help any crewmen who were still aboard, working on repairs. My heart feels like lead in my chest. Beside me, Hit curls her hands into fists.

"We should look for survivors," I say at last.

We ready our weapons in case the Morgut have sent a ground team—yet why would they? They can continue the blitz from above. The missiles aren't toxic, so the natural beauty will rebound in time—and by then they will have claimed the lush, tropical paradise, a replacement for their own dying world. Once they establish a foothold on Venice Minor, fighting them will be more difficult. For all we know, they might breed fast enough to compensate for the troops lost in grimspace, and then we'll be back where we started—with no solution in sight.

Still, I power up my laser pistol, wanting it charged and ready in case we run into trouble. Silently Hit does the same. We move through the burning graveyard with the scent of smoke and scorched metal in our nostrils, compounded by a chemical burn that makes breathing difficult. There's no telling what might be in the air, but I don't have any air scrubbers handy. The little ship we left in offered no special equipment, and there's nothing left intact here on the ground.

"Any movement?"

Grimly, Hit shakes her head, continuing to pick a path through the wreckage. It looks as if we lost all our ships. How many dead? So far, we see no signs that anybody survived the attack. As far as I know, my mother didn't have an emergency bunker. Nobody would reckon that as a necessity on Venice Minor.

My timing was off. I didn't get here fast enough. *They'll find some way to blame you for this*, a cynical little voice says.

I shake my head, trying to silence it. The Conglomerate isn't like Farwan, I tell myself. *If I'd been here, I only would've died with them. No help in that.* But maybe it would've been better for me. More than most, I know the pain of surviving.

There is an awful gravitas in standing at ceremony after ceremony, listening to a holy man intone words that are supposed be comforting but instead merely remind you that you've been left behind.

Not this time, I tell myself. *You'll find them.*

In slow, stealthy movement, we complete our circuit of the perimeter. No bodies, but I recognize the stench of burned meat. It lingers in the air, people who became ash in a white-hot instant. They rain down on us in the aftermath, clinging to our skin and hair, the dust of the ones we loved drifting in ladders of light. This is a wound too grave for weeping, a silence of the soul burned as black as a night without stars.

"Where's the *Dauntless*?" Hit asks.

The question gives me pause because I didn't notice it as we scouted the area. With the others, I saw enough of their destruction to recognize the fragments. So maybe they got away. I cling to that hope. They might have been going up to fight even as Hit and I raced down. *Please, please let that be true.*

"I'm not sure."

"That might be a good thing."

"Our ship won't fly, but it has the only working comm in the area." I name our biggest challenge as we head back to the tiny vessel.

"We could try hiking out of here in hope the rest of the planet has fared better."

As if in answer, the horizon lights up with the impact of more missiles—an awful red glow that burns like twin desert suns, deeper than Gehenna's permanent sunset and far more sinister. They're going to kill everyone on the surface. Complete extermination, as if we're merely pests that prevent them from taking possession. I suppose I should be grateful they aren't eating us; maybe we've taught them at last we're an enemy to be reckoned with, not mindless meat, but that elevation of status comes with a high cost. They'll assume this area has been saturated sufficiently unless they learn otherwise, so we don't have to worry about renewed bombardment here.

"They're still bombing," I say needlessly.

Even if they weren't, I'm not up to a long walk just yet. The nanites haven't had a chance to finish repairing all the damage I did during the long immersion in grimspace, while I reprogrammed the beacons. So I merely shake my head. Hit seems to understand my limitations, as she drops the suggestion without argument.

"If I rest some, I can keep up with you later," I add.

"That leaves the problem of food and water."

Fortunately we're on a hospitable planet, not like Lachion or Ithiss-Tor. We can find fruit and fresh water nearby. The insects and hungry indigenous life will make survival a challenge, but it's not insurmountable. The Morgut ships overhead, on the other hand, trouble me, but I've told our allies not to risk jump travel, which means Venice Minor won't be seeing Conglomerate reinforcements—and maybe that's for the best. In wartime, they talk of acceptable loss; from my training, I know that commanders are prepared to lose up to thirty-three percent of their troops—and when the representatives present this as a victory, that's how they'll describe the people who died here—but right now it doesn't feel tolerable to me at all.

There hasn't been time for my message to reach Tarn or for him to respond. Which means Hit and I must focus on finding shelter and staying alive until the Morgut finish the eradication of our species. After that, I don't know what the hell we'll do—steal a ship, maybe. At least with my implants, I have the advantage of understanding Morgut speech and some of their technology. I might be able to explain to Hit how to fly one of their scout ships, assuming we aren't caught and eaten first.

"It's gonna be a rocky few days," Hit says.

"I'm aware."

"The jungle's not secure, with the fires still burning." Her dark gaze roves around the rubble, looking for safe harbor.

We both know we can't roam too far from the ship. At this point, stealing a Morgut scout vessel and rendezvousing with the rest of the Conglomerate fleet offers our best chance for survival. I can't feel March, but this time, it's because of the physical distance between us. That's what I tell myself, anyway. *It doesn't mean he's dead. He's probably on the* Dauntless *with Hon and Loras.*

You better hope they don't jump. If they do, you'll lose everyone on board.

Icy terror crawls down my spine. *Please, please let them be in orbit, fighting the good fight. If they are, maybe . . .*

"Do you remember the *Dauntless* comm code?" I ask Hit.

Regret colors her expression as she shakes her head. Damn. I don't recall either. If Rose were here, I have no doubt she could tell me. She was a good comm officer, but we lost her even before we landed on Venice Minor. I remember Doc's grief, and sorrow steals through me. War has no regard for love.

"Maybe we can find part of the *Triumph*'s computer and link it to ours," she suggests. "It should have records of past communications."

I hope her technical expertise surpasses mine, because I can't do that. But spending as much time with Dina as she does, it's not surprising that some of the knowledge has sunk in. For all I know, she helps the mechanic with repairs in between the nuzzling and softly whispered words.

"Let's look."

The *Triumph* wreckage lies nearby, and we creep toward it in silence. Together, Hit and I sort through the metal and burned components. I try not to think of Kai; he died long ago yet haunts me still. I imagine the ones we've lost as ghosts who prowl about the edges of the light, waiting for us to join them. Sometimes that's terrifying and sometimes it's reassuring, a promise of homecoming.

At length, she produces a chunk of the computer trailing wires and says, "I think this is it."

More explosions light that bloody glow in the distance. We're too far from ground zero to hear the booms or feel the earth shake; the Morgut are moving off now, systematically destroying the defenseless resorts and private homes. I wonder whether they had any real warning, or if they went from relaxing massages to dying in abject terror. There are no RDIs here, no ground resistance at all apart from Hit and me. Right now that seems like an impossibly tall order.

"Do you feel like we saved the Conglomerate only to lose everything that matters?" I ask her quietly as we pick a path toward the downed skiff.

"Only if Dina died here," Hit answers. "*If* she did, then I'll find a way to end the Morgut. I will hunt them to extinction and then delete all their records, all their writings. They will pass unremembered." Her coldness gives me chills.

But I feel more or less the same way; I'm just less articulate about it. "If I've lost March, then I'll help you."

She doesn't hesitate as she drops through the open door to the cockpit. I come in on the other side and squat on the ceiling, watching as she snips and intertwines the wires. Sparks fill the air, simmering white-hot, and then dying with a hiss as connection begins.

"Got it. Cycling through old logs now."

Over crackles of static, I listen as Rose patches the calls through. Her voice echoes from beyond the grave, more memories I cannot shake. "You have Hon from the *Dauntless* requesting a connection."

"Patch him through," March says.

Mary, how it hurts to hear his voice, even blurred with electronic interference. It makes me feel as if he's one of my ghosts, and I can't give in to grief before I find the answers. Hit plays the log until she successfully extrapolates the comm code, a matter of some urgency, as there's no telling how much longer this wreck will have sufficient power to send—or receive—messages. Hit cues me with the go-ahead and I angle my head as best I can toward the comm array. The video's not working, but as long as we have audio, it should suffice.

"Hit and I have returned to Venice Minor. We've encountered no survivors. Our ship's disabled, but we don't see the *Dauntless* amid the wreckage, so we hope you survived the initial bombing. If you're still in direct comm range, we implore you not to jump, as your navigator won't be able to interpret the signals. At best, you'll wind up far from your intended destination. At worst, you'll be lost for good. Until we hear back, we'll be waiting on the surface, so please advise with intel about the battle and our new orders."

Unless they court-martial us for going AWOL. But it isn't time for disciplinary action; we're in the middle of a war, for Mary's sake. Once the dust settles, then I'll take my punishment, but I'm not letting them touch Hit. I'll lie if I must.

After a nod from her indicating she has nothing to add, I say, "Send."

A ping from the comm indicates it's resolved the link, which indicates they're up there, somewhere. Who's on the *Dauntless*, we cannot know. Then from the damaged console comes an alarming beep, accelerating in speed. Even I know what that means. Frantic, I scramble out of the cockpit, cutting my palms on metal shards as I pull myself out. Hit grabs my hand and we sprint full-out away from the skiff.

ABOUT THE AUTHOR

Ann Aguirre is a national bestselling author. She has a degree in English literature and a spotty résumé. Before she began writing full-time, she was a clown, a clerk, a voice actress, and a savior of stray kittens, not necessarily in that order. She grew up in a yellow house across from a cornfield, but now she lives in sunny Mexico with her husband, two children, two cats, and one very lazy dog. She likes books, emo music, action movies, and *Dr. Who*. You can visit her on the Web at www.annaguirre.com.

Also Available from

Ann Aguirre

Blue Diablo
A Corine Solomon Novel

Eighteen months ago, Corine Solomon crossed the border and wound up in Mexico City, fleeing her past, her lover, and her "gift." Corine, a handler, can touch something and know its history—and sometimes, its future. Using her ability, she can find the missing—and that's why people never stop trying to find her. People like her ex, Chance.

Chance, whose uncanny luck has led him to her doorstep, needs her help. Someone dear to them both has gone missing in Laredo, Texas, and the only hope of finding her is through Corine's gift. But their search may prove dangerous as the trail leads them into a strange dark world of demons and sorcerers, ghosts and witchcraft, zombies—and black magic.

**"Gritty, steamy and altogether
wonderful urban fantasy."**
—#1 *New York Times* bestselling author Patricia Briggs

Available wherever books are sold or at
penguin.com

R0019